#Find the Girl
All that
Glitters

Find the Girl series

FIND THE GIRL
FIND THE GIRL: ALL THAT GLITTERS

#Find the Girl
All that Glitters

LUCY AND LYDIA CONNELL

Written with Katy Birchall

PENGUIN BOOKS

.PENGUIN BOOKS

UK | USA | Canada | Ireland | Australia
India | New Zealand | South Africa

Penguin Books is part of the Penguin Random House group of companies
whose addresses can be found at global.penguinrandomhouse.com.

www.penguin.co.uk
www.puffin.co.uk
www.ladybird.co.uk

First published 2019

001

Text copyright © Lucy and Lydia Connell, 2019
Cover images copyright © Shutterstock

The moral right of the authors has been asserted

'The Sound of Music' lyrics were written by Oscar Hammerstein II

Set in 10.5/15.5 pt Sabon LT Std
Typeset by Jouve (UK), Milton Keynes
Printed and bound in Great Britain by Clays Ltd, Elcograf S.p.A.

A CIP catalogue record for this book is available from the British Library

ISBN: 978-0-241-34029-5

All correspondence to:
Penguin Books
Penguin Random House Children's
80 Strand, London WC2R 0RL

www.greenpenguin.co.uk

CHAPTER ONE

NINA

'Nina!'

I wake with a start, rudely jolted from my dream by Nancy shouting my name. I blink sleepily as she barges into my bedroom and stands over me with her hands on her hips.

'You're hiding something from me,' she says accusingly.

'What?' I say, completely dazed and still half asleep. 'What's wrong? What time is it?'

'You are hiding a secret from me, Nina Palmer,' she states, giving me a stern look. 'My twin sense is going off like no tomorrow.'

I reach for my phone on the bedside table and groan when I see the time.

'Your twin sense is going off at six a.m.? Any chance you can turn it off for a bit, so I can get a lie-in?'

'Something has been niggling at me for days and then suddenly this morning I woke up realizing why: you're keeping a secret from me!' she says, prodding me as I pull the duvet over my head. 'Now, can you please tell me what it is, so we can all move on with our lives?'

'I'm not hiding a secret from you,' I lie, my voice muffled into my pillow. 'Leave me alone.'

I should have known she'd work it out. I've never been good at keeping secrets.

If I even THINK about the secret, I blush furiously. When your cheeks go bright red for no reason, people tend to guess something is up. And it's even worse when someone asks me directly about the secret and I'm supposed to lie. I'm a terrible liar. My brain goes completely blank.

I know all this for a fact because last term I had to hide a HUGE secret from everyone, including my identical twin sister, Nancy. The fact that I managed to keep it as long as I did is a miracle. The thing is, now I have another secret. A new secret. And if I thought that hiding a secret from Nancy when we were barely speaking to each other was difficult, hiding one from her when we're inseparable is near to impossible.

'The niggling feeling began a few days ago,' Nancy continues, perching on the edge of my bed. 'You remember we were having breakfast before school? And you said, "Mum, the post is here." Do you remember that?'

'No.'

'Well, you said, "Mum, the post is here", and then do you know what happened? You went bright red. And not in the normal way that you go bright red, but in a different way. And this morning the reason why hit me. You blush a different shade when you're keeping a secret!'

HOW DOES SHE EVEN KNOW THIS?!

WHY do my cheeks have a specific shade of red that gives away when I'm hiding something?! Why can't I just blush like a normal person?

And, seriously, the other day Nancy noticed for the FIRST TIME that we have a painting of a horse hanging by the stairs – 'in my head, it's been a cow all this time' – despite the fact it's been up on the wall since the day we moved in almost SEVEN YEARS AGO.

But when my cheeks go a very slightly different shade of pink she's suddenly Sherlock Holmes.

'You have lost your mind,' I say as convincingly as possible. 'I have no idea what you're going on about.'

'Why would my sister blush for no reason? That was my first clue,' she says, combing her fingers through her shiny, blonde hair.

Even though we're identical twins, Nancy and I have different approaches to our appearance. Nancy is glamorous, with flawless make-up and glossy hair that always sits perfectly, however she's styled it that day. I'm useless with make-up and, no matter how many times Nancy tries to teach me, I don't know which brush to use for what or why there need to be so many base layers or how to use straighteners to curl my hair (which, I have pointed out to Nancy on several occasions, doesn't even make any sense).

'The next clue,' she goes on, 'was yesterday's incident.'

'Nancy, is there any chance we can continue this conversation at a normal hour? It is a *Saturday*. It's been a long week at school, what with all the homework they're piling on in the lead-up to our GCSEs this year, and I could do with some downtime,' I point out, hoping that my pleas will eventually work and she'll drop it.

Deep down, I know that it will never work. When Nancy is on a roll, there's no chance of stopping her.

'Yesterday morning, when Mum dropped us off at school and I asked you if everything was OK because you seemed a bit distracted, you replied, "Yes, why?"'

She watches for my reaction, her eyes wide with excitement, as though she's just blown the case wide open.

I sigh. 'And?'

'You said, "Yes, *why*?"' she repeats, looking exasperated. 'If you weren't hiding something and I asked you whether you were OK, you'd reply "Yes" or "No". But, because you're hiding something, you added the "why" to make sure I hadn't caught on to whatever it is you're hiding. Do you follow?'

'No.'

'Do you want to know what I think you're keeping from me?' she asks. 'I think you, Nina Palmer, have been signed to a record label or something! Am I on the right lines?'

There's a moment's silence before I burst out laughing.

'WHAT? That is ridiculous! Why would you even *think* that?' I say through giggles.

'I don't see why that's so outrageous a theory,' she huffs defensively.

'It's completely mad.'

'As mad as you secretly dating Chase Hunter, the famous lead singer of Chasing Chords, my favourite band in the world, for months without anyone knowing, not even the press?' She raises her eyebrows. 'You remember *that* little secret of yours?'

I hesitate. She has a point.

I still have moments when I don't quite believe what happened last term, as though I might have made it all up in my head. I didn't exactly plan on falling in love with a pop star. The only reason I'd heard of Chasing Chords was because Nancy was obsessed with them and used to blare their music out on repeat all the time, not to mention the fact that she ran a fan-fiction website completely devoted to the band.

I, on the other hand, spent most of my time listening to my favourite composer and pianist, Austin Golding, hoping I might one day play the piano as well as he does.

Nancy and I are VERY different, and not just when it comes to our music taste or talents with a make-up brush. She's popular and funny, whereas I am completely useless in social situations. Up until last term, those differences meant that we barely spoke to one another, even though we were in the same class at school, and when we had to speak at home, with Mum's ever-hopeful encouragement, it always ended in an argument.

But then I was forced to go to a Chasing Chords gig with Nancy and I accidentally bumped into Chase Hunter, the lead singer. I'd never met a boy like him. Which isn't exactly that surprising because, before then, I'd barely *spoken* to a guy before, except for my best friend, Jimmy. But I never really saw Jimmy as a *boy*; he's just Jimmy. I didn't have the confidence to talk to any boy I liked and I always got tongue-tied with new people and felt super self-conscious. Not with Chase, though.

From the start, I felt comfortable around him; we had so much in common that the conversation just flowed without me having to think about it. Sitting there on the pavement on a random London street, I could have talked to him for hours. He was just so different from how I assumed the lead singer of a pop band would be. He wasn't self-centred or materialistic; he was funny, smart and kind. Not to mention really good-looking.

I don't know why someone like him would be the least bit interested in someone like me in the first place, but somehow he was. That night we met, when I had to rush off without giving him my number, he started this huge campaign on social media to track me down using #FINDTHEGIRL. Thanks to me dropping my purse, all he knew were the details on my bank card: Miss N. Palmer.

Secretly spending time with him was amazing, but things got bad because Nancy believed she was the girl Chase was looking for. Even though we weren't exactly friends, I still couldn't bear the idea of hurting her by telling her the truth. It got harder to find the right time to tell her as the term went on because we started to hang out again, and I was terrified that if she knew about Chase she'd hate me again.

I still feel a stab of pain in my stomach if I think about the day she found out about us at school. The paparazzi had got a photo of Chase and me on a date without us knowing and it spread over social media like wildfire. Nancy looked so betrayed when she saw it. We had a huge fight when Mum was driving us home, which I can't remember all that well because someone bulldozed through a red light straight into our car.

Nancy doesn't like talking about the accident.

Whenever it comes up in conversation, she gets this funny look on her face and changes the subject as quickly as possible. I think Nancy found it all much harder to deal with than me. As the other driver went into my side of the car, I took most of the hit and ended up being put into a medically induced coma. I guess, for me, it was like being in a really deep sleep, whereas Nancy was conscious of everything and had to see me like that.

While I was recovering, she went into protective-older-twin overdrive and barely let me out of her sight, sorting everything on my behalf and telling me what to wear so I wouldn't be cold. Honestly, it was hilarious, but it was also really nice because it was exactly how we used to be before we let ourselves grow apart. Growing up, Nancy was the confident, outgoing one and I would hide behind her, letting her take charge and calming her when she got too silly.

The truth is, the accident brought us closer together. I guess the idea of losing one another made us realize just how lucky we were. Now, we love how we're so different and I can't seem to do anything without checking Nancy's opinion first. I couldn't be without her.

Although I could probably do without the early-morning wake-up calls.

'I know what you're not telling me!' Nancy suddenly cries, clicking her fingers. 'Chase said the L-WORD! Oh my god, Nina, tell me everything! How and when did he say it and did you say it back?'

'Wait, what? No!' I protest, almost choking on my own spit. 'He hasn't said –' I lower my voice to a whisper – '*the L-word*. Neither of us have.'

'There's no need to whisper like he might overhear us, Nina. He's a hundred miles away in London, so I think we're safe,' she says, rolling her eyes. 'What's the big deal about telling him you loooooove him?'

'It isn't a big deal,' I say, trying to act casual but fully aware that my cheeks are glowing red. 'He just hasn't said it yet. So, I haven't either.'

I want to ask Nancy whether she thinks it's weird that he hasn't said it yet, but it's just so embarrassing talking about it. It's not like I haven't thought about it. I've *almost* said it several times, at the end of phone conversations or at the end of our dates. Once, I was looking into his beautiful blue eyes and admiring his long dark eyelashes, and was so distracted that I started blurting the first bit out and had to change the sentence into something else: 'I love . . . pens,' I'd said quickly, which was so stupid, but I'd panicked and it was the first thing that came into my brain. Chase had looked at me strangely and then said that he too loved pens, so I think I got away with it.

Still, he has said he's *fallen* for me before and he definitely acts like he's in love with me.

But it would be nice for him to actually say it. Then I could say it back and stop worrying about saying it accidentally.

Unless, he's not in love with me and that's why he's not saying it.

'Nina, pay attention! You're in a weird daze,' Nancy says, making herself comfortable on the bed. 'So, if it's not a record label deal or Chase saying the L-word, then what is this big secret? I'm not going to leave your bedroom until you tell me.'

'What's going on?' a voice says from the doorway.

I groan as Mum comes into my room, plonking herself on the end of my bed and planting a kiss on Nancy's forehead.

She smiles. 'I didn't expect you to be up at this time on a Saturday,' she says.

'Neither did I,' I grumble.

'My twin senses were going,' Nancy explains as I roll my eyes.

'Oh, how exciting!' Mum gasps, leaning forward eagerly. 'What were they telling you?'

Mum is the biggest believer in the idea that twins have a special telepathic connection. Whenever she catches Nancy and me looking at each other in a certain way, she'll yell, 'You're doing the twin thing! Right now! I can see it happening!' She even thinks we can read each other's mind when we're not in the same room. The other day when I was in the kitchen and Nancy was in her room, she asked me what Nancy wanted for dinner.

'I'm not sure – you want me to go upstairs and ask?' I said.

'No, no,' she replied, before her eyes went all wide. 'Why don't you do your twin thing? Can't you sense what she wants?'

I had to go into a long explanation about how we couldn't ACTUALLY read each other's mind, but she refused to believe me.

'My twin senses were telling me that Nina has a big secret and she was just about to tell me what that is,' Nancy says matter-of-factly.

'I'm just in time then!' Mum beams at me. 'What's your secret, Nina? Are you dating another famous pop star? Or perhaps a Hollywood actor this time. Maybe both!'

'Very funny.' I sigh, as Nancy and Mum giggle together. 'No, Mum, I'm still dating Chase. He's actually coming over this evening for dinner, if that's OK?'

'How very un-scandalous of you. But of course he's always welcome here; you don't need to ask. Go on then – tell us what's going on. Nancy's twin senses are never wrong. Although –' she pauses, holding up her hand and changing to her serious-Mum voice – 'if you don't want to tell us, then you don't have to. There's no pressure. You are entitled to your privacy.'

'Oh, really? I'm entitled to my privacy, am I? Nancy has been on at me to tell her my secret for the past half-hour.'

'AHA!' Nancy cries. 'So you admit you have a secret!'

I let out a long sigh. It is time to admit defeat.

'Fine – you win. There *is* something I'm not telling you.'

I reach under my pillow and pull out an unopened envelope addressed to me. They both stare at it with eager curiosity. The envelope is expensive, thick paper and my name is written across the front in swirling letters.

'Oh my god, what's that?' Nancy asks, her eyes widening. 'Are you . . . are you going to HOGWARTS?'

Mum bursts out laughing at Nancy's joke.

'Thank you for appreciating my comic genius, Mum,' Nancy says, ignoring my unimpressed expression. 'But seriously, Nina, what is it? It looks important.'

'It's a letter I've been waiting for. It arrived yesterday morning.'

'That's why you blushed when you asked about the post the other day! And why you were so distracted yesterday!

I REALLY AM A GENIUS!' Nancy declares. 'My twin senses are out of control. I should have my own show.'

'You really should, darling,' Mum agrees sincerely. 'What's the letter, Nina?'

I take a deep breath. 'It's from Guildhall School of Music and Drama. I found out that they've introduced a weekend music programme that runs through the term. It's a sort of introductory course to their summer school programme. It starts next week. Anyway, I auditioned last minute and –'

'What?' Nancy interrupts, looking stunned. 'You auditioned? *When*?'

'Just after New Year. Chase took me. It's not that I didn't want you to come,' I say quickly. 'Chase was the one who told me about the course in the first place and then he practically dragged me to the audition, and I made him promise not to tell anyone because I knew I wouldn't get a place.'

Nancy smiles. 'OK, that's very . . . *Nina* of you,' she says. 'Was it scary?'

I nod, thinking back to that day. When Chase pointed out the course to me, I couldn't believe it. It looked amazing and, more than anything, I wanted to get a place on it.

But I also couldn't bear the idea of auditioning. I was too scared. I felt so torn; I filled out the application and then spent a whole day with Chase at my computer, trying to build up the courage to send it. I felt sick as soon as I pressed send and then checked my emails every five seconds, convinced I'd made a huge mistake and the Guildhall teachers would probably be crowded round the computer, laughing their heads off at my application.

But then an email popped up in my inbox a couple of days later inviting me to audition at the school in London. Just the idea of it made my whole body tense up in fear, and the fact that this was for a course at the school I'd spent my life dreaming of attending made things ten times worse. As Chase lives in London, he'd promised to meet me off the train and take me to the school so at least I wouldn't have to do it alone.

When the day came, I almost didn't get off the train when it pulled into London Liverpool Street station. I sat still in my seat, wondering if I should just wait for the train to head back to Norwich again. I somehow found the courage to get off and walk down the platform to where Chase was waiting by the barriers.

'Are you ready?' he said, linking his fingers through mine and leading me towards the taxi rank. 'You can do this, Nina, I know you can.'

I would never have got to Guildhall without him.

'What was it like?' Nancy asks, prodding my leg under the duvet. 'The audition. Were there judges and buzzers and stuff?'

I laugh. 'No, Nancy. It wasn't a reality singing show. There weren't any buzzers or judges. But it was still terrifying. I had to perform two pieces, then have an interview about why I thought I deserved a place on the course. I had no idea what to say, so I completely messed it up, rambling on about my love of music. Such a boring answer.'

'I'm sure it was better than you think it was.'

'That's what Chase said. Anyway, I don't think I've ever felt that nervous. Ever.'

'Not even when I forced you to play the piano in front of a big crowd on New Year's Eve without giving you any warning?' Nancy says.

'This was worse,' I tell her. 'On New Year's Eve, I didn't have to play in front of Caroline Morreau.'

'Who?' Mum and Nancy chorus.

'The director of music at Guildhall and one of the school's piano teachers. She is a famous pianist with several bestselling classical albums and she also happens to be leading this course.'

I feel a wave of nausea just thinking about when I walked into the audition room and saw Caroline standing by the piano, writing something down. I froze to the spot. I knew she was the director of music there, but I had NO idea that *she* would be the one conducting the audition.

'Miss Palmer,' she'd said in this clipped, expressionless voice, gesturing to the piano stool. 'Take a seat.'

After a few moments of staring at her while she got back to writing notes, I'd forced myself to walk over and sit down.

'Your first piece, when you're ready,' she'd instructed, moving away and sitting on a chair to the side.

I hadn't known what to do. My hands were shaking and my heart was thudding so hard against my chest that it was making my ears ring. I swallowed, a cold sweat breaking out on the back of my neck, and tried to unscramble my brain, desperately trying to remember all the tips Chase had given me over the past few weeks for getting over my crippling stage fright. But Caroline Morreau was right there, in the corner of my eye, waiting for me to perform, judging me. I couldn't play in front of her. I could barely play in front of anyone. But I especially couldn't play in front of *her*.

Caroline had sat patiently waiting and, after a while, cleared her throat.

'Are you nervous, Miss Palmer?' she'd asked, her voice neutral.

My mouth too dry to answer her, I'd nodded.

She had then picked up her chair and walked across the room with it to a space behind the piano stool, her heels clacking loudly on the floor as she went. She placed the chair against the wall behind me and sat down, so I wouldn't be able to see her when I faced forward.

'Try now,' she'd said. 'Take your time. There's no rush. Deep breaths. Play what you can.'

It had sort of worked, too. I had swivelled back round to look at the keys and now I couldn't see her in the corner of my eye. All I could see was an empty room. I did as she said and tried to get my breathing under control, feeling less pressured to play straight away. When I'd felt slightly calmer, I'd lifted my fingers to the keys and begun my piece. After a shaky beginning, I got into it a bit more and by the time I reached the end I had almost forgotten she was in the room with me.

It wasn't the best I'd ever played, but I'd got through it.

'Wow, it's so impressive that you auditioned in front of someone like that,' Mum says, her eyes brimming with tears. 'I'm so proud of you, Nina. I can't believe you kept this all to yourself!'

'So,' Nancy begins, glancing back to the letter, 'is that letter going to say whether you got a place or not?'

I gulp. 'Yep.'

'And you haven't opened it yet?'

'Nope.'

'Why not?'

I bite my lip and look down at the envelope. 'I'm scared to.'

Nancy leans forward and takes my hand, squeezing my fingers and looking me right in the eye. 'Nina, the fact that you had the guts to audition is amazing. If you don't get a place on this one, who cares? You'll try again for the next. Either way, you're going to have to open the envelope.'

We suddenly hear a sniffle from the end of the bed and turn to look at Mum.

'Oh, girls,' she says, dabbing her eyes with her dressing gown. 'I'm so proud of you.'

'Nancy,' I say, as she rolls her eyes at Mum, 'can you open it?'

'Really? Are you sure?'

'Yes. I can't do it.' I pass it to her confidently. 'Just open it and tell me.'

'OK then.'

She tears open the envelope and pulls out the folded letter inside, her forehead furrowed in concentration as her eyes scan down the page. I try to read her expression, but I can't work it out. A lump forms in my throat and my palms suddenly feel very clammy. I so *badly* want this.

'Well?' I croak, staring at her. 'What does it say?'

'Nina,' she says, a grin spreading across her face. 'You got in.'

CHAPTER TWO

NANCY

CHASE!

CHASE?! WAKE UP!

CHASE ARE YOU
THERE?!?!?!?!

CHASE WAKE
UUUUUUUPPPPPPPP!!!

HELLOOOOOOOOO?!?!

Hi Nancy

Oh hi!! Yay! You're awake!!

I sure am now. Have you
ever heard of weekends?

If you don't want to be
disturbed, put your phone on

silent, pal. And hello, you're
a pop star. Aren't early
mornings part of the job?

Yep, when we're touring or
working. The band is having
some well-earned time off,
remember?

CHASE, NINA GOT IN!

TO THE GUILDHALL COURSE!

Are you serious? That's
amazing news!!

Not that I'm surprised. I'll
call her now

NO OMG DON'T CALL
HER!!!!!!

Whoa, OK, why not?

BECAUSE then she'll know
I've been messaging you

I've decided to throw her a
SURPRISE party this
evening. You know, to
celebrate

Find the Girl: All that Glitters

That's really cool of you! I'm
in. You need any help?

I know you're supposed to
be coming over for dinner
tonight, right? Stick to that
story. But I need you to come
to Norfolk early and keep
her busy for the day. That
way I can sort everything out
without her noticing that I'm
organizing things. That OK?

I'll cancel my plans and
make my way there later
this morning. I'll think of
something

You can maybe go to the
beach and drink hot
chocolate or whatever
cringe things you guys do
that make the rest of us
want to throw up

You're so sweet. Are you
going to have the party at
your house?

Nancy

I have a better idea for the
venue actually. I'll let you
know if it works out. Btw, I
saw you on the Graham
Norton Show last week and
I'm not sure about that shirt

What was wrong with the
shirt?

I think blue is more your
colour. Not . . . vomit yellow

It wasn't vomit yellow! It
was mustard. Cool mustard

Sure. Mustard. Whatever
you say

I LOVE that shirt

OK

I looked GREAT in that shirt

OK

Come on. Was it really that
bad?

Yes

Anyone ever tell you you're
very blunt?

I prefer the word honest

Fine, I won't wear that shirt
again

See you later, Colonel
Mustard x

I am so proud of Nina. I'm not even mad that she didn't tell me about the audition because it's just so HER to convince herself there's no point in telling anyone because she won't get a place. Just like last term when she didn't want to do the school talent show because of her stage fright and she thought she was really bad at playing the piano blah blah blah and then what happened in the end? She WON.

Her getting a place on the Guildhall course is the perfect opportunity to throw her a big party. And, to be honest, I think everyone at school could do with a party this weekend. We've only just come back from the Christmas holidays and already the teachers have piled on the homework as well as constantly warning us about how our GCSEs are right round the corner. Every morning, Mrs Smithson, our form teacher, has droned on about how it may only be January but exam season will be here soon enough and early preparation is key.

It's really quite depressing.

So, when I message Layla and Sophie, the most popular girls in our class, and tell them that I'm throwing a party for Nina tonight and to spread the word that everyone is invited, they reply straight away saying they'll be there.

I still feel a bit awkward around Layla and Sophie, though. We used to be best friends and did everything together. But then, when the whole thing about Chase and Nina came out, Layla wasn't very nice to me about it. It made me realize that our friendship wasn't really a proper one. Sure, we both loved make-up and clothes and Chasing Chords, but, apart from that, we were very different when it came to values and stuff. Friends are supposed to support you and love you no matter what – I didn't exactly get that vibe from Layla. I think it was more a status kind of thing. We were both popular, so therefore we were friends. And Sophie just tagged along.

Anyway, it's not like we had a big fallout and we hate each other or anything. We're still *friends*, just not close ones.

If you'd told me a few months ago that I would end up becoming best friends with Nina again and her friend Jimmy, I would have laughed in your face. But that's exactly what's happened. I can't do anything these days without consulting them.

Which was why, as soon as Nina left the house, telling me that Chase wanted to spend the afternoon together to celebrate the news about Guildhall, I got on the phone to Jimmy and told him to come round immediately.

'Jimmy!' I yell as he comes through the door. 'We have so much to do – I'm freaking out!'

'Whoa, whoa, whoa,' he says, laughing. 'Calm down. We've got a good few hours, Nancy. Plenty of time.'

'Did you speak to the record-shop lady?' I ask. 'Hannah?'

'Haley,' he corrects. 'Yes, I did.'

I try to read his expression. 'Aaaand?'

He grins. 'She said it's no problem for us to hold Nina's surprise party at Neptune Records tonight.'

'YES!'

Neptune Records is this really old, dusty record shop on our small village high street that, for some reason, Nina loves. She spends loads of time there and has all these vinyl records up on her wall in her bedroom. As soon as I decided to throw her a party, I knew that Neptune Records would be the PERFECT venue. It was much easier to organize it there than try to keep her out of the house for the whole day without her getting suspicious. And not only is Neptune Nina's favourite place in Norfolk but she also told me that she bumped into Chase there after meeting him for the first time at his concert, so I know it means a lot to her. It was like fate or something.

'Let's go to Neptune now,' I say to Jimmy, pulling my coat on. 'I'll message Layla and Sophie and let them know the venue so they can tell everyone else. And we can go to the bakery on our way and get a congratulations cake.'

'Is your mum at the shop today?' Jimmy asks, holding open the front door. 'We should say hello on our way past.'

When our dad left all those years ago, we moved to this village in Norfolk and Mum opened a shop on the high street, something she'd always dreamt of doing. It's about as difficult to describe the shop as it is to describe Mum. She likes to wear big bows in her hair, full skirts and VERY loud colours, the whole shebang. And her shop is equally wacky. We get a lot of tourists visiting the village, especially in the summer as it's quaint and near the coast, so Mum's shop is filled with bits and bobs that might appeal to them, like paintings by local artists, postcards of the beach, hand-painted Norfolk-themed teapots and other weird things.

I know that last year Mum was struggling a bit with sales, but since the news got out that her daughter is dating Chase Hunter of Chasing Chords, she's had an influx of customers.

'I had to shoo a group of girls out at closing time,' she told us the other day. 'They'd been waiting in the shop for two hours, hoping Chase or Nina might stop by. They had to keep buying things to have an excuse to hang around. Great for business but, goodness me, they're dedicated!'

I laughed when she told me that, partly because of her baffled expression, but also because it wasn't that long ago that I was one of those girls. I was Chasing Chords' biggest fan. I was so devoted to them that I even had a fan-fiction blog. I used to write stories about the band all the time and spent most of my free time tracking them on social media, making sure I was completely up-to-date with their every move. Chase Hunter was my phone background and I even printed out and framed a tweet the band once sent me in reply to a comment about their latest single.

Which, now that my sister is dating Chase, all seems a bit creepy.

Over the holidays, I took down any Chasing Chords memorabilia I had around my room, including the framed tweet and a picture of Chase. It would be a bit weird to keep a picture of my sister's boyfriend on my desk. My phone background is now a picture of Nina and me pulling faces at each other. I also decided to shut down the blog. I may still love the band's music, but I wasn't exactly going to continue writing stories about the boys now that we're friends.

I've got to know Chase well over the last few weeks and through him have met the band, including Miles, the drummer. Who has nice arms. And nice eyes.

Not that that's important. Just an observation.

Anyway, now that I know Chase, the dream fantasy I had about him has gone right out of the window. There's no denying he's hot and everything, but the idea of fancying him is really gross. He's my twin's *boyfriend*. We get on very well but we definitely aren't compatible.

No offence to him, but he's got this whole broody, serious thing going on, which is great and everything, but the other day I made a HILARIOUS joke about Nina's obsession with the composer Austin Golding and Chase didn't even laugh. He just waited for me to finish laughing at my own joke and then went, 'Oooh, actually, Austin Golding's latest composition is quite nostalgic of a bygone era, blah blah blah.'

I zoned out straight away but Nina was totally engrossed.

'Oh my goodness, Nancy Palmer!' A woman wearing a Stevie Wonder T-shirt beams at me from behind the counter of Neptune Records as I walk through the door, before racing round to give me a big hug. 'I haven't seen you since you were a little girl and you first moved to the village. I'm Haley.'

'Hi, Haley, thank you so much for letting us hold the party here,' I say, glancing round. It's exactly how I remember it, with the same dusty old-book smell.

'Not at all. Nina comes here all the time.' She puts a hand on her heart and sighs. 'Jimmy told me about Guildhall when he phoned about the party. I'm so proud of her! She didn't say a word to me about it when she was in here the other day.'

'She didn't tell anyone,' Jimmy says, coming through the door behind me and putting down the bags of decorations that we just bought. 'We didn't even know she was auditioning.'

'I can't believe how brave she is. Just the word "audition" makes me feel nervous,' Haley says before putting her hands on her hips. 'Right, well, we can get to work decorating the place. We officially close at five, but I can try to close earlier if you'd like the party to start before then.'

'No, don't go to any trouble. I can tell everyone to get here by five, if that's all right with you, and I'll message Chase to ask him to bring Nina along a bit after that.'

Haley nods. She has a customer in the shop at the moment, standing at the back and flipping through a stack of old records, but I've noticed that he's glanced over at Jimmy and me curiously several times. Haley follows my eyeline and then turns back to me with a knowing smile.

'You know that's Max Rogers, right? Nina's piano teacher.'

'No way.'

'I knew I recognized him from somewhere!' Jimmy says.

'He's in here all the time, too. Let me introduce you. Max!' she calls out, gesturing for him to come over. 'Max, I assume you can guess from her appearance, but this is Nancy, Nina's twin sister, and Jimmy, her friend.'

He shakes my hand. 'It's nice to meet you, Nancy, and of course, Jimmy, we've met before at school. Good to see you. Haley was just filling me in about Nina's Guildhall place. It's brilliant news. I couldn't be happier for her.'

'She kept it secret from you, too?' Jimmy asks, amazed.

'Oh, yes – but, knowing Nina, that doesn't surprise me.' He chuckles as we all nod in agreement. 'I'm looking forward to hearing about her audition. It's so wonderful to see her growing in confidence and going for these opportunities. I think we have you to thank in part for that, Nancy.'

I stare at him. 'Me?'

'She mentioned it was you who encouraged her to enter the school talent show last year and I believe you were the one who set up that outdoor concert at New Year in Norwich,' he explains. 'Nina is a very talented pianist, but she's always suffered from stage fright. I've been trying for a long time to get her to play in front of an audience and she was always too afraid. Things are changing now. I couldn't be happier that people are starting to take notice of what she can do.' He puffs out his chest proudly. 'I'll be telling everyone I know that my star student has got a place on a Guildhall course.'

'Everyone *will* know after tonight.' Haley grins. 'Nancy is throwing Nina a surprise party here to congratulate her.'

'Ah, well, she deserves it.' He smiles warmly at me. 'It was very nice to meet you, Nancy, and tell Nina I look forward to hearing all about it in our lesson next week. I'll see you soon, Haley.'

He gives us a wave and heads towards the door. Just as he's about to leave, I stop him.

'Uh, Mr Rogers, wait,' I say hurriedly, a thought suddenly popping into my head. 'You should come to the party here tonight. If you've got nothing on, I mean.'

'Good idea! Nina would love that!' Haley exclaims, clapping her hands together.

'Yeah, she would. She's always going on about how you transformed her piano playing and stuff,' I say, Jimmy nodding beside me. 'I think she'd want you here to celebrate her achievement with everyone. Without you, it might not have happened.'

'And since you're here already, Max, you can stick around and help us with the decorations,' Haley points out, nodding at the bags by the door.

Mr Rogers looks so taken aback at the invitation that he doesn't say anything for a moment, standing stock-still in the doorway.

'Well, that's very kind of you, Nancy,' he says eventually. 'I'd love to.'

A few hours later the shop is decorated with bunting and balloons, and a large CONGRATULATIONS banner hanging across the back wall. The aisles are bursting with people from our school year chatting excitedly, admiring the cake sitting on the counter and enjoying Jimmy's home-made fruit-juice punch. Haley is at the counter looking pained as Layla pesters her to change the music playing from a Beatles album to the current chart.

Jimmy comes to stand next to me. 'You know, I have a feeling that Nina is going to really hate this,' he says with a chuckle. 'She's never been one for surprises. I still don't think she's forgiven us for setting her up to play the piano to an audience with no preparation at New Year.'

'Yeah, she may not have been happy about that surprise at first, but in the end it was a total win,' I point out. 'The video of her and Chase playing together went viral and she became the hottest new music talent out there. If she was a bit more media savvy and let me create an Instagram account for her, she'd be getting music deals left, right and centre. It's like Mr Rogers said: it's about time people started taking notice of what she can do.'

'Looks like she's doing just fine without social media,' Jimmy says. 'I can't believe how many people are here tonight, last minute! And, speaking of Mr Rogers, I think it's really nice that he could stick around for tonight.'

'Yeah,' I say, spotting him chatting to Mum on the other side of the room. 'He's so proud of Nina. When he was helping me tie up the banner, he asked me if I wanted to take up piano lessons because, if I had even a smidge of her talent, he'd want me to give it a try.'

'Oh, really? And what did you say?'

'The truth: that I don't have ANY talent. So he should give up on that one.'

Jimmy laughs. 'You never know. I can see you in an orchestra. The cymbals perhaps? Or tambourine?'

'I'll think about it.' I smile, before checking the time on my phone and craning my neck to look around the shop. 'Do you think everyone is here who should be? Nina and Chase will be home soon.'

'I think so.'

'Are you sure? There might be some last-minute arrivals.'

Jimmy looks at me curiously. 'Are you *hoping* for some last-minute arrivals?'

'Don't know. I just don't want anyone coming in late or at the same time and ruining it. Maybe I should text some people and check if they're coming or not.'

'Uh-huh.' Jimmy nods, giving me a knowing look. 'And exactly *which* people are you going to text and check to see if they're coming?'

I shrug, checking my phone for messages. 'No one in particular.'

'You're not going to text a certain drummer of a certain band to see if he's dropping by?'

My cheeks immediately start burning. 'What do you mean?'

'I mean Miles, the drummer of Chasing Chords,' he says with a mischievous smile. 'Don't think I didn't see that spark between you two at New Year. And you've been talking about him non-stop ever since.'

'WHAT? I have NOT.'

'Yes, you have. I don't think you even realize you're doing it, but every now and then his name will crop up into conversation.' He puts his hands on his hips and makes his voice high-pitched, launching into a ridiculous impression of me. ' "I like your shirt, Jimmy; it's a bit like the one Miles wore in that Chasing Chords music video." "I don't understand how anyone can not like *Jane Eyre*. It's my favourite book and I think people like Miles, who say it's boring, need to read it again because they're clearly deluded." "Jimmy, do you think Miles will be coming to the party tonight? I hope so because I looooooooooove him." '

'Firstly, that was a terrible impression of me. And secondly, you've made all that up. I never speak about Miles and I do NOT love him. I barely know him!'

'Tell me again what you said earlier when we were choosing the cake flavour at the bakery?' he asks, wearing a smug expression.

'What does Nina's cake have to do with this?'

I suddenly feel very warm. I need to ask Haley to turn the heating down in here.

'I suggested the carrot cake and you said no, we should go for the Victoria sponge because everyone likes that and not everyone likes carrot cake . . . like Miles,' he says triumphantly. 'Admit it, you've got Miles on the brain.'

'I will not admit it. And, anyway, I have no idea if Chase invited him tonight; I just said that he should ask the rest of the Chasing Chords members in case they were around and they wanted to come along on the off-chance,' I tell him casually, flicking my hair behind my shoulders. 'Clearly they were all too busy as none of them are here. Which is fine. I don't mind. I didn't even notice.'

Suddenly, my phone vibrates in my pocket with a message from Chase.

Walking down the high street

now . . .

'QUICK!' I yell. 'THEY'RE COMING!'

There's total chaos as everyone scrambles to get into position. Haley turns off the music and Jimmy rushes to get the lights so Nina won't be able to see into the shop through the window. I quickly grab the cake from the counter and hold it up proudly by the door, while Jimmy loudly whispers for everyone to get ready with the party poppers he handed out earlier.

We hear Nina's voice just outside the door.

'I told you it would be closed, Chase. Look – all the lights are off. Come on, we can come back another time. I'll ask Haley to hold whatever record you want.'

'I think we should try the door and check, just in case.'

The door creaks open, ringing the old bell above the shop door.

'That's weird,' Nina says, stepping into the darkness. 'Haley must have forgotten to –'

'SURPRISE!' we all chorus as the lights switch on, making her jump about ten metres in the air.

34

'WHAT THE –'

'Surprise, Nina!' I cry, stepping forward with the cake. 'Congratulations on getting on to the Guildhall course. We're all very proud of you!'

'Nancy!' she gasps, looking so shocked that I can't stop giggling. 'I can't believe this!'

'You should have seen your face!' I say as I pass the cake to Chase so she can give me a hug. 'Priceless.'

'You organized all this?' She has tears in her eyes as she takes in all the decorations, before waving at Haley across the room. 'How did you do all this in one day?'

'She had plenty of help,' Jimmy says, nudging me with his elbow and throwing an arm round her. 'It was all Nancy's idea to have it here at Neptune, though.'

'The best idea!' Chase grins at me. 'Where could be cooler to have a party than a record store?'

'Thanks for keeping Nina busy, Chase.'

'It wasn't too tricky in the end,' he says, running a hand through his messy hair. 'I suggested that we go to some cool places so she could do some photography. I'm guessing she'll have to put that hobby to one side for a bit while she focuses on her music. Turns out there are a LOT of cool places to photograph in Norfolk. Who knew that one tree in one field could look so different to another tree in a field very far away?'

I laugh. 'Poor you! Where did you drag him, Nina?'

'Hey! You said you were enjoying seeing the beautiful countryside!' Nina says, as he kisses her on the head. 'I took him on that walk we used to do with Mum when we first moved here – do you remember?' She reaches for her camera that's in her bag. 'It's still just as beautiful, Nancy – you should come with us next time.'

'There's going to be a *next time*?' Chase says under his breath to Jimmy, who stifles a laugh.

'As much as I'd love to look through the endless photos you got on that camera of a bunch of trees and cows, you should probably go say hi to all your friends,' I point out, winking at Chase as I take the camera from her hands.

She smiles. 'Oh, yeah. Seriously, Nancy, I can't believe you organized this. Thank you.'

She gives me another hug and then goes to say hi to a group of girls from our year behind me who are waiting to congratulate Nina and also stare open-mouthed at Chase. I notice it happens a lot as the two of them make their way through the room and wonder how Chase is so good at acting completely normal, pretending that people aren't just openly gawping at him. As I watch him, I think that it's probably a good thing that the other band members of Chasing Chords couldn't make it, because that may have been a bit much for a lot of our school friends. If one of them is causing this amount of staring, then all the band here would have been disastrous.

'Well done, Nancy – this is great!' Sophie smiles, bopping next to me. 'Such a good surprise! Do you think Chase would mind having a selfie with me?'

'Ugh, don't be so embarrassing, Sophie,' Layla says, rolling her eyes and flicking her glossy brown hair behind her shoulder. 'Try and play it cool. He must get so bored of all that.'

I smile to myself, knowing that if Chase offered up selfies, Layla would be first in line. Last summer, back when Layla and I were best friends and did everything together, I thought I saw one of the actors from *High School Musical* walking down Oxford Street when we were there doing some shopping. As soon as I said it, Layla squealed, 'Hold my bags!' and hurled her shopping into my arms before sprinting down the road after him.

It turned out not to be him but some random guy who looked a bit like him. Layla was so annoyed she'd wasted such energy on a nobody that she was in the worst mood for the rest of the day.

It was worth it for me though, just to witness that extraordinary reaction.

'Nina has done really well,' Sophie says, still bopping absent-mindedly to the music. 'She's like . . . going to be a famous musician, right? Like Chase? I mean, she must hang out with music people in the industry all the time! SO cool.'

I shrug. 'I think she's more into classical music.'

'Do you get to meet anyone through her and Chase?' Sophie asks eagerly.

'Yeah, course,' I find myself saying. 'I'm quite close with all of Chasing Chords now.'

I don't know why I still feel a need to try to impress Layla and Sophie. But, for some reason, I don't want them thinking I'm *completely* irrelevant. Yeah, Nina is the one dating the famous pop star, but when it comes down to it I know more about Chasing Chords than Chasing Chords know about Chasing Chords.

Seriously. Ask me anything.

And anyway, technically, the whole I-know-people-in-the-music-biz thing is not a total lie. I *have* briefly met Mark, the band's manager and Chase's uncle. I've got his contact details from when Nina was in a coma after our car accident and Chase was worried I might not be able to reach him at any point, so he gave me Mark's number.

I've hung out with Miles a few times now, too, if you count New Year's Eve, the time I barged past him to get into the Norwich studio, and also that time a while ago when he thought I was a crazed stalker claiming to be the one Chase was talking about in the #FINDTHEGIRL campaign. (Well, I *was* claiming to be her, but I really did think he was talking about me. Hello, I'm 'Miss N. Palmer' too and I'd been at that same concert where he and Nina met. And also I was obviously NOT a crazed stalker. Just an enthusiastic fan.)

'That's awesome that you are friends with the best band EVER.' Sophie beams. 'Do you think we can all hang out some time? I have, like, a hundred of their T-shirts I want them to sign.'

'Maybe,' I say, nodding. 'Now Nina will be on her course in London at the weekends, I'm not sure how often I'll be seeing Chase and the band.'

'So, what are you going to do, Nancy?' Layla suddenly asks, taking a sip from her drink.

'What do you mean?'

She looks at me as though I'm really slow. 'You just said it. Nina will be off every weekend in London on this amazing course, so it's not like she's going to have that much free time. Don't you guys do everything together these days?'

'Yeah, but I'm sure I can survive a few weekends,' I say confidently. 'I'll see her in the evenings.'

'But any spare time she does have, she'll want to spend with her pop-star boyfriend, right? Or doing her music practice. This course is a big deal; it's a proper London music school. She's going to be off in London being successful and you'll be here. I don't know –' she pauses and shrugs – 'if it was me I'd feel a bit . . .'

She searches for the right words and Sophie finishes her sentence for her.

'Left behind?'

'Yeah,' Layla agrees. 'Left behind.'

'I . . . well, I hadn't really thought about it like that,' I answer quietly, watching Chase and Nina laughing together on the other side of the room.

'Oh well, they say that change is good,' Layla says breezily, before waving at someone behind me. 'We'll see you in a bit, Nancy. Great party, by the way.'

When the party has finished and after we've helped Haley clear up, I get home and lie in bed trying to sleep but I can't get Layla's words out of my head, which is ridiculous. I'm not being left behind. I'm really happy for Nina. She deserves to go off and be successful. You can't stay in the same place forever; things are always going to change. That's just life.

And it's like Layla said. Change is good.

Right?

CHAPTER THREE

NINA

As soon as the taxi pulls up at Guildhall, I feel like I might throw up.

Nancy offered to come with me on the train to London and help settle me in for the first weekend of the course, but I told her not to be so silly. I didn't want her to waste a chunk of her weekend holding my hand and, anyway, Chase is meeting me, so it's not like I'll be on my own. But, now that I'm here, I wish more than anything that Nancy was with me, calming my nerves and making me laugh.

I pay the taxi driver and lift my bag out of the car, staring up at the brick building with 'GUILDHALL SCHOOL OF MUSIC AND DRAMA' written in bold white letters across it. I can't believe I'm here. I can't believe I got a place on this course. I'm so lucky to be able to spend every weekend for the next few weeks in this very building. Others would kill for this opportunity.

So, WHY do I just want to go home?!

'Come on, Nina,' I say to myself, taking a deep breath. 'You can do this.'

I check my watch. Chase should be here by now. He said he'd meet me outside, so I put my bag down and wait at the side of the building, people-watching to pass the time.

I'm pleased that there are no paparazzi here at least. Chase had warned me that there might be, as they'd easily be able to track down what time the course started on the first day and be waiting for me to turn up. Even though we'd managed to keep my audition secret from the reporters, the fact that I'd got a place on the course had somehow been leaked to the press.

None of us know how they found out, as I made sure to tell Nancy not to put anything on social media about it. While I wait, I have a momentary panic when I think I see someone with a camera pointing the lens in my vague direction, but when people move out of the way, and I'm able to get a good look, I can't see anyone.

A few minutes later a tall boy around my age with short brown hair, wearing skinny black jeans and Wayfarers even though it's a cloudy day, walks towards Guildhall, a bag slung over his shoulder. He does a double take when he notices me standing there, as though he recognizes me, but if that's the case then it doesn't look like he's all that happy about it. Unimpressed, he raises his eyebrows and does a small shake of his head as he passes me, heading under the archway and through the glass doors into the school's reception.

I feel instantly mortified. Why would a complete stranger react like that? I instinctively run my hands through my hair in case it's sticking up stupidly or something and I hadn't noticed. I reach for the compact mirror in my bag and check my make-up that Nancy did for me this morning, but it looks as perfect as when she'd just finished, nothing smeared or smudged.

As more and more people stroll past me into the building, I grow impatient, constantly checking my phone. Chase was meant to be here half an hour ago and we're supposed to have signed in by now. I can't bear the idea of facing people like that sunglasses boy on my own, but I also don't want to be late on my very first day. Finally, my phone beeps with a message from Chase.

> Hey, I'm so sorry, I won't be able
> to make it. Stuck in a meeting
> that's overrun and can't leave!
> Good luck for your first day,
> you'll smash it! Xxx

It's so stupid but I feel like crying. I can't believe he's not coming. He promised he'd be here. And he could have told me sooner, rather than letting me stand around waiting for him. It was his idea for me to audition for this course in the first place and now he's left me to handle it on my own.

No, Nina, that's not fair, I tell myself, shaking my head at my own thoughts. *Everyone else is able to walk into Guildhall on their own, so this should not be such a big deal.* I tell myself that over and over until I find the courage to pick up my bag and walk towards the glass doors.

'Hi,' I say quietly as I reach the reception desk. 'I'm Nina Palmer.'

'Sorry?' the receptionist says, looking up from the computer.

'I'm . . . N-Nina Palmer,' I repeat a little louder, my cheeks growing hot.

At moments like this, I wish I had the confidence of Nancy. She wouldn't have waited for anyone. She would have marched in on time and announced herself without any qualms whatsoever, excited to get going and make an impression on some of the best music teachers in the country.

I can't even say my name without tripping over my words.

The receptionist smiles warmly. 'Ah yes. Welcome to Guildhall. Here's your room key; you'll be sharing room fourteen with Grace Bright. The induction is going to start soon, but you can leave your bag in your room, then you'll need to be in the Milton Court concert hall in ten minutes. And don't forget your music from your audition.'

She holds out the key, but, as soon as I take it from her, I drop it. Feeling like a complete klutz, my whole face is burning with embarrassment as I bend down to pick it up. Ignoring my clumsiness, the receptionist shows me on a map how to get to the halls where my room is and points me in the right direction.

I go back outside into the cold and follow the map down the road and round a corner to the halls. Some other students are hurrying down the stairs as I enter, already on their way to the induction, but I keep my eyes to the floor as they go past chatting. I'm too nervous to introduce myself. As I reach room fourteen, the door swings open and a girl with curly dark hair and bright eyes stands in the doorway.

'You must be Nina!' she says, beaming at me. 'Hi, I'm Grace.'

'Hi,' I squeak as she gestures for me to come in.

'Are you fussy about which bed you're on?' she asks. 'I shoved my bag on that one by the window, but I really don't mind where I am, so say if you have a preference.'

I shake my head, my stomach doing somersaults of nerves. I put my bag on the bed that isn't taken and go over to the window, looking out at the courtyard I just crossed from the road. I see more students leaving our building and swallow the lump in my throat. They all look intimidating. Even though I know I'm going home tomorrow, I still feel homesick. I wish Chase could be here, or Nancy, or Mum. It all feels a bit too overwhelming.

'Are you OK?' Grace asks, watching me curiously.

'Yeah. Just a bit nervous.'

She smiles kindly. 'Don't worry – I'm nervous, too,' she says. 'I keep telling myself it's just a couple of days but I guess being here –' she gestures at the room – 'I know it's stupid because it's only the weekends and it's not like we're actual students at Guildhall, but I feel completely terrified as though I don't deserve to be here.'

'Same,' I admit.

'Let's go to the concert hall for the induction. Have you got your sheet music from your audition?'

I fumble for my Austin Golding music and clutch it close to my chest like a safety blanket as Grace leads the way out of the room and along the corridor to the stairs.

'So, you're a pianist, right? I saw that video on YouTube of you playing the Chasing Chords song "Ghosts" at New Year. Wow, you're talented! You play with so much feeling – it's amazing!'

'Oh, no, I'm not that good,' I assure her as we cross the courtyard and head down the road. 'It seems like a tricky song to play but actually –'

'Nina,' she laughs, interrupting me gently, 'you're allowed to take a compliment. You wouldn't be here on this course if you weren't great at playing the piano.'

'Are you a pianist, too?' I ask, steering the conversation in a different direction.

'I wish,' she says. 'I'm a singer. One day, I want to be on the West End.'

'My sister and I love the West End.' I smile. 'I love playing songs from the big shows.'

'You have any favourites?'

'Have you heard of *Half a Sixpence*?'

She breaks into a wide grin. 'I love that show.'

'One of my favourite songs is "If the Rain's Got to Fall". Nancy and I are obsessed with it.'

'I'm a *Dreamgirls* fan myself. If you haven't seen it, you need to. I've seen it five times,' she says, before pointing up to a building on our left. 'I think this is Milton Court.'

A man waiting at the front of the building directs us to the hall and, as Grace pushes open the door, we both stop and look around us in complete awe. The hall is so grand and vast, with its high ceiling and hundreds of audience seats facing a wide, brightly lit wooden-floored stage. A long lighting rig hangs high above it.

'Whoa,' Grace gasps before turning to me, her eyes wide in amazement. 'This isn't at all terrifying.'

'It's incredible,' I whisper, staring at the group of teachers standing on the stage, talking to one another. I gulp, spotting Caroline Morreau among them.

Some of the seats in the first few rows are taken by fellow students on the course, who glance up at us as we choose two seats behind them. I shrink as low as possible into my seat as soon as I'm in it. Even though I've just met her, I'm so glad that I was put in a room with someone as nice and friendly as Grace.

The two boys in front swivel round to face us and I realize that one of them is the guy in sunglasses I saw earlier. The boy next to him has dark brown, curly hair and those large, round tortoiseshell glasses that all the popular people in my school wear.

'It's Nina, right? Nina Palmer?' the sunglasses boy says in a low voice.

'Yes, and this is Grace,' I say, as she gives a wave next to me.

'Right,' he says, looking like he doesn't care that much. 'I'm Jordan.'

'James.' The boy in the tortoiseshell glasses smiles.

I instinctively like James. Jordan, not so much. And it turns out my instincts could not be more right.

'You're the one dating Chase Hunter,' Jordan states. 'The lead singer of . . . what's that band?'

'Chasing Chords,' Grace tells him excitedly. 'I love their music. Chase writes all the songs, doesn't he? The lyrics are so good and such creative melodies.'

Jordan snorts.

'Sorry,' he says, clearly not sorry at all. 'No offence to your *boyfriend*, but pop songs aren't really my thing.'

'No worries.' I shrug, not wanting to start the weekend with any negativity. And anyway, until I went to a Chasing Chords show, I thought the same way. I was as ignorant and snobbish as Jordan before I really listened to a Chasing Chords song.

'So, did he just make a call then?' Jordan asks me breezily.

'Um, did who make a call?'

'Chase,' he says, looking at me as though I'm stupid.

'Sorry, I don't know what you –'

'That's why you're here, right?' he says loud enough for other students around us to glance over in curiosity. 'Because you're famous.'

'No, I'm not famous,' I reply.

'It must be nice just to be able to click your fingers and get what you want, just because you're dating a pop star,' he says with a thin-lipped smile. 'I guess it's true what they say: it's not *what* you know – it's *who* you know.'

'Hey,' Grace says, frowning at him. 'Nina didn't get on this course because she's dating Chase Hunter. Haven't you seen the video of her playing? She's a talented pianist.'

'Sure,' Jordan says, rolling his eyes. 'But it doesn't exactly *hurt* to let someone like Nina on the course, right? Good publicity and all that. I'm just saying that some of us had to work hard to get on this course, whereas *others* can get places using their connections.'

'I auditioned,' I say, growing flustered at all the attention. 'I didn't get in because of Chase.'

'But he took you to the audition. I saw him here that day.'

'Well, yeah, but . . . but he just wanted to be here for me; it's not like he knows any of the teachers here.'

Jordan's eyes flicker to the sheet music resting on my lap and a smirk crosses his lips.

'You played Austin Golding for your audition? And you still think you got in *just* on your playing? The last time I played any of that simple, popular music, I was about five years old. Guildhall is a place for serious musicians,' Jordan says, turning back to face the stage. 'I'd hate to think it had lowered its standards by giving someone famous a place when they're not good enough.'

I bite my lip and stare down at my feet, desperately trying not to cry.

'Ignore him,' Grace whispers, before raising her voice to make sure he hears the next bit. 'Unfortunately, you get a lot of jealousy in music.'

But Jordan just sits there, looking ahead and smiling, completely indifferent to her comment.

I feel grateful to Grace for standing up for me, but I'm also completely mortified. The first day hasn't even started and already everyone thinks I don't deserve to be here. Jordan's words sting and I can't get them out of my brain. I tell myself that there's no way that the teachers at Guildhall would care about things like who I'm dating, and they would only judge on talent, but Jordan has made me feel uneasy.

And, even worse, everyone else will be thinking that now.

'Good morning!'

Caroline steps forward to the front of the stage. Her dark hair is tied back from her face and she is wearing bright red lipstick and a smart black dress. I realize that in all her concert clips I've seen on YouTube, and on the front of all her album covers, she's always been wearing black. I'm also not sure I've ever seen her smile.

'I am Caroline Morreau, the director of music. Welcome to the Guildhall weekend music course. Over the next few weeks, you'll spend every weekend learning from the very best in the business, giving you a taster of what it's like to be a student here. We believe that you are the musicians of the future, who will one day study full-time with us –' she pauses to scan our faces and everyone sits up a bit higher in their seats – 'but, most importantly, you're here to develop your passion for music and the arts. This first weekend, you'll be learning the ropes. Next weekend, we'll have some exciting announcements and that's when the real work begins.'

There's a murmur of anticipation through the hall before she continues.

'This afternoon, you'll be introduced to your teachers and begin your lessons, but we thought we'd start with a performance from each of you; your audition pieces were just too good not to share with your peers. So, without further ado, let's see what you can do.'

I go completely numb.

'Is she serious? I can't . . . I can't go up there and perform,' I say in a panic to Grace, who is busy getting her sheet music in order. 'I can't. She knows I can't. I could barely play just to her in the audition.'

'Of course you can,' Grace says, turning to me in surprise. 'You're a brilliant performer. I've seen you in action, remember?'

'No, Grace, I can't.' I clutch her wrist, shaking my head. 'That thing I did at New Year was with Chase and it was a complete one-off. I get stage fright. Really bad stage fright.'

'We'll go alphabetically by surname so, Grace Bright, you're up first,' Caroline announces, leading a round of applause.

Grace stands up and shifts past me into the aisle, walking towards the stage. She hands her music over to Caroline, who takes it to the piano while Grace goes centre stage.

As Grace starts to sing, I'm so mesmerized by her voice that for a moment I forget about how scared I am and become completely engrossed in the song. She looks so confident and comfortable on that stage; the idea of her doing anything else in life seems immediately absurd. Her song comes to an end and the audience burst into applause. The fear washes over me again.

'You have the most beautiful voice,' I tell her when she returns to her seat. 'Why aren't you already performing on the West End?'

She giggles and thanks me as Caroline calls the next person up to perform. I get more and more nervous as time goes on, desperately trying to think of an excuse to get out of this. Maybe I could pretend to be sick. Or say I don't want to do it. But this is *Guildhall*. If I mess this up or refuse to perform, they'll kick me off the course – and my dream of attending this school one day will be over.

I close my eyes, trying to stay calm. They didn't say we'd have to perform our audition piece on the first day. No one warned us about this. I can't do it. I can't.

Yes, you can.

I hear Chase's voice in my head, just as he's said it a million times these past few weeks whenever he's encouraged me to play something in front of family or friends in an effort to help me get over my stage fright.

Just take a deep breath and remember that this is what you love doing. Forget the audience, play for yourself.

But his voice is drowned out by Jordan's name being called and the round of applause as he sits down at the piano.

'He's a pianist,' I groan to Grace.

'I think you two might be the only ones on the course,' she says. 'There's not many people left to perform and, judging by the fact those two over there are holding a flute and a violin, I'm going to guess that those are their instruments and they're not just holding them for the hell of it.'

Jordan begins to play. He's brilliant. He's a hundred times better than me. I don't realize that my mouth is hanging open for his whole performance until he finishes and I need to swallow because it's so dry.

'Nina Palmer!' Caroline calls out next as Jordan goes to sit down, receiving a high-five from James.

I stay in my seat and Grace gives me a nudge with her elbow. As I get to my feet, I drop my sheet music and Jordan lets out an audible sigh.

'Here we go,' he says, under his breath.

Grace helps me gather up my music. 'You'll be OK, Nina,' she whispers encouragingly. 'You're just as brilliant as he is, if not better. Go and prove it.'

I stumble up to the stage and put my music on the piano, getting it back in order. The hall falls silent. The piano stool scrapes loudly across the floor as I move it into position and I apologize out loud to no one in particular.

'When you're ready, Nina,' Caroline says, before going to stand on the side of the stage behind me.

I try to remember everything that Chase has said about stage fright, about taking a deep breath and focusing on just doing what I love, but the music hall is so big and I can feel everyone's eyes boring into me. My fingers are shaking so badly as I rest them on the keys that I accidentally press a random note before I start playing, the sound reverberating around the hall in the silence.

'Sorry,' I say again. No one says anything. They're just waiting.

I know I can't just sit here; I have to start playing. So, I do. But my nerves are in pieces and I noticeably mess up in several places throughout the song. My performance is terrible, like I've never seen the music I'm playing before. When I get to the end, I'm so relieved it's over that I don't hold the last note properly or wait for the crowd's reaction. I leap to my feet, almost knocking over the piano stool, and scrunch up my music from the stand, rushing to get down the steps off the stage and back to my seat as quickly as possible.

There is a stilted, half-hearted round of applause, as though no one is quite sure whether to clap or not. I sit down and can't hold back my tears any longer. They flow freely down my cheeks. Caroline clears her throat and calls the next name. Grace shoots me a sympathetic look and reaches over to pat my hand.

Jordan speaks loud enough to James so that everyone, including me, can hear.

'Looks like famous connections can only get you so far. Talent always wins out in the end.'

CHAPTER FOUR

NANCY

I turn round as someone taps me on the shoulder at my locker. It's a girl from a couple of years below.

'Hi, Nina,' she says, as a group of her friends hang back giggling. 'I'm sorry to bother you, but I just wanted to ask how you got this look?'

She holds up her phone screen. It's a picture of Nina standing outside Guildhall on a celebrity gossip website underneath the headline:

NINA MOVES CENTRE STAGE!

Chase Hunter's girlfriend hits all the right fashion notes as she starts her part-time music course at Guildhall School of Music and Drama!

'I'm Nancy,' I correct, being sure to smile at her so she doesn't think I'm annoyed.

'Oh,' she says, looking disappointed.

'But I actually did her make-up and hair that day, so if you want to make a note in your phone I can tell you what products I used.'

'That's OK,' she says, putting her phone away. 'I'll ask Nina when I see her.'

'Are you sure?' I ask. 'She's kind of useless with make-up. I don't think she'll be much help whereas I can tell you exactly how to get this look. The highlighter is actually a new find and it's so good, if you just –'

'That's OK,' she interrupts, before heading back to her friends, where I overhear her say, 'It's not Nina – it's the other one.'

My jaw drops to the floor as I watch them scurry away. *The other one.* I feel a stab in my stomach as her words echo round my brain. Since when was I . . . *the other one*? Only a few months ago I was one of the most popular girls in school and everyone was asking me for style tips and encouraging me to do vlogs on how to get the perfect curls using straighteners. How did this happen?

Jimmy comes round the corner and starts laughing at my expression.

'OK, what happened?' he asks, leaning on the locker next to mine. 'The last time I saw you looking this shocked was when that pigeon almost landed on your head the other day.'

'Nothing,' I say hurriedly, too embarrassed to tell him the truth. 'How are you?'

'Good. I've chosen our next book for book club. You want to know what we'll be reading this month? It's a classic and it looks brilliant.'

'Jimmy,' I sigh, taking some textbooks from my locker and slamming it shut, 'how many times do I have to tell you that I am NOT part of your book club? If you can call it that, considering the only two members are you and your dad.'

'You know, it's lucky that we're friends now, otherwise I might be insulted by comments like that one.' He grins, falling into step with me as I head towards my form room. 'I just thought, after all those texts you sent me last weekend, you might want to reconsider my generous offer to join my book club so you had something to focus on.'

'What do you mean?' I ask, stopping in the doorway of my classroom.

He raises his eyebrows. 'Are you serious? Do you know how many times you texted me last Saturday?'

'I don't know.' I shrug. 'A few.'

'A few?' He tips his head back and laughs loudly. 'You messaged me fifteen times telling me in various ways how bored you were.'

'No way. That's not true. I was not that bad.'

He smiles. 'I speak the truth, Nancy Palmer. I counted.'

'Yeah, well, whatever,' I huff defensively. 'Mum was at the shop all day and Nina was on her course. I was only checking *you* weren't too bored without Nina around.'

'How thoughtful of you,' he says, folding his arms and then giving me a look. 'You do know that Nina's course is for a few weeks, right? It's not a one-off.'

'Yes, of course. Why?'

'What are you going to do this coming weekend when she goes off to London?'

'I don't know,' I say, suddenly realizing that I have no plans AGAIN. 'I'll have to think of something.'

'Maybe it's a good opportunity to try something new,' he says. 'Have you signed up for any of the career talks this term?'

I shake my head.

'You should,' he says encouragingly. 'There's some quite good ones. A newspaper editor is coming in next week, which I think will be really helpful. You should come with me.'

'You're thinking of going into journalism?'

'Yep, I've got it all planned out,' he says. 'I'll study English at Oxford, intern at a major publication during the holidays, run the student newspaper in my final year, then land a competitive job at a huge news corporation, write ground-breaking investigative reports and insightful features, working my way up to become editor-in-chief by the time I'm thirty.'

I laugh. 'Wow, you really do have it all planned out. How do you know exactly what you want to do?'

'I guess writing and debating has always been my thing. Or being "very opinionated", as Mr Barber wrote in my report.' He grins. 'So, journalism makes sense.'

'OK, well, what if you don't have a talent. What happens if you're just –' I search for the word – '*meh*. I can't think of anything I'm good at or really stand out in. It's not like I really have any hobbies. Before, if I had some spare time and I was bored, I'd think up a story for my Chasing Chords blog, but I can't exactly do that now.'

'Why don't you do some vlogs?' Jimmy suggests. 'People at school are always asking you for make-up tips, right?'

I grimace, thinking of the 'other one' incident only a few minutes ago.

'Not any more. I don't think I'd get any hits unless Nina was on it and I can't exactly ask her to help me out with vlogging; it's not like she has the time. Argh, Jimmy, what am I going to do this weekend? Last weekend was the WORST. I had nothing to do. I'll go mad if I have to sit around the house on my own again with nothing to distract me except homework.'

Jimmy looks pensive for a moment as students in my form barge past us into the classroom.

'I know!' he says, his expression brightening. 'You could help your mum in the shop.'

'PLEASE tell me you're joking.'

'What?' He laughs at my horrified expression. 'It is not that bad.'

'Yeah, so while Nina is up in London on her amazing music course, being papped by photographers with her envy-inducing make-up and drinking hot chocolate with her pop-star boyfriend, I'm supposed to sit in my mum's shop in the middle of nowhere all day? No thank you. That will make me feel more left behind than ever.'

The bell rings, signalling the start of registration.

'I better go or I'll be late; I'm on my last warning,' Jimmy says. 'I'll see you at morning break and, in the meantime, consider the book-club offer. You could spend your Saturday lost in the world of Thomas Hardy if you want!'

'I'll think about it,' I call after him as he races down the corridor.

I sit down at my desk at the back of the room. I used to sit over by the window with Layla and Sophie, but since the events of last term I've moved across to a desk that I now share with Nina. It took a lot of persuading to get her to agree to sit at the back of the class as she used to like being up front, but I put my foot down on that one and she eventually relented. I have a reputation to uphold.

At least, I thought I did before this morning's events.

Our form tutor, Mrs Smithson, comes in with her coffee and settles us all down, telling Layla to put her phone away before it's confiscated. Mrs Smithson is yet to confiscate Layla's phone despite threatening to do so at least three times a day.

'Where's Nina today?' she asks, noticing the empty seat next to me.

'I'm here!'

Nina comes bustling through the door and hurries over, plonking her books on the desk with a loud thud and sliding into her seat, pushing her hair out of her face.

'Where've you been?' I whisper, as Mrs Smithson ticks the register.

'Practising.'

'Again? You've been practising non-stop all week. I've barely seen you.'

'I know, but, like I told you, Guildhall is intense. I'm definitely the worst. If I don't improve, they'll kick me off.'

'Nina, don't be silly – you're a total star. You should have a little more faith in yourself.'

I can tell she's so stressed by it all that she's not listening to a word I say. Mrs Smithson finishes checking the register and clears her throat, standing at the front of the class.

'I have an exciting announcement to make,' she says. 'Today, we are launching a competition and the prize is really quite something. Last week, the headmistress was at an event and she happened to meet someone who had a very interesting job. A creative director at the Disney Channel in London. And guess what? This Disney creative director has offered an internship for students to work alongside her and learn the ropes during the Easter holidays!'

I sit bolt upright. An internship working at the Disney Channel? That would be AMAZING. I've loved Disney for as long as I can remember and it would be a dream to work there one day. I stick my hand as high up in the air as possible.

'Nancy, I see you already have a question?'

'How do we apply, Mrs Smithson?'

She smiles. 'I was getting to that. The headmistress thinks this is, of course, a fantastic internship but also thought it might be quite a fun opportunity to start a new school competition to get your creative juices flowing.'

'Wait a second,' Layla says, looking unimpressed. 'We have to *win* the internship through a competition?'

'That's correct.'

'What do we have to do?' shouts someone at the front.

'Disney is looking for a creative and innovative intern, or interns – those who are knowledgeable about media and have a good connection with an audience. So, we thought it would be fun to start a competition for . . . the best new website!'

'We have to create a website?' Layla wrinkles her nose. 'About what?'

'Ah, that's the whole point,' Mrs Smithson enthuses. 'You need to get creative and think of something exciting and different! Towards the end of term, the headmistress will whittle down the entries to those she thinks are the most outstanding and then we'll put it to the school for a vote. The website that gets the most votes wins. And its creator, or creators, get to spend their Easter holidays behind the scenes of the Disney Channel! You can either create the website yourself or as a maximum group of three. The creative director has said that she's willing to take on up to three students.' She claps her hands excitedly. 'What a fabulous thing to put on your CVs!'

'And I bet you get to meet loads of celebrities!' Sophie adds.

Mrs Smithson nods. 'This certainly isn't the sort of opportunity that comes along every day, and I already have a bet on with the other teachers that the winning student will come from my form. I have by far the best and most creative class in the school.'

Nina catches my eye and we share a giggle.

'So, the most popular website will win?' asks Timothy Davies, one of the boys sitting at the front of the classroom. 'Will it be measured by the number of hits it gets by the time it's judged?'

'There will be many factors. The websites that get through to the final will be judged on things like how many hits they have got, as you say, Timothy, but also things like the quality of content, their appearance, and what they deliver that's different to anything else. Once the final sites have been decided on it's up to you, the students, to judge the websites and vote for the one that you like the best.'

'Isn't it going to be tricky to do this alongside all our homework?' a girl named Ellie points out. 'And the internship will be during our GCSE revision time.'

'Ah, yes, well I thought of that,' Mrs Smithson says solemnly. 'This is purely voluntary, so it's only if you think you have the time around your revision. And, as for the internship, it's a week that has been offered, leaving plenty of holiday time to do your revision before your exams in the summer term. Now, speaking of revision, however exciting the competition is, I want to spend the few minutes we have left of form time to run through some excellent revision tips. If you have any more questions about the competition, feel free to ask me at the end or in break times.'

As she turns her back to us to begin writing on the board, I lean in to Nina.

'That's a pretty cool prize, isn't it? Imagine working with a creative director at the Disney Channel. You'd get to see how everything works and how it all comes together.'

'It would be great experience,' she agrees, copying Mrs Smithson's bullet points into her notepad. 'But it's not for me.'

'You're not even considering the competition?'

'I have so much on; I can't think about a competition when I'm trying to juggle schoolwork and Guildhall stuff,' she says. 'And, anyway, I wouldn't know the first thing about creating a website or have anything to say on one.'

'Jimmy is going to love this. Just before class started, he was telling me about his plans to become a journalist. This could not be more perfect for him.'

'Nancy Palmer,' Mrs Smithson calls out from the front of class, 'please don't think that because you're at the back of the room I can't hear your whispering. I assume that you and Nina are busy discussing the excellent revision tips I'm currently writing on the board for your benefit?'

I get my head down and start copying the bullet points, but I'm distracted by the idea of getting to go behind the scenes of the Disney Channel. I can totally see myself wearing one of those cool headsets that people in TV always wear and coming up with new creative ideas for bringing in an audience.

My heart sinks. Why am I letting myself daydream about this? I can't create a website. The Chasing Chords fan-fiction thing was just a blog, just loads of fangirl stories, not really a proper website. And what would I even say? Up against people like Jimmy, who actually know what they're doing, I'd have no chance of winning. I should just forget about the competition and concentrate on these very helpful revision bullet points. I should not let myself think about working at the Disney Channel.

'Nancy?'

I jolt my head up. I'd been lost in a vision of me sitting at a table with a load of creatives and producers, saying, '*Come on, people, I need ideas! Let's get brainstorming!*' I hadn't even heard the bell ring or noticed everyone packing up their stuff. Nina is already standing, her bag over her shoulder, giving me a strange look.

'Sorry,' I say, sliding my chair back. 'I was distracted.'

'No kidding.' Nina smiles. 'You've got biro on your cheek from where you were leaning on your hand.'

I hurriedly get my pocket mirror out and examine my face, attempting to rub the blue smudge off my foundation.

'I'll see you in the next lesson,' she says, checking her watch.

'You're not going to wait for me? I'm coming now – I just want to get this biro off.'

'I'm going to see if I can catch Mr Rogers in the music room to ask him a question about this new piece I'm trying out; I'm really stuck on a section. Can you let Miss Sanders know I'm on my way?'

'Sure,' I say, as she thanks me and rushes off.

I finish getting the pen off my face as best I can and then shove my books under my arm. I'm the last one to leave the classroom and Mrs Smithson stops me as I reach the door.

'Nancy,' she says, clicking the cap on to her board pen, 'before you go, I wanted to ask – what do you think about the competition?'

'I think it's cool. It's a great prize.'

She smiles. 'Yes, I thought you'd be interested in it.'

'Yeah, well, I've always loved Disney movies. Nina and I were obsessed with them growing up and . . . I'm still obsessed with them, I guess. Whoever wins that prize will be seriously lucky. I hope it's Jimmy. He works really hard and it's his big dream to go into media, so he really deserves it.'

'And not you?' Mrs Smithson says, tilting her head slightly in surprise.

'Huh?'

'I thought that you'd be interested in entering the competition and winning the prize. It's right up your street.'

'Mrs Smithson, I think you've got me muddled up with someone else. I couldn't win a prize like that. Are you sure you're not thinking about Nina?'

'I'm quite sure, thank you, Nancy,' she says, leaning back on her desk and folding her arms. 'You've got a wonderful flair for writing; don't think I haven't noticed.'

I blink at her. What is going on? Has she fallen over and bumped her head? A flair for writing? I mean, English probably is my best subject because I love reading, but I hardly ever get As on my essays, unlike Nina or Jimmy.

'Um, Mrs Smithson, I don't have a wonderful flair for writing. Don't you remember the essay I wrote last term on *Jane Eyre*? I got a B minus and *Jane Eyre* is my favourite book, so I don't think I'm going to get any better than that.'

'I'm not talking about essay writing. I'm talking about *creative* writing,' she explains, watching me carefully. 'I saw all the blog posts you did for that band.'

'You read my Chasing Chords fan-fiction stuff?'

'Oh, yes.' She chuckles. 'I didn't know about it until the commotion last term and I thought I'd have a little read of

68

what you'd been putting all your effort into, as you certainly weren't putting much effort into your classwork. Well, it was very enlightening. The stories were creative and entertaining. I read quite a few and ended up a Chasing Chords fan by the end of it. That Chase Hunter really does have incredible cheekbones, doesn't he?'

She gets this dreamy look on her face.

Gross.

'It's really good of you to bother reading those stories, but I was just messing around.'

'Ah, but that's what I'm trying to tell you,' she says, waggling her finger at me. 'You weren't just messing around. You created a brilliant website because you were passionate about the subject. I think that with your ability to write captivating content and your natural ability to grow an audience, you have as good a chance as anyone in this school of winning this competition. It would be nice to see you give it a go at least. Have you considered a career in the media? I think you should.'

'Mrs Smithson, I appreciate your encouragement and everything, but Nina is the twin with all the talents and cool lifestyle, so I think everyone would be more interested in what she has to say. Anyway –' I glance at the clock above the board – 'I better get going otherwise I'll be in trouble.'

'I hope you'll think about what I've said. It would be a shame for you to give up before you've even given it a try.'

'OK. I'll think about it.'

'And, Nancy,' she says, stopping me again from racing out of the door, 'you need to remember that you may be twins, but you and Nina are each your own person. It's wonderful to see Nina really flourish after years of shying away and hiding in your shadow, but don't let that become an excuse for you to hide away in hers.'

'A competition? How exciting!' Mum exclaims, clapping her hands in the oven gloves. 'So, are you two going to enter it?'

'Nina's too busy with everything going on and I wouldn't stand a chance,' I reply, laying the table. 'Although Mrs Smithson mentioned . . . Never mind.'

'Go on,' Mum says encouragingly. 'What did Mrs Smithson say? That you two are the most talented beings on the planet and I am the luckiest mother in the world?'

'Um, no?' I say, staring at her like she's lost her mind. 'Because that would be weird. She just said something about how I should think about entering because she liked my Chasing Chords blog. That's all.'

'What's that about Chasing Chords?' Nina says, looking up from her scribbles across some sheet music. 'Sorry, I wasn't listening – what are we talking about?'

'The competition that Mrs Smithson told us about today,' I remind her, sharing a smile with Mum. 'Are you going to work on that through dinner, too?'

'No, I'll put it away for a bit,' she says apologetically, putting the music back in its folder and sliding it across the table. 'My eyes are going funny, anyway. Every time I shut them, all I see is black music notes.'

Mum shrieks with laughter. Like, really loudly. Way louder than normal.

'That wasn't that funny,' Nina says, staring at her, 'was it?'

'No, it wasn't,' I confirm. 'Mum, are you OK?'

'Of course, my beautiful ducklings!' she trills, putting our plates in front of us.

'Sorry, did you just call us . . . beautiful ducklings?' Nina asks as I pretend to stick two fingers down my throat. 'Did something happen at the shop today, Mum? Because you seem to be in a very good mood.'

'Why wouldn't I be in a good mood? I'm having dinner with my wonderful girls, my beautiful little ducklings,' Mum says, sitting in her chair and lifting her fork. 'Dig in! I hope you like it!'

I catch Nina's eye and know exactly what she's thinking. Something is going on with Mum.

Over the past couple of days something has changed about her. She's been in a permanent good mood, nothing has bothered her, and she's been overenthusiastic about absolutely everything. She's holding herself differently, too; she's walking a bit taller or something and her face is all . . . glowy.

And I think I may have an idea why.

'Mum,' I begin, 'have you . . . met someone?'

Nina gasps. 'That's it! I've been trying to put my finger on it. Mum! Tell us immediately.'

Mum blushes to her roots and smiles so shyly that I'm worried her lips might disappear into her face. 'What? Don't be silly, girls. I'm just in a good mood, that's all.'

'No, that is not all,' I say firmly. 'You're acting super dreamy and happy, just like Nina did when she first started dating Chase secretly. Remember? Everyone noticed the change. And now you're doing the same. Who is this man?'

'Honestly, it's like I'm being grilled by MI5!' Mum exclaims. '*Fine*, I . . . I have met someone.'

'I knew it! Maybe I should be a detective,' I say, making Nina laugh. 'So, who is he?'

'No one,' she replies, not looking either of us in the eye. 'We're just talking. It's nothing. I don't want to talk about it. Yet.'

'All right – we'll drop it.' Nina grins. 'But I think it's really exciting.'

'Same,' I agree. 'And also a bit disturbing.'

'Oh, girls.' Mum chuckles, rolling her eyes.

She gets up, flustered, to get something out of the fridge and, while she's gone, Nina leans across the table.

'By the way, Nancy, I think you should enter the competition.'

'Huh? Don't be stupid.'

'Mrs Smithson is right. You should give it a try.'

I sigh. 'Come on – what would I create a website about? There's no way I'd win.'

'Nancy, earlier when I got to class and you thought I wasn't listening, you told me that I should have a little more faith in myself. Maybe it's about time you listened to your own advice,' she says, shooting me a grin. 'What's the worst that could happen?'

CHAPTER FIVE

NINA

'Welcome back.'

Caroline looks at us from the middle of the Guildhall concert-hall stage. As everyone else eagerly sits up at her greeting, I sink, hoping she can't see me. After last weekend, I'm too embarrassed to even look at her. She must think she's made a terrible mistake letting me on this course. I wish that the director of music at Guildhall didn't also have to be my piano teacher.

'I trust you've all had a good week and have been practising the tasks your various teachers gave you.'

A shiver runs down my spine. It is safe to say that the lessons I had on Saturday and Sunday last week with Caroline did not go well. She had barely said a word as I played the three Austin Golding pieces I'd brought with me. She'd just asked me to play them over and over without any commentary, until the end when she told me that she now knew what we needed to work on in the lead-up to the showcase and it was 'a long, long list'. Which was *very* comforting to hear.

I am not looking forward to my lesson this morning.

'Before I let you rush off to the music rooms, I want to tell you something,' Caroline says. 'Last weekend, I promised that I would have an exciting announcement to make today. The performance showcase at the end of the course will be an opportunity for your friends and family to witness your improvement and development, but it is also an opportunity for myself and the other Guildhall staff to select one of you to win an automatic place on our summer school.'

The hall erupts into a ripple of gasps and excited chatter. I should be ecstatic at such an idea, but instead it's like a knife twisting into my stomach. Getting a place on the summer school would be an incredible advantage when it came to auditioning to be a student here full-time. Mr Rogers and I have always talked about it. But now I know the other talent that's out there, the level of competition and the kind of people I'd be up against. I know that I don't have a hope of being selected by Caroline. I'd made it clear to everyone that I was a second-rate pianist and Jordan was the one with the potential.

'Oh my god, Nina, how amazing is this?' Grace squeals next to me, clutching my arm. 'Can you imagine getting an automatic place? Not having to worry about auditioning? My heart is beating so fast.'

'So, if you weren't already nervous about the showcase, you should be now,' Caroline continues. 'Right, off to your lessons. I'll be coming to your group rehearsal this afternoon, so will see you all then.'

As she walks off the stage, her heels clacking across the wood, Grace stands up and grabs my hand, attempting to drag me to my feet.

'Come on, Nina – let's go! We can get the best practice rooms before this lot barge their way in. I have a LOT to work on.'

'I have a lesson now,' I tell her, reluctantly standing up.

'Oh,' Grace says. 'With the Matchmaker?'

Even though I'm not feeling in the best mood, I can't help but laugh as Grace reminds me of the nickname we came up with. After I returned to our room from my disastrous first lesson, Grace patiently listened to me explain how badly it had gone and then had looked really thoughtful.

'Caroline Morreau is terrifying. She reminds me of someone, you know. I just can't put my finger on it. Something about the way she holds herself and her permanently unimpressed expression,' she'd said, before sitting up and clicking her fingers, as if a light bulb had gone on in her head. 'I know! The person from *Mulan*!'

'The Disney film?'

'Yes, you know that scene with the teapot.'

'I can't remember. We need Nancy, my sister, here. She's an expert when it comes to Disney. She'd be able to tell you straight away.'

'You know,' Grace had continued, refusing to give up, 'at the beginning of the film when Mulan is sent to impress that really strict, snooty woman to see if she'll make a good wife. Come on, and they sing that song about bringing honour? And the cricket gets in the teapot? I KNOW!' she'd suddenly yelled. 'THE MATCHMAKER!'

We'd then fallen about with laughter and when Grace managed to get the clip up on her phone we'd laughed even more until my stomach ached. It had been a stroke of genius that had made me feel much better and forget about how terrible my day had been.

'Oh no! Now we're not going to be able to get that out of your head!' Grace had said through tears of laughter. 'Every time we see her, we're going to think about it!' She'd then stood up and pretended to hold a clipboard with a slapstick frown before doing a spot-on impression of the first time the Matchmaker makes an appearance in the film – 'FA MULAN!' – causing a fresh round of giggles.

I'm so lucky to have been put in a room with Grace. Apart from her, I haven't really made friends with anyone else on the course, not that there's been much opportunity. On the first day, we'd had so many different back-to-back inductions that we were all completely exhausted on Saturday night, so no one was hanging around in the common room. Everyone went straight to bed. Fortunately, that also meant I'd been able to avoid horrible Jordan, although I caught him whispering to a group of friends and then all of them looked over in my direction when we were in the canteen.

I haven't told anyone at home about Jordan's comments and how awful my first performance was. I didn't want to tell Nancy because I knew she'd get super protective and I wouldn't have been surprised if she'd booked herself a train to London straight away to come and give him a piece of her mind. As much as I'd like to see that, it just felt like making a big fuss and I really don't want her worrying.

I thought about telling Chase. But then I got scared that he might admit Jordan was right and he *had* pulled a few strings to get me on the course, and I didn't want to know.

I told myself I was being ridiculous; I know that Chase would never do that. But I still didn't want to tell him. What good would it do? The only result would be that it would make him angry on my behalf and he's too busy at the moment to have to bother with something so petty. Not that I know exactly why he's so busy. Chasing Chords are having a break in between working on songs and tours, and Chase was really looking forward to having some downtime. I thought we'd be spending loads of time together, but that hasn't happened at all.

'It will be so nice,' he'd said at New Year. 'I can come to Norfolk and see you in the evenings after school, and at weekends we can go on proper dates.'

But so far, in the weeks off that he's had, he's only managed to come to Norfolk for two evenings and we've hardly had any weekend dates. I thought we could spend time with each other last Sunday when my course finished, before I got the train back to Norwich, but he was only able to meet me for a hot chocolate at the station before rushing off. His uncle and manager, Mark, was taking him for a posh dinner and he had to get back home to change.

I was a bit hurt that he was cutting short his time with me to spend it with Mark. He sees Mark all the time and he knew that my first Guildhall weekend hadn't been exactly how I'd dreamt it.

But still. Seeing him was really nice and he'd promised to drop by this evening. I just have to get through the day. The thought of seeing him at the end of it is the best motivation I can find.

'Ah, Nina. Come in,' says Caroline, after I tap tentatively on the music-room door.

I shuffle past her and sit at the piano stool, propping my sheet music on the piano.

'Have you been practising, Nina?'

At the sound of her clipped voice, any lingering sense of humour I had about the whole Matchmaker thing disappears. I feel so tense that when I try to speak my throat seems to have closed up.

'Yes,' I say quietly.

She stands beside the piano stool, towering over me.

'This isn't the piece we were working on last week,' she states.

'No, I thought I'd try something different,' I explain, remembering Jordan's comment about Austin Golding being too easy. 'If that's OK?'

My question is met with silence. 'Yes,' she says finally. 'It's good to try something new. Let's see how you go.'

I gulp and position my fingers on the keys. I've chosen Edvard Grieg's *Notturno*, Op.54, No.4. It's a very beautiful piece and one I overheard Jordan practising last week. It's also very difficult.

Mr Rogers had been a bit confused when he arrived at our music lesson this week to find me already at the piano, studying the newly bought sheet music for us to work on. He did a double take when he saw my Austin Golding sheet music squashed into the bin in the corner of the room.

But when I explained that I needed to work on something that actually stood a chance of impressing the Guildhall teachers, he nodded in understanding and we set to work on *Notturno*. It was disastrous. I could barely play the first few bars without making a mistake.

'You see?' I'd told him. 'I can't do it. It's too hard. I don't know why they let me on this course. Jordan was playing this off by heart.'

'You've played pieces of this standard before,' Mr Rogers had replied. 'You've told yourself you can't do it and that's why you're making mistakes. Usually, you'd never expect to be able to play this piece perfectly straight away. If you could, there would be no point having lessons with me and no point in lessons with Caroline Morreau at Guildhall. Take a deep breath and let's try that section again. Take it a bit slower this time and listen to the music. Enjoy how pretty it is.'

'How can I enjoy how pretty it is when I keep messing it up?'

'A piece doesn't need to be technically perfect to be enjoyable,' he'd said, and he'd chuckled.

I had a feeling that Caroline Morreau did not share the same optimistic opinion. Seconds into the piece, she holds up her hand, stopping me. To say that she has a different teaching style to Mr Rogers is an understatement. Where he is warm and encouraging, she is cold and blunt.

'Don't play for me,' she says after a moment's silence.

'Sorry?'

'Don't play for *me*,' she repeats.

'Um.' I stare at the music, feeling the heat rising up my neck and fully aware that my face is probably the shade of a tomato right now. 'But –'

'Try again.'

I start playing and she lets me get to the bottom of the first page this time, having made several mistakes on my way, before her hand comes flying out, signalling for me to stop. She closes her eyes and breathes in dramatically. We stay in silence for what feels like hours, but it's only a few minutes. When she opens her eyes again, she hits me with a hard stare.

'Try. Again.' She pauses. 'Stop apologizing. Start from the top.'

I hesitate, confused because I haven't said anything at all; I didn't apologize. Is she hearing things?

'When you're ready,' she prompts.

I tentatively start to play.

'Stop!' she cries, holding up her hand. 'On your feet, Miss Palmer.'

I jump upright and stand as straight as possible, as though following the instructions of a terrifying army captain.

'Walk around the room. Just walk.'

I stand frozen to the spot, staring at her. 'S-sorry?'

'Walk around the room,' she instructs. 'Come on,' she adds, gesturing for me to join her as she begins to glide around the room in a circle.

WHAT DO I DO?

'Miss Palmer! Start walking.'

I do as I'm instructed, walking round the room behind her in silence, feeling like a complete idiot and wondering

82

how exactly this is helping my piano playing. We continue with this activity for about two minutes before she stops so suddenly that I almost go straight into her back.

'Do you see?' she says, stepping aside so that I'm facing the long mirror on the wall by the door.

I stare at my reflection.

'Um. It's me?' I squeak, praying that that is the simple answer she's looking for.

'Yes, this is you.' She gestures to the mirror. 'Look at how you stand. Shoulders hunched forward. Eyes to the floor unless forced to look up. Your whole body is closed. I can see that you are sorry before you say you are sorry. Your body language is apologizing for you even being in the room. This is how you play.'

Oh. So, that's what she meant by apologizing.

I look back at the mirror. She places her hands on my shoulders and prompts me to roll them back so that my back straightens. She then lifts my chin with her finger.

'Beautiful. *This* is how you should play,' she says, signalling for me to sit back at the piano.

I try to keep my chin up and my body open while I play, but when I fumble the notes I automatically close up, my eyes falling, wishing I could sink into the ground. After a few more miserable attempts at the piece, our lesson comes to an end and I rush to the door as fast as possible.

'Practise, Miss Palmer.'

'I will,' I reply, although I'm not exactly sure what I'm supposed to be practising: the music or walking with my head up stupidly high.

I go straight to the practice rooms to look for an empty one when I turn a corner and walk into Jordan on his way to see Caroline.

'How did it go, Nina?' he sneers, attempting to get a glimpse of the music in my hand. 'More Austin Golding? Or perhaps you're getting better and can move on to some lovely Chasing Chords pop music. I think their songs feature in those *Easy Piano for Beginners* books.'

Trying to ignore him, I push past and he gets a look at the title at the top of the page.

'Grieg's *Notturno*, I see,' he says, his sneer replaced with a thin-lipped smile. 'Ambitious. I wonder where you got the idea to try that? I suppose imitation is the sincerest form of flattery. Well, if you need any tips on the hard bits, don't hesitate to ask. I often play it as a little warm-up before I try any challenging pieces.'

He heads to his lesson, chuckling to himself all the way down the corridor. I get to an empty piano room and slam the door behind me, leaning against it and having a moment to collect myself. I can't let him get to me. I look down at the sheet music and shake my head. He's right. I should be able to play this without thinking. I feel so embarrassed that I thought playing pieces by a contemporary composer like Austin Golding might impress anyone here at Guildhall.

I'll have to work twice as hard over the next few weeks. Attending Guildhall one day is my dream and I'm not going to mess that up now.

I just wish I didn't feel like a failure already.

'So, how is it all going?' Chase asks later that day.

We're sitting in the kitchen near my room, drinking mugs of hot chocolate. I wanted to go out to meet him but he insisted on coming to Guildhall. He wanted to see what it was like and where I was staying. I decided not to say anything about him popping by as I didn't want any nasty comments from Jordan or for anyone to make a fuss, so I asked him to come after we'd all had dinner, knowing that everyone would be in practice rooms working on their music for tomorrow's lessons.

'It's OK. I'm struggling a little with the performance side of things.' I sigh, clasping the warm mug in my hands. 'I'm sure you won't be surprised to hear that.'

Chase gives me an encouraging smile. 'Being onstage isn't easy.'

'It's embarrassing how bad I am. You can't be a concert pianist if you can't play to an audience.'

Chase shrugs. 'Which is why you're here: to work on that. Nobody is perfect, Nina. Not even Caroline Morreau.'

'I know that, but I don't think she's all that impressed with my progress so far,' I admit. 'She made that clear this afternoon.'

As well as our solo pieces, we're going to perform a group orchestral piece in the showcase at the end of the course, so while our one-on-one lessons are in the mornings, our afternoons are made up of group practices, which involve all the students. In our group rehearsal after lunch, we'd gathered in this huge orchestral room ready to work on the piece that we'll be performing together at the end of the showcase. There were two piano parts: Piano One and Piano Two.

Without saying a word, Caroline held out the Piano One part to Jordan and the Piano Two part to me.

'Guess it's talent before celebrity. No hard feelings,' Jordan had said, taking the music sheet from Caroline and going to sit at the piano closest to the orchestra.

I clutch my mug of chocolate tightly as I recall how small he'd made me feel in that moment.

'What happened?' Chase asks, watching me curiously. 'How did she make it clear that she's not impressed with you?'

'Nothing. It doesn't matter,' I say, forcing a smile. 'Anyway, enough about me – what's going on with you?'

'What do you mean?' he asks, shifting uncomfortably in his seat.

'How are you? How's your week been?' I give him a funny look as he stares down at his mug. 'Chase, why are you acting so cagey all of a sudden?'

'I'm not.'

'Yes, you are.' I laugh. 'I just asked how you were doing and now you're barely looking at me.'

'I've had a busy week, that's all.'

'I know, I've hardly heard from you,' I mention pointedly. 'What are you so busy doing? I thought you were supposed to be having some time off. Nancy's been keeping me updated with what the rest of the band are up to; she's shown me all their Instagram pictures and, from the looks of it, they're having a really nice time seeing friends and family, going off on holiday. How come you're not doing the same?'

'They're not the ones who write the music,' he replies.

'So, you've been busy writing music? Chase, you're supposed to be taking some time out for yourself. It's not good for you to never give yourself a break. I thought we were going to be spending time together.'

'We are,' he snaps. 'I'm here now, aren't I?'

His tone stings and neither of us says anything. The silence is unbearable.

'Sorry,' he says eventually, reaching across the table. 'I didn't mean that the way it came out.'

I nod, letting him take my hand.

'And I'm sorry I've been busy. I know I promised that we'd be hanging out a lot,' he says in a gentler voice. 'I'll make it up to you, OK? Trust me.'

'OK,' I say, attempting a smile. 'It's fine. I've hardly got any time anyway, with this taking up all my weekends and practising in between. Homework, too.'

'We'll make the time,' he says firmly, and the knot in my stomach begins to unravel. 'I wasn't expecting this week to be so busy, but I'm really happy to be here now with you.'

He gets up and walks round to stand behind me, leaning forward and wrapping his arms round me, his chin resting on my shoulder. I turn my head to his, pressing my forehead against his cheek. I think about asking him more questions about why he's been so busy because, despite apologizing, he still hasn't explained what it is that's been taking up all his time. But I don't want to ruin this moment.

Unfortunately, Jordan does instead.

The door to the kitchen swings open and he strolls in with his mug, stopping dead in his tracks when he sees us at the table. He purses his lips and walks round to the kettle, filling it from the tap and putting it on in silence. I can't believe my bad luck. Of all the people to walk in here while Chase was with me, it HAD to be Jordan. I'm embarrassed that he's seen us together, as though it's somehow further proof of his ridiculous theory that Chase is the reason I'm on the course. I quickly nudge Chase's arms off me.

With no idea who Jordan is or what he thinks, Chase acts exactly how he normally would if anyone had walked into the kitchen.

He smiles, holding out his hand to Jordan. 'Hey, I'm Chase.'

Jordan glances at his outstretched hand and for a horrible moment I think he might not take it, which would make things more awkward than ever, but thankfully, after a few moments' consideration, he does.

'Jordan,' he says coolly.

'Are you on the music course with Nina, too? Or are you an actor? I know there's a drama course on too, isn't there?' Chase says enthusiastically, unaware of any tension.

'I'm on the music course. I'm a pianist.'

'Cool.' Chase nods. 'You must be really good, like Nina.'

I notice Jordan's bemused eyes flicker towards me, but he doesn't say anything. The kettle pings and he pours the boiling water on to the teabag in his mug.

'Are you enjoying the course?' Chase continues, leaning against the counter. 'I've always wanted to go to Guildhall.'

That sparks Jordan's attention and I regret not dragging Chase away the moment Jordan walked through the door. I quickly get up from my chair and put my mug and Chase's into the dishwasher.

'*You*, Chase Hunter, wanted to go to Guildhall? A music school?' Jordan asks.

'Yeah, I know,' Chase admits with a self-deprecating smile. 'The band thing kind of happened by accident and I actually always thought I'd end up going to study music somewhere like this. I guess it's never too late. Maybe one day I'll be able to get on a course like this one.'

'But Guildhall is for *proper* musicians,' Jordan says slowly, as though explaining something simple to a child who isn't getting it.

Chase stares at him. 'What did you say?'

'Come on, Chase – let's go,' I say hurriedly, grabbing his hand and dragging him from the kitchen and down the stairs, out into the cold.

'Who was that guy?' Chase asks, shoving his hands in his pockets. 'What did he mean?'

'He's just . . . difficult. It doesn't matter.'

'Are all the people on your course like that?'

'No. Only him. He's a bit of a loser.'

'Yeah, just a bit,' Chase grumbles, shaking his head. 'I hope you don't start thinking like him.'

'What? Chase, how can you even say that?'

'I don't know,' he says. 'If enough people tell you that pop music isn't "proper" music, maybe you'll start believing it.'

I take a step closer to him and link my fingers through his.

'Don't be silly. I think you're amazing.'

I feel him physically relax and he squeezes my fingers tightly, before pulling me to his chest.

'I think you're amazing,' he says, and sighs. 'And I'm sorry I can't stay longer.'

'It's OK. I should go get some practice in before bed,' I say, checking my watch.

We stroll together towards the road and he hails a taxi, kissing me goodbye.

'Chase,' I say, stopping him as he opens the car door, still distracted by our earlier conversation about how busy he is. 'You know you can tell me anything, right?'

He smiles, my stomach turning to butterflies as usual at the sight of those dimples.

'Of course.'

But as the taxi pulls away and I watch him disappear down the road, I can't shake the feeling that Chase is hiding something from me.

CHAPTER SIX

NANCY

'Mum, what is *this*?'

'Well, what does it look like? It's a pair of earmuffs! If you could pop them all on that stand by the door, that would be very helpful.'

I hold the object at arm's length and wrinkle my nose. The headband is bright neon green and on each end there's a fluffy earmuff in the shape of a giant seashell. I put the first one on the stand as instructed and reach down into the box to pull out some more. I can't believe I'm spending my Saturday like this. I'm working at the weekend *voluntarily*. But last night when we got back from school and Nina started packing her bag, ready to head off for another weekend in London, I got a horrible sinking feeling. That feeling of being left behind. Of having nothing to do. Of feeling . . . purpose-less. As I watched Nina neatly fold her clothes and get her music in order, I realized that, unlike everyone around me, I have nothing figured out. Nina is all about her music, Jimmy has a clear path set out in journalism, Chase is already a star who is on his way to even bigger things . . .

How come everyone has life goals except for me?

It made me feel really sad thinking about it. Usually, when I'm feeling down, I go into my room and play music until I feel better. Music has always been able to make me feel good about myself. Not the classical relaxing stuff that Nina is always trying to get me to listen to, but pop music like Chasing Chords' albums, my favourite show songs or movie soundtracks. After the car accident last year, I had some trouble sleeping, but music helped me through that. I've even created various playlists depending on what kind of mood I'm in.

But, no matter what songs I listened to, nothing cheered me up. I still felt like I was sitting around, wasting valuable time, completely directionless. I had to *do* something. I didn't want to spend all weekend feeling that way, so I ended up taking Jimmy's advice and asking Mum if she needed any help at the shop. This way, at least I'm busy and I'm not constantly scrolling through Instagram, seeing how amazing and fulfilled everyone else's life is compared to mine.

Although, now that I'm here staring at a pair of seashell earmuffs, I'm not really sure what I was thinking.

'I've bought a lot of coastal-themed products recently,' Mum tells me enthusiastically. 'Tourists come from far and wide to see our beautiful Norfolk coastline and quirky things like that always sell well.'

'I find that hard to believe,' I mumble. 'Who would ever buy these? And then actually wear them?'

'They look a lot better on,' Mum insists, walking over and grabbing a pair to model them. 'You see?'

I burst out laughing. 'You look *ridiculous*!'

With a mischievous smile, she takes another pair from the box and pops them on me.

'Now we both do!'

'Very funny!' I smile, pulling them off and throwing them back in the box as quickly as possible. Luckily, there were no customers in the shop to witness my humiliation. 'So, are you going to wear these on your date tonight?'

Mum blushes, taking the earmuffs off and carefully placing them on the stand.

'I thought I'd ask you to help me pick what to wear later actually,' she says. 'When we get home. Would that be OK? I have a few outfits in mind, but I feel so out of the dating game that I'm not really sure what sort of thing I should be wearing for a dinner date.'

'Don't be silly, Mum – you should wear what you want. But of course I'll help you out. I've got nothing else to do, anyway,' I add.

You know things are bad when your mum has a Saturday-night date and you don't. Mum still hasn't told us anything about this guy she's dating, even though Nina and I did our best at probing her all week. Every time we slid in a question about where they met or what he looks like or what his job is, she'd bat us away and remind us that it was very early days. If things got more serious, then MAYBE she'd give us some more information.

I don't know why she feels the need to be so secretive about it. Nina and I think it's brilliant that Mum is dating someone. She hasn't been interested in anyone since Dad left, and he walked out on us YEARS ago.

She never talks about it unless we ask, but it took her a long time to move on from Dad. He was her first love; they were childhood sweethearts. She really believed they'd be together forever and, when he left, I think she thought he would come back. I guess one day it dawned on her that wasn't going to happen, so she packed us up and moved us here to Norfolk.

Sometimes I think about that time and realize how amazing Mum is. It can't have been easy going through a divorce, moving house and basically having a complete life overhaul while trying to look after two children on your own.

I get so angry at Dad, thinking about those days. How could he leave us like that? Just walk out and then pretend that Nina and I don't exist? I have all these happy memories of him before he left that I wish I could delete from my brain. He worked long hours and we didn't see him much during the week as he'd travel a lot for work too, but we would have these amazing days in London at the weekend where we'd go for dinner and then see a show, and he'd have organized all of it. He's the whole reason Nina and I love musicals. And it was Dad who got Nina into the piano in the first place. He encouraged her to take lessons and to practise every evening, telling her that she was going to be his big superstar.

Sometimes I wonder whether I'm making these memories up, because he can't have been very happy for him to not only leave us but also to make almost no effort to see us afterwards. A Christmas card every year. That's it.

When it arrived in the post this year, I recognized his handwriting and tried to put it in the bin straight away but Nina wouldn't let me. She got all funny about it and when I asked her why on EARTH she'd care about some flimsy Christmas card from him, she didn't say anything – she just read it a few times and put it up on her desk in her room. I don't understand why she'd want to keep it.

'Let her,' Mum had said to me gently, when Nina was out with Chase and I had voiced my opinion on the matter. 'It means something to her.'

'A stupid Christmas card? He hasn't tried to visit us in years, and she thinks him sending a Christmas card to us is meaningful? I'm surprised he even gets our names right.'

'Nina is different to you. She's more sensitive. For her, that card is a connection to her father.'

I'd rolled my eyes very pointedly, but decided that Mum was right and I should let it go. Nina could do what she wanted, but, as far as I was concerned, I didn't *need* a connection to the man who walked out on his family and never looked back.

I think it's great that Mum is dating someone new. Although, obviously, if things get more serious, I'm going to need to do some proper vetting of this guy. Mum deserves the best.

'Is your date picking you up this evening?' I ask casually.

'No, Nancy,' Mum replies, shooting me a knowing look. 'And don't try to be sly – I know why you're asking that. We're meeting at the restaurant, so he doesn't have to worry about being asked a million and one questions by my mischievous daughter at the front door. I don't want to put him off this early on.'

'Hey!' I huff. 'I would be nothing but politeness itself.'

'Sure,' she says, smiling to herself as she checks some paperwork. 'I just need to pop into the back for a bit. Are you OK to man the shop on your own?'

I nod and she disappears, leaving me to finish the earmuff stand. Once I'm done, I flatten the empty box and take it behind the counter. As I bend down to put the cardboard by the door to the back office, the bell above the shop door rings. I straighten up, ready to welcome the customers.

My jaw drops when I see who it is.

'Hey, Nancy,' Layla says, walking towards me with Sophie happily trotting along behind her. 'You're not answering your phone.'

'I have to leave it behind the till when I'm working,' I explain, completely baffled. 'What are you doing here?'

'There are some really cool things in this shop,' Sophie says, picking up handmade candles from a shelf and smelling each one. 'Do we get a discount?'

'I'm not sure, but I can ask. Were you after something specific?'

'Actually,' Layla says, frowning as Sophie tries on a hat with two green pom-poms on it, 'we're not here to buy anything. We were looking for you. When you didn't answer your phone, we tried Jimmy and he said you were working here today.'

'Oh my goodness,' Sophie says, putting the pom-pom hat to one side. 'Are those fish key rings? My dad would love one of these!'

'Sophie, can you focus please?' Layla says in a strained voice.

'Sorry,' she says, her eyes drifting longingly to the key rings.

'Nancy, we have a proposition for you,' Layla begins importantly. 'We've been thinking about the school competition that Mrs Smithson announced this week, and we have decided to enter it.'

'You have? *Why?*'

'Duh! Did you not hear what the prize was? Working with a creative director at the Disney Channel is pretty much the coolest job ever,' Layla says, flicking her hair behind her shoulders. 'We need to win.'

'But isn't it a lot of extra work?'

She shrugs. 'How hard can it be? It's just setting up a website and we'd tell everyone to vote for us. Simple.'

'Okaaaaaaay. So, why are you telling me this?'

'We want you on our team,' Sophie says, beaming at me. I stare at her. 'Huh?'

'We've got it all worked out,' Layla says. 'We're going to launch a really beautiful, classy lifestyle website. It's going to have everything on there that anyone could possibly need. Fashion, hair, make-up tips; guides to throwing the best parties; the best new music recommendations. Basically, everyone at school always asks us these questions anyway – why not put it on to a website for them? People would love it.'

'The music bit is where you come in,' Sophie jumps in, leaning forward next to the till. 'We know you like writing about stuff like that because of the Chasing Chords fanfiction site.'

I hesitate. 'But why would you want me to help you? I mean, after what happened last term . . .'

I let my sentence fizzle out and there's an uncomfortable lingering pause as Sophie and Layla glance at each other. No matter what they say about my writing skills and music knowledge, it's weird that they want me to join their team. Our friendship has changed drastically and things are still kind of awkward between us. There are LOADS of people in our year who are good at writing about music who they could ask.

'We just said why we want you.' Layla shrugs again. 'We both already have so much to do on the website; we don't have time to do the music section, too. You like music so we thought we'd ask you first. Also, you have good contacts.'

'Contacts?'

'Chasing Chords!' Sophie grins. 'You're friends with the best band EVER. We'd find out about music stuff before anyone else! Think how AWESOME that would be.'

'So, what do you think?' Layla asks, tapping her fingers impatiently on the counter.

'I don't know,' I answer honestly. 'I don't know whether I'd have the time with homework and other stuff.'

I don't say the other reason for not wanting to join their project: that I'd have to spend plenty of my spare time hanging out with them.

'Other stuff like . . . working in your mum's shop?' Layla says, watching me carefully.

'This is a one-off. Mum really needed the help.'

'That's OK,' Sophie says cheerily. 'We can always ask Nina.'

'*Nina*?' I say, not even trying to hide how astounded I am at the suggestion. 'Did you say Nina? As in my sister, Nina?'

Layla nods. 'Yeah, that Nina.'

I let out a loud 'HA!' but neither of them is laughing. 'Is that a joke? You're thinking of asking Nina to join you in creating a lifestyle and hot music website?'

'Why is that so weird?' Layla says, folding her arms. 'Nina is dating *Chase Hunter*. She's basically the most popular girl in school. She's famous and she has incredible music contacts, especially now that she's hanging out with Chase and showbiz people in London. The only reason we wouldn't ask her is that she'd probably be too busy, but it's worth a try to see if she's interested.'

'Hang on.' I hold my hands up. 'Did you just say Nina is the most popular girl in school?'

'I bought the same headphones she has the other day,' Sophie informs me. 'I saved up for them and they are *amazing*. She was so right; they totally transform the sound.'

'And she recommended this highlighter when I asked her which one she uses,' Layla says, gesturing to her perfectly made-up skin. 'I can't believe I didn't know about this one before. It's so much better than my last one.'

'Oh my god, and her shoes,' Sophie says excitedly, before I can interject that it was ME who did Nina's make-up and ME who told her which highlighter to use. 'Did you see what that style columnist said about those high-tops she was wearing to Guildhall last weekend? Geek chic. Apparently, Chase got her those trainers for Christmas. So cute of him! I already asked Mum if she could get me some for my birthday.'

'Whoa, whoa, whoa!' I practically yell. 'I got Nina those trainers. Not Chase. Me. I got them for her.'

'The thing about style is that it's not really what you're wearing, it's how you wear it,' Layla says, ignoring me, with Sophie nodding slowly and sincerely in agreement; it's as though Layla has spoken the wisest words of the century.

I can't believe what I'm hearing. I know that Nina is dating a pop star, so obviously the interest in her is going to go up a notch, but I had NO idea that it was this mad. Sophie is buying things because Nina is wearing them. NINA. I love Nina more than life, but the other day she almost bought a beige polo neck. A BEIGE POLO NECK.

Thank goodness I was there to stop her.

And this whole idea of Nina joining Layla and Sophie to create a lifestyle website together is completely laughable. Nina doesn't have a clue about that kind of thing and she doesn't even care. For example, at the amazing surprise party I threw for her, she pointed at the bunting on the wall and went, all baffled, 'How did you get that to stay up there?'

AND THEY WANT HER TO GIVE PEOPLE TIPS ON HOW TO THROW THE BEST PARTIES?!

I know that she'd never do it. I know that she can't stand Layla and Sophie, so that alone would stop her from being a part of it. I know that she doesn't have the time to enter this competition. I know all this.

And yet . . .

I feel terrified at the idea of her doing this and not me. If in some fit of blind madness, Nina agreed to join their team, I would be more left behind than ever. I'd really have

NOTHING left. Nina would be doing all these incredible things, and what would I be doing?

Hanging up key rings in Mum's shop every weekend?

'Anyway, we thought we'd ask you first but if it's a no then we can –'

'I'm in,' I hear myself say.

Layla raises her eyebrows. 'Yeah?'

'Yeah.' I nod firmly. 'I want to launch this website with you. And I want to win.'

'Yes!' Sophie squeals, clapping her hands. 'This is going to be SO much fun!'

'We'll have our first staff meeting on Monday and launch the website soon after that,' Layla says. 'We need to think up a name for the site and get as much content as possible up so we can get lots of interest quickly. I've already got plenty of ideas for layout and we need to come up with some good vlogs, too. As soon as people at school hear that us three are creating this amazing website, they'll be wanting to see it as soon as possible. We want to drown out the competition from the start.'

'OK,' I say, slightly impressed by Layla's new businesswoman persona. 'I'll think up some ideas for the music section over the weekend and we can brainstorm.'

'Great.'

There's a commotion behind me and I turn round to see Mum coming through the office door carrying a huge box, which she plonks down on to the counter.

'Hello, girls,' she says, sounding as surprised as I was to see Layla and Sophie in her shop. 'Have you come to see Nancy working hard?'

'We were just talking about our new project,' Sophie informs her. 'A website for the school competition.'

'You're going to enter the competition?' Mum asks me with a wide smile. 'That's wonderful news!'

'Nancy is going to be the music editor for our hot new lifestyle site,' Sophie continues.

'Oh!' Mum tries to hide her astonishment at this news. 'You're entering the competition together.'

'We'll see you at school, Nancy,' Layla says, looking bored and getting ready to go.

'It was very nice to see you both. Nancy can get to work putting these out for me,' Mum says, tapping the box.

'What is it?' Sophie asks, going up on to her tiptoes to try to peer in.

'These are fantastic,' Mum enthuses, and, before I can stop her, she pulls out a hat that she proceeds to put on her head.

'Is that hat in the shape of a . . . *lobster*?' Layla asks.

'Isn't it really something?' Mum chuckles, wiggling her head so the pincers sticking out of each side of the hat wobble.

Layla smirks. 'It sure is.'

'OK, well, see you on Monday,' I say hurriedly, jumping round the counter and ushering them out of the shop. 'Can't wait to get things started.'

They wave goodbye and I wait until the door has safely shut behind them, before turning to glare at Mum.

'You *had* to put the lobster hat on.'

'Yes, I did,' she says, giggling away. 'Those girls could do with smiling once in a while. They take themselves much too seriously. And, besides, a mother is entitled to embarrass her daughter every now and then. It's our right and privilege.'

'Yeah, well, I'm sure I'll get some marvellous comments from them both about the lobster hat on Monday.' I sigh.

'Nancy,' Mum begins, her expression turning serious, 'are you sure this is a good idea? Going in on a website with them?'

'They've got a good idea and we might actually have a chance of winning.'

'You're more than capable of winning on your own,' Mum insists. 'I know you don't think you are, but it's true. And those girls . . . well, I know that you've had your ups and downs –'

'Mum, it's fine,' I interrupt. 'Trust me, I need this. It's not like I have anything better to do and it would be good to have something to focus on while Nina is gallivanting about London, becoming super successful and famous. I want to do this project.'

'Fine, fine, it's your decision,' she says, sliding the box of hats towards me. She takes off the one she's wearing and puts it on my head. 'You look adorable. Now, get to work.'

I smile, lifting the box from the counter and carrying it to the stand. The bell above the door goes again while I'm busy arranging the hats and I hear a familiar voice, which makes my heart jump into my mouth.

'Hey, Nancy.'

I spin round to see Miles, the drummer from Chasing Chords, grinning from ear to ear.

'What are *you* doing here?'

'It's nice to see you, too,' he says, before nodding over at my mum. 'Hi, Ms Palmer.'

'Miles!' she says, coming over to give him a big hug. 'You look *very* handsome!'

Oh my god. Kill me now.

'Thanks!' He laughs, as she beams at him. 'How have you been?'

'I'm good, thank you. Nancy told me all about your trip to Singapore; she was showing me all the pictures on your Instagram! Did you have a lovely time?'

'*Mum*!' I hiss. She is so engrossed, she doesn't hear me.

'Nancy showed you *all* my Instagram pictures, did she?' Miles says, raising his eyebrows at me. 'I had a great time, thank you. I was visiting my mum's family out there.'

'And then Nancy showed me the photos of you in your hiking boots on your long weekend in the Lake District!' Mum continues, completely oblivious to how she's making me look right now. 'We used to go walking all the time;

there are some lovely countryside walks around Norfolk. You would love them! Maybe Nancy could take you sometime.'

She looks at me and winks.

WINKS.

'A countryside walk would be great. I look forward to it,' Miles says, absolutely relishing the situation.

She nods and then the shop falls into an awkward silence.

'Well!' Mum says, clicking her fingers suddenly. 'I'd better get back to my paperwork. I'll leave you two in charge of the shop. Nancy, I'll be in the office.'

I make sure not to look at her as she saunters off, so as not to give her the opportunity to wink at me again. The office door shuts behind her.

'So,' Miles says, putting his hands in his pockets, 'you've been stalking me, then?'

'What?' I turn back to the hatstand and pretend to be busy arranging it. 'I haven't been stalking you.'

'It sounds like you showed your mum a LOT of my photos,' he says, strolling over to lean on the shelves next to me. 'Kind of stalker-y.'

'She got mixed up. It was Nina showing her those photos. It sounds like you've had a good break, though.'

My face is literally on fire. Thank goodness for foundation, otherwise I would be the colour of a beetroot right now.

'Ah, Nina showed her the photos,' he says, nodding. 'That makes sense. How was Nina's party? Sorry I couldn't make it.'

'Oh, weren't you there?' I ask casually. 'I didn't notice; there were so many people. It was a lot of fun.'

He smiles. 'Yeah, Chase said.'

'What are you doing in Norfolk?' I ask, running out of things to pretend to arrange on the hatstand, so I move to sort the key rings.

'We met that Norwich producer about ideas for new songs and I thought it might be fun to drop by and see what the fuss was all about. Chase is always talking about your lovely, quaint village.'

'That's nice.'

'I could do with a tour guide, though.'

'You want me to point you in the direction of the tourist information office?'

I glance up to see him smiling at me. My stomach does a weird flip thing. I really don't know why I ever thought Chase was the hottest guy in Chasing Chords. Miles is much cuter. And he looks really good in a denim jacket over a hoodie. Like what he's currently wearing.

Stop it, Nancy, I think, desperately trying to ignore how good he looks. Because I know for certain that Miles will NEVER be interested in me. I am the opposite of Nina, and she's the one who boys in bands fall hopelessly in love with. I'm just the 'other one', remember?

'I was actually thinking that *you* might have some spare time to show me around. According to Chase, there's a good record store here.'

'You mean Neptune Records? Nina loves it there. That's where we held the party for her.'

See? This is a perfect example of why Miles would never be interested in someone like me. I am not a record-store person. *Nina* is a record-store person.

'How about I go there for a bit and you come find me on your break? We could go for lunch and catch up. I have some time before I need to head back to London.'

'OK,' I say. 'Sounds good. See you then.'

It is not a date, Nancy. He only needs to kill some time and he knows no one else here. He is not asking you out. Stop the butterflies flying around like crazy in your stomach.

He grins, before heading back to the door.

'See you then. And by the way,' he says, stopping in the doorway to turn back to me, 'do you know that you're wearing a lobster on your head?'

CHAPTER SEVEN

NINA

'We're leaving.'

Caroline is waiting for me at the music room as I arrive on time for my Sunday morning lesson, her long black coat slung over her arm.

'You're leaving?' I ask. 'Where are you going?'

'No, I didn't say I'm leaving. I said *we* are leaving,' she replies, before glancing at the music in my hands. 'You won't need that today. Come with me.'

She pulls her coat on as she marches down the corridor with me following closely in utter confusion. No one said anything about field trips. And I'd spent all last night practising for this morning. I could barely feel my fingers by the time I got to bed.

'Caroline, where are we going? Do I need my bag or anything?' I ask, as we head out into the cold.

'We're going to the drama department.'

I stop in my tracks. 'What?'

She continues walking, unaware that I'm no longer following her. After a few paces, when she glances behind and notices I'm not on her heel, she stops and turns, gesturing for me to come towards her.

'What are you doing, Nina? Come on, the cold is not good for the pianist's fingers.'

'Did you say the drama department?' I ask, not wanting to move.

'I did.'

'Why are we going there?'

'Why do you look so scared?' She watches me curiously. 'I thought you were here because you wanted to learn. Don't you trust my teaching techniques?'

'Of course!' I say. 'But, it's just . . . I'm the worst person in the world at drama. Don't you remember my performance at the start of the course? Me and the stage don't exactly mix.'

She walks over to stand in front of me. 'If you really want to get the most out of this music course, you need to learn to trust me, Miss Palmer. Now, come on. We're going to be late.'

With that, she turns and marches towards the drama wing. I have no choice but to follow her.

I feel slightly cowed by Caroline, but at least I'm not the only one having trouble with her teacher. Yesterday, before group practice, Grace told me that her singing teacher asked her to stop singing in a silly accent.

'I was singing in my own accent,' she'd complained. 'I didn't know what to do! So, I . . . well . . .'

'What did you do?' I asked, completely enrapt.

'I started singing in a Scottish accent.'

I'd burst out laughing and at first she'd told me off, saying that it wasn't funny, but eventually she started laughing too and then we couldn't stop.

'After you, Nina,' Caroline says, holding open the door to the drama wing. I follow her down a corridor and she stops at a door on our right. 'Are you ready?'

'I have no idea,' I answer honestly. 'I don't know what I should be ready for.'

'Make sure your phone is on silent.'

She opens the door to a large rehearsal room with a back wall of mirrors and some chairs placed at the front. A group of drama students dressed in black leggings and T-shirts are milling around, chatting. A few of them look up when we walk in but then turn back to their conversations. Sitting on one of the chairs is a man in his forties reading a dog-eared and heavily highlighted book. He glances up as Caroline approaches and a smile spreads across his face. He stands to greet her and I notice that, like his students, he's not wearing any shoes.

'Thank you for letting us sit in,' Caroline says, giving him a kiss on both cheeks. 'It's very good of you.'

'Always a pleasure,' the man says, looking over her shoulder to smile at me. 'This is her?'

'Nina, this is Sam. He's a movement teacher here.'

He reaches out to take my hand in a firm handshake. I keep my eyes fixed on the ground, terrified that he's going to ask me to join in with his class. At times like this, I'd rather be invisible.

'Nice to meet you, Nina. Ah yes,' he says, sharing a knowing look with Caroline. 'I see what you mean.'

She nods. 'I told you.'

'Have a seat, Nina,' Sam says, gesturing to one of the chairs. 'We're just about to start.'

I sit down. Caroline takes off her coat and sits next to me, as Sam steps to the front of the class and claps his hands. Immediately, the students stop talking and move to stand in their own spaces across the room facing him.

'Caroline,' I whisper, leaning towards her, 'what's going on? Why are we here?'

'I only want you to watch,' she says, her eyes scanning the students. 'That's all. You might find yourself learning something. Sam is a superb teacher.'

'But these are drama students. They're learning *acting*,' I say as quietly as possible while Sam calls out for everyone to take a deep breath. 'This stuff has nothing to do with playing the piano.'

Caroline slowly turns to look me straight in the eye.

'Do you think so?'

She turns her attention back to the class, so I assume that she's not expecting an answer to her question.

'I heard you all practising your monologues in drama class earlier,' Sam announces. 'Wonderful. The words were spoken beautifully. But I can tell you this: the hardest bit about your performance won't be speaking the monologues. It will be the walk from the wings on to the stage and into your current position, facing the audience. So, with that in mind, think about how you are standing right now. Are you standing *alive*?'

What is he talking about? Of course, they're alive! I glance at Caroline. She's nodding softly, like she agrees with him. Like he's asked a question that makes sense. Maybe I didn't hear him right.

'Become aware of how you are standing,' he continues.

The students start shifting slightly: some are rolling their shoulders back, others are stretching their hands out and wriggling their fingers. All of them have become taller.

'Beautiful,' Sam declares. 'This is all we will be doing in today's class. Standing.'

I look at Sam's back as though he's mad and he must catch the reflection of my expression in the mirrors because he stops to look over his shoulder.

'Yes, just standing,' he says directly to me before turning back to the class. 'We need to get you used to simply standing in the space.'

As he takes a walk about the room to inspect everyone's standing position, Caroline takes the chance to whisper to me.

'You look confused.'

'It's just . . . I thought you said he was the movement teacher.'

'Yes, that's right.'

'But . . . isn't standing still the opposite of movement?'

'Look at his students,' she says, nodding at them. 'Do you think you could stand like they are doing now? If I asked you to get up and stand like that, this very moment?'

I take in the girl in front of me. She's standing with her shoulders back, her chin high, staring straight at the wall behind me. She looks so *open*. She knows I'm sitting right here watching her, but that's not affecting her at all.

'No,' I whisper back. 'I couldn't do that.'

She looks satisfied with my answer. 'Sam is teaching his students to learn how to *be* in the space, before he develops their movement. That is what I want you to practise. Nina, your homework for this week is to stand.'

'Sorry?'

'I want you to stand,' she repeats, her eyes locked on Sam as he makes his way around the classroom. 'I look forward to seeing how you've progressed next Saturday morning.'

'What?' Chase asks, almost spitting out his sip of hot chocolate. 'Your homework is to *stand*? Like . . . just stand still?'

'Yep. And it's harder than you think. I tried it right before I met you. I stood in the middle of my room and I felt weird straight away. Like really aware of how I was standing and then I felt stupid and had to sit down or do something.'

'Wow,' he says, putting his cup down. 'That's weird.'

I nod in agreement, doing another quick glance around the cafe to make sure no one is watching us and no phones are pointing in our direction. We picked a table in the corner on purpose and so far no one seems to have noticed us.

Ever since that photographer got a photo of me waiting for Chase outside Guildhall on my first day, I've been completely paranoid that there might be more of them lurking around the school, hoping to get a picture of us. We decided to go to a small cafe that Chase had found down a road a bit out of the way, somewhere no one would expect to find a pop star. I was really happy when Chase messaged asking if we could meet between my morning lesson and afternoon group practice, but I've felt constantly on edge that someone might spot us. The last thing I needed was Jordan walking in and seeing us together again.

'It's nice to spend time with you,' Chase says, his smile accentuating his cheekbones. 'I've missed you.'

'Same. I miss not talking every night.'

It comes out a little more pointed than I intend and I can tell from his pained expression that I've ruined the moment. But it's also true. Since we started dating, even when we had to keep it secret from everyone, we spoke almost every day. This past week, he's taken much longer than usual to reply to my messages, and then he's been either too tired in the evenings to be able to chat much, or out at some kind of music event so unable to talk.

'Nina, you were right last week. I haven't been completely honest with you,' he says suddenly. 'I want to tell you something. I should have told you a while ago, but I wanted to make sure it was the right time.'

He leans forward, his gentle blue eyes meeting mine. My breath catches in my throat and my heart does a weird fluttery thing, because maybe this is the moment. Maybe he's about to say it.

The L-word.

'Nina,' he begins, a smile creeping across his lips, 'I think I'm going to go solo.'

The warm fuzzy feeling vanishes. My eyes instantly fill with tears, my heart thudding so loudly against my chest that it feels like everyone in the cafe can hear it.

'You're . . . you're breaking up with me?'

'*What*?' He looks horrified. 'NO! Why would you think that? Nina, I don't mean solo from you! I mean, solo from the band!'

'Oh!'

I'm so relieved that I lean back in my chair and press a hand on my heart, taking a minute to let his words sink in and blinking back the tears.

'I can't believe you thought I was breaking up with you,' he says, shaking his head. 'And also, I'm going to tell you now, that if anyone breaks up with you using the words

"I'm going solo" then you should NOT be with that person in the first place, because they are an absolute idiot.'

I laugh, my heart rate gradually slowing down, and he reaches over to take my hands in his. I don't know how his hands are always warm and mine are always freezing.

'Wait, so, Chasing Chords is breaking up?' I ask, as he shifts his chair to be closer to me.

'No, they don't know anything,' he explains, his forehead furrowed. 'I haven't said anything to anyone. It was Uncle Mark's idea and the more he talked about it, the more it kind of made sense. I've always said how the Chasing Chords music is great, but it's not exactly my style –' he pauses, to push my hair behind my ear – 'I remember telling you that the first night we met. I spilled my guts out to you, a complete stranger.'

'I thought Mark was the one against you ever going solo from Chasing Chords, considering he's the band's manager,' I point out, trying not to get distracted by his fingers brushing my cheek and instead stay focused on this HUGE piece of news he's just told me out of the blue. 'You were terrified of telling him about wanting to do your own stuff. You said he'd never understand.'

'That was before our little New Year's Eve acoustic concert in Norwich.'

'But you didn't tell him about it for that reason,' I say, confused. 'Nancy had to organize the whole thing without him catching on.'

'And then it went viral and suddenly there was this huge interest in me as a solo singer-songwriter,' Chase explains, before adding with a sly smile, 'Mark is a businessman, remember?'

'You've had interest from your record label?'

'And others. That's why I've been so busy. As soon as that video went global, Uncle Mark says he got a lot of producers asking to work with me on a solo album and calls from some labels wondering if I'd consider signing with them or whether I would be sticking to the Chasing Chords' one. He told them I was open-minded about the whole thing.'

'Did he ask you first?'

'No, he didn't have to,' he says with a shrug. 'He's always known that I've never been entirely happy with the Chasing Chords sound and that the band's fame took me by surprise. I think he's been afraid of that for a while, but now it might work to his advantage. A new record deal and a whole new career path.'

'Chase,' I say, realizing I'm so taken aback by the news that I haven't actually congratulated him yet. 'I'm so proud of you.'

'Thanks, Nina. I'm just sorry I've been out of it for a bit. We had all these meetings and then Uncle Mark made me go to a load of music events for "networking opportunities".' He rolls his eyes. 'Anyway, those parties made calling you a little bit more difficult and by the time I got home you'd be asleep.'

'So, have you had a formal offer? Is it definitely happening?'

'It's mostly only meetings at the moment.' He runs a hand through his hair. 'I've found it all really stressful. Exciting, but stressful. My main concern is the band. If I do sign to a label as a solo artist, what am I going to tell them?'

'They'll understand,' I say gently. 'They're your biggest fans. And everyone knows you write all the songs. Miles went to that acoustic concert in Norwich; he must know that you'd eventually go solo.'

He nods. 'Yeah, but it still feels like I'm betraying them somehow. Going behind their backs. Miles is a good songwriter, too. He's helped me out on a few of the tracks.'

'Don't go behind their backs, then,' I suggest. 'You could tell them what's going on. It will give them a bit of time to get used to the idea before anything becomes official.'

'I can't just sit them down and say, "Guys, I'm shopping around for a solo album." They'd think I was leaving them and the next thing you know, it'll be all over the news that Chasing Chords is splitting up.' He closes his eyes before he goes on. 'I'm not ready for that. I don't want to leave the band behind yet. They're my best friends. I want to do my own thing, but I'm also not done with Chasing Chords. It's greedy, isn't it?'

'It's understandable,' I say, placing a comforting hand on his arm. 'You can do both.'

'Maybe. That's why I want to sign to a label as a solo artist before I tell the rest of the band. That way, I'll have all the answers ready for their questions. I can assure them that the label I have signed to, whether it's our existing one or a new one, knows that I have a responsibility to the band, too, and is happy to make sure both careers can work around each other. Uncle Mark has promised me that he'll get it all in writing.'

'Then you don't have to worry. Everything will be fine.'

He smiles at me. 'Thanks, Nina. I should have told you sooner. It was so overwhelming and I wasn't sure at first that anything would come of it. But things have started getting serious.'

'Don't worry. I'm so, so proud of you.'

'I know I don't need to say this,' he begins apologetically, 'but please don't say a word to anyone. It's still early days and if anybody found out before the guys –'

'You really *don't* need to say this. Your secret is safe with me.'

He smiles so broadly at me that his dimples become even more pronounced, which makes me break into a wide grin. His hands gently cup my face and he leans in to kiss me.

'I'm so lucky to have you,' he says in a serious voice, as he pulls away.

'Likewise,' I say dreamily, in a bit of a daze from the kiss. You'd think I'd get used to it.

He laughs softly. 'Maybe when I go solo, you can be my personal pianist and we can tour together. I promise I won't make you practise just standing.'

Chase's Guildhall joke suddenly jolts me out of my trance.

'Oh my god, what's the time?' I ask frantically, reaching for my phone. I've been so caught up in our conversation that I haven't been keeping an eye on the time. I look at my screen and I feel sick. I have three minutes to get to our group rehearsal for the end-of-term showcase. I won't make it in time. 'I'm going to be late!'

I stand up so fast that I send my chair flying backwards. I grab my bag and coat, and race towards the door.

'They won't mind. You lost track of time; it happens,' Chase says, following me out as I rudely push past someone coming into the cafe. 'Just say you were with me.'

'That will make things a *hundred* times worse.'

Chase looks at me strangely. 'Why?'

'I don't have time to explain right now. Look, I have to go. I'll –'

I stop mid-sentence as I notice someone down the road looking straight at us. Chase turns to look behind him, following my gaze.

'What? What is it?' he asks, turning back to me.

I blink to make my vision clearer. The person has disappeared round the corner. It must have been a trick of the light. It could have been anyone.

It can't have been *him*.

'Nina?' Chase looks concerned. 'What is it? You're freaking me out. You've gone really pale.'

'Nothing,' I say, shaking my head. 'I thought I saw someone, but it wasn't them.'

'Who did you think you saw?'

'Never mind.' I collect myself and stand on my tiptoes to kiss him goodbye. 'I have to go. I'll call tonight on my way home to Norwich,' I say, before rushing down the street towards the music building.

'I have something on tonight,' he calls out after me.

I don't have time to stop to reply. When I get to Guildhall, I'm drenched with sweat from running. I stop at the door to the orchestra room and catch my breath, listening out for a good moment to walk in and creep to my piano at the back. *Maybe*, I think as I wipe my forehead and peer through the little window in the door, *maybe they haven't noticed I've been missing.*

If I was Piano One, they definitely would have noticed, but, considering my part is hardly important, there is a small chance that I can sneak in without it making any difference.

I wait until the conductor has his back to the door and is practising with the first violins and then I creep in, tiptoeing around the orchestra and sliding on to my piano stool. Jordan looks unbearably smug, but I think I've got away with it.

I'm wrong.

'Thank you for joining us, Nina,' a voice rings out as the violins finish their section.

Caroline is in the session and has been sitting in the corner. She stands up to address me, making the whole orchestra spin in their seats to watch my reaction.

'You're seven minutes late,' she states. 'Do you not take these rehearsals seriously?'

'Of course,' I say timidly, wishing everyone would stop staring.

'And is everyone's time not as important as yours?'

'No! I mean, yes! I mean . . .' I pause, my brain blurry as I try to work out the best thing to say. 'I lost track of time.'

'I see. Did you have somewhere better to be?'

'According to Twitter, she did,' Jordan announces, holding up his phone.

There's a picture of Chase and me kissing in the cafe, taken through the window. Someone must have seen us from the street and taken it without us noticing.

Everyone starts giggling as I try as hard as possible not to cry in front of them.

'Thank you, Jordan, but I don't remember asking your or Twitter's opinion on the matter,' Caroline says sharply.

Jordan's face drops and he quickly shoves his phone into his pocket. The room falls silent again and Caroline turns her attention back to me.

'You might want to take a moment to think about how many people wanted to get on this course and didn't, because we gave that place to you,' she says. 'Don't be late again.'

I nod, too afraid to speak. She moves to sit down and the conductor clears his throat, before telling everyone to take it again from the top. Now that they are all focused on their music and facing the other way, I am free to silently cry behind them, shielded by my music propped up on the piano.

Jordan glances at me as hot tears stream down my face.

For a moment, I think I see a glimpse of surprise, and then sympathy, in his expression. But he turns away and doesn't look at me for the rest of the lesson.

No one does.

CHAPTER EIGHT

NANCY

I can't stop thinking about Miles and it is driving me NUTS.

It's so stupid because I know that he's not into me in that way, but every time I try to push him from my brain he finds a sneaky way to get right back in there. I wish Nina was here so I could be distracted, and I do think about calling her, but I check the time and know that she'll be on her way home from London. There's no point.

I lie on the sofa watching an old Mary-Kate and Ashley movie in the hope that it will distract me but I can't concentrate on it at all. My mind keeps wandering back to yesterday, analysing everything he said and did.

'ARGH, stop it!' I say out loud to myself.

'Everything all right, darling?' Mum yells from the kitchen. She's in one of her artistic moods today and is in the middle of drawing an empty milk bottle.

'Fine, thanks, Mum. I was just talking to myself,' I reply.

'You know,' Mum says, coming through from the kitchen and sitting down on the sofa next to me, 'there's something rather fascinating about that empty milk bottle. If you really take the time to look at it.'

'I'll take your word for it,' I say, leaning forward to reach for the remote and pause the film. 'Are you going to tell me *anything* about your date last night, then?'

Even though she's refused to give me any details, I can tell that her date went well because she's been floating around in a daze, humming tunes from musicals all day. She even decided to do some baking this morning, and now I've eaten about a hundred cupcakes because they're there right in front of me with pink icing and sprinkles and everything.

'Are you going to tell me anything about *your* date?' she retorts.

'Huh? What date?'

She looks at me as though I'm mad. 'Your date with Miles! The hunk from Chasing Chords.'

'OK, please don't ever use the word "hunk" again. And that wasn't a date!'

'He made the effort to come to your little Norfolk village and ask you out for lunch,' she says, raising her eyebrows. 'That sounds like a date to me. Don't think I didn't notice the flirtation between you two. I was pressed up against the office door with a cup to my ear, listening to every word you said.'

'MUM!' I throw a cushion at her. 'You know that's an invasion of privacy.'

'Well, I wanted to see if my theory was correct! And I was right. You like him.'

'OK, conversation finished. I'm going back to my movie,' I say, my cheeks burning hot.

'If you tell me about your date, I'll tell you about mine.'

I let out a long sigh. 'Mum, it really wasn't a date. He just happened to be in Norwich to meet that producer and Chase had obviously told him about Neptune Records. He wanted to go and visit it because I guess that's what talented people like Chase, Miles and Nina do in their spare time. Flick through dusty old records. He was being polite asking me out for lunch. Maybe he felt sorry for me.'

'Why would he feel sorry for you?' she asks, her eyebrows knitted together.

'Plenty of reasons,' I say. 'Mainly, everyone else knows what they're doing and I'm left behind, with no direction.'

'You have plenty of direction! It's all right not to have your entire life worked out by the age of fifteen, Nancy.' She chuckles. 'Your path will work itself out.'

'Mum, do you know what someone at school called me the other day?'

She takes a stab at guessing. 'Nina?'

I roll my eyes. 'Well, yeah, that happens all the time, but that's not what I'm talking about. They referred to me as *the other one*. The other one! As though it didn't matter what my name was. Nina is the main twin and I'm the other one. I HAVE to get my name back on the map. Don't worry, though – I have a plan.'

'I see. And what's the plan?'

'The website,' I state proudly. 'The one I'm going to launch with Layla and Sophie. As soon as we have that up and running, everyone is going to be talking about it and my amazing music section. I'll be popular again, win the competition and have an amazing time behind the scenes of the Disney Channel. I will no longer be irrelevant. I'll stand out again. It's an excellent plan.'

Mum nods thoughtfully. 'It sounds like you've got it all worked out. Did you tell Miles about this plan?'

'No, why would I tell him? And, anyway, I only thought of the plan this morning. I hadn't come up with it yesterday.'

'I just thought that he'd probably have the same thoughts about the plan that I do.' She smiles warmly at me. 'You already stand out beautifully, Nancy. You don't need to be popular or launch a successful website or get an internship for that.'

'Mum,' I groan, 'you're my *mum*. Of course, you're going to say that. Didn't you hear my story about what I was called at school the other day? My life is currently a big fat nothing. I need to do something about it otherwise I'll go crazy.'

'Well, I have to say, it's lovely to see you so dedicated to the competition, but as long as you do it for the right reasons,' she says. 'So, if you didn't chat to Miles about the website, what did you talk about?'

'Not much. Mainly how nice it's been for him to have a little break from the band. He's excited to start work on some new songs for the band with Chase, though.

'It was quite funny actually,' I went on, 'because while he was talking I saw he had a tiny spider on his shoulder and when I pointed it out he yelped and jumped up, knocking the table, which then made his drink spill everywhere. It was HILARIOUS. I couldn't stop laughing and he was like, "Nancy, it's not funny! Get it off! Where's the spider gone? WHERE IS IT?" And his panicked expression just made me laugh ten times harder until I was crying.

'By now everyone in the cafe was staring at us and this old guy went, "There's no spider there, mate. It's gone." And then Miles thanked him and sat back down and I was still laughing, and he started to see the funny side and then he started laughing, too.

'Anyway, we got him a new drink and I told him that he shouldn't feel embarrassed because that teeny tiny spider was, after all, potentially a MASSIVE TARANTULA in disguise and he could have DIED.

'But in the end he got his own back because, as we walked out, there was a pigeon on the street pecking at a chip and I got the heebie-jeebies and then had to admit my fear of pigeons, and the whole time we were walking Miles kept yelling, "NANCY, DUCK! A PIGEON FLYING AT

YOUR HEAD!" and I kept ducking in a panic, but obviously he was joking.

'I told him about that whole boy-who-cried-wolf thing and that he shouldn't joke about such serious stuff, but whatever – he seemed to find it VERY funny. Then he made a call for a car to pick him up to take him back to Norwich station and I teased him about being this precious celebrity who couldn't take public transport, and he was so insulted that he cancelled the car and insisted on taking the bus. Which I obviously had to take with him because he's so useless; he was trying to get on one going in the complete opposite direction. It was quite cute actually.

'Wait –' I pause and turn to look at Mum – 'what was the question again?'

She smiles at me in a knowing way. I stare back.

'What? Why are you looking at me like that?'

'Nothing,' she says. 'It sounds like you had a good day.'

'It was fine,' I say quickly, realizing I'd just been talking for ages about pigeons and spiders. 'More importantly, how was your date?'

'Oh, Nancy, it was simply wonderful,' she says, her eyes going all misty. 'We had such a fun night. We went to this little Italian restaurant and the food was delicious, and there were no awkward pauses in the conversation at all! It's refreshing to meet someone and be so comfortable around them, you know? And then he suggested we go dancing and I told him that I did happen to be the 1988 East Anglia

Amateur Dance Competition Mambo Champion, as you know, but that I hadn't been dancing properly in years, so off we went to this club.'

'You went to a *club*?'

'Yes, I did, and let me tell you, darling daughter, I can still shake up a dance floor.'

'OK, Mum, you need to stop talking now, otherwise I'm going to need therapy,' I say, as she starts giggling. 'It sounds like you really like this guy. Any chance I get to meet him?'

'Not yet,' she says stubbornly. 'It's still too early to be introducing him to my children.'

'We're not children any more, Mum,' I assure her. 'We can handle it, you know.'

We hear the sound of the key in the door. After a few minutes, Nina comes into the sitting room, headphones round her neck as always, and slumps down into an armchair, closing her eyes.

'Hey, Nina,' I say, chuckling. 'You look tired.'

'I am exhausted.' She opens her eyes to smile at us. 'But I'm happy to be home.'

'How was Guildhall?'

'It was OK.'

Mum and I share a look. Mum quickly grabs the plate of cupcakes and holds them out for her. She takes one gratefully and begins to nibble round the edge.

If someone was struggling to tell the difference between me and Nina, a good way would be to give us some kind of treat, like a chocolate bar or baked product, and watch how we go about eating it. She eats those things as though she's some kind of squirrel, nibbling the edges and saving the best bit until last, like she's really thought it through. I just go for it without any thought whatsoever and then have to sit for ages, enviously watching her finish hers.

'The invitation to your big showcase arrived in the post yesterday,' Mum says, causing Nina to wince. 'You're such a star, Nina! I'm very excited already.'

'Great,' Nina says as enthusiastically as she can muster. 'I don't know what I'm going to play. It has to be something amazing. I suppose I can think about it while I practise standing.'

'Practise standing? Ooooh, are you going to play the piano standing up, like Jamie Cullum? You know, when he gets really into the jazz and kicks the piano stool away. That would be AWESOME.'

'No, Nancy, I have to play serious stuff,' she says, laughing at me. 'How was your weekend?'

'Nancy is teaming up with Layla and Sophie for the website competition,' Mum tells her. 'And she's going to win it and become a big Disney star.'

'You're *what*?' Nina looks stunned. 'Why are you teaming up with *them*?'

'Because they asked and, when I thought about it, it seemed like a good idea,' I say. 'I think we may have a

133

chance of winning. It's a lifestyle website and I'm going to be the music editor, as well as helping with fashion and style tips. You know, like on my Instagram.'

Nina nods, her face pensive. 'I guess that is quite a cool idea and really good experience. Jimmy is entering the competition too, although I don't think his will be a lifestyle website, so you don't need to worry.'

'What's his website going to be?'

'I don't know,' she admits, rubbing her neck. 'I haven't had the chance to speak to him all weekend. I'm a terrible friend. How was your date, Mum?'

'I was just telling Nancy about how lovely it was,' Mum says, smiling broadly.

'Do we get to meet him this week?'

'Nancy asked that, too, and I'm afraid I'd like to wait a little bit longer before I introduce him to my girls.'

'Yeah, probably a good idea,' Nina says. 'We don't want Nancy scaring him off.'

I narrow my eyes at her. 'You know, I just threw my cushion at Mum, but otherwise I'd be throwing it at you right now.'

'Here we go, darling,' Mum says, handing me the cushion.

'Thanks, Mum.' I throw it at Nina, who catches it, laughing, before throwing it straight back at me.

'Why don't you ask Nancy how *her* date went?' Mum says to Nina.

'You went on a date? With who? You didn't tell me about this!'

'It was *not* a date,' I emphasize, shooting Mum a glare, but she smiles happily back at me. 'Miles popped by the shop yesterday and we went for a quick lunch before he had to head back to London, but it was just a catch up. Mum, if it gets back to Chase that I'm calling it a date, he'll tell Miles and it will be MORTIFYING.'

Mum giggles. 'All right, all right - it was "just a catch up",' she says unconvincingly.

'Do you want me to throw the cushion at you again?'

'What was Miles doing in Norfolk?' Nina asks.

'He was in Norwich for a meeting with that producer. You must know that already though, right? Chase must have been there, too.'

'Oh. Um. Yes, yeah, he must have been,' she says, looking distracted.

I'm about to tell her all about the spider incident, because I know that will cheer her up, when the doorbell goes.

'I didn't know Chase was coming this evening, Nina,' Mum says, pushing herself up off the sofa and heading out of the room.

'He's not,' Nina replies. 'Maybe it's Jimmy. Or perhaps it's Miles, "popping by".'

'Don't you start,' I huff. 'Maybe it's Mum's new *boyfriend*.'

We hear Mum open the door and there's a few moments of silence before we hear her shutting the door.

'That's weird,' I say, as Nina nods in agreement. 'Did she just slam the door in someone's face?'

Nina gets up and peers out into the hallway at the front door.

'No,' she informs me, coming to sit back down again. 'She's out there with whoever it is as well. Must want to talk to them in private.'

'It HAS to be her boyfriend!' I squeal. 'Shall we spy on them? We can finally see who it is!'

'How are we going to do that?' Nina points out, laughing at my excited expression. 'There's no good vantage point of the front step anywhere in the house.'

'Are you sure?'

'Yes. The first time Chase came over, I was so nervous and excited that I ran to every window that looked out that way to check whether or not he was here yet and none of them look directly on to the front step.'

I blink at her, taking in this new information. 'Wow, Nina. I knew you were a loser but I did not know you were THAT bad.'

'Give me back that cushion to throw at you again.'

The door opens and we hear Mum say, 'Come in,' before there are footsteps in the hall.

'She's introducing him to us!' I hiss at Nina, sitting up and checking my hair. 'Try to act normal!'

'*You* try to act normal!' she whispers back, jumping up and racing across the room to sit with me on the sofa.

Mum appears in the doorway as Nina plonks herself at my side, and we both smile at her in what is hopefully an angelic and non-intimidating way.

'Girls,' she says, looking ghostly pale. 'Someone is here to see you.'

She steps aside to let them in. A sandy-haired, tall man wearing a sharp, tailored suit comes into the sitting room, offering us a watery-eyed smile.

It's him.

He looks a bit different now, obviously, having aged. And his hair is shorter than I remember. But it's definitely him. Standing right in front of us, after all this time.

'*Dad*,' Nina whispers, instinctively grabbing my hand.

I take it and hold it tight.

'Hi, girls,' he says timidly. 'Wow. Look at you. You're so grown up.'

There's a long pause as we just stare at him and he looks down at his feet, unsure of what to do. I've thought of this moment before. What it would be like to see Dad again after all these years. I even googled him a couple of times and then would sit staring at his stupid business profile, before closing the page and telling myself not to do that again. I used to go through all the things I'd say to him in my head, a long list of mistakes that he made and moments that he's missed.

Now that he's finally here, right in front of me, I have no idea where to start. Is this actually happening? Is he really here? What do you say to someone after almost seven years? When the shock begins to subside, I'm hit by a flood of overwhelming emotion.

I suddenly have a massive headache and want to cry.

'Why are you here?' I blurt out, anger starting to bubble up uncontrollably inside me. 'What are you doing here? You left.'

'I know. You have every right to be angry. But I . . . well, I know it's your birthday coming up and I had a sort of epiphany, I suppose.' He takes a deep breath. 'I'm here because I want to be back in your lives. I've been a terrible father and I know I don't deserve it, but I want a second chance to be a dad. I've missed you. I've never stopped thinking about you.'

We all stare at him, his words hanging in the silence.

'Sorry, I know this must be a bit of a shock,' he adds.

'You had an *epiphany*,' I say eventually, shaking my head in disbelief. 'Are you serious? *That's* what you're leading with?'

'I . . . I know this is all a bit sudden,' he says in an uneasy voice. 'But –'

'You can't just turn up here!'

'I didn't know the best way of going about this,' he says, his brow deeply furrowed. 'I thought about calling, but it didn't seem right not to come in person. Look, it's no excuse, but when I left your mother I was very young and stupid. I got caught up in work. I have a very high-stress job and I lost sight of what was important.'

'Right,' I say. 'And it has taken you all these years to realize that.'

'Like I said, it's no excuse,' he admits, nodding. 'Over the years it got harder and harder to build up the courage to come to you and ask to be a part of your lives again. I didn't think you'd be interested after everything I've missed.'

'You were right.'

'But,' he continues, powering on despite my comments, 'the only thing I can do is hope that you'll forgive me and let me make it up to you. Finally.'

'Well, thanks, but no thanks. We don't need you. Mum has done everything by herself and you can't simply decide to come back whenever you feel like. That's not how parenting works.'

'I know, and Karlene is an amazing person.' He smiles at Mum but she isn't looking at him at all. She's just watching us with a concerned expression on her face. 'I'm not expecting to click my fingers and be a dad again. I only wanted to come here today and ask you to consider it. You can take your time. However long you need. I had to come and see if I still had a chance to be your father.'

He pauses, before his face lights up, looking at Nina.

'I saw you playing the piano on YouTube, Nina. I was so *proud* of you. And so disappointed in myself. Disappointed that I'd missed so much of your lives because of my selfishness and cowardice. I should have done everything in my power to be there for you when things didn't work out between your mother and me. After seeing that video, I made a New Year's resolution to try and contact you again, and it's taken me a few weeks to build up the courage, I suppose. But here I am.'

'Did you read a book on all the right things to say to the daughters you walked out on or something?' I ask, prompting him to look back down at his feet. 'Because we're not buying any of it.'

'I'll go now. I just wanted to see you and . . . well, I hope you'll think about it.'

I notice he's looking at Nina when he says this and not me.

He glances at Mum. 'Karlene, you've got my phone number and email address. And my London address if any of you wanted to see me at all. Nina, I know you're down there a bit these days. I saw in the paper that you'd got into the Guildhall weekend course. Anyway, you have my details. If you want them. I really hope I'll be hearing from you.'

He slowly turns to go.

'I'm really sorry. For everything,' he says quietly. 'I'll show myself out.'

He walks out into the hallway, his footsteps echoing in the silence before he leaves us, the door slamming shut behind him.

CHAPTER NINE

NINA

'I can't believe he thinks he can just walk back into our lives!'

Nancy kicks at the sand and a couple of pebbles go flying. She pulls up her coat zip against the breeze and stuffs her hands in her pockets. I hate seeing Nancy this upset but at least she's talking about it.

She hasn't spoken much at all in the last few days, ever since Dad visited the house. This would seem strange to most people as Nancy is usually the talkative one and I'm the quiet one, so you'd think when something big happens in our lives we'd handle it in the exact opposite ways to how we do. When Dad walked out all those years ago, I really wanted to talk about it but Nancy refused. She would get angry at me if I ever brought it up, as though she was trying to push it out of her brain and forget that it ever happened.

Since seeing Dad at the weekend, she hasn't been herself. Not that any of us have, if I'm honest. Mum has been trying to pretend like she's completely fine but she must have got such a shock when he turned up out of the blue.

'I'm so sorry, Mum,' I said that night.

'It's not your fault, Nina,' she'd said with a weak smile. 'I'm absolutely fine. You're the ones I worry about.'

But it was my fault.

Not Dad turning up out of the blue, obviously, but it was my fault she didn't have any preparation. Because I'd seen him. Outside the cafe where I was with Chase, before I had to rush back to Guildhall. I'd seen him, right there, watching me. I had convinced myself that it hadn't been him, that it was just a trick of the light and, besides, he was so far away, how could I be sure? But in my gut I'd known that it was my dad, standing at the end of the road, staring at me, disappearing as soon as I recognized him. He must have come to see if I really was at Guildhall School of Music and Drama, so close to his house, and then spotted me by chance.

I know he lives just down the road because I searched for the address he'd left with Mum, and there it was on the map, only a ten-minute walk from Guildhall. I almost fell off my chair when I saw pictures online of the kind of houses and flats in that area. They're super posh and expensive. I guess Dad's business does pretty well.

'He showed up at our house, without even calling first!' Nancy goes on. 'Who does that? What if we'd not been in? It seems very arrogant to show up like that, expecting everyone to be home.' Nancy's brow is creased in anger as she stares out at the sea.

'The boys are coming back,' I say, nodding towards Chase and Jimmy who are walking towards us with hot chocolates.

Chase gives me mine and then wraps his arm round my waist, while Jimmy passes one to Nancy. It's really nice to have Chase here. I hadn't been able to get through to him on Sunday to tell him what happened and then he was in meetings all day Monday, only able to message during the day rather than call, and I didn't want to tell him about Dad in a text. Once we'd spoken that evening and I'd filled him in, he'd promised to come and see me one evening this week after school to cheer me up.

I'd had to wait a few days as he had so much on, but he's here now and that's all that matters. I invited Jimmy and Nancy to join us for a stroll on the beach after school because I thought it might help cheer Nancy up too, and give us an opportunity to talk about it and get it all out in the open with people we trust.

'I can't believe you two came here on your first date,' Jimmy says, smiling at Chase. 'Wasn't it like October or something? You must have been freezing!'

'It was actually a bit like how it is today,' Chase says, taking a sip of his drink. 'Nice and empty. I taught Nina how to skim stones.'

'That's not how I remember it.' I laugh. 'You picked up a perfect stone for skimming and just threw it into the water with no skill whatsoever. And you'd been so confident in the lead-up, too. I seem to remember you describing yourself as quite the *champion* when it came to skimming stones.'

'I'm pretty good at skimming stones,' Jimmy declares, scanning the beach for any smooth pebbles as we walk.

'Challenge accepted.' Chase grins, showing off his dimples. 'What about you, Nancy? Any good?'

'Terrible,' she says apologetically. 'Nina's really good. Mum taught us when we first moved here after Dad left.'

'I can't believe your dad came here on Sunday,' Jimmy says in a gentle tone. 'It must have been so weird for you.'

'Yeah, it's mad that he just showed up,' Chase says. 'I don't know what I'd do if my dad turned up at my house with no warning. I'm not sure I'll ever be able to forgive him for walking out on me and my mum.'

'You're not the only one,' Nancy says, kicking another pebble and sending it skittering across the sand. 'I hope he doesn't come back. I don't want anything to do with him.'

She looks at me pointedly as she says this and I know what she's thinking. She wants me to agree with her. She wants me to say that I never want to see him again. She wants me to promise not to contact him, not to meet up with him in London.

But I won't. I don't know what I want to do, but my gut is telling me to give him a second chance.

'Do you really want to let him back into your life after he left us?' Nancy asks, without me saying a word.

It's so unnerving how she can read my brain like that.

'I don't know. Maybe. It's complicated. My brain feels all jumbled and confused.'

While I'm saying this, I notice Chase glance at his watch and I get a pang of irritation, but I push it aside and focus on how good it is that he's here.

'I'm not surprised,' Jimmy says. 'It's kind of a big deal.'

'He knows absolutely nothing about us,' Nancy says bitterly. 'Nothing. How can he catch up on all the years he's missed? Just sit there while we read off a reel of our biggest moments throughout our lives? I don't think he even knows about the car crash last term. His daughter was in a coma and he had no idea!'

'How's your mum coping with it?' Jimmy asks. 'It must be stressful for her to see him again after all this time.'

'She seems all right, I think,' I say. 'She keeps asking us about it and encouraging us to talk to her rather than bottling anything up.'

'Would she mind if you met up with him?' Chase asks, moving his arm from my waist as his phone beeps in his pocket. 'I reckon my mum would be really angry if I tried to see my dad.'

'If anything, it's the opposite,' I point out. 'I get the feeling that, after the initial shock of him showing up, she's quite happy that he wants to be a part of his family again. She's always worried about us not having a father figure and she doesn't want us not to have a dad because it didn't work out with them.'

'That's the phrase he used,' Nancy says coldly. 'The other night, he said, "It didn't work out," as though it was some kind of puzzle. But it's not. He left. It's simple. He walked out. He doesn't get to just walk back in whenever he feels like it. Why has he come back now?'

'It was his New Year's resolution,' I reply, glancing at Chase who is reading a long email on his phone.

'What was?' Jimmy asks, finishing his hot chocolate.

'Re-bonding with his daughters,' Nancy answers, rolling her eyes. 'Imagine telling people that at a party.' She puts on a voice. ' "So, my New Year's resolution is to join the gym. What's yours?"; "I'm going to track down the daughters I walked out on and ask to be their dad again. I wonder who will stick to their resolution the longest." It's so ridiculous. I think there's something more to it.'

'Sorry,' Chase interjects, holding up his phone screen as a call comes through. 'I need to take this. I'll catch up in a second.'

He answers the phone and hangs back while we carry on along the beach. I try not to be annoyed but I am. Giving me a few hours one evening doesn't seem like that much to ask, especially when such a huge thing has happened in my life. I know that this is an important moment in his career, I get it, but couldn't he focus on me for a little bit?

But then I think of when he called last night and I didn't pick up because I was in the middle of working on a new piece to play to Caroline on Saturday. I had spent ages researching the most difficult piano pieces out there and then picked one that would be bound to impress everyone, even Jordan, if I could get it right. I meant to call Chase back, but, by the time I was done practising, it was midnight and he'd already texted me an hour before, saying he was going to bed.

I can't exactly be angry at him for being busy, when I'm so busy myself. We needed to somehow make our moments of free time coordinate better.

'They must be writing lots of new songs at the moment,' Nancy says.

'Huh?'

'Chasing Chords,' she prompts, nodding back towards Chase. 'I'm guessing that's why he's so busy. He writes them all, doesn't he?'

'Um, yeah, I think so.'

'I don't know how he does it, writing all those songs,' Jimmy muses. 'It takes me ages to write anything for my website and that's only words, let alone making them all poetical and meaningful, and then match some catchy melody. I have a whole new respect for writers these days.'

'I thought you wanted to be a journalist. Haven't you always had respect for writers?' Nancy says with a small smile, the first I've seen since we walked out of the school gates this afternoon. I knew it would be a good idea to invite Jimmy along.

'Yes, but I did not realize how stressful it is, writing under pressure! It's impossible! Impossible, I say!' he cries dramatically, flinging his arms up in the air like a total drama queen and making Nancy and me laugh. 'I've only written two articles so far, ready to upload, and they've taken a lot of time and concentration to put together. I haven't even got started on the layout and design of the website yet.'

'What's yours about?' Nancy asks curiously.

He wags his finger in her face and she swats him away.

'Nope, Miss Palmer! I'm not telling you one thing about my genius project, and do you know why? Because we are competitors. Media rivals!'

'That's true,' she says as he sticks his tongue out at her. 'But I'm going to find out what your site is about when you launch it at the end of the week, so why don't you just tell me now?'

'And how do I know that you won't go straight to Layla and Sophie, your best friends, and tell them all about my wonderful ideas that they'll then copy straight away, having no original or creative bone in their collective bodies?'

'I actually disagree with you there,' Nancy says haughtily. 'They are creative in their own ways. Layla can get creative with make-up and Sophie once suggested I write a story about Chasing Chords set in a world of dinosaurs and robots. That's definitely imaginative thinking outside the box. And they're not my best friends, thank you very much. You two are.'

Jimmy stops dead in his tracks and places a hand on his heart, closing his eyes and inhaling deeply, before shoving his empty hot chocolate cup at me.

'Here we go,' Nancy says, rolling her eyes at me.

'Did you hear that? Did you *hear* that?' Jimmy cries out. 'I am Nancy Palmer's best friend! What an honour! She has finally embraced her nerd roots.' He flings his arms round her. 'Who could have guessed that this would be in our future? That the most popular girl in school would declare herself my best friend. You remember that time you said very openly that you didn't mind which group the teacher put you in, but you didn't want to be in a group of three with me and Nina?'

'In my defence,' she says, 'you two were drawing on each other's faces with marker pen. And, besides, I'm not the most popular girl in school any more. I barely exist there.'

I'm about to probe her on what she means, but Chase comes running up to fall into step with us again.

'Sorry about that. It's really hard to get Uncle Mark off the phone. What were you saying about your dad before Mark called, Nancy?'

Nancy's face falls at the mention of Dad again.

'I can't remember.'

'You were saying you thought there was more to it than the New Year's resolution,' Chase reminds her. 'What do you mean by that?'

'Oh yeah.' She sighs. 'It just seems odd that he's turned up now. If it was a resolution and he wanted to get the new year off to a good start by making up for his past mistakes, wouldn't he have come to see us weeks ago? He mentioned Guildhall, so maybe it's that. It's convenient that Nina is in London more or something.'

'Have you thought about seeing him when you're down in London at the weekends?' Jimmy asks me.

I nod gently, purposefully not looking at Nancy's expression.

'I've thought about it, but I don't know if I will. I guess Nancy and I need to chat it through and make the decision together.'

Nancy lets out a groan. 'Nina, are you seriously considering meeting up with him?'

'A lot of my memories of music include him and I can't ignore that,' I reason. 'He was the one who first sat me at a piano.'

'So? Chase's dad first sat him at a piano at the age of four and he's not trying to re-bond with his dad!'

Jimmy shoots Chase a look. 'It's weird how much she knows about you.'

Chase nods. 'Tell me about it. I didn't realize I had a distant cousin who is some kind of famous cheesemonger until she told me about it.'

'Anyone who has ever read your Wikipedia page knows about the cheesemonger,' Nancy huffs, crossing her arms.

'I only know the stuff that Chasing Chords fans know. I don't know any personal stuff like how you butter your bread before using peanut butter, which Nina told me about. By the way, that's gross.'

'Everyone butters their bread before putting peanut butter on!' Chase claims defiantly.

Jimmy wrinkles his nose in disgust. 'No, they don't! What's wrong with you?'

'Nancy,' I say, trying to focus on the topic of Dad now that I've finally got Nancy talking about it, 'all I'm saying is, I don't think we should be completely closed to the idea of seeing him. Don't you remember how much fun we used to have? How encouraging he was?'

'Not really,' she says.

I know she's lying because she's angry, and I can understand that. But she remembers as well as I do.

I remember so vividly the day he took us to London to see a show, but he made us go there really early for a big surprise he had planned. We had barely seen him all week because of work, and he'd been away travelling for his business the weekend before. Nancy and I could barely sleep on the Friday evening because we were so excited about our family day out the following day.

On the train we begged him to tell us where we were going, but he just tapped the side of his nose and said it was a surprise. And then he made us all take a guess. Nancy, as usual, yelled out so many funny possibilities that other people on the train started to laugh along with us and one woman in the seat in front of us even turned round to have her own guess.

'The aquarium, perhaps?'

'Boring! Are we going to go have tea at the Ritz with all the celebrities?' Nancy had asked, making the lady chuckle.

When we got to London, he took us to this really posh street and then, as Mum walked along with Nancy behind us, he had pulled me ahead and stopped in front of a huge door.

'Ready, Nina?' he'd said, and then we'd walked in.

It was an amazing piano shop, which sounds silly, but for me it was like walking into heaven. I'd never seen anything like it. I had gasped, taking in all the shiny pianos, my fingers itching to play on the biggest one by the window. It looked like the one all the famous pianists played in their grand-hall concerts. A smartly dressed woman had then come over and asked us if she could help.

'We're looking for the perfect piano,' Dad had said, putting a hand on my shoulder. 'This is Nina and she's going to be a big star some day.'

The woman had smiled warmly at me and then told us to go ahead and have a try on any piano that we liked. Dad and I went from piano to piano, pressing the keys and pretending that we were interested in the grand pianos that never would have fit in our house. It's one of the happiest memories I have, especially of Dad. I didn't care that he never actually ended up getting me a piano, even though he'd said that to the lady. I don't know if he'd never intended to or whether he just never got round to it, but it was still one of the most wonderful days I'd ever had.

Although, now that I think about it, I don't remember what Nancy and Mum were doing while Dad and I were running around that shop. I wonder where they went. I don't even remember them being there, but they must have been.

Chase's phone starts ringing, jolting me from my memory.

'Sorry,' he says again, answering the call and walking a few paces away from us.

'He really needs to tell Mark to give him a break,' Nancy says, watching him.

'I know.' I hesitate. 'Nancy?'

'Yes?'

'Do you remember that weekend when Dad took us to the piano shop?'

She nods. 'Yes.'

'Before we went to see *The Lion King*?'

'I remember, Nina.'

'What did you and Mum do? While Dad and I were playing on the pianos?'

She lifts her eyebrows. 'That's random.'

'I was just thinking about it and how much fun I had that day, trying all the pianos with Dad. Did you and Mum go around playing all the pianos, too?'

'No, we didn't. We sat waiting by the shop door and when you were playing the third or fourth one Mum went over to Dad and asked if he could wrap things up. He told her that we should go do something else for a bit and you two would come find us.'

'Oh. What did you end up doing?'

'We didn't end up doing anything,' she says. 'We stayed and waited. I hadn't seen Dad for weeks at that point because he'd been on a work trip the weekend before, remember? He arranged the day out so we could spend some time together before he went on another week of meetings in Germany afterwards. I didn't want to go anywhere without him.'

I stare at her. 'Oh.'

'Hang on, isn't there that photo in your sitting room of you two wearing matching Minnie Mouse outfits in front of *The Lion King* poster? Was that the day you're talking about?' Jimmy asks. 'You two were seriously adorable back then. Shame you grew up, really.'

As Nancy gives Jimmy a playful shove, Chase comes back to join us with a funny look on his face. I know what he's going to say before he opens his mouth.

'I'm so sorry, I –'

'Have to go,' I say, finishing his sentence for him.

'Something's come up,' he says gently, putting his arm round me. 'I tried to get out of it but you know what Uncle Mark's like. He says it's important; I'll tell you about it later.'

'I thought you were staying for dinner,' Nancy says, sharing a look with Jimmy. 'Mum's made cheese-and-potato pie.'

'Next time,' he says, giving her and Jimmy a hug before returning to my side. 'Mark's sorted a taxi for me and it's meeting me at the cafe, so I should head back. I'll try to call you later. Here –' he places a small shell inside my palm that he must have picked up while he was on the phone, a reminder of our first date when he gave me one then, too – 'I wish I didn't have to go.'

I nod and he leans down to give me a quick kiss, before hurrying back along the beach. I look at the shell in my hand. I think it's meant to make me feel better but it doesn't.

'Is everything OK?' Nancy asks. 'Between you and Chase, I mean.'

'Yes, course,' I reply, closing my fingers round the shell. 'Everything's great.'

She nods and doesn't bring it up again the rest of the evening, but Nancy has that funny way of being able to read my mind.

And she knows that I'm lying.

CHAPTER TEN

NANCY

Sometimes I wish I could just shut down my brain.

I'd like to turn it off for a bit and not have all these thoughts and worries running through my head all the time. Imagine how relaxing that would be, to have a few moments of nothing. My attention span has never been brilliant, but at the moment it's non-existent. I can't concentrate on anything and I get distracted very easily, before I realize I haven't heard one word of the conversation I'm supposed to be part of.

I'm not very good at handling stressful situations, even though I pretend that I am. When we were little and anything bad or stressful happened, I would be the one taking the lead and Mum would always say things like, 'I'm so pleased Nina has you, Nancy.' But the truth is, Nina is much better at dealing with stuff like that. She likes to analyse things, which means she thinks it all through very carefully, even when it hurts to do so. I prefer to avoid that at all costs.

I think that's one of the reasons we drifted apart after Dad left. I did everything in my power to forget all the hurt he had caused and so I threw myself into building a new life here, distracting myself from the past with all the exciting things in my present, like becoming captain of all the sports teams, going to fun parties and hanging out with confident, popular new friends. Nina took a different tack. She basically dropped off the grid, becoming so introverted and hidden away that it was impossible to have a conversation with her.

She kept clinging on to the past. She wanted to talk about Dad all the time, which was annoying. And then she would get upset if I went shopping with a new friend without her, even though I had invited her and she'd said no. So I stopped inviting her. She wanted to listen to the music Dad used to play in the car, instead of the current charts, and she became obsessed with playing the piano, as though if she got good enough that might tempt him to come back.

I was angry at her for holding on to him when he'd so easily let us go.

Which is why I'm so wary of Dad coming back now. It seems strange that he'd show up with no warning whatsoever after so many years and expect us to welcome him back with open arms. Who does that?

'*He* does,' Mum had said a few nights ago, when Nina was in her room practising on her keyboard and I was helping Mum dry up. 'He could be very spontaneous like that. I used to admire that quality in him. For someone so ambitious and career-driven, it was rather lovely that he had an unpredictable side to him.'

'Did you think he'd ever come back? That he'd ever want to be part of our lives again?'

She'd stopped what she was doing and taken a few moments to think about her answer.

'Honestly, no. For the first couple of years, I thought he might want to look after you girls at least some weekends when he wasn't busy working or travelling. I always made sure that he knew he was welcome to do that. No matter how I felt about him, it was never my plan that you would grow up without a father. But his enthusiasm petered out, a bit like it did with everything. Well –' she'd smiled sadly – 'with me at least. I thought that he might be interested in making contact with you when you were older, in your twenties maybe. When there would be less responsibility for being a parent. Maybe that's why he's come back now. You're grown up. Seeing Nina playing the piano with Chase on that video must have stirred some emotions for him. He always thought she could make it as a musician and he was very encouraging of her. It must be nice for him to suddenly see her doing so well after all these years of wondering whether she was even still playing.'

'That's if he gave us any thought at all. I don't get it, Mum. How can you be so calm about it? He left you to cope with two kids on your own.'

'I'm not angry any more,' she'd said firmly. 'I've come to realize that he did us a big favour. He is a brilliant businessman and a terrible family man. If he wants to make an effort with you and means it, and you both want that, then I'm pleased. I really hope he means it.'

'You have your doubts.'

She'd given me a wary look. 'I don't know him well enough now to judge it. I'm always going to be cautious when it comes to him, Nancy, and protective of you. That's all I care about. If he sticks to his promises this time round, then I'm all for it.'

I had nodded and changed the subject, tired of feeling irritated all the time. I know I've been in a terrible mood all week and that I've been difficult to be around, but I keep thinking about that moment when he walked into the room. I've played it over and over in my mind. It seems so surreal now.

'HELLO! NANCY!'

I snap my head up at the sound of Layla's screeching voice in my ear.

'Sorry! I was in a daze,' I say, sitting straighter and paying attention.

'No kidding,' she grumbles, putting her hands on her hips. 'You haven't contributed anything to this meeting and I just asked you a question about TEN times!'

'Twice,' says Sophie.

'What is with you?' Layla asks, ignoring Sophie. 'You've been acting strange all week.'

'Have I? Oh, it's nothing,' I say. 'I've had a lot on my mind with homework and stuff. Anyway, what did I miss?'

Layla booked our form room after school, so that we could have a website meeting, having officially launched it yesterday. *All That Glitters*, a name I'd suggested, was now up and running. Layla and Sophie had already done a lot of the design before I came on board and, I have to say, it looked very good. Layla had posted a make-up vlog, which had gone down well, and together we'd put together an article on party essentials, which I thought was really strong. Sophie had done a hilarious vlog about learning to do the worm, which, considering she can't do anything close to it, was extremely entertaining. That had got the most hits so far, something she was very proud of.

My contribution was a 'Welcome to the Music Section' article, talking about the sort of thing readers had to look forward to. It wasn't exactly my strongest work, but in my defence I had been a bit distracted this week.

Something that clearly hasn't gone unnoticed.

'We were discussing ideas for driving up hits to the website,' Layla tells me grumpily. 'It's an important conversation, Nancy. We need everyone to pull their weight.'

'Got it,' I say in my most serious voice. 'Hits for the website.'

'Yes, we have to be clever about this,' she continues, pacing at the front of the room as though she's the prime minister working out how to win the next election. It's actually quite funny to watch her, but laughing at Layla in her current state is out of the question.

'We have some good competition,' Sophie points out. 'Your friend Jimmy's website is really cool.'

'It is? How do you know? He hasn't launched it yet.'

'I logged on to his school account and checked it out,' Sophie says breezily. 'It's a very striking design and his articles really made me think, you know? Like, he has so many interesting debates about important school stuff. Did you know that they only have one vegetarian option in the canteen? That seems unfair that vegetarians don't have as many options. They should have at least two. When he launches his website tomorrow, I'm going to sign that petition of his.'

I stare at her. 'I have SO many questions right now.'

'About the canteen options?'

'No, Sophie! Questions like, what are you doing logging on to someone else's account? And how do you even know how to do that?'

I like Sophie, I do. But, having gone through a period of being very close friends with her, I can tell you with confidence that she's got her head in the clouds a lot of the time and the idea of her HACKING into someone else's account in order to get a glimpse at our competition makes absolutely NO sense.

She shrugs. 'It's not rocket science, Nancy. I know his email address, so I just worked out his password and I was in. It only took me a few attempts. His password is "judetheobscure1", all lower case. He's been carrying around that book a lot lately, so I gave it a try. I think he changes his password to whatever he's reading at the time. He is such a geek.'

'Whoa,' I say, looking at Sophie in a whole new light. 'I never knew you had it in you.'

'Had what on me?' she says, suddenly panicking and checking her arms and shoulders. 'What do I have on me?!'

'No, genius, had *in* you. Not on you,' Layla says, rolling her eyes, before turning back to me. 'Sophie's report of Jimmy's work is worrying. *All That Glitters* isn't gaining as much interest as I predicted it would at this stage.'

'Layla, it's been up for a day,' I say, smiling at her. 'Shouldn't we give it a bit more time before we panic about it?'

'What world do you live in, Nancy Palmer?' she retorts, clicking her fingers repeatedly in my face, making me lean right back in my seat. 'This is the twenty-first century! Things move fast! If you don't make an impact, you might as well pack up your bags and go home!'

As she makes her way to the whiteboard at the front, I lean towards Sophie.

'Has Layla just had an energy drink by any chance?' I whisper.

'No,' Sophie assures me. 'But she's had three coffees.'

'That explains it.'

Layla writes 'BRAINSTORM' in the middle of the board and circles it, before turning back to us and pointing the pen right at me.

'You!' she says. 'Give me an idea!'

'Uh . . .'

'Come on, think! This isn't a joke!'

'I know!' I say, trying to control my giggles. I really think she's convinced herself via copious amounts of coffee that she's some kind of chief executive working out a multi-million-pound deal and not a teenager working on a school competition.

'I think we need more vlogs,' Sophie suggests. 'People respond more to video online now. I was thinking we should do some "How To" vlogs, like "How to avoid boring, weird people at a party" and stuff like that.'

'Good!' Layla cries, turning back to the board and writing 'MORE VLOGS'. 'Nancy, do you have any ideas for music vlogs?'

'I do actually,' I say, pleased to be able to bring something to the table. 'I was thinking of doing a vlog series called "The song that means something". In short video clips, I would ask people in school, including teachers, to tell me a song that really means something to them and why. It's music-themed but also gives an insight to each individual.'

Layla looks at me with a pained expression.

'I'm not sure that's quite the vibe we're going for,' she informs me. 'Anything else?'

'Oh. Um. Sure, there was something – what was it again?' I stall for time, trying to think up an idea. Layla's enthusiasm and seriousness seems to be infectious and I genuinely feel like I'm in a boardroom, under pressure and about to be fired. 'Oh yeah, OK, how about "Best live performances through the ages". Quite a good nostalgic idea?'

Sophie nods encouragingly, but Layla hangs her head, as though I've severely disappointed her.

'Nancy,' she begins, clicking the cap on to the pen and coming over to stand in front of me.

'Yes?' I gulp, her shadow looming over my table. I suddenly feel very small.

'Maybe we weren't clear enough about your role on this website. What we want from our music editor is *brand-new material*. Hot new stuff. People don't care about other people's favourite songs! They want celebrity news. Information that they can't get from anywhere else. That's how we're going to drive up hits. Because we are leaders. We are shepherds. We are not sheep.'

'We are SO not sheep,' Sophie reiterates.

'Right, we're not sheep.' I nod, pretending I know what they're talking about. 'But how am I going to get that kind of information?'

'By asking your friends, the members of Chasing Chords.'

'What?' I look from Layla to Sophie to check they're being serious, and neither of them look as though they're joking. 'You want me to ask them for celebrity news?'

'Absolutely! They're sure to know everything about everyone. Pop stars always do,' Layla states, as though she's an expert on the subject. 'I bet they have loads of good stories.'

'You can ask them to make an appearance on the vlog!' Sophie suggests. 'We were thinking that you could do an exclusive interview with them about what they've got coming up. People here would LOVE that and we'd definitely win.'

'Exactly,' Layla agrees. 'A few juicy stories about celebs and the Disney Channel internship would be in the bag. No one would even care about Jimmy's vegetable petitions or whatever they are.'

'Hang on,' I say, jumping in before they can get carried away with this idea. 'I can't just ask them to give me exclusive news and stories about their friends in the business.'

'Why not?'

'Because . . . Chase is my friend now. And the rest of the band, too. I'd feel weird asking them questions about stuff like that. They get enough of that from sleazy reporters. They don't need me asking them about personal things to splash across a website. I'd much rather write about music in a different way.'

Layla and Sophie share a look.

'Nancy, why do you think we asked you to join our team?' Layla frowns at me. 'You told us that you were the one with the contacts. Otherwise we could have asked Nina. You said that you were the best for the job.'

'Well, yeah, but I didn't . . . I didn't really think about this side of things.'

'Maybe we've made a mistake thinking you could handle this. Come on, Sophie.'

Layla packs away her things and slings her bag over her shoulder, while Sophie gets up and gathers her books.

'The meeting is over?' I ask, stunned at the reaction.

'Yes, the meeting is over,' Layla hisses. 'Because you're not taking this seriously. Clearly, you don't want to win.'

'I do want to win,' I protest. 'I really do! I want to be a success at this but –'

'Nancy, if you want to be the best at something, you have to ruffle a few feathers. That's life. And, unlike your sister, you're obviously not made for the cut-throat world of winning,' Layla says in a strop, marching towards the door. 'At least Nina isn't afraid to go after what she wants. You can't even jump the first hurdle!'

I sigh. 'Layla, wait. Don't leave. I can think of something better than –'

'Better than a world-famous band giving you an exclusive story about their next single? I don't think so,' she declares. 'I really believed that you would be the key to us winning this competition. But you don't want it badly enough. Sophie and I really want this, Nancy. That internship is an incredible chance for our futures, but if you're happy to stay where you are, not bothering to try –'

'That's not fair, Layla. This is ridiculous!' I say, throwing my arms up. 'I don't know why you're making such a big deal of it.'

'I told you, Sophie,' Layla says, swinging open the classroom door. 'She's more suited to selling lobster hats.'

She stalks out of the room and Sophie turns to me apologetically.

'She's in a bit of a mood,' she explains quietly. 'Just think about it, yeah?'

'Yeah,' I say, slumping back in my chair. 'Tell her I'll think about it.'

'Cool!' Sophie grins at me. 'What a great meeting!'

She waves goodbye and then runs out, chasing Layla down the corridor to deliver the news. I bury my head in my hands, trying to remind myself that Layla can say a lot of things she doesn't really mean – although I'm starting to believe some of those things myself.

I get out my phone and look at my Instagram, which I haven't updated in a while. I notice that I've lost some followers. Only a few months ago, I was doing so well on social media that a brand sent me a pair of shoes to wear in a post. I click on to Layla's page – her followers have gone up and the last photo she posted was before our meeting started. It's of her at her laptop with a serious expression. The caption says: '*Ready to get to work #allthatglitters #newwebsite #lifestyle #bringonthechallenge #motivation #followyourdreams.*' It already has a ton of likes and comments, praising her for her work ethic and for being so inspiring.

I make a face at my phone and go back to my feed, scrolling down. Everyone is doing something. Whether it's work posts, like Layla's, or pictures at some amazing event. They're all doing *something*. I'm doing nothing. Maybe Layla is right. Maybe I'm doomed to end up stuck here. Selling lobster hats.

I get to Miles's latest picture and smile. It's a good photo from their last tour. He's at his Chasing Chords drum kit and the photographer has captured him in the middle of twirling a drumstick. Underneath, he's written the caption, 'Love my job #throwback #ChasingChords.'

I put my phone in my bag and lean forward, resting my forehead against my arms on the table. A voice suddenly comes from the doorway, making me jump.

'Hey, Nancy.'

'Jimmy! You gave me a heart attack!'

He comes to sit down at the desk next to me, with a bemused expression.

'What are you doing here?' I ask him, checking the time. 'School finished an hour ago.'

'I was working on my website in the computer room,' he explains, before eyeing me suspiciously. 'What are *you* doing here?'

'Same. I just had a meeting with Layla and Sophie. I thought I'd hang back to . . . uh . . . brainstorm. Anyway, have you launched your website yet? I hear it's amazing.'

He frowns at me, confused. 'Who told you that? I haven't shown it to anyone.'

'Uh . . . um . . .'

Oh god. I can't tell him about Sophie. Otherwise, he might get angry and tell a teacher, and that might scupper our chances. COME ON, BRAIN. THINK OF SOMETHING. DON'T LET ME DOWN NOW.

'You told me,' I say.

'I told you?'

'Yeah, during our walk on the beach, you told me it was amazing. Remember?'

To my complete surprise, he grins and nods.

'Ha, yes. I do think I referred to myself as a genius.'

PHEW. Well done, brain.

'I'm going to launch it tomorrow, I think,' he continues. 'I wanted a bit of content up there first before I unleash it for all to see. If people like it, they'll want more straight away. It's an impatient world.'

I smile. 'You sound like Layla. You should have seen her during our meeting. It was like a whole new person. I have to say, I'm kind of impressed. Now that I've seen her in action, I can picture her becoming a CEO.'

Jimmy glances at her scribbles on the board. 'How did the "brainstorm" go, then? I hope you came up with more ideas than "more vlogs".'

'Actually, it didn't go all that well,' I admit, realizing I may as well tell the truth as it's Jimmy. 'It turns out I'm not very good at all this music-writing stuff.'

'I don't believe you,' he says without hesitation. 'You kept that Chasing Chords website going without any help from those two, and that took a lot of creativity. And you've always talked about how much music means to you. You were always blasting music out of your room at all hours.' He shoots me a mischievous smile. 'I remember Nina and I always getting annoyed at you when we were trying to work in her room and you'd be playing some new album on repeat at the highest volume so the whole street could hear. Then over dinner afterwards you'd go into SO much detail about each song, analysing every lyric and shooting down any comment Nina or I made about it being "manufactured music". This was before we were BEST friends, of course.'

'I remember.' I sigh. 'Yeah, well, Layla and Sophie don't want me analysing music lyrics. They want *real* music stories about the artists themselves. Layla wants me to ask Chasing Chords for their help, but I don't want to do that.'

'Why not?'

'You don't think that's bad?' I say, taken aback by his casual reaction.

'You're trying to be a music editor, right? You happen to be friends with a really famous band. It would be strange to ignore that. I'm sure they'd be happy to at least give you an interview or something. Why wouldn't they want to help you with a school project?'

'I thought it would be weird to ask them.'

'I don't think so. If they don't want to do an interview, the worst that will happen is they'll say something along the lines of, "Sorry, Nancy, we don't want to do an interview." And that will be it.'

'I guess I could ask.'

'You can't be a journalist and not ask any questions,' Jimmy says, laughing as he gets to his feet. 'Taking risks is all part of the fun. Trust me, I'm worried that I might be expelled when I launch my website tomorrow, but you can't get to the top without ruffling a few feathers.'

'OK, now you're literally repeating Layla word for word.'

'Worrying,' he says, stopping in the doorway. 'If Layla's making sense, then this competition really is having a positive effect on the school. I'll see you tomorrow and don't forget to check out my website first thing. We may be competitors and everything, but you did say I was your best friend.'

'Are you ever going to stop teasing me for the best-friend thing?'

He looks thoughtful. 'Nope.'

'See you tomorrow. Oh and, Jimmy? Maybe you should change your password.'

'Huh?'

'I . . . read an article about it. Yeah. It's really important to stay on top of changing your password regularly. Just a thought.'

'OK.' He laughs, giving me a funny look. 'Thanks for the really random tip.'

When he leaves, I get out my phone. I take a few deep breaths, collecting myself, and then tap on Miles's name in my contacts. It starts to ring.

'Hello?'

Oh my god, it's him! I hang up immediately.

For goodness' sake, Nancy, OF COURSE IT'S HIM. YOU JUST CALLED HIS NUMBER.

And now I've hung up on him! Like some crazy stalker! WHY DID I DO THAT? Argh, what do I do, what do I do, what do I do, what do I do, what do I do, what do I do, what do I do, what do I . . .

My phone starts vibrating. It's him! Calling back! I stare at it in utter panic and then my brain kicks in, making me answer before he hangs up.

'Hello?' I say as casually as possible.

'Hey, Nancy,' Miles says. 'I think you just called but it got cut off.'

The sound of his voice is already making me feel VERY sweaty.

'Oh, really?' I croak. 'I didn't call you – it must have been an accident. I think my pocket called you, ha ha ha.'

It is so obvious I'm lying. And WHY did I even lie in the first place?! He already gave me the perfect excuse that it cut out! I could have gone with losing signal! WHY didn't I go with that?!

'So, whassup?' I say, putting on a weird Bugs Bunny voice.

Oh god. What am I doing? I have NEVER used 'whassup' in my life. And I have NEVER attempted a Bugs Bunny voice before. Why does Miles have this effect on me?!

'Not much,' he replies, kindly pretending that I didn't just put on a Bugs Bunny voice. 'How's everything with you? It was nice seeing you in Norfolk.'

'Yeah. Yeah, that was cool. Um, not much is going on with me. I'm working on this big school project, but it's kind of boring. I need to phone Mum actually to come pick me up, I'm still sitting here in a classroom like a big loser, ha ha ha, so I'll be heading home soon.'

THIS. IS. NOT. GOING. WELL.

'I was thinking of calling you actually,' Miles says, again kindly not making fun of me for rambling. 'There's this party on Saturday night. I wondered if you wanted to come . . .'

'Huh?' I croak.

'A big music label is throwing it – you know Emerald Entertainment? – and they invited Chasing Chords for some reason, even though we're technically signed to one of their rivals. But Chase and Nina are going – did she mention it?'

'I . . . uh . . . I think I do remember her saying something last night, but I was distracted by this cat sitting outside our window.'

Seriously. Why do I even bother talking?

'Cool, I love cats,' he says, going with it. 'You'd love my cat, Buttercup. But, anyway, Chase mentioned you were having a bit of a tough time at home. I heard about your dad.'

'Oh. Yeah. Weird.'

'I bet. I reckon you could do with some cheering up, so what do you think? You could make your way down to London on Saturday and we could all go together.'

'You're seriously inviting me to the Emerald Entertainment party?'

'Yeah, I am,' he says, and I can hear from the way he says it that he's smiling. 'Seriously.'

It's strange how life can be. One moment, you've got your forehead flat on a desk, wondering how on earth you are going to get celebrity news for your brand-new website and win a really important competition that will prove to everyone that you're not, in fact, a big fat nothing.

And the next moment, a famous drummer is inviting you to a glamorous music party packed with celebrities.

'Nancy?' Miles jolts me out of my musing. 'Would you like to come on Saturday?'

'You know what, Miles,' I say, looking out of the window at the sun breaking through the clouds. 'I'd love to.'

CHAPTER ELEVEN

NINA

'That was AWFUL!'

I wince, dipping my head so that I'm hidden from view by the piano's music stand. Thankfully, the conductor of our group rehearsal isn't talking about me, personally. At least I hope he's not. The group practice has just finished for the day and he's shaking his head in despair.

'You are all out of time,' he says, throwing his hands up in the air. 'You're not a team! How can I work with you if none of you will work together? I hope it will be better tomorrow, otherwise I will not be in a good mood.'

We sit in silence as he finishes tutting and then says, 'DISMISSED!' before shutting his music book and marching out of the room, muttering something about amateurs. Caroline, who's observed the session again, doesn't add anything as she follows him. I was fifteen minutes early today.

With the teachers out of the room, the atmosphere relaxes, although not in a particularly nice way.

'You played that last page at the wrong tempo,' a violinist snaps at the girl next to him. 'It made us all out of time.'

'That wasn't my fault,' she says defensively. 'It was the wind section.'

'Maybe we wouldn't be out of time if we could hear ourselves,' a boy holding an oboe declares, before looking over his shoulder at Jordan and me. 'All I can hear is the stupid tinkering of the piano!'

'Hey, you should be grateful. I covered for you when you messed up the middle section,' Jordan says, glaring at him. 'And, if you ask me, we should be blaming the vocals, which were completely flat that last time.'

The room descends into uproar as everyone starts defending themselves, accusing others and voicing their opinions, talking over each other and getting louder and louder as they realize no one is listening to them. I sit where I am, grateful to be at the back, hoping that no one is about to lay into me.

It's been a tough week.

'Hey, hey, HEY! Everybody, stop it!'

Grace's voice rings out so clearly that everyone stops and turns to look at her. She's climbed up on to her chair and addresses the room.

'This is exactly what he was saying! We aren't working like a team when we play, remember? And we're sure not acting like one now! If we're going to play this piece well in the showcase, which we all want to do, then we need to respect and listen to each other. Come on, I know there's a lot of ego when it comes to the arts, but how about we don't live up to the stereotype. There has to be a way we can make this work. Right?'

I beam at her, catching her eye as she finishes her speech. I'm just thinking about how I wish I could be as confident and clear-headed as Grace, when I notice her trying to tell me something with her eyes. She's encouraging me to speak. The room is completely silent. Oh no. I try to convey a message back with my eyes. *No, no, no, don't make me do this.* Her eyes are now practically bulging out of her head as she pleads with me to stand up and agree with her.

I have to. I don't want to, but I have to. Because I'm so in awe of her and she needs my help right now.

'Um,' I begin quietly, rising from my piano stool.

But I stop, because Jordan is already on his feet.

'Grace's right,' he says, making everyone turn to look at him. 'We need to be working together. No wonder it's all over the place.'

Grace looks as surprised as I do at his words. I should feel grateful for him speaking up, so I didn't have to have all that attention on me, but I feel disappointed that I didn't leap to my feet as soon as Grace finished speaking. It should have been me backing her up, not Jordan. If Nancy had been here instead of me, she wouldn't have hesitated for a moment when it came to standing up with her friend.

'Look,' Jordan continues, relishing the opportunity to lead the troupe, 'for what it's worth, violin section, you sounded incredible to me. When you come in after my introduction, I almost forget to keep playing – it's so beautiful.'

The violinists all smile at him. He glances at Grace and she gives him the thumbs up.

'And woodwind section, wow. So beautiful and delicate, those little trills you do on the third page? It blows me away every time. Vocals, I'm sorry I said you were flat. I would be too, if I had to sing myself hoarse all day. Everyone else here has instruments that we can pick up and put down –' he pauses, glancing at the grand piano he plays – 'well, maybe not pick up . . .'

They all laugh at his joke.

'Seriously though, we all know that the singing is the bit that's really going to hit the audience.'

At this point, the whole orchestra is nodding along, and the singers look so touched by Jordan's words that I think some of them even have tears in their eyes.

'The point is, we're all very talented in this room. Otherwise we wouldn't be here. But we've been so focused on ourselves and our own music that we haven't been listening to anybody else's. I reckon it's about time we did.'

The room bursts into applause and there are even some cheers and whoops.

'So, here's what I propose,' he tells his captive audience. 'I think tomorrow morning, before our individual lessons, we meet here and give it a try again, really listening and respecting what our fellow musicians are doing. Everyone in?'

More applause and cheering, along with some stray shouts of 'YEAH!'

'Good. And I have another idea. As Grace quite rightly pointed out, we haven't been working as a team. That doesn't surprise me. I don't know most of your names and it's hard to play as a team when I'm thinking of you as your instrument and then a number. Isn't that right, Flute Two?'

Flute Two laughs and then nods in agreement.

'So, instead of us all escaping to our individual practice rooms, I reckon we have a little gathering in our halls! It's time for a party.'

The room erupts into excited cheers before giving Jordan a standing ovation as he high-fives a group of woodwind players surrounding him. Everyone starts talking excitedly about the party as they pack up and Grace makes her way across to me.

'Who knew?' she says, waiting for me to get my music together and watching Jordan as he talks to his new adoring fans. 'I hate to say it, but he's gone up in my estimations.'

'It was you who started it,' I comment. 'You were amazing. If it wasn't for you, then none of this would be happening.'

'It was nothing. I was just tired of all the shouting. And a very similar thing happened with my football team last year, so I've had practice.'

'You're on a football team?' I ask, impressed. 'I didn't know that.'

'I didn't know you were a photographer.' She grins as I blush to my roots. 'I saw that book on your bed at lunchtime, filled with all those shots of beaches and fields and a few of that hot boyfriend of yours. Is photography a hobby? Because some of those pictures were really cool.'

'Grace!' Jordan calls out, coming over to us with James before I can answer her. 'Thanks so much for putting an end to all that stupid bickering.'

She smiles back at him. 'Thank *you* for winning over the crowd,' she says. 'I think we could really do with a party. You're right, it's weird that we haven't all hung out together.'

'So, you're coming?' James asks hopefully, his eyes lighting up.

'Course! We're in the same block, so it's hardly an inconvenience.'

Jordan's eyes reluctantly flicker to me. 'What about you, Nina?'

I really, REALLY wish he hadn't asked.

'I can't. I have something on.'

'Aw, can't you cancel?' Grace pleads. 'This is the first party we're having and probably the last, knowing how hard everyone here usually works at the weekend.'

'Let me guess,' Jordan says, 'you're going to a celebrity party?'

They all look at me. I can't lie. There's no point. It will be all over social media as soon as I arrive there with Chase.

'Actually, it is. But I'd much rather be at this party.'

'Then come to our party,' Jordan says. 'It's simple, Nina: don't go to the celebrity party, come to the Guildhall party with people you're supposed to be working with. It's not like you HAVE to go to that one. You'd just rather spend the evening with attention-seeking Z-listers than us.'

'That's not true,' I say quietly.

I can't expand on it because otherwise I'd have to tell them *why* it's so important to me to go to this party. I'd have to tell them that it feels like Chase and I have barely spoken this week and that every time we get the opportunity to be together it's precious. If I go to a different party tonight, then I won't see Chase all weekend. And who knows if I'll see him next week? Or the week after? We seem to be struggling to fit in phone calls, let alone meeting face-to-face.

But I meant it when I said I'd rather be at the Guildhall party. This course is so important to me and I don't want to miss out.

'I have to go to this party with Chase,' I repeat, thinking up a solution. 'But only for a bit. I'll show my face and then come join you at yours.'

Grace's eyes light up. 'Really? That would be so great!'

Even Jordan looks mildly impressed at my compromise, but then shakes his head.

'I'll believe it when I see it,' he says, before heading towards the door. 'We had better go get ready. See you at the party, Grace.'

'Bye, Grace,' James adds, looking a little flustered before following his friend, tripping over his feet as he goes.

'You're really going to come?' Grace asks when they've left. 'Because you can't expect me to put up with Jordan all night without having you there to roll my eyes at whenever he says something stupid.'

'I promise I'll be there.' I laugh, linking my arm through hers. 'I'll text you when I'm on my way. And, for what it's worth, I think James has a little crush on you. Also, Jordan was genuinely impressed by your handling of the situation just now. So maybe tonight he'll be pleasant to you and it won't be so bad.'

'Maybe. Miracles do happen,' she says, laughing as we head outside to walk back to our halls. 'And, if you want my opinion, I think he's pleased that you're going to show up this evening. Even though he won't admit it, I think deep down he respects you as a pianist.'

'Deep, deep down.'

'Deep, deep, deep down,' she says.

We burst out laughing again, but as we turn the corner I stop in my tracks. Dad is standing a few metres away, leaning against the wall and typing on his phone.

'You OK?' Grace asks, following my line of gaze. 'Who is that?'

'My dad.'

She looks at him and then back at me. 'And . . . that's a bad thing?'

'I don't know.'

'Oh.'

Dad looks up from his phone and spots me, a smile spreading across his face as he shoves his phone in his pocket and walks towards us.

'Hi, Nina,' he says, before holding out his hand to Grace. 'Hello, I'm Nina's dad. Are you on Nina's course?'

'Yeah, I'm Grace. Nice to meet you.' She looks to me for instruction but I don't know what to do so she decides to improvise. 'Nina, I'll . . . shall I meet you back at our room?'

I hesitate and then nod.

'See you in a bit. Call if you need,' she says, heading off down the road and leaving us to it.

'I thought we could go for dinner,' Dad says hopefully.

'I can't.'

'Oh.' He stares at his shoes. 'All right.'

'I have . . . It's a party,' I explain, my whole body tense. 'A music label is throwing it. I'm going with Chase.'

'No, no,' he says hurriedly with a bright smile. 'It sounds brilliant. An excellent networking opportunity, you should absolutely go. I should have known you'd be busy. It was a long shot.' He looks at his watch. 'How about a drink before you have to go? There's a nice little cafe around here. We could go and grab a hot chocolate. It used to be your favourite.'

I smile. 'It still is.'

'I thought as much.' He grins. 'How about it?'

I hesitate. I don't know what the right thing to do is. I wish Nancy was here. She always knows what to do.

'That would be nice,' I say.

'Brilliant!' he exclaims. 'Let's go – it's not far.'

'I should give Nancy a call though.' I pull my phone out of my pocket. 'She's on her way to London for the party. She was going to get her train around now. So we could wait and then all go together. Nancy and I can make our way to the party afterwards.'

Dad shifts uncomfortably. 'I'm not sure that's such a good idea.'

'Why not?'

'You say she's just getting the train now?'

'I don't know, I can't remember. She may already be on it.'

'Even so . . . it's a long way from Norwich, a couple of hours at least, and by the time she got here you'd probably have to leave.

I think Nancy may also need a bit more time getting used to the idea of me again and I don't want to waste this opportunity, while she thinks about it, to spend time with you and hear all about your music course. I want to do this all together, but I don't think Nancy is ready yet. Maybe it's best that we just keep it us two for now.'

I know he's right. It will take Nancy hours to get here, by which point we'd have to leave, and he's right that she'd not want to go for hot chocolate with him anyway. I know all this. But I still wish she was here. I put my phone back in my pocket.

'Lead the way.'

'Jordan sounds like a character!' Dad chuckles, reaching for a napkin. 'Some of the things he says sound outrageous. Not that it surprises me that he's trying to chip away at your confidence bit by bit. Self-doubt is a sure way to failure and the music industry is a competitive world.'

'I'm only just discovering that,' I say. I sigh, leaning back in my chair.

I'm glad that the cafe Dad chose is different to the one Chase and I got photographed in. I don't trust that place any more. This one is really fancy and Dad had spoken to one of the staff as soon as we walked in, making sure we got a table where we couldn't be photographed.

'This is great,' I'd said, sitting at the table and noticing it was away from the crowds and hidden from view. 'What did you tell them?'

'That, in case they didn't notice, I was with THE Nina Palmer, the famous musician, and we didn't want any fans of you or Chasing Chords taking pictures of us stuffing our faces with pastries,' he'd said, and then he had grinned, making me laugh.

Since we sat down, time has flown. At first, the conversation was a bit stilted as I felt so weird being here, having a hot chocolate with my dad. My *dad*. But thankfully he's better at this sort of thing than me and he started talking about music, which meant the conversation just started flowing because it was something we are both passionate about. We'd got on to the subject of Guildhall and I'd ended up telling him everything about how terrible I was at performing, my stage fright, the showcase and, of course, Jordan's constant jibes.

'When I applied for the course, I didn't even think about the other people who'd be on it with me. It didn't come into my brain that they might resent me because I was dating a pop star.' I shake my head. 'It seems stupid now.'

He smiles. 'No, it doesn't. Unfortunately, not everyone is as nice and trustworthy as you are. You're going to have to harden that shell if you're going to make it.'

'I don't know. Maybe this course is a way of life telling me that I'm not cut out to be a musician, that I don't have it in me.'

'You don't really believe that, do you?'

'It's crossed my mind.' I shrug. 'If there are people like Jordan out there, I don't stand a chance. I'm not even close to his standard.'

'Nina, you're looking at this all wrong,' Dad says, leaning forward and clasping his hands together. 'I'm glad someone like Jordan is on this course. It's good motivation for you. There's nothing like a bit of competition. That's how I grew my PR business. When my old company didn't work out, my ex-business partner started doing really well, which helped spur me on to work harder, be more ambitious – and what do you know? My business grew at double the pace and, in the end, a lot of his clients started working with me. His success gave me the motivation I needed not to give up.'

'Wow, that's amazing. I always wondered how you started your business.'

'Yes. It was hard work and, obviously, its success came at a cost . . .'

He looks upset as his sentence fizzles out, and I don't know whether to say something. I can't tell him he's wrong, because that would be a lie. But I also don't want us to have a miserable time because I'll need to leave soon to get ready for the party. I think about how to comfort him, but in the end he doesn't need me to. He suddenly clears his throat and his expression brightens.

'Anyway, enough about me. I'm interested in you and this dazzling career of yours!'

My cheeks burn at his praise. 'No, don't be silly.'

'Nina, why don't you believe in yourself? You always used to hide behind Nancy. You're a very talented young woman and I have witnessed that. Thousands of people have seen it for themselves, when you played alongside Chase.'

'You're wrong. I'm not that talented, not compared to the other students. I've dreamt my whole life of training at Guildhall and here I am, getting a taster of what it might be like, a chance to impress future teachers, and I'm failing.'

'Time to start succeeding then,' Dad says simply.

'You make it sound easy.'

'And you make it sound unachievable,' he retorts, with a knowing smile. 'I know you can do this, Nina. Everyone does. That's what's making Jordan scared.'

'Believe me, Jordan is –'

'Quivering in his little boots,' Dad finishes.

I laugh. 'Why would he be scared?'

'Because you're better than him. Maybe not technically, but that can be taught. What you can't teach is whatever it is you have. Natural talent. You're entrancing when you play. Jordan, I can tell from the little you've told me of him, is not. He's a good pianist, I'm sure, but he won't sell albums and he won't top charts. You, on the other hand, will. I've always known that. What do Chase's record label have to say about you?'

'What do you mean?'

'You must have spoken to them. Have they noticed your potential? Have you had any meetings at all?'

I shake my head, trying to work out if he's joking or not.

'Why not?'

'I . . . I don't know. Why would they want to have meetings with me?'

'Nina,' he says, rolling his eyes, 'have you heard anything I've said today? You'll have to invite them to your showcase.'

'Chase's management team? WHY would they want to come to my Guildhall showcase?'

'So they can see how talented you are and then sign you,' he explains, before getting a waiter's attention and ordering another espresso.

'Now,' he continues, 'have you got a manager?'

I'm so taken aback that I choke as I sip my hot chocolate, coughing and spluttering so much that my eyes water.

'Did you say a manager?' I wheeze.

'That's exactly what I said.'

'No, I don't.'

He nods thoughtfully, placing his hands together in his lap.

'I could be your manager, if you like,' he suggests.

'B-but I thought you were in PR,' I stammer, bowled over by this whole conversation. 'And, anyway, why would I need a manager?'

'Being in my line of work has many transferable skills and I've always thought I'd be good at music management. It essentially combines my two passions: talent and business,' he says, slowly tasting his espresso. He adds a sugar lump and stirs. 'Nina, you are in an excellent position right now. You've got incredible contacts. For example, this party tonight. Think of the people who will be there. Some of the most powerful in the business and they'll all know who you are. You're dating Chase Hunter and you're one to watch as you happen to have a place on an acclaimed music course. You just need guidance.'

'And . . . you want to guide me?'

'I want you to think about it. Whether you realize it or not, you're embarking on a career. That YouTube video was only the start, but things like that get forgotten if you don't make good use of them. It might be handy for you to have someone looking out for you.'

'Right. Thanks.'

He smiles broadly at me. 'I truly believe that you can beat that Jordan person. You know what the best revenge is?'

'Shutting his fingers in the piano lid?'

He laughs. 'Not bad. But I was thinking of something else. The best revenge on Jordan would be for you to win the showcase, get signed and sell a million records before he's even finished his performance. But we need to work out how to get you to stand out. I'll have a think.'

He finishes his espresso and asks for the bill, checking the time.

'You need to head off if you're going to get to your party.'

'Yeah, I should go. Thanks for all your advice. It's been really good to talk about it. I haven't really been able to with anyone else,' I admit.

'It's an honour. I'm proud of you, Nina.'

Tears fill my eyes. I try to blink them back but I can't, and one falls down my cheek.

'Are you OK? Did I say something wrong?' he asks in a panic.

'No, no. The opposite,' I say, wiping the tear away with my sleeve. 'I always wanted you to be proud of me.'

'Don't you remember what I told the lady in that piano shop all those years ago?' he says, reaching out and taking my hand. 'I said, "This is Nina and –"'

He looks at me encouragingly, his eyes twinkling. We finish the sentence together.

'"She's going to be a big star some day."'

CHAPTER TWELVE

NANCY

As the taxi draws up to the party, I feel a gigantic, excited knot in my stomach.

There is a red carpet leading up to the glass doors of the Emerald Entertainment building and at either side of it are hordes of photographers, ready to take pictures as guests arrive. I nervously check my outfit and then my make-up for the hundredth time. I wish I wasn't alone, but I arranged to meet Miles at the party as there was no point in him coming to meet me at the train station. It would be easier for me to hop in a taxi and go straight there. I'd hoped to go with Nina because Guildhall is really near Liverpool Street station, but she wasn't picking up her phone or answering any messages.

Where is she? Her group practice finished ages ago and then she told me she'd be going back to her room to get ready. I didn't want to hang around waiting for her at the station, in case she was already at the party, so I decided to make my own way here. But now, seeing all these photographers and a long red carpet, I totally regret that decision. I could really use someone's arm to lean on.

No, seriously, I actually need someone's arm to lean on, because these heels are already killing me.

I was sent them last term when my followers on social media were increasing so much that I got noticed by one of my favourite brands, Silhouette, and they sent these shoes as a gift to post on my Instagram. I wore them to the Chasing Chords secret gig – which turned out to be an important event in the end, because Nina and Chase met that night – and everybody said they looked amazing in my comments. That, I remembered. What I had conveniently forgotten was that by the end of the night I couldn't feel my little toe and I had to wear blister plasters for days afterwards. Oh well, they look good.

I have to admit, all of me looks good tonight. I've spent the entire day getting ready. Mum helped me pick out the perfect outfit, a black tuxedo minidress which looks amazing with my sea-blue heels. My hair is naturally poker straight, but I straightened it anyway and added perfectly matching extensions that I'd ordered online. I'd then swept it back into a high sleek ponytail, which was very satisfying to swish about as I walked. I'd gone for dramatic eye make-up to complete the look, with shimmering gold eyeshadow, dark eyeliner with a perfect feline flick and full fake eyelashes.

Mum had taken a hundred photos on my phone and then I'd spent the two-hour train journey picking the best one, getting the filter just right, editing it and then posting it with a caption about going to the Emerald Entertainment party. As soon as I posted it, I got a phone call from Layla.

'What are you DOING?' she'd cried down the phone frantically. 'You need to edit that post IMMEDIATELY.'

'Why?'

'You haven't added the link to *All That Glitters*!'

'Oh. Right.'

'Honestly, Nancy, you need to start thinking about these things. Say that you're about to go to the Emerald Entertainment party and that you'll be posting all the latest hot gossip from the party on our website later! That way, our audience can start getting excited and they'll be ready to click through as soon as you write about it!'

'Got it – I'll edit it now,' I'd assured her. 'Sorry, I don't know why I didn't think of that.'

'Get your head in the game,' she'd said, before hanging up.

I never thought there would be a day when Layla would quote *High School Musical* lines at me in a serious capacity. At least she'd forgiven me for the disastrous meeting this week. She and Sophie were so excited about me going to the party and I'd promised them I wouldn't come back with nothing. I promised that to myself, too. This is a huge opportunity and I really don't want to mess it up.

'Here we are, miss,' the black-cab driver announces, pulling up at the top of the red carpet. 'This looks like it's going to be quite the party.'

'It is.' I smile warmly, paying the fare.

I take a deep breath, watching the photographers notice the taxi and crane their necks over each other to see who it is. I can't believe I'm at THE Emerald Entertainment event. It is the music party of the year. Anyone who's anyone will be here.

The door swings open as someone comes to help me out and I gratefully take their hand, steadying myself on my heels before I start the walk along the carpet. The camera flashes explode as soon as I step out of the car and I'm hit with a barrage of blinding lights and yells from the photographers. I remember when I helped Nina leave the hospital after the accident along with Chase and there had been loads of paparazzi waiting for us – it was just like that all over again and I am reminded why celebrities always wear sunglasses. It is very difficult to walk normally with those splodges you get in your eyes after a camera flash.

But I also love it. Because feeling like someone important and wanted is a really good feeling. I glide confidently towards the glass doors as the photographers ask me to stop, so they can get a full picture of my outfit. Placing one hand on my hip, I stop and face them, flashing a big smile and hoping my lipstick hasn't smudged.

That's when I actually stop to listen to what the reporters are yelling.

That's when I realize.

'Nina! Who are you wearing?'

'Nina! Why haven't you arrived with Chase?'

'Nina, is it true your relationship is on the rocks?'

'Nina, how's music school?'

Oh my god. They think I'm Nina.

My smile is frozen in place. I don't know what to do. I have to tell them. Otherwise, when she arrives with Chase, it will be even more mortifying.

'I'm . . . I'm not Nina,' I say, my voice wobbling.

'What?' The photographers shout back at me, begging me to come closer to repeat what I said, desperate for Nina to answer their burning questions.

'I'm not Nina,' I repeat, glancing towards the glass doors where a doorman and a woman are waiting, watching this humiliating scene.

'She's not Nina!' A photographer yells for the others to hear. 'It's not Nina! It's the other one! It's her twin.'

As his voice rings out, the cameras are lowered and the murmurs of disappointment ripple through the group. They're not looking at me any more; they're chatting to each other about whatever they were talking about before I arrived. It's like someone flicked a switch and I no longer exist.

Flustered and ashamed, I lower my head and walk as quickly as possible towards the door. I walk so fast that I trip on my ridiculously high heels and am thankfully caught just in time by the doorman's arm, saving me from falling flat on my face. There is a titter of laughter from those of the paparazzi behind me who notice.

'You all right?' the man says as I regain my balance.

'Fine,' I mutter, my ankle throbbing. 'I'm Nancy Palmer.'

'Nina's twin.' The woman smiles, looking down the list on her tablet. 'Welcome to Emerald Entertainment. Enjoy your night.'

The man holds open the door for me and I walk into a grand reception room, where I'm directed down a corridor and through the doors into the party. The room is bursting with people, a couple of whom look my way as I walk in and then, when they realize I'm no one important, go back to their air kisses and conversations. The music is blaring and, with low lighting and hundreds of people, I don't know how I'm ever going to find Miles in here. Just by scanning those standing nearby, I spot two famous pop stars, an actor and a model who I follow on Instagram. Hardly the crowd you can simply stride on over to and introduce yourself.

I make my way to the corner of the room and lean back against the wall, still feeling shaken from what happened outside. I don't know why I'm surprised. Why would the photographers have wanted a picture of me? It's not like I'm famous, I know that. So, why do I feel like crying?

Maybe it was those horrible words uttered by the photographer, a label I'm scared of being stuck with forever: *the other one*.

I guess that's the curse of having a perfect twin like Nina. Always feeling a bit smaller.

'Nancy!'

Miles appears in front of me. I have never been so happy to see anyone in my life.

'There you are,' I say, relief flowing through me. 'I didn't know how to find you in this massive crowd and I wasn't sure if you'd be busy and –'

'Wow,' he says, staring at me with a smile spreading across his face.

I'm not sure I've seen him smile like that before. It's different to his usual teasing grin. It's more serious somehow. If that makes sense.

'What?' I ask, worried that I've got eyeliner smudged down my face.

'You . . . you look beautiful,' he says.

'Oh! Um. Thanks.'

'I see your hair has magically grown a few inches since I last saw you,' he says, the familiar mischievous grin returning. 'What products do you use?'

'I'll send you the list.'

'Do you want a drink? The sparkling elderflower is a fantastic vintage.'

I laugh. 'That sounds perfect, thank you.'

'I'll be back in a second,' he says, before leaning in to kiss me on the cheek. 'Don't go anywhere.'

He disappears back into the crowd, leaving me in a bit of a daze. It's really unfair of him to do things like that. Firstly, because he smells very good and leaning in towards someone like that can cause their brain to go fuzzy with how good he smells. Secondly, when he kissed me on the cheek, his face was very close to my face. Obviously. And his cheek kind of grazed my cheek and made my stomach do that somersault, butterfly thing.

'Nancy, are you OK?' a voice says over the music.

'Nina!' I cry, grabbing her hands and pulling her in for a hug. 'I'm so glad you're finally here!'

'Why are you standing in the corner with a weird, dreamy smile on your face?' she asks, giggling. 'You look a little strange, no offence.'

'I was just thinking about . . . things,' I say, before cunningly changing the subject. 'Where have you BEEN? You know, you left me to do the red-carpet thing on my own. And it was the worst experience of my life.'

'It was? I thought you'd really enjoy that kind of thing. You're always going on about how you'd love to walk a red carpet some day.'

'Yeah, well, it wasn't exactly how I imagined it.'

She gives me a knowing look. 'Did you fall over in those stupid shoes?'

'No! Of course not. Why would you say that?'

'Because those shoes destroy your feet and I specifically remember telling you not to wear them. I know how hard it can be to walk in a straight line with a mass of people trying to get your picture and in those things I imagine it's even worse.'

'At least I'm not wearing trainers,' I point out, glancing down to her feet.

'Hey! They're *sparkly* trainers,' she says defensively, pointing her toe. 'And someone VERY stylish helped me pick these on a recent shopping outing.'

'Uh-huh, I can tell that person was VERY stylish, indeed.' I grin. 'And don't you forget it. I like your make-up. Very natural.'

'That's because it is. All I'm wearing is mascara,' she admits with a grimace. 'I was in a rush and I still don't know how to use all those fancy products you gave me. I needed you.'

After the night I've had so far, it's really nice to hear her say that.

'Nancy, about tonight,' she continues, 'I'm going to have to –'

'Hey,' Chase says, looming into view and pulling Nina towards him before she can finish whatever it was she was about to tell me. 'Where have you been? There are so many people here wanting to meet you. Hi, Nancy. Nice hair!' he says, before frowning in confusion. 'Wait, how does it grow so fast?'

'I won't make fun of you for not knowing that I'm using extensions if you don't make fun of me any more for that time I fell over showing you and Nina my favourite Beyoncé move.'

'Deal,' he says, realizing his mistake and bursting out laughing. 'It looks good. Nina, how come you're so late? I called you so many times.'

'Me too,' I say.

Nina gets a funny look on her face and pushes her hair behind her ears.

'Actually, I was with Dad.'

'What?' I ask, thinking I hadn't heard her correctly over the loud music.

'I was with Dad,' she repeats, her eyes locking with mine. 'He was waiting outside Guildhall when my group rehearsal finished.'

'Why was he waiting for you?' Chase asks, taking the words out of my mouth. 'Had you called?'

'No,' she answers, looking at me. 'I had no idea he was going to be there.'

'Wait,' I say, trying to get my head round this. 'He was waiting for you outside Guildhall and then, what? You guys went and . . . hung out for a few hours?'

She nods, biting her lip. 'Yeah. I swear, Nancy, I didn't plan it. And I was going to call you and see if you could make it but the timing was wrong. You would have just been on the train on the way down here and by the time you'd arrived we'd have had to leave to get here on time.'

'What did you talk about?' Chase asks, glancing at me with concern.

'We only went for hot chocolate and talked about music and stuff. Nothing important. I think he just wanted to see us and have a normal conversation.'

'Not us, *you*. He wanted to see you,' I say.

'Nancy, I'm sorry, I didn't know what to do and . . . Are you mad?'

I look down at my sea-blue shoes. I'm not sure how I feel. I think I am mad but I'm not entirely sure why exactly. I'm not sure which bit of it I'm mad at. He does live very close to Guildhall. When Nina wasn't around, I sneaked a look at the address he'd given Mum and googled it. It was in a really expensive part of town and barely a ten-minute walk from her school. It makes sense that he'd try to see Nina when she's so close.

'Why didn't he call you first?' I eventually say, avoiding her question. 'Don't you think that's weird? He hasn't seen us in years and he thinks it's OK to show up at your music school? Why didn't he have the courtesy to arrange a meeting with us both, rather than take you completely by surprise so that you're pretty much forced to see him? He didn't give you the choice.'

'I don't think he thought of it like that,' she reasons. 'I think he knew I was in London and wanted to make the effort.'

'Why doesn't he want to make the effort with both of us? Should I expect him to be waiting outside school in Norfolk this coming week? Or is a two-hour train journey a bit too much of an ask for reconnecting with your daughters?'

Nina looks down at her shoes.

'Hey, come on – let's enjoy tonight,' Chase says, attempting to lighten the mood. 'We're at this incredible party and it would be a shame to waste it. Right?'

'Yeah,' Nina agrees, watching me anxiously. 'It would.'

'Chase!'

Mark, Chase's uncle and band manager, appears flustered at Chase's side.

'What are you doing stuck here in the corner?' he grumbles. 'You're supposed to be working the room.'

'Uncle Mark, you remember Nancy,' Chase says, nodding towards me. 'And Nina just got here.'

'I need you to come with me now,' Mark growls, ignoring him. 'The CEO of Emerald Entertainment specifically said she wanted to meet you.'

'Seriously?' Chase's eyes widen. 'Whoa.'

'Whoa, indeed,' Mark says in a strained voice. 'I've been looking for you for ages. You don't want to keep someone like that waiting. Come *on.*'

Chase turns to Nina. 'Will you come with me? I'm nervous. The CEO, Nina!'

'Sure,' she says, taking his hand. 'Nancy, are you coming?'

'I think I'll stay here,' I say, avoiding eye contact. 'Miles is coming back with drinks.'

'Nancy –' she begins.

'We have to go, now,' Chase says, dragging her into the crowd. 'Otherwise we'll lose her.'

She mouths 'sorry' to me, following Chase as he attempts to make his way around groups of guests towards where Mark and the CEO are, right in the middle of the room. I stay where I am, dodging out of people's way as they try to squeeze past. I'm still in shock about what Nina has just told me. I can't believe she's spent the afternoon with Dad. Without me. I know it's not her fault and that he sprung the meeting on her, but still. That doesn't make it hurt any less.

Mum said he was spontaneous, but that seems calculated.

I'm so engrossed in my thoughts that I don't realize Miles is back until he's right in front of me, wiggling my drink under my nose.

'Sorry it took so long,' he says, as I thank him. 'There are a LOT of people here.'

'Yeah, it's really busy,' I reply, distracted.

'Hey.' He peers at me with a furrowed brow. 'Why are you so down? What did I miss?'

'I'm not down.'

'Yes, you are. When I left you, you were smiling and laughing, swishing your unicorn ponytail without a care in the world. And now I'm back and it's like you've got the weight of the world on your shoulders, so spill.'

I can't help but smile. 'Unicorn ponytail?'

'Yeah, it looks like the tail of a unicorn.'

'I'll take that as a compliment,' I say with a laugh.

'You should – it was meant to be.' He nudges me gently. 'Come on, what's going on? Did that weird guy from *PopRock Magazine* start asking you questions? Because he's lurking somewhere and trust me, if anyone can put you in a bad mood, it's him. He once asked why our songs had no good melodies, and whether we agreed that they all sounded the same.'

'No, I haven't had the pleasure of meeting him yet.' I sigh. 'It's Nina. She just arrived and the reason she's late, and why neither Chase nor I could get hold of her, is because she was hanging out with our dad.'

'What? Really?'

'Yeah.' I nod, pursing my lips. 'Apparently, he showed up at her door and they decided to have a nice hot chocolate together. Without me.'

'Are you OK?'

'I don't know. I feel annoyed, but that's unfair because I said to Nina that I wasn't interested in having him back in my life, when I knew that she felt the opposite. But I'm not sure if I meant it, you know? I was still trying to work it out. Anyway, it makes sense that he'd want to make an effort with her and not bother with me.'

Miles looks confused. 'Why do you say that?'

I shrug. 'Nina's the special one. They always bonded over music. When he was around, I mean. That was like, their "thing". He and I don't have anything like that to bond over.'

'You love music, too, don't you?'

'Yeah, but I'm not a musician. I like listening to music, that's all. Hardly a talent that a dad can be proud of.'

'Come on, Nancy – he's your dad. You don't need to have something to bond over. Of course he'd be interested in getting to know you again.'

'I don't think he is,' I admit, taking a sip of sparkling elderflower, hoping Miles won't notice that my eyes are welling up. 'He's only interested in Nina. Just like everyone else. And so they should be.'

Miles watches me, and we stand in silence, listening to the loud, thumping music and the excitable chatter of all the party guests around us. I feel my phone vibrating in my clutch and check it, seeing a flurry of messages from Layla and Sophie asking if I've got anything good yet. I shove my phone back in my clutch and click it shut.

'I know the whole dad thing sucks, but I don't want to see you like this,' Miles says eventually. 'If you want to leave, I understand, but maybe there's a way of cheering you up. That was the reason I invited you along here tonight in the first place, so, tell me how I can put a smile on your face.'

'Don't be silly, Miles,' I say, nodding towards the group of models huddled together in front of us, who keep looking at him and giggling. 'You should be mingling and enjoying this big party. You don't need to babysit me. I'm sorry for ranting at you; I didn't mean to.'

'I don't feel like I'm babysitting you. I enjoy our chats,' he says with an infectious grin. 'You want me to crack a few jokes to cheer you up? I have some great ones up my sleeve, although, I have to warn you, sometimes it takes me a while to remember the punch lines.'

'As brilliant as that sounds, there is something you might be able to help me with,' I say, deciding to bite the bullet. 'Did I tell you about my school project?'

'Nope, but school projects are ALWAYS fascinating.'

'This one actually is,' I say. 'I've launched a website with a couple of my friends and if we win the competition for the best new site, we get to spend the Easter holidays backstage at the Disney Channel, learning the ropes from the creative director.'

'OK, that's awesome. What school is this? I want to go there.'

'Anyway, I'm the music editor of *All That Glitters* – that's the name of the website – and I need some content for my section.'

'Hang on,' he says, his eyes brightening. 'Please tell me you have launched another Chasing Chords fan-fiction site.'

I roll my eyes. 'No, that's not what this is.'

'I actually have several bones to pick with you about your old one. How come Chase got to play the lead in all the stories? I was always the sidekick. Except for that one where I bumped into the girl on the beach and we fell in love while surfing and swimming with turtles. That one was good. I didn't like the one where I was attacked by a swarm of bees, but I checked the date of that story and you wrote it just after we first met, which is encouraging.'

'Argh.' I bury my head in my hands, feeling the heat rising through my face. 'Please stop! It's so embarrassing! You told me you hadn't read them.'

'Hey, they were really good, no kidding!' He laughs, pulling my hands from my face. 'Tell me about this new website.'

'We need more hits, otherwise we don't have a chance of winning,' I explain. 'I thought maybe tonight I could get some music news to put up.'

He nods thoughtfully and then spots someone, turning to me to say, 'Hang on,' before launching himself at them. I can't see who it is as Miles's big head is right in the way. After chatting to them quickly, he makes his way back to me with the person in tow.

I almost choke on my elderflower drink when I realize it's Tyler Hill, one of my favourite singers. I was listening to her music on the train on the way here.

'Tyler, this is the journalist I was telling you about.'

'Nancy, it's nice to meet you,' she says, kissing me on the cheek while I try to remain calm. 'I'm a big fan of your sister. Chase introduced me to her a moment ago; they're a lovely couple.'

'Hurugh,' I say, nodding. The corners of Miles's mouth twitch as he tries not to laugh at how starstruck I am.

'Miles says you're looking for content for your new website? Well, I am launching a fashion line this summer and it hasn't been announced yet. I was going to leak the story tonight to that guy from *PopRock*, but then he asked me why I keep trying to bring back blue eyeshadow and now I don't think he deserves the story.' She smiles at me. 'Would you like the exclusive?'

'YES,' I cry, before composing myself and clearing my throat, much to Miles's amusement. 'I mean, yeah, sure, that would be great.'

'I'll email you the details now. What's your address?'

She sends me the information, gives me some quotes and lets me take a picture with her to accompany the piece, before kissing me on the cheek again and emphasizing how nice it was to meet me.

'Thanks so much, Tyler,' I gush. 'I don't know why you're giving me this amazing exclusive, but I can't thank you enough.'

'Not at all. I look forward to seeing the story – and good luck with your new website. It's nice to support up-and-coming music journalists. Besides,' she says, glancing at Miles and then back to me, 'Miles couldn't stop going on about you.'

And, with that, she glides off into the crowd.

'Oh my god, I can't believe that just happened,' I squeal.

'Yeah,' Miles says, looking bashful.

'Thank you so much, Miles. I owe you big time! People are going to go crazy at school when they see this story.'

'So, you're happy?' he asks hopefully.

'Very,' I say. 'Our website might have a chance of winning with content like this! You're the best.'

'No worries.' He beams at me. 'As long as you don't go writing stories about me on that website, I'm happy to help. I don't want to see any of my many secrets splashed about for your school pals.'

I give him a look. 'And what many secrets might you have, Miles?'

'Oh, I have a few.' He holds his glass up. 'Cheers. To having a good night.'

'To having the *best* night,' I say, clinking my glass against his. 'Thanks to you.'

He smiles at me and suddenly I don't care about everything else going on. I don't care that I felt so down earlier in the night that I wanted to go home and cry. I forget that my dad doesn't seem to be interested in me. I forget that I've felt really lost lately.

With Miles standing here, smiling at me in that way he does, everything feels like it's going to be OK after all.

CHAPTER THIRTEEN

NINA

'Just one more,' the photographer promises, moving a step to the right and crouching slightly, before clicking the button. 'Got it. Perfect, thank you.'

He then spins round and taps the shoulder of Tyler Hill, the pop star Chase introduced me to earlier in the evening, asking her for some photos.

'I can't pose for any more pictures,' I tell Chase, rubbing my jaw. 'My face is aching from all this smiling. How do you do it?'

'You may not have noticed, but I don't really smile in pictures,' he says. 'I go for a sexy, smouldering vibe.' I burst out laughing as he pretends to pose for another picture. 'You see?'

'Yes, very sexy,' I say, rolling my eyes.

'Don't laugh, Miss Palmer! It's taken me a couple of years to perfect that look.'

'Time well spent.'

He smiles, brushing a stray lock of hair off my face and tucking it behind my ear.

'Actually, it's nice to see you laugh,' he says. 'I was worried you'd be in a bad mood all night. You barely said a word to Rachel.'

'Rachel? So you're on first-name terms now with the CEO of Emerald Entertainment,' I tease.

'She specifically said to call her Rachel; you were there. She was impressive, wasn't she? Imagine being in charge of all this,' he says, gesturing around the room. 'Some of the most successful musicians in the world are signed to Emerald Entertainment.'

'Maybe you'll be next.'

He runs a hand through his hair. 'Maybe. I think the rest of the band know something is up. Miles was asking me loads of questions earlier. You didn't say anything to Nancy, did you?'

'Of course not,' I say, slightly hurt at the accusation but he doesn't notice. 'You asked me to keep it secret. What sort of thing was Miles asking?'

'He was saying how we didn't get an invitation to the last Emerald Entertainment party and was it weird that we have to this one. I told him that we must officially be on the map. But they obviously invited us because Uncle Mark has been putting feelers out to see if they'd be interested in me as a solo artist. I can't believe they're even considering it. The fact that I'm on Rachel's radar means a lot to me. Signing to Emerald would be incredible. It sounds like she'd let me have a lot more control over things, you know? Which has always been the problem with Chasing Chords. I have to stick to that sound. But here I'd be able to try something new.'

'When are you planning on telling the band?' I ask, bringing him back to the point. 'It's silly for it to be so secretive.'

'Isn't that the guy from the Armani adverts behind you?' Chase asks, completely ignoring me. 'He seems shorter in person.'

'Chase, I know it's difficult, but you have to tell them some time. If Mark is talking to lots of people in the industry about it, then it might get back to the band before you've mentioned it. And that would be even worse. What happens if someone brings it up tonight?' I say, spotting Mark talking to Rachel again before they both look over at Chase with smug expressions. 'Your uncle seems to be on a mission to get you signed to Emerald before the clock strikes midnight. Maybe you should tell the band sooner rather than later? Don't you think?'

'I'll tell them when it's the right time, Nina,' he says, brushing the question aside.

'It's never going to feel like the right time. You have to –'

'I got it, Nina,' he snaps.

I recoil, stung by his tone. 'Don't get angry, Chase. I'm only trying to help you to do the right thing.'

'And what about the right thing with your dad and Nancy?' he asks, irritated.

'What has that got to do with anything?'

'I just think it's a bit strange that you're telling me to do the right thing, when you didn't even call or text Nancy to let her know that you were having a hot chocolate with your dad this afternoon.'

'I told you,' I say, lowering my voice, worried that people around us might be able to hear, 'when he showed up, Nancy was getting on the train. She never would have made it in time and it would have made things complicated.'

'Sounds like a convenient excuse to me.'

'You're being unfair.'

'And you're getting angry because you know I'm right. You took the easy path. You didn't let her know because then you could go enjoy your hot chocolate with him, without feeling guilty. You should have at least texted her to let her know or checked that she was OK with it,' he says in frustration, before letting out a long sigh. 'Just like I shouldn't be so cowardly about talking to the rest of the band about trying a solo career, right?'

We stand in silence as the party continues around us. I don't want to admit it to myself but he's speaking the truth. I should have let Nancy know earlier. I feel terrible about it now. Her face dropped when I told her where I was, as though she'd been punched in the stomach. She tried to act calm and collected, but I knew she was hurting. I can't regret going for a hot chocolate with Dad, though. Nancy doesn't want him around, I know that. She's said so. I just have to learn how to handle it better. Be honest with her about meeting him and invite her along, even when I know that she'll turn it down.

'Sorry,' Chase says eventually.

'Me too,' I say, hating that we've argued. 'I know you'll find the right time to tell the band. It's a difficult situation. I shouldn't be pressuring you to rush something so delicate.'

He nods. 'I guess I'm so excited about the solo side of things that reminding me that I need to let down my closest friends just bums me out and I don't want to think about it.'

'I understand.' I check my watch and see that it's getting late. 'I need to leave soon and get back to Guildhall.'

Chase frowns. 'What? You can't leave. You only got here half an hour ago.'

'I know,' I say apologetically. 'But I have to get back to a party that they're having in our halls at the moment. I promised.'

'Hang on, you want to leave this party where you are with me, to get back to a party full of people like that Jordan loser and all the others who you spend the whole weekend with? Nina,' Chase says, grabbing my hand, 'we've hardly spent any time together.'

'When I told them that this party is why I couldn't be at *their* party, they weren't exactly impressed. I bet they've seen all the pictures already of me walking in on that stupid red carpet and are all making fun of me with popcorn or something.'

Chase lets go of my hand. 'So, you're embarrassed to be here with me in front of all your *serious* music friends?'

'No, of course not. That's not what I meant,' I say, placing my hand on his arm. 'Chase, the music course is really important to me. I don't want to feel like an outsider, that's all. I want to make the most of it. I want them to know that I've earned a place on that course, just like they have.'

'All right,' Chase says, nodding slowly. 'I shouldn't be selfish and keep you to myself. I've missed you, that's all. I thought we'd be spending tonight together.'

'I know, I'm sorry. I have to let them know that I'm as committed to working as a team as they are. I feel like I'm letting them down. And anyway,' I say, glancing to where Mark is now standing with an important-looking man in a sharp suit with an impressive beard, 'I think your uncle has plenty of people for you to talk to while I'm gone.'

Mark catches Chase's eye and eagerly gestures for him to join their conversation.

'Yeah, you were complaining about smiling a lot – think how I feel.' He grimaces. 'Let me know when you're back there safe, OK?'

'I will,' I promise, giving him a peck on the cheek. The photographer is still lurking and neither of us are keen to be captured again in what one gossip column coined a 'Passionate Chase Embrace'!

'Nina, one more thing,' Chase says, before I attempt to make my way to the door through the crowd. 'You shouldn't have to prove to anyone that you've earned a place to be a musician and to develop your craft. That's why you're there on the course, isn't it? You're there for you, no one else. That's all that matters.'

I smile up at him. 'Thanks, Chase.'

Mark arrives at his side and Chase turns to introduce himself to the bearded man in the suit. I realize that I'm getting in everyone's way, so I start walking towards the door, trying not to knock over everyone's drinks as I squeeze through the gaps. I need to find Nancy to let her know that I have to leave, a conversation I'm not exactly looking forward to having. If she's already angry at me for having a drink with Dad without her, she's going to be even more upset that I can't stick around at the party.

I'm only halfway to the door when I bump into Miles.

'Hey, do you know where Nancy is?' I ask.

'I'm looking for her, too.' He smiles, scanning the crowd. 'Last time I saw her she was going to upload her feature, but she should be back in the party somewhere now.'

'What feature?'

'A little exclusive that we got from Tyler Hill. She called one of the girls in your class, Layla, I think it was, and told her about her chat with Tyler and the story she'd given her for the website. I think people in Australia may have been able to hear the screams that came down the phone.'

'That sounds about right.' I smile, pleased that Nancy has had a good time and I hadn't ruined her night.

'Anyway, that Layla person made her go and upload the story straight away. She said she'd come and find me afterwards, but I haven't seen her.' His eyes suddenly light up as he looks back in the direction I'd just come from. 'There she is! She's standing near Chase.' He holds out his hand for me to take. 'I'll lead the way.'

I groan, wishing I didn't have to make my way back into the centre of the crowd, but I take his hand as I can't leave without saying goodbye to Nancy. Luckily, it is much quicker with Miles leading the way.

'There she is,' Miles says, only a few clusters of people away from Chase.

Their group has now been joined by Rachel, the CEO of Emerald Entertainment, and Miles looks impressed when he sees who Chase is surrounded by.

'Whoa, Chase is doing well at this whole mingling thing,' he says, looking over his shoulder to smile at me. 'Let me say hi quickly and then we can barge our way through to Nancy. She's just there.'

Chase and Mark are too engrossed in their conversation with Rachel and the bearded man to notice us standing right behind them, and it suddenly hits me what they might be talking about.

'Miles,' I say hurriedly, tugging on his hand and at the same time trying to catch Chase's eye to let him know that we're nearby, 'let's get to Nancy. You can say hi to Chase in a bit.'

But I'm too late. As we get closer, Rachel is talking and we can just about hear her conversation over the music.

'I think there's a lot of potential in your solo career, Chase,' she's saying.

Miles tenses next to me.

Oh no.

'And I'm pleased you're interested in branching out from your label. I look forward to more talks with you both,' she continues.

'Yes, I've always been a fan,' the bearded man joins in. 'Rachel, Mark and Chase have some brilliant ideas for his album. We've just been talking through them.'

Before I can stop him, Miles has spun round and is making his way back through the crowd.

'Miles! Wait!' I call out after him, but he ignores me. I'm about to go after him when I feel a hand on my arm and turn back to see Nancy next to me.

'There you are!' she says, her eyes wide with excitement as she holds her phone up for me to see. 'Have you heard about what Miles did for me? Look at my piece on our website. See how many comments it's got all ready!'

'That's great, Nancy,' I say, my heart dropping as I see Miles storming out of the door.

'I think that's more than Jimmy had on his recent piece,' she squeals. 'And it's only been up a few minutes. Maybe I can get some more stories from tonight – let me know if you hear of anything newsworthy. There's got to be some more secrets in this room.'

'Sure.'

'Hey, isn't that Chase? What's going on?'

She points towards the front of the room where there's a raised level space, set up for a band to play and a microphone stand at the front. Rachel is at the microphone with Chase standing at the side of the stage. Rachel clears her throat into the microphone and nods pointedly at someone at the back of the room. The music is turned off and the room descends into a hush.

'Good evening and welcome to Emerald Entertainment,' she says, prompting applause and waiting for it to die down before she continues. 'As you know, our very own Tyler Hill will be performing her latest single for you later tonight!'

The crowd cheers and Tyler graciously waves from where she is standing with a group of friends.

'Oh my god, I'm going to live-stream that,' Nancy whispers to me. 'The website hits are going to be off the charts.'

'But before that performance,' Rachel continues, 'I'm pleased to say that I have just managed to convince Chase Hunter to perform his song "Ghosts" for us tonight! It took a bit of persuading to get him to play without any warning, so let's give him a very warm welcome. I present Mr Chase Hunter!'

'This is brilliant!' Nancy gasps, cheering along with everyone before craning her neck to search the crowd. 'Where's the rest of the band? Where's Miles gone? He should get up there and join Chase!'

'Miles isn't here,' I say quietly. 'Chase is doing this on his own.'

But Nancy doesn't hear me. My voice is lost in the eruption of noise from the crowd as Chase takes his place in the spotlight, solo.

'You made it!'

Grace bounds over to me as I walk through the door of the party, but her expression drops when she sees my face.

'Uh oh, what happened?' she asks, looking worried. 'Did you fall on your face in front of the photographers or something?'

'No, nothing like that,' I assure her, taking off my coat and hanging it over the back of a chair, before changing the conversation. 'How's this party been?'

I'm desperate to be distracted from my night so far. I still can't get Miles's face out of my head when he overheard that conversation. He looked so shocked and so hurt at the same time. And then when I'd told Nancy halfway through Chase's solo performance that I was leaving to come back to Guildhall, she'd looked really disappointed. I couldn't even make myself feel better by saying that she had Miles for company in the knowledge that he had left. I'd had to leave her there on her own filming Chase for her website, making her promise to text me when she was at the station and safely on a train home.

'It's been so nice getting to know everyone,' Grace enthuses over the music blaring from speakers that someone has set up on a table. 'Let me introduce you.'

She leads me over to a group of students who are sitting on the sofa, chatting. Jordan is on the other side of the room, deep in conversation with someone; when he glances up and spots me, he looks surprised.

'Nina, this is Nico, also known as Flute Two; and this is TJ, Cello One; and this is Florence, aka Oboe Two.' Grace grins as they all wave at me. 'Everyone, this is Nina Palmer.'

'Otherwise known as Piano Two,' I add, coming to sit with them.

'Grace was saying that you were at an Emerald Entertainment party just now,' Nico says, his eyes wide with awe. 'That is so cool. There must have been so many amazing musicians there.'

'I'm not sure they're the type of musicians you'd be impressed by,' I admit, but he responds with a confused look.

'We don't all think like Jordan, Nina,' Grace says. 'He's being stupidly pretentious when he says celebrities aren't real musicians.'

'He said that?' TJ seems amused.

'Yeah,' she says, nodding. 'And he was rude about Chasing Chords.'

'I love Chasing Chords!' Florence says to my complete surprise. 'I listen to their first album all the time. Their song "Talk to You" is my favourite. I can't believe they didn't release it as a single.'

'Jordan is jealous that he doesn't have a record deal himself,' Grace says to me. 'You shouldn't listen to anything he says.'

'Yeah, last weekend I overheard him telling someone that the cello was an easy instrument to play compared to everything else,' TJ says, shaking his head. 'I stepped into the conversation and offered him my cello, saying that he was very welcome to play it right there in front of everyone, considering it was so easy. He suddenly got *very* quiet and had to rush off "for a thing" –' he pauses as we laugh – 'That guy is all talk. Don't let him get to you, Nina.'

I smile gratefully. 'Thanks, I'll try not to. I'd find it easier if I wasn't so behind on this course, on top of everything else. In Caroline Morreau's eyes, Jordan is leagues above me.'

Florence snorts. 'You think you're behind? You haven't heard the story about my lesson this morning yet.'

'Why? What happened?' I ask, already smiling as the others giggle infectiously.

'She turned up to her oboe lesson . . .' Nico begins, waiting for her to finish the sentence.

Florence lets out a long sigh before adding the punchline. 'Without my oboe.'

'Seriously?' I laugh. 'Did you have to go back to get it?'

'No, my teacher told me that if my oboe wasn't the first thing on my brain that day, I didn't deserve a lesson with him,' she says, rolling her eyes. 'I'm pretty sure he thinks I'm an idiot who got on the course by accident. Not that I blame him. I'm starting to think along those lines, too.'

'I feel the same way.' TJ nods, giving her a comforting pat on the arm. 'In my lesson this morning, my teacher told me that I played like I'd never seen the piece before, even though I've been practising it all week, and that he wasn't sure I had any rhythm. Which is really comforting, being a musician and everything.'

'Sometimes I wonder why they even offered me a place on this course,' Nico chimes in. 'Today in group rehearsal, I was by far the worst and I could see Flute One giving me evils the whole time. Since I started Guildhall, I've felt like I can't get anything right.'

Nina

'You know what,' I say, stunned at what I'm hearing, 'I feel *exactly* the same way. I thought I was the only one!'

'So did I,' Florence says. 'It's nice to know I'm not alone.'

'I hate to compliment him, but Jordan's idea to have a party and get to know each other was brilliant,' I admit, the others nodding along.

'Yes, we now know something very important that we didn't before.' Grace grins. 'At least we're all in this mess together.'

CHAPTER FOURTEEN

NANCY

'Excuse me,' a girl says, sidling up to me with her phone in her hand. I recognize her from Year Nine. 'But could you tell me how you got your hair like this? I think you look amazing.'

'Have you got the right twin?' I ask cautiously, slamming my locker shut. 'I'm Nancy.'

She glances back nervously at her friends, who are huddled behind, giggling.

'Yes, it's you I wanted to ask.' She holds up her phone to show the photo of me and Tyler Hill on my website. 'I can't believe you and Tyler are friends. That's the coolest thing ever.'

'Oh!' I say, smiling. 'Yeah, that was a great evening. And, in terms of the hair and outfit, I'm going to be uploading a vlog on to *All That Glitters* this evening with all the details of how to get that look, so make sure you check it out.'

'Yes!' she exclaims. 'Are you going to be doing more stories like this one? Like, do you get to hang out with Chasing Chords and go to all these big parties in London?'

'Kind of,' I say. 'I mean, there will definitely be more stories like this one coming soon.'

'Thanks so much, Nancy! You're amazing!' she gushes, hopping up and down on the spot. 'We're your biggest fans. Have a good half-term!'

She runs off to tell her friends, who all chatter excitedly as she fills them in on my upcoming vlog. I grin, strolling down the corridor and feeling on top of the world again. My plan is working. I am no longer hopeless, going nowhere, destined to a gloomy existence in my sister's shadow. I have *fans*.

All That Glitters completely exploded with my exclusive from Tyler. Not only did I become the most popular girl in school overnight, but real celebrity publications and newspapers picked up the story and published it too, using the phrase, 'as reported on *All That Glitters* by Nancy Palmer'. Some of them even got in touch with me to congratulate me on the exclusive and gave me their details in case I got any other stories like that in the future and wanted to write for them on a freelance basis.

'We're always looking for new, ambitious talent,' one editor said in an email. 'And it would be good to have someone on the inside.'

New, ambitious talent! Someone on the inside! And she was talking about ME.

Our website was all anyone could talk about for the last week of school leading up to half-term. It wasn't just people at school checking it out either; it had got thousands of hits, especially when Tyler put the link on her Instagram page, telling her fans about her new fashion venture. I don't think I've ever seen Layla look happier than the day after the party when she and Sophie turned up at my house and began dancing around the sitting room, chanting, 'We're going to win, we're going to win!'

All week, I got stopped walking down the corridor on the way to lessons or stared at across the canteen, as my celebrity status got discussed. Suddenly Nina wasn't the only one with A-list friends. I was a serious music journalist who got invited to Emerald Entertainment parties and given exclusives by global pop stars.

Even Mrs Smithson noticed the change and told me she was really pleased I'd decided to enter the competition and to 'keep up the good work'.

Which, by the way, is easier said than done. The only problem with having a massive hit on our website was that everyone expected more, something that Layla wouldn't stop going on about. She kept talking about keeping up the momentum, but the only way to do that was to get more exclusive stories from pop stars and, despite what everyone thought, I didn't exactly spend my evenings in such company.

'Nancy, wait up,' Layla says, falling into step with me.

I'm still basking in the fact that the girl from Year Nine and her friends are my self-proclaimed biggest fans.

'Hey, Layla, how excited are you for half-term? I can't wait to have a week off.'

'Yeah, but we have a lot to do on the website. Have you got any new ideas for another post?'

'I'm going to do the vlog on how to get that make-up and hair extensions look from last Saturday. I'll make sure that's up tonight.'

'Great. We've had a lot of messages from PRs in the music industry sending us press releases now that we're on their radar. Are you able to go through those tonight? You said you would this week.'

'Yeah, I'll read them this weekend.'

'You really need to stay on top of stuff like that, Nancy,' she scolds, as I hold open the door and we head outside, down the school steps. 'By the time you read through it, it's probably old news and not worth publishing. And content should really be uploaded daily, otherwise our audience will start getting their content from somewhere else. We could really do with some more news.'

'You did that really good vlog on the best way to decorate a scrapbook, and your denim jackets article only went up this week. And I thought Sophie uploaded that hilarious video of her attempting to prank you this morning,' I point out. 'That's quite a lot of new stuff in a week.'

Layla looks at me like I'm mad. 'Are you joking? That's *nothing*. Most lifestyle websites have new content twice a day at least!'

'Yeah, I know.'

Layla holds out her arm in front of me, bringing me to a sharp halt.

'*Do* you know, though, Nancy? Do you really?' she asks rhetorically, coming to stand face-to-face with me. 'Haven't you noticed the difference at school? How people respond to us? *All That Glitters* has come to mean something to them and we can't let them down. We have to keep it up. Otherwise no one will be talking about us and everyone will be talking about Jimmy and his half-term protest at the town hall.' She rolls her eyes.

'I think the protest is actually a really good idea. Did you know that they've closed down two libraries in the town centre? Jimmy was a member of one of them and he was telling me that Doris Lessing once visited there.'

'Nancy, can you please FOCUS!' Layla cries in frustration. 'I'm not talking about Jimmy and his protest; I'm talking about us and our project. You need to get some more music news and pronto, otherwise everything we've done so far will be forgotten! Nancy, think what we can do if our website goes big time!'

'What do you mean?'

'I mean,' she begins, her eyes sparkling, 'we could actually be talking about our future careers here, and not just a school project for the Disney Channel internship. Nancy, if our website takes off, like, really takes off, we'll have our own *brand*. And when you have your own brand, you can do anything. Fashion lines, make-up ranges, sponsored YouTube videos and Instagram posts. You need to think about the big picture!'

'Wow! You really think we could do that?'

'Hello, look at the difference in one week alone! The photo of you and Tyler has put us firmly on the map. People are looking to us for inspiration and our website is officially a big deal.' She grins at me encouragingly. 'We need to keep it that way.'

'I'll try and get some music news this week,' I say, filled with fresh determination. 'I could call the PRs and try to get some news out of them before they send press releases to everyone else.'

'Or, you could call Miles?' she says, stepping aside and allowing me to continue walking towards the school gates. 'He might have something.'

'Yeah, good idea,' I lie.

There is NO chance I'm phoning Miles.

I don't know what happened at the party but he disappeared without even saying goodbye. I know he's famous and everything, and doesn't exactly have time to worry about saying goodbye to people like me when he decides to leave a party, but I thought we were having fun together and he made out like he was happy to stay with me for the night. Once I'd uploaded my story to the website, I came back into the party and couldn't find him anywhere. He missed out on all the good bits, too, like Chase's amazing performance. If he had stayed, then we might have been able to persuade Chasing Chords to take to the stage, which would have been amazing.

Nina said she didn't know where he was, but I couldn't shake the feeling that she knew more than she was letting on and she just wasn't telling me. Maybe she was trying to protect me from something, like Miles went to meet a girl for a date or maybe he met someone he liked at the party.

When I got on my train back to Norwich, I'd thought about texting Miles to make sure he was OK and to check I hadn't done anything wrong. I started typing my message, but then I'd realized how embarrassing it would be if he really was out with someone else. I didn't want it to look as though I was expecting him to stay at the party with me. It's not like I was there as his date. He'd invited me as a friend.

So I'd left it and then woken up the next morning to a message from him apologizing for rushing off. 'Something came up,' was all he said on the matter. We've been texting a bit since, but he seems distracted and I know that he's busy but I thought . . .

I don't know. It's stupid. But I thought that MAYBE there was something *there*. Between me and Miles, I mean.

I feel so comfortable around him and he makes me laugh a lot, and I got the feeling that he liked spending time with me and then there was that smile of his when he saw me all dressed up. It seemed like he maybe didn't smile that way at anyone else.

But, as I've told myself a hundred times this week, if there was, I don't know, some kind of actual *spark* or whatever, wouldn't he have noticed it, too? Wouldn't he have stayed with me at the party rather than leaving without a word? Wouldn't he have asked to see me again sometime soon?

I must have been wrong. About the spark.

'Hey,' Jimmy says, running up to me as I open the front door of Mum's car. 'My dad is stuck at work – can I come to yours for a bit?'

'You know you never need to ask,' Mum says out of the window.

He smiles, sliding into the backseat. 'Is Nina at music practice?'

'Actually, she's not,' Mum says, looking round me to nod at Nina walking towards us from the front steps. 'I've persuaded her to practise at home this evening instead. As it's officially the start of half-term, I thought she could do an hour upstairs and then come join us for a movie night. You're welcome to join in too, Jimmy.'

'Good idea, Mum,' I say, waving at my sister as she hops in the back. 'I've missed our movie nights. Nina, are you game for a Disney classic?'

'We'll see how my practice goes,' she says cautiously. 'I have a lot to do for tomorrow. I'm trying a new piece to show Caroline as a potential for the showcase.'

'I thought you showed her the new piece last week,' Mum says, as she pulls out into the school traffic.

'This is a different one.'

'Don't you need to pick one quite soon?' Jimmy asks. 'The showcase is in a few weeks, right?'

'Don't remind me. I pick a new one every week and none of them seem to be working for me.'

'I don't understand,' I say, fiddling with the radio. 'You have so many pieces that you're amazing at. Why don't you pick one of those? Like the one you played for the school talent show last year.'

'I can't just play something I like; it has to be something that blows them away. It has to be something different.' She lets out a long sigh. 'Except I need to find what it is and that is proving VERY difficult.'

'Doesn't Caroline have any suggestions?' Mum asks.

'She's said that it has to come from me,' Nina explains. 'She can't choose for me. I have to connect with a piece and then pick that one. So far, I haven't connected with any.'

'You'll find something,' Mum says, shooting her a smile in the rear-view mirror. 'And how is your website coming along, Jimmy? Nancy took me through it the other day and I was extremely impressed.'

'It's going OK,' Jimmy says, before adding, 'although it's been a bit overshadowed this week by Nancy's latest post.'

'Everything's been overshadowed by that article,' Nina agrees. 'It's all anyone can talk about. I didn't even know who Tyler Hill was when Chase introduced us at the party, but everyone else at school seems to.'

'That is a very Nina thing to say.' I laugh. 'She's ever so slightly majorly famous.'

'And now Nancy is, too. I can't believe they posted about your story on Buzzfeed AND included a link to your website.' Jimmy sighs. 'I'd kill for that kind of publicity.'

'It's been popular, but it's a tough act to follow,' I point out. 'As Layla was just reminding me, I need to come up with something equally good in the next few days. Otherwise it will be a bit of a one-hit wonder.'

'Welcome to the world of journalism,' Jimmy says with a smile. 'It's always about the next story. Or so I've been told.'

'Yeah, well, I can't muck this up. Firstly, if I do, Layla will kill me. And secondly, I've finally found something that I can do to make people proud. Like you have, Nina. So, for the sake of my future, I have to make it work.'

'Hang on,' Nina says, as we pull into our drive. 'What do you mean you finally have something to make people proud?'

I shrug, getting out of the car and slamming the door shut behind me. 'You know, it's obvious to everyone that you're going places. I want people to think that about me, too. I don't want to be left behind.'

We're interrupted by our neighbour Mrs Byrne, who opens her front door and calls out to Nina.

'This arrived for you in the post today, when you were all out,' she says, coming over with a box. 'It had to be signed for.'

'Thanks, Mrs Byrne,' Nina says, taking the parcel. 'I wonder what it is.'

Once we're in the house, we head into the kitchen and Mum puts the kettle on, while Nina gets a pair of scissors to cut through the packaging.

'What is it?' Jimmy asks, leaning over her shoulder. 'Did you order something and forget about it?'

'Jimmy, have you met Nina?' I laugh. 'Internet shopping with her is one of the most frustrating processes I have ever had to experience.'

'It's hard to pick things when you can't see them in person,' she insists, opening the box. She gasps at its contents. 'Whoa!'

'What? What is it?'

She pulls out a brand-new Canon camera, the latest model. I am so jealous that I might explode. It's the EXACT camera that's recommended for professional vloggers and I'd been looking at it online recently, imagining how incredible my videos for *All That Glitters* would be if

I had one of those. I knew I could never afford it or ask Mum to get it for me because it was so expensive.

'Nina!' Mum exclaims. 'Did Chase send you that?'

'Maybe,' she says, admiring it with total awe. 'I can't believe he would do this! It's so thoughtful of him. And this is way over the top! It's not even my birthday yet.'

'There's a note,' Jimmy says, pulling a card out of the box and handing it to Nina. 'What does it say? Read it out. Unless it's gross lovey-dovey stuff, in which case, feel free to paraphrase,' he adds with a wink at me.

Nina's expression transitions from amazement to shock as she reads the card.

'Nina?' Mum asks. 'Are you all right? What did Chase say?'

'It's not from Chase,' she says, lowering the card and picking up the camera.

'Who's it from then?' I ask.

'Dad,' she says.

The kitchen falls into silence. Mum stares at her.

'Your father sent you that camera?'

'Yeah.' She nods slowly. 'He wants me to use it to start a YouTube channel. He thinks it would be helpful for my career. That's what he's said in the card.'

'Dad sent you the camera,' I repeat quietly, still taking it all in. 'Did . . . did he say anything about me? Read it out loud.'

It's a stupid question that I already know the answer to, but I torture myself by asking it anyway. If he'd meant it for me, it would have been both our names on the parcel.

'It doesn't really say anything,' Nina says, looking uncomfortable. 'It's just about music stuff.'

'Read it aloud,' I repeat, getting flustered. 'If it's just music stuff, then it doesn't matter if we hear it, does it? Jimmy, you can read it.'

Jimmy picks up the card and, with a nod of reluctant approval from Nina, begins to read it out, '*Dear Nina, I'm so proud of you and everything you've accomplished. This is to help with your future achievements. Maybe you could use this to launch a music channel. I'm sure it would be a big hit with your growing fan base. Love, Dad.*'

'Wow,' I croak, clenching my jaw. 'He's really, really trying to get in your good books, isn't he?'

'I think it's only because when we met I told him that I was finding Guildhall a little tougher than I'd expected and he . . . well, he really wanted to help me. That's all,' Nina says quickly. 'But we can share it.'

She slides the camera across the table to me, but I push it back.

'No, he sent it to you. It's yours. And he can't buy his way back into my life. He's going to have to make a little bit more of an effort than posting a camera.'

'Please don't be upset. He's proud of your achievements, too.'

'I don't have any achievements,' I mutter.

'That's absolutely not true,' Mum says firmly, reaching across to squeeze my hand.

'He doesn't know about your amazing website yet, Nancy. He'll be blown away when he sees what you've done,' Nina says, desperately trying to make me feel better. Her over-the-top effort makes it all the more embarrassing. 'If he knew about it, then he'd have sent this for both of us to use. When you see him, you can fill him in and then he'll be really interested and want to help with that, too.'

'He doesn't know about the website because he hasn't asked,' I say, feeling a lump form in my throat. 'He hasn't tried to get in contact with me once since he's come back to say that he'd wished that I had been there, too. I guess he's too busy choosing expensive cameras to help your music career.'

'I can't accept it,' Nina says, looking to Mum. 'I'll tell him that I can't. I don't want it if it's going to upset you both.'

Mum opens her mouth to say something, but I cut her off.

'It doesn't upset me,' I say with a shrug. 'He can do what he wants. I'm happy for you. You should keep it.'

'He clearly doesn't know Nina very well anyway,' Jimmy offers. 'I can't imagine you launching a YouTube channel. You get embarrassed if I try to take a picture of you for one Instagram post.'

'I don't know,' she says, biting her lip. 'Maybe it would be a good thing.'

'What? Are you serious?' I ask, stunned at this reaction. 'You hate that kind of thing.'

'Yes, but Dad's right. I need to change things if I'm going to do well. Maybe I need to start putting myself out there, and stop being so afraid. Like he did with his PR business.'

Mum raises her eyebrows. 'He told you about that?'

'Yeah.' She examines the camera lens distractedly. 'Maybe a YouTube channel would help me tackle my stage fright and get me noticed by the right people.'

I can't believe what she's saying. It's so unlike her.

It sounds pathetic but the hurtful thing is that I've been on at her for ages about setting one up. Ever since that video of her and Chase went viral, I kept saying that she had the perfect platform to launch her own channel, but she always laughed and told me it wasn't her thing. And now Dad has come along out of nowhere with a fancy camera and she's suddenly interested?

'But I won't keep it if you don't want me to,' she says firmly, putting the camera down and meeting my eyes.

'No, like I said, you should keep it,' I reply, turning round to get some mugs from the cupboard and blinking back the tears that are starting to form. 'You deserve it.'

'Really? Are you sure?'

'I'm sure.'

Nancy

When I turn back to face her with a fresh smile, the tears have disappeared. Because, if anything, that stupid camera has spurred me on more than ever. Not only am I going to win this competition, but my website is going to be huge and then I won't be nothing. Then Dad will want to help me with my big, successful career.

Then maybe he'll be proud of me, too.

CHAPTER FIFTEEN

NINA

Dad tells me to lie to Nancy.

At first, I say that I can't do that; I have to tell her the truth. We don't keep things from each other, and she can tell when I'm lying anyway. But it's a difficult situation and the more I think about it, the more it makes sense not to mention it to her and pretend I'm heading to London early for something else.

I don't know what Dad has got planned but he invited me to come up to London on Friday evening, rather than Saturday morning like I've been doing. He has an idea for my showcase and wanted to work on it before my Saturday morning lesson. But that means telling Nancy and Mum why I am heading up an evening early and, after seeing Nancy's face when the camera arrived last week, I don't think I can bear telling her that Dad and I have organized something together without her *again*.

If I do tell Nancy, I'll have to invite her along. It would be horrible not to. But, if she does come, she'll be sitting there while Dad and I work on the showcase music and it would be like the piano shop all those years ago, which just isn't fair on her.

'Maybe we delay the showcase stuff and tonight we all go for dinner together,' I suggested over the phone to Dad when he'd called that Friday morning. 'I think she'd really like to see you, no matter what she says. She has a tendency to put on a hard front, but I think she was sad to hear that we went for a hot chocolate together.'

'I thought you wanted to focus on your showcase,' he said.

'I don't want to go behind Nancy's back again. She needs time, but I think she would come around to the idea of you being back in our lives. You're our dad. She's very protective of her family, that's all. But, if I tell her that you want to go for dinner with both of us in London tonight, I think she would be interested.'

'Nina, I would love to go for dinner with you and Nancy. I really would. But could we do it another time? Because I've already organized something for you for this evening and it would be very difficult to rearrange. And don't you want as much time as possible to get things ready for the showcase? It's not that far away now, is it?'

'No, it's looming.' I remembered the last time I had to get up on that Guildhall stage. 'I definitely need all the practice I can get. I still haven't chosen the music I'm going to perform.'

'No need to panic – that's what tonight is for. So, I appreciate it's difficult with Nancy but if you're serious about your music, which I think you should be, then I really think it's best if we leave dinner for another time.'

'I'll just have to lie to her and Mum,' I'd said, burying my head in my hands. 'I'll . . . I'll say I'm meeting Chase.'

'Great, sorted!' was his cheery response. 'I have to go into a meeting now, but I'll meet you at Guildhall at seven p.m. And you booked the music room like I asked?'

'Yes, I booked that earlier in the week.'

'I can't wait to see you, Nina.'

'Same,' I replied, before hanging up.

Now, I'm looking in the mirror and practising what I'm going to say to Nancy and Mum, and how exactly I'm going to say it. Maybe I should just tell them that I'm meeting Dad to go through music things, then Nancy might not mind. But I thought that might have been the case last weekend, when I rang her to tell her that Dad had messaged asking if I'd like to go for a hot chocolate after my group rehearsal again.

'Is this going to be a weekly occurrence, then?' she'd asked.

'I don't think so. I won't go if you don't want me to.'

'Why didn't he let you know earlier so I could come into London and join you?'

'I think he thinks you don't want to.'

'He gives up easily then,' she'd said, sounding dis-appointed. 'Whatever, Nina – do what you want and go for a hot chocolate with him. But maybe remind him he has two daughters, not one.'

And then she'd hung up before I could reply. I'd spent the whole of half-term week trying to work out if she was mad at me for going. She doesn't like talking about it and, whenever Dad is brought up in conversation, I can see a twinge of sadness in her expression, no matter how well she pretends not to care.

The main thing she does keep probing me about is why I'm not questioning him all the time. Why I'm not grilling him about why he left, whether he ever missed us, why it took him so long to come back.

'If he took me for a hot chocolate, that's what I'd be doing,' she'd said over dinner one evening. 'I wouldn't be bonding with him over music. I'd be expecting some answers after all these years.'

Maybe she's right. Maybe I should be angrier with him for walking out, and maybe I should be asking him questions so I better understand exactly what happened.

But I don't want to. It has been so nice getting to know him again. I love talking to him about music and filling him in on Guildhall and hearing everything he has to say. I love him talking about old memories, like last weekend when he reminded me of my first-ever performance. It was a Saturday morning concert at school and it was only in one of the small music rooms in front of a few parents, but I was so nervous that I hid round the side of the building and Dad had to persuade me to come in.

'You were so stubborn,' he'd chuckled as he recalled it. 'You told me that if I made you play the piano in front of the people in that room, you would be sick. And guess what happened?'

'No!'

'Oh yes.' He'd burst out laughing. 'You sat shivering away on the piano stool, played a few notes and then threw up everywhere! So, trust me, I know you think you're terrible at performing now, but you have greatly improved since then.'

He'd told me other stories too and it had been so nice to just sit there, laughing over old memories, like we were a normal father and daughter meeting for a hot chocolate and a catch up. If I started probing him about why he left and everything else, then I would lose that feeling, and I didn't want that yet. I knew we'd have to get round to it sometime, but I wasn't ready. I want to savour all these new memories, where he can tell me lovely, silly things about my childhood and then help me with my problems. Like dads are supposed to.

I look at my reflection in the mirror and shake my head at myself. I can't believe I'm even considering lying to Nancy about meeting Dad tonight. But what would be the point in telling her? She can't come anyway because it's a music thing, so it would essentially be rubbing it in her face.

'I wish there was a simple solution,' I say out loud.

There's a knock on the bedroom door and Nancy pokes her head round.

'Are you talking to your reflection?' she asks, when she sees me standing in front of the mirror.

'No. Yes. Sort of,' I say, gesturing for her to come in. 'I was thinking out loud.'

'About simple solutions?' she says, coming to sit on my bed. 'What's the problem? We can work it out together.'

'It's OK, it's stupid. Music stuff,' I say, brushing it aside. 'What are you up to?'

'I was going to ask the same question. I wondered if you wanted to do a little study group together,' she says hopefully. 'We could work in the kitchen or in my room? I was just about to get some popcorn ready before I get started.'

I smile. 'Sounds good. I am so behind on GCSE revision. The exams seem a way off, but then I remember they're next term.'

'I know. Crazy.' She notices my bag half-packed at the top of my bed. 'Are you already packed for tomorrow?'

'Actually –' I take a deep breath and pretend to organize some folders strewn across my desk – 'I'm going to London tonight.'

'You are? But normally you go on Saturday mornings.'

'Yeah, but I thought I would do some music practice at Guildhall this evening. Take advantage of having a proper piano to play on. This way, I can get some practising in tomorrow morning, too.'

'Oh, OK – yeah, that makes sense.' She nods. 'Are you going to see Chase as well?'

'I think I'm seeing him tomorrow night.'

'Is everything OK with you guys? Mum and I were saying that we were expecting to see him a bit over half-term but he hasn't come here at all. And you've only been to London once this week, and you weren't even there the full day.'

'He's been busy writing music, that's all,' I say hurriedly. 'He needs to focus right now on that. We're fine.'

At least, I think we're fine. Things are better this week than they were.

They hadn't been so great after the Emerald Entertainment party. I had been on such a high after the party at Guildhall and woken up the next day feeling like a huge weight had been lifted off me. Speaking to TJ, Nico and Florence with Grace had reminded me that it was OK not to be the perfect musician yet – that's why we were there in the first place.

Chase had called just before my music lesson with Caroline, and I'd been so eager to tell him about the party that as soon as I'd picked up I'd launched into an excited speech about how wonderful the other students were at Guildhall, now that I'd got to know them, and how I felt a fresh wave of determination.

He said that he was pleased I had a good time, but his tone was so down that I realized something was wrong, and then when he went, 'Did you know that Miles overheard me talking about going solo?' my stomach dropped.

I had completely forgotten to tell Chase about Miles. I'd meant to message him at the Guildhall party, but I'd been having such a good time and then was so tired going to bed that I'd forgotten.

Chase was really upset, wondering why I hadn't given him the heads-up so he could go and find Miles the night before. Apparently, Miles wasn't talking to him and he didn't even know where he was. I felt terrible, especially when Miles was supposed to be my friend too, and I'd forgotten about him while I was having a good time at a party. Things between Chase and me the week following that had been a bit off – I think he was still annoyed at me for not telling him straight away about Miles. They're barely talking at the moment; Miles is so upset with him.

Anyway, during my half-term, Chase and I decided that we desperately needed to have a day together, just us, so that we could both cheer up.

'On one condition,' Chase had said after we made the plan to meet in London and have a fun day out. 'Neither of us can talk about work.'

'Deal.'

It had worked perfectly. We went around London doing loads of touristy things, like visiting the Tower of London and then looking at the amazing yachts on St Katherine Docks, picking out which ones we'd like to own. He'd worn his hoodie and cap, so he wouldn't get recognized, and it was like it was when we were secretly dating, when for those few hours that we'd see each other we'd forget that he was this big famous music star and I was lying to all my family and friends. We could just be us.

'I've missed this,' he'd said, and grinned when I bought him an I HEART LONDON cap to wear for the day, stuffing his old one in my bag and plonking the new one on his head.

'You've missed me making you look ridiculous?'

'Not so much.' He'd laughed, catching a reflection of himself in the shop mirror. 'I've missed hanging out and acting like teenagers, I guess.'

'We are teenagers.'

'Exactly. Easy to forget sometimes,' he'd said, before taking an I HEART ENGLAND cap from another stand and going to the till to buy it for me.

After that day, I'd felt better about everything. I knew we both had a lot of pressure on our shoulders at the moment and we had to expect it to be difficult, especially not living in the same city, but that didn't stop me from worrying that he might decide it was *too* hard and give up altogether. He hadn't been able to get away from the studio another time this week, but he promised me Saturday night, so that was something. I'm a little embarrassed that Nancy and Mum have noticed, though.

'It must be so difficult writing songs,' Nancy says, leaning back on my duvet. 'I don't know how he does it.'

'Yeah, I don't either. He's very talented.'

'I can't wait for some more Chasing Chords songs. I've listened to the old album so many times that I reckon I know all the words to every song. I could do with some new material. But don't tell Chase that – I don't want his head to get too big.'

I smile. 'I won't.'

She notices the camera tucked into my bag and pulls it out for a closer look.

'Have you done any videos yet?'

'No, I would tell you if I was going to,' I assure her. 'I'd need your help in creating a YouTube channel; I wouldn't have the first idea how to go about it.'

'Yeah, I figured that. But then I thought Dad might set it up for you.'

As she mentions him, I feel immediately tense, as though she knows that I'm not telling her the full truth about tonight.

'Nah, I'd want you to help me. And anyway I'm still not sure if I want to do it. Maybe once the Guildhall course is over and I have more time.'

'Maybe. I asked Mum about his PR business, by the way,' she says, putting the camera back in my bag. 'You mentioned it the other day when the camera arrived and I wanted to know what you meant.'

'He didn't tell me much,' I say, not wanting her to feel as though we've had all these deep conversations. 'It came up really briefly.'

'Did he tell you that he stole all the clients from his old business?'

'What?' I put the book I'm holding down and stare at her. 'No, he didn't steal them. His ex-partner was doing really well after their first company didn't work out and that pushed Dad to work harder. Then his business grew.'

'That's not how Mum put it.' She shrugs. 'According to her, their company was doing just fine. He didn't tell his business partner, who was an old friend, that he was launching a new one. He spoke to all the clients in secret and then went ahead and launched it, taking those clients with him. His partner had to move to a different sector; it put him completely out of business. Obviously it was a smart move by Dad though, because he did so well. If you want to look at it that way. He also lost one of his best friends, but I guess loyalty isn't exactly his strong point.'

'Oh,' I say, wondering why he hadn't told me any of that. 'Right.'

'All I'm saying is, be careful, Nina,' she says, getting up and walking towards my bedroom door. 'He's left you once. I reckon he'd be capable of doing it again.'

'It's different now. He knows he made a big mistake and he's trying to make it up to us.'

'He's trying to make it up to *you*,' she says pointedly. 'I don't want you getting hurt again.'

'Nancy,' I say before she heads downstairs, 'is that why you don't want to get close to him now? Because you're scared he'll hurt you all over again?'

'Maybe,' she says. 'Aren't you?'

I wait outside the Guildhall music department for half an hour until I decide I might as well go in and wait for Dad inside where it's warm. Even though spring is definitely on its way, it's still quite cold out, so I go into the music practice room and check my phone again to make sure he hasn't messaged to let me know he's running late.

Nothing.

I take my sheet music out from my bag and place it on the stand, lifting the lid of the piano and wiggling my fingers, ready to start playing. I smile to myself, thinking how weird it is that, no matter how badly it seems to be going right now, I still can't wait to play the piano. Without thinking, I place my fingers down on the keys and, ignoring the sheet music, I start playing one of my favourite Austin Golding songs that I know by heart. I haven't played any of my favourite composer's music in weeks and I remember how good it feels, how much I love it.

I'm so engrossed in the music that I don't notice a face at the window watching me play until I come to the end and the door creaks open. Holding the door open with his foot, Jordan crosses his arms.

'If you're going to play something as simple as Austin Golding at the showcase, then I really do have that summer school place in the bag,' he sneers.

'What are you doing here?'

'I've been coming to Guildhall every Friday night to practise before the weekend begins. You'll find that most of the really dedicated students have. I was annoyed when I found out this room had been booked for the evening.' He checks his watch. 'You have it for another hour, right?'

'Yes,' I say, noticing the time and realizing that Dad is now an hour late.

'I'll let you get back to your "piano for beginners" music, then,' he says, giving me a salute as he leaves the room.

I wait until I can no longer hear his footsteps echoing down the corridor before I close the piano and get up to leave. It's childish of me, but I didn't want to give him the satisfaction of having the best practice room, even though there's no point in me being here now anyway. As I gather my music together to leave, Dad comes through the door followed by a woman I don't recognize.

'Nina, I'm so sorry we're late!' he says, coming over to give me a hug. 'I got stuck at work because of this huge deal I'm working on and, argh, I won't bother to bore you with the details but unfortunately it would seem a few of my staff are completely incompetent. I have to do everything myself.'

'No worries,' I say, pleased to see him but very aware there's a strange woman in the room too. She is slowly turning round on the spot, taking in every aspect of the room and breathing very deeply.

Dad sees me staring at her and claps his hands together suddenly, making me jump.

'Nina, I would like to introduce you to Simone. Simone, this is my daughter, Nina.'

Simone looks as though she's just come from reading people's futures in a circus tent. She is wearing a long, flowing woollen poncho with multicoloured tassels all down it, and her heavily lined eyes are framed by large, round, orange-framed glasses. Her brown hair is tied up loosely by a scarf and she has enormous, dangling earrings that swing about her neck every time her head moves.

'Yes, this is a good space,' she says, nodding vigorously.

'This is your surprise, Nina! Simone is one of the top music teachers in the country. She's worked with every famous pop star you can think of,' Dad says proudly, while looking at his phone. 'She's going to help you with the showcase.'

'She is? Sorry, I mean –' I turn to address her – 'you are?'

'Your father tells me you need help climbing the ladder of success,' she says, waving her arms up dramatically and forcing me to dodge backwards so I don't get hit in the face. 'I am the person who will get you there. Any famous pop star you can think of, I was the one who put them on the map.'

'Um . . . OK,' I say, looking to Dad for help but he's too distracted by his phone.

'Let's start with your diaphragm, because if you want to sing like a goddess then you must breathe like one!' she shrieks, flouncing to the middle of the room.

'Oh, I don't sing.'

'You shall,' she says, closing her eyes and inhaling deeply. 'You shall!'

'No, sorry, I think there's been a mistake,' I say, laughing nervously. 'I'm a pianist, not a singer. I'm playing the piano in the showcase.'

'Nina, if you want to win this thing, you're going to have to think differently,' Dad says, before running a hand through his hair and yelling at his phone, 'WHY doesn't anyone in my office have the ability to take some initiative?'

'Dad, what are you talking about?' I ask, taking a step away from Simone, who has now flopped forward so that her hands are dangling by her feet and appears to be murmuring some kind of chant to herself.

He looks up from his phone and then gestures at Simone.

'This is how you're going to beat everyone else and how you're going to get over your stage fright. Simone will sort you out. You're not just a pianist – you're a *full package*. A singer-songwriter. It's a good idea, right?'

He taps the side of his head smugly.

'No, it's not a good idea,' I tell him, panicking. 'Look, sorry, Dad, but I'm not a singer. And, even if I was, I can't even play the piano in front of an audience – how are you expecting me to sing in front of one?'

'That's why Simone is here.' Dad puts his hands on my shoulders. 'Follow her instructions and those talent scouts won't know what's hit them.'

'What talent scouts?'

'Ah, second part of your surprise.' He grins. 'There are going to be talent scouts in the audience of your showcase! And they're there to see you. It's all arranged so you don't need to worry about any of that – you just focus on doing your thing. Oh, which reminds me, when are you going to launch that YouTube channel? I didn't send you that camera for nothing.'

I stare at him in horror as he gets back to his phone. *Talent scouts* are going to be in the audience. As if I wasn't nervous enough already, now I have to worry about performing in front of talent scouts? I'm not ready for this.

'Dad, I don't –'

'Ah, I have to take this,' he says apologetically, holding up his phone screen to show a call coming through. 'I have to go. Have fun though – I'll call you tomorrow to hear how it goes.'

'Wait, you're leaving? I thought we were spending the evening together.'

'I have too much work to do, but you're in good hands.' He smiles, squeezing my arm. 'Simone is what we need to get the ball rolling. Ah –' his phone stops and starts ringing again – 'I really have to take this. Good luck, Nina!'

'Wait, Dad –'

He answers the phone and leaves the room. Simone summons me to stand in front of her and tells me to follow her lead. Lifting her hands high above her head, she stretches out her fingers and then flops forward again, swinging her arms from side to side. Not knowing what else I can possibly do in this moment, I attempt to do the same.

As I hang there with my head by my knees, swinging my arms left to right, I hear a loud cackle by the door. I glance up to see Jordan peering through the window of the door, laughing so much that he's wiping his eyes. I straighten up immediately, but it's too late. I know I won't hear the end of this. I bury my head in my hands, dreading tomorrow.

And here I was thinking things couldn't get any worse.

CHAPTER SIXTEEN

NANCY

A cow is looking at me in a very suspicious manner.

'Is it just me, or is that cow about to charge?' I ask nervously. 'I'm not a big fan of the glare she's giving me.'

'You're thinking of bulls,' Miles replies, laughing as he holds out his hand to help me jump over a puddle. 'That cow is minding her own business and you're traipsing through her field. No wonder she's glaring.'

'I wouldn't be traipsing through her field if you would let me have my phone back so I can check my map,' I huff, putting my hands on my hips. 'We're lost because of you.'

'What's the point in a countryside walk if you're going to stick to roads?' He grins, throwing his hands up. 'This is what it's all about! Fresh air and proper fields.'

He watches in amusement as I carefully dodge another muddy puddle.

'You know that the point of boots is that you can walk through puddles, right? They're waterproof. They're designed to withstand tiny patches of water,' he points out.

'Why are there so many puddles in this field, anyway?' I ask, ignoring his comment. 'It must have rained so much overnight. I told you we should have stayed in a nice cosy cafe or gone to the milkshake bar. Then we could be inside and warm right now, and not being stared at by angry cows.'

'And miss out on hearing you scream every time you see some kind of animal in nature?' He laughs. 'Never. Coming here was the best decision I've made in a long time.'

When Miles rang and asked if he could come for one of those countryside walks across Norfolk that Mum had mentioned weeks ago in the shop to him, I thought he was joking. But then he turned up at the station, wellies in tow, ready to 'enjoy the real outdoors'. I tried talking him out of it but he was set on the activity, and now here we are, in the middle of nowhere. He put the phone rule in place an hour or so ago when he wanted to take a path through a woodland that wasn't on my map. He confiscated my phone and said that today we would be following our instincts, rather than going by a digital map. It turns out that path led to another weird, creepy woodland path, which led to a huge field with a public walkway, which led us to another field and now to this field.

I have to admit, at this stage, I'm a little bored of fields.

'I'm glad you're enjoying this,' I say grumpily, tripping over a stray mound of grass and steadying myself. 'Not exactly how you'd expect a pop star to spend his weekends.'

'Actually, this is just what I needed. I had to get out of London; it gets very claustrophobic there.'

'How is that possible? It's massive.'

'I know.' He shrugs and puts his hands in his pockets. 'I felt like I needed some space to breathe. Thanks for inviting me here for the weekend. I seriously appreciate it.'

'If I'm honest, you kind of invited yourself,' I point out. 'But I'm pleased you did. It's really nice to see you. It's been a while since the party.'

He nods and makes his way over to the wooden fence at the edge of the field. Hoisting himself up, he sits on it, resting his muddy boots on the lower rail, and looks out across the field.

'Hey.' He grins and ushers me to come and join him. 'You have to see this view.'

'Is it just a load more fields?' I sigh, making my way through the squelchy mud and climbing up on the fence, before plonking myself next to him and leaning on a post. I'm right, it is a load more fields, but it's also really beautiful looking out across them. It's so peaceful and quiet, except for the odd moo from a grumpy cow. We sit in silence for a moment, enjoying the view.

I know that he purposefully avoided me bringing up the subject of the party but I don't want to push him on it. When I asked him on the phone why he needed to get out of London so badly, he went on about needing space to breathe and a break from everything going on.

I had asked him what it was exactly that was going on and he'd said it was nothing.

'Is it something to do with why you suddenly left the party?' I'd asked, taking my chances, but he'd brushed that question aside, moving on to a different subject.

I didn't want him to think he couldn't tell me stuff so I tried a different tack later on in the conversation, when he was thanking me again for letting him come to Norfolk this weekend.

'It's really no problem,' I'd assured him, trying to pretend I wasn't dancing round my room in excitement. 'As long as it's OK with everyone else that you're spending the day away from London? You know, as long as it doesn't annoy anyone in particular.'

'Who in particular would be annoyed by me leaving London for the day?' he'd asked.

'Oh, I don't know. Your girlfriend or someone.'

In my head, it was supposed to come out very cool and collected, as though it was a casual, fleeting thought. Not a big deal, just a normal thing to say. But, as soon as I said the words, I regretted them straight away. It was so OBVIOUS what I was asking and then, because I was panicking about how transparent I'd been, my brain went into overdrive and I started saying things that didn't even make sense, which made everything ten times worse.

'Or your family. Girlfriend or family. Or friends. Anyone you might have made plans with at the weekend. Because that's what you do. Make plans. I mean, not you specifically, although I'm sure you do make plans. I mean, you plural. Like, people. People make plans at the weekend with their friends and family and girlfriends. If they have them. Like, I make plans at the weekend with Mum or Nina or Jimmy, and if I went off for the day, like you're planning on doing, they might wonder where I was and stuff. So, I'm just checking that no one will be wondering that for you.'

I'd paused for breath and then asked myself what on EARTH I was EVEN SAYING.

'I don't have a girlfriend,' he'd replied calmly.

And then he carried on talking about something else, as though I hadn't given the weirdest speech of all time.

Anyway, I'm glad my strange rambling didn't put him off and he's here now.

'It must have been amazing growing up here,' he says wistfully, pushing his hair away from his eyes.

I don't know why, but the way he does it is entrancing and I don't realize that I'm staring, admiring that thick dark hair and how nice his side profile is, when he turns and catches my eye. I quickly look ahead, out over the fields, pretending that I'm nonchalantly admiring the view and my cheeks aren't burning with embarrassment that he caught me gawping at him.

'Did you go on a lot of walks?' he asks.

'Um, yeah, we did. Mum was really into her walking when we first moved here. I think because it was good exercise and distraction as she tried to move on from Dad. We spent a lot of time running about the countryside trying to cheer her up and forget about him.'

'How are things with your dad?'

I shrug. 'Not great.'

'Have you seen him again?'

'No, but Nina has. She sees him every weekend. He's helping her achieve her dreams.'

I look down at my boots and try to kick some of the mud off.

'You don't want to see him?' Miles asks carefully.

'I haven't really been given the chance. I know I shouldn't be surprised considering the history, but he's taken the easy path. Nina is in London every weekend so he just ambushes her. He knows she's so nice and so in awe of him, no matter what he did in the past, that she'll go along with it. She always put him on a pedestal.'

'Have you asked to join them?' Miles suggests. 'Maybe Nina could tell him to stop randomly showing up and actually organize something properly so you can be there, too.'

'Nina has suggested that, but I get the feeling he's not so keen. I'll just spoil the lovely time they have together.'

Miles frowns. 'That can't be true.'

'Why isn't he showing up here then? He's made no effort with me and yet is buying Nina expensive cameras and hiring singing coaches for her. I bet he knows about my website but he hasn't sent me anything to help towards that.'

'Wait, slow down,' Miles says. 'What's this about a singing coach? Nina doesn't sing, does she?'

'He thinks it will help her win the Guildhall showcase if she has more strings to her bow,' I explain, rolling my eyes. 'Apparently, Dad thinks it will impress these talent scouts he's organized to come to her show. But I thought she was supposed to be impressing the Guildhall teachers, not talent scouts. I don't know. I asked her to stop telling me what Dad thinks and to tell me what she thinks and she went completely silent. I know she doesn't want to do it.'

'She should tell him that,' Miles says sternly. 'She is good enough to win without adding another string to her bow, or whatever you said.'

'That's my point exactly, but she doesn't believe that. She thinks Dad knows best. They have their own little music bubble and I'm stuck here. On the outside.'

I kick my boot against the rail again and a lump of mud comes flying off.

'You're not *stuck* here,' Miles says gently. 'And you're not on the outside. You've got your mum and Nina. And me. You've got lots of other bubbles to be in.'

I laugh. 'Yeah. I guess that's one way of looking at it.'

'How does your mum feel about Nina spending all this time with your dad?'

'I'm not sure. I think she finds it a little weirder than she lets on. And I know she's hating that he's not making any effort with me, because she keeps asking me if I want to talk about it and how I'm feeling, blah blah blah. At least she's got this guy that she's dating. He seems to make her very happy.'

'You know anything about him yet?'

I shake my head. 'She is being very secretive, but I know she'll tell us when she's ready. It will be nice to meet him and make sure he ticks all the boxes.'

Miles winces, before chuckling to himself.

'What? Why are you making that face?'

'Because I can imagine that you'd be the kind of person who would actually show up with a clipboard and a list to make sure he does genuinely tick all the boxes.' He laughs.

'Yeah, well, wouldn't you if it was your mum?' I say defensively. 'She deserves the best. He has to be perfect. It's nice to see her dating again, though. You know, she hasn't really since we moved here.'

'She was too busy dragging you and Nina on countryside walks.'

'Something like that.'

I smile as a memory flits across my mind and Miles nudges me.

'What? What are you thinking about?'

'It's stupid.'

'Go on.'

'It's just . . . well, when we first got here, sometimes Mum would get a bit down. Understandably. She was amazing at being upbeat and positive most of the time, but sometimes something would remind her of Dad and she'd get this look on her face. I hated seeing her get that look. Nina has the same one. Their faces just cloud over with sadness.'

'What, and you don't have that expression?' he asks curiously.

'They overthink everything. Mum and Nina, I mean,' I explain. 'Anyway, I'd see Mum get this look on her face because she'd see a flower or something and it would remind her of the time Dad once bought her that kind of flower . . . you know, that sort of thing. And Nina would start getting really sad, too, so I had this . . . stupid thing I would do to cheer them up.'

'Yessss? And that was?'

I bury my head in my hands, laughing. 'I can't believe I'm about to tell you this.'

'You can't not tell me now. I've never been more intrigued,' he says. 'Come on, Nancy. What did you do to cheer up your family when they were down?'

I take a deep breath. 'I would run around the field and pretend to be Maria from *The Sound of Music*. The bit where she's running across the hills at the beginning. It was so silly but it would make them laugh every time. It never failed to cheer them up. I haven't thought about that in years, but now I remember so clearly running around the grass in circles, belting out that "hills are alive" song.'

'I see,' Miles says, his dark eyes shining. 'Any chance of a demonstration?'

'No. Absolutely no chance.' I hold my hand out and look up at the sky. 'I think it might be about to rain. I felt a raindrop then. We should start heading back.'

'Oh, come on! You can't tell me about this Maria-from-*The-Sound-of-Music* thing and not actually act it out.'

'Yes, I can. I'm not showing you.'

'I can't picture it.'

'Yes, you can.'

'I need cheering up.'

'No, you don't.'

'I'm going deep into my thoughts. I'm getting a clouded look on my face. Nothing will cheer me up at this stage apart from Maria from *The Sound of Music*, lead role played by Miss Nancy Palmer. Moving to the West End next spring.'

'Nice try, Miles, but it's not happening,' I say stubbornly.

'Why? Are you embarrassed? I'll sing it first if you like and then you can come in. Join in when you're ready.'

'What? No.'

'Let me get the right starting note and then you bring in the harmonies.'

'Miles! I am not singing any harmonies with you! What are you doing?'

He hops down from the fence and takes a few paces forward.

'I'm getting into character. I'm assuming that you didn't just sing at your mum and Nina; that you did the moves too? You said you ran across the field, like Maria ran across the hilltop.'

'I wish I had never told you,' I groan, as he clears his throat. 'And it really is starting to rain. I definitely felt a raindrop that time. What are you doing? I'm not going to . . .'

Before I can finish my sentence, Miles throws open his arms and begins to bellow '*The hills are aliiiiiiiiive*' while running round on the grass in a wide circle. I burst out laughing, almost falling backwards off the fence.

'Come on,' he says, pausing his performance to grin at me. 'You're supposed to have joined in by now with your beautiful vocals!'

'You look ridiculous!' I say through wheezes, as he launches into the second line of the song and runs round in another circle.

When a cow begins mooing along with his completely out-of-tune singing, I'm laughing so hard that I'm bent over double on the fence, clutching my stomach. It starts to rain but neither of us care.

'The cows are coming in on the harmonies you are neglecting,' he says, coming to a stop and holding his side. 'Also, side note: Maria must have been in really good shape to do all this running and singing at the same time.'

'That was beautiful.' I grin, applauding him as he takes a bow. 'Truly, I've never seen anything like it.'

'Well, you were right about the rain and you were right about a good Maria impression making people laugh,' he says, as I wipe the tears from my eyes with my jacket sleeve. 'It clearly works.'

'And here I was thinking that you were merely a drummer for Chasing Chords. I had no idea that such vocal talent lay beneath the surface.'

'Yeah, I keep that VERY well hidden,' he says, coming to lean forward on his arms across the fence. 'I let Chase steal all the thunder.'

As he talks about Chase, I notice his expression changes and he looks suddenly troubled, as though he's just remembered something. He pulls up the collar of his jacket.

'Everything OK?' I ask. 'You want to get out of this rain?'

He gives me a look. 'It is gently spitting. I can hardly feel it.'

'Well then, if you were putting on a sad face in order to try to get me to repeat your excellent performance, I'm afraid to tell you that it's not going to happen.'

He smiles up at me, resting his chin on his hands.

'Fine, I'll let you off this time,' he says. 'It's very sweet that you used to do that to cheer your mum up. She must have loved it.'

'I used to do it when she was mad at me too. If she started talking about a bad report I'd got or something, I'd burst into song and start running around. Even if we were in public.'

'So, it wasn't just a performance confined to the muddy fields of Norfolk?'

'Nope. I remember she was furious at me once when I skipped a lesson. When she started talking to me about it in the middle of a busy shopping centre, I turned into Maria and ran around singing about the hills. The other shoppers loved it and Mum had to forgive me; I was simply too adorable.'

He laughs. 'That is genius. Music and public humiliation. No one could stay mad at you with such a combination.'

My phone beeps in his pocket and I give him a pleading look.

'What if it's an important message? It could be from Nina! Please, I promise I won't look at the map and we can stay lost in these fields for no reason, even though it's about to tip it down.'

'Fine,' he says, passing me my phone.

I groan when I see it's a message from Layla:

> Just a reminder to update the
> music section today! We need
> good stuff FAST. Jimmy's website
> is storming ahead. THIS CANNOT
> HAPPEN

'What is it?' Miles asks, as I gladly hand the phone back.

'Layla's on at me about the website. My Tyler story is old news now and I haven't exactly been able to match it. Our hits are continually dropping and I think it's all my fault. I can't seem to find anything good to report on. I feel so stressed about it.'

'Why don't you write about what you were saying when we passed that busker at the station? You said all that stuff about how much joy they can bring to passers-by. That would make a nice piece.'

'I don't think that would be good enough.'

'What about what music means to you?' he offers thoughtfully. 'How it can bring people together?'

'I'm not sure anyone would read that stuff. They want things a little more celebrity-based and exciting,' I explain. 'I have to think of something or *All That Glitters* won't win the competition and everything I have going for me will be gone. This is exactly the reason Dad isn't interested and Nina is the twin that everyone cares about.'

'*What*?' Miles blinks at me. 'Explain.'

'What else am I good at? This is it. I've found something I can do really well and people have begun to notice me again. But I haven't been able to follow the Tyler story up with anything and so they're all losing interest again. Next week it's being judged and that's it. Game over.'

'So what you're saying is, you need a new story to make things better?'

'Yeah. You got any music friends with some new, big exclusive?' I ask hopefully.

'I do. I really do. I have a huge scoop!'

I feel a rush of excitement that he may be able to help. He points my phone at me and starts filming.

'This is a BIG exclusive, for your eyes only. Nancy Palmer, THE Nancy Palmer, has kidnapped a ridiculously good-looking drummer and is now holding him hostage, completely LOST, in a field of suspicious cows. Nancy, what do you have to say for yourself?'

I narrow my eyes at him as he gives me a thumbs up.

'Ready for your close up? I'm zooming in on your face!' he whispers loudly. 'Say something.'

'It's raining on my phone. Put it away.'

Miles gasps dramatically, before flipping the camera to selfie mode and filming himself.

'She is truly mysterious. Will I ever make it out of here alive?'

I jump down from the fence and come into shot with him.

'The truth of this story is that MILES is the one kidnapping ME, an innocent civilian, who isn't allowed to look at her map and find us a way HOME before we both get soaked.'

He raises one eyebrow at the camera in an attempt to look suspicious. 'Will we ever really know the truth?'

'OK, stop recording now. You've made your HILARIOUS point. Now, I have this stupid video stuck on my phone, taking up valuable space. I thought you were going to give me an ACTUAL story.'

'Wait, I have one more thing to say,' he argues, as I grapple for my phone and snatch it out of his hands. 'Spoilsport. I wanted what I have to say to go on the record.'

'Oh really? And what's that? Another exciting exclusive about mud being on your boot or something?'

'No,' he says, his tone suddenly serious. 'That you're wrong about Nina being the only twin that people care about.'

My eyes meet his and he smiles at me in that different way that he does. In the way that makes my stomach flip and my heart thud loudly against my chest.

He takes a step closer and, with no hesitation, he leans down and kisses me.

CHAPTER SEVENTEEN

NINA

'Can I be honest with you?' Jimmy asks.

I lift my head up from where it's been resting on the piano keys to look at his face on my phone screen.

'Why not? At this stage, I really have nothing to lose so you can say whatever you want.'

'OK.' He takes a deep breath. 'You need a break.'

'Jimmy,' I groan, 'that is the LAST thing I need. I have so much to do. I can't take a break now.'

'Yes, you can. You need to. You remember that English exam last year? The one I worked so hard for that I messed up because I was tired and running on no energy? You remind me of how I looked then. Which, by the way, was terrible.'

'Maybe I regret allowing you to be so honest.'

'I was always going to be honest, whether you allowed me to or not,' he says, grinning. 'And you did wake me up at a ridiculous hour to talk, so you can't expect me to be that nice at this time in the morning.'

'It's only eight a.m.'

'On a Saturday. And we've been talking for forty minutes. But I forgive you. I need to try and get one last push for the website before voting closes, anyway. Have you voted?'

'No.'

'Why not? It's so easy, Nina – the link is on the email that got sent round and it's on the school homepage. All you have to do is click on it and it takes you straight to the voting page.'

'That's not the part of voting I have an issue with.'

'Don't tell me you're letting your personal life get in the way of your professional judgement,' he says, giving me a stern look.

'What am I supposed to do, Jimmy? Choose between you and Nancy?'

'Yes – everyone else has to. And hopefully they're voting because of the content and the general excellence of the websites rather than on a popularity or personal basis.' He sighs, knitting his eyebrows together. 'Otherwise I don't have a chance. Not only is their website really quite good, but Layla, Sophie and Nancy are celebrities at school. I could have sworn I heard someone gasp when Nancy walked past them the other day. How can I compete with that? No one gasps when I walk past.'

'I'm sure that's not true. And, if you want, I'll start gasping every time you walk past,' I say, stifling a yawn. 'And your website is brilliant. It's going to be a very close call.'

Nancy had been certain that *All That Glitters* wouldn't make the shortlist for the student body to vote on. The competition was strong and, as much as she'd tried, she hadn't been able to track down a good story to add to the website at the last minute, so their hits were much lower than they had been, something that wasn't going to look good to the judges. Jimmy's hits, on the other hand, were gradually growing every day, much to his total shock. Then the school announced this week that they were widening their vegetarian selection because of his petition. His website was really making a difference.

Not that Nancy's wasn't brilliant. It really was. I know Layla and Sophie had been giving her a hard time about getting some good music gossip, but, in my opinion, it didn't really need it. The vlogs and articles that Nancy had uploaded about other things were great – she has a really unique style of writing and she doesn't even realize it. I'm pretty sure it's her music section that helped the judges make their decision. It's so much stronger than the rest of the website – not least because her posts are actually helpful, like the one she wrote on the best music tracks to study to. And this week she'd uploaded an amazing feature about what music means to her. I loved it.

Music affects us in so many ways, she wrote at the end of the piece. *It makes us happy, it makes us sad, it makes us understand something we're yet to feel, and it gives us hope when we feel we're alone. Music reminds us that even when we feel left behind or on the outside, it doesn't mean we're powerless or that we're fighting our corner by ourselves. Music connects us to each other, whether we want it to or not.*

I wanted to print that passage out and stick it everywhere around the house, but Nancy wouldn't let me, so in the end we compromised and she let me print out one copy and keep it by my bed.

I wasn't surprised when Mrs Smithson punched the air as she announced that *All That Glitters* was in the final against Jimmy's site. Judging from the dirty looks Mrs Smithson has been giving Jimmy's form teacher this week, I'm going to guess that they have some kind of bet going because she is much more enthusiastic about one of her form winning an internship than you'd expect.

Layla, Sophie and Nancy went mental when they found out that they were through to the final two. Everyone in our class started clapping and cheering, and Layla stood up to blow kisses at everyone while Sophie launched into a weird celebratory dance. Nancy looked as though she might burst into tears; she really couldn't believe that she had done it.

'You really could win!' I'd yelled as I gave her a big hug.

'Finally!' she'd yelled back before going over to Layla and Sophie's desk to squeal along with them.

Obviously, it doesn't put me in the easiest of situations as now I'm under pressure to vote for Jimmy or Nancy, and I have no idea how I'm going to choose. I was hoping neither of them would ask me if I'd voted and then I might have been able to go under the radar, but I should have known I wouldn't be able to get away with it.

'Taking into consideration that you're talking to me right now and not Nancy, how about you vote for me, as clearly I am here for you in your times of need?' Jimmy says with a mischievous grin. 'That seems fair.'

'I actually spoke to Nancy first,' I admit. 'She couldn't chat for long though, as Layla has already rung her a million times and wanted Nancy to get round to her house as soon as possible.'

'So, they're definitely doing a last-minute push?' Jimmy says, suddenly sitting upright and looking nervous. 'I have to go, Nina. I need to write a piece thanking my readers for their support and listing all the changes my website has made to the school so far. Just to remind everyone how important it is to keep my website going!'

'That's a good idea.'

'Yeah, well, it probably won't help, but at this stage it's the best I can do, along with begging people to vote for me. Knowing those three, they'll have something sneaky up their sleeve.'

'Good luck.' I smile at my screen. 'You deserve this. Sorry for being a bit out of it recently, but I hope you know I'm proud of you.'

'Course,' he says. 'Likewise. Oh – and, Nina, a reminder that you could do with a rest, otherwise I'm scared you'll have some kind of breakdown. You've got too much on your shoulders. Do you have a bit of time before your lesson with Caroline?'

'Yes, a few hours.'

'Good. Go do something different.'

I sigh. 'You really think that will help?'

'You've been at that piano since the early hours. If you haven't got it now, it's not going to hit you this morning. Get a breath of fresh air or see some sights. Just make sure you're not at a piano for a bit. That's my non-professional, non-musician, simply-best-friend advice.'

'Thanks, Jimmy,' I say, waving goodbye. 'You're the best.'

'I know,' he says, shooting me a grin before the call ends.

I grab my jacket and head out of the door, knowing that Jimmy is right. I have to get out of that practice room before I lose my mind. I've been trying Simone's physical and vocal exercises every day, to see if I really do have it in me, like Dad said.

I don't. Of course, I don't. And that means I have wasted another week on music that isn't working. I am running out of time.

I head back to our block of rooms and, as I go up the stairs, Jordan and James happen to be coming down them.

'How are the moves coming along, Nina?' Jordan sneers, flopping forward dramatically and swinging his arms from side to side. 'Have I got it right? Is this how I'm going to win?'

'Isn't that joke getting a bit old?' Grace calls out, coming down the stairs behind him with Florence, TJ and Nico. 'Seriously, Jordan, you tried that all last weekend and the laughs weren't exactly forthcoming. I think you should get some new material.'

Jordan's smug expression is pleasingly wiped from his face, while James's expression brightens as Grace approaches them.

'Anyone would think you were threatened by Nina,' TJ comments, leaning on the bannister.

'I hope that's some kind of joke,' Jordan spits.

'If so, then it's about as hilarious as one of yours,' Grace murmurs, making the others snigger.

James howls with laughter. Jordan glares at him. He stops laughing very quickly.

'Word on the street is that you haven't selected your music for the showcase yet,' Jordan says, returning his attention to me. 'Time's running out, don't you think?'

Without waiting for a reply, he pushes past me down the stairs, leaving James to reluctantly follow and give Grace an awkward wave as he goes.

'If Jordan gets a place on the Guildhall summer course, the art of music is doomed,' Florence says, shaking her head. 'Are you all right?'

'Yeah. I'm sorry you had to stand up for me. I should be able to say what I think to him, but somehow he makes me feel so inferior.'

'Yeah, one of his limited talents.' Grace raises her eyebrows. 'What time were you up this morning? Are you coming to breakfast?'

Nico smiles encouragingly. 'We're heading there now if you want to join.'

'Actually, I've been practising but I'm on strict orders by my friend Jimmy to have a break, so I think I'm going to head out for a bit. My brain feels a little bogged down lately. Jordan's right, you know. I haven't selected the music yet. Can you believe that?'

'Yes. It's not easy picking music for an important showcase like this. There's a lot of pressure and it sounds like Jimmy is a wise man. You can't have your brain all bogged down while you make that decision.'

'I only decided on mine last night if that makes you feel better,' Florence admitted, shrugging.

'Any advice?' I ask hopefully. 'How did you all choose your music for the showcase?'

'I actually rang my music teacher from school,' Grace says, laughing. 'I know it sounds a bit weird, but she knows me so well that she was able to guide me. She helped a lot. Do you have someone like that?'

'Yeah, I do. My piano teacher. But I've told him about Guildhall during my lessons at school and he hasn't said anything about what piece to play.'

'Have you asked him?' TJ says.

I hesitate. 'No. I don't think I have. I've just given him the new piece I'm considering each week and he's helped along with it.'

'Maybe he doesn't think you're after guidance from him. You should ask him outright,' Grace suggests. 'My teacher was surprised that I went to her but really eager to help. She said she thought I'd be too "big time" to ask her advice.'

'I'll give that a try, thank you,' I say, trying to remember whether Mr Rogers had ever truly given his opinion on any of the pieces I'd brought to him.

'No worries,' she says, heading down to breakfast with the others. 'Good luck with it!'

'Let us know how it goes!' Florence calls as I head upstairs.

When I get to my room, I shut the door and slump down on to my bed, calling Mr Rogers straight away. I realize after I've pressed the call button that it's quite early to be calling a teacher on a Saturday morning, but luckily when he answers he doesn't sound unhappy about it.

'Nina?' he says. 'Is that you?'

'Hey, Mr Rogers, I'm so sorry to disturb you. I forgot it's quite early. Do you want me to ring back later?'

'Not at all, I'm just on my way to Neptune Records.'

'Oh! Say hi to Haley for me.'

'I will,' he says. 'So, Nina, how can I help you? Did you want to book in another music lesson this week?'

'No, I'm actually calling for your advice.'

'Go ahead. I'm listening.'

And so I launch into my predicament of choosing a piece of music for the showcase, thinking that's all I'm going to tell him. But, without meaning to, I end up talking about Chase as well, and then I go into Dad being back on the scene and, before I know it, I'm telling my piano teacher my entire life story down the phone on a Saturday morning as he heads to a vinyl shop.

He doesn't complain though and he doesn't stop me once to ask any questions or anything. He just patiently listens to everything I have to say, without me pausing for breath.

'And now I feel so lost,' I conclude. 'I'm still not over my stage fright. Chase was meant to help me with it but, as you know, he's busy with his own thing. And I don't think I can sing in front of everyone, so I'll be letting my dad down and the talent scouts will have wasted their time. I've spent my entire life dreaming of being here, only to ruin any chance I have of coming back. I must be Caroline's worst student of all time. I don't know what to do. I wondered . . . I wondered if you had any advice about what music I should choose for the showcase. I'm sorry for not asking you before.'

'You never need to apologize to me, Nina. It's been fun working on your new pieces this term. It's always good to experiment and push yourself out of your comfort zone. Instead of telling you what pieces I think you should play for the showcase, do you mind if I ask you a question?'

'Of course not.'

'Why do you love playing the piano?'

'Huh?'

'Why is it that you love playing the piano?' he repeats. 'Forget music school, forget Chase, forget your dad. Why is it that you turn up to your music lesson every week with me?'

'Um. I don't know. I can't explain it.'

'Have a think and give it a go.'

I take a deep breath and attempt to find the words. 'I guess I've always loved playing, ever since I first started. I don't know – it's just part of who I am. That's always how it's been.'

'That's what I thought. And exactly what you need to hear.'

'I'm sorry, Mr Rogers,' I say, lying back on my pillows and rubbing my forehead. 'I'm a bit confused. What did I need to hear?'

'The teachers at Guildhall aren't there in the audience of the showcase to see what you can do. They're there to see *who you are*. Think about the hundreds of people who audition for these courses every year; think how many people they've heard play Bach's *Prelude in* C. It's not simply a matter of pressing the right keys; it's the *feeling*. Like you said, playing the piano and music are part of who you are. And the Guildhall teachers must have seen that in the audition and *that's* why they wanted you.'

'So, when Caroline took me to that movement class . . .'

'From what you told me, it sounds like she was showing you that you have a right to be up on that stage, just like every other student does, as no one else but yourself. That's your space. Don't apologize for being there. It's a hard thing to do to make yourself open and vulnerable to an audience, but that's what music is. She told you that you apologize with your body language for merely being in the room, yes?'

'Yeah.' I remember. 'That's right.'

'Why are you apologizing for doing what you love? You're so worried about what Caroline Morreau, the great pianist, thinks of you that you're too afraid to let yourself connect with the music you're playing. And I think she could tell. You were playing the notes but you weren't really feeling what it was all about.'

'And I've been like that with every piece of music this term?'

There's a pause.

'Mostly, yes. But, as I said, it's good to try new things and I've been proud of how you've come along technically. I've never seen anyone work harder.'

'So, what do I do now?'

'You fall in love with playing again,' he replies simply. 'Stop playing for everyone else. Play for you.'

I let his words sink in and in the background I hear that wonderfully familiar sound of the old bell ringing above Neptune Records' door as he walks in.

'Thanks, Mr Rogers,' I say, exhaling. 'You've been very helpful.'

'Any time, Nina. I'll see you next week.'

'See you next week.'

I hang up and lie there for a minute. It feels as though a blanket of calm has just been thrown over me. For the first time in weeks, my mind seems clear. I've been trying so hard to play the piano well that I haven't really been *playing* the piano.

If that makes sense.

This whole time I've been trying to impress Caroline when I should have been playing for me! I leap up from my bed and know that I need to get straight back to the practice-room building. I feel elated as I rush down the stairs, throwing open the door and –

'Nina!'

I run straight into Chase, who has to put his arms out to stop me from toppling over.

'Hey!' I beam, never happier to see those sparkling blue eyes of his. 'What are you doing here? I thought we were meeting tonight.'

'I wanted to tell you in person.' He gives me a strange look. 'What's different about you?'

'What do you mean?'

'Something's different,' he says, a smile on his lips. 'You seem . . . taller. And your face is all bright and glowy.'

'I feel taller. And brighter and glowier. Chase, I've got it. Mr Rogers has helped me to see what's been going on this whole time. I haven't been playing the piano!'

Chase frowns. 'You what now?'

'I haven't been *playing* the piano!'

'Nina, have you fallen over and banged your head?' he asks, bending slightly to look closely into my eyes. 'You've barely stopped playing the piano in the last few weeks. I'm surprised you haven't turned into a piano.'

'It's a long story,' I say. 'But it doesn't matter because I think I know what I'm going to do for the showcase now and I . . . Hang on. What do you mean you wanted to tell me in person?'

'What?'

'When I asked what you were doing here, you said you wanted to tell me in person. What did you want to tell me?'

'Oh, yeah, well,' he says, shuffling his feet. 'I thought I'd drop by this morning because I really want to enjoy our date night tonight, and I didn't want this to spoil it. So I thought I'd tell you now and then you can be angry all day and forgive me by the evening.'

'Okaaaay? That sounds worrying.'

'Nina, the news is coming out,' he says quietly, glancing around him to make sure no one is listening. 'We're going to announce that I'm going solo. I'm signing with Emerald Entertainment. It's official.'

'That's amazing!' I cry, jumping into his arms.

He laughs and spins me round, kissing me as he places me back on my feet.

'I can't believe it's happening. It's really happening.'

'I can.' I grin up at him. 'You deserve this. I'm so happy for you! And the rest of the band?'

'We've worked it out,' he says happily. 'Miles has finally got his head round it and, once he did, the rest of the band followed. I should have been honest with them right from the start. We've had some really good talks about it and I think they see it from my point of view. They want to support me. That's why we're going to announce it as a band at a press conference. Together.'

'I'm really happy for you, Chase – this is great news. Why would you think that would make me angry?'

His eyes drop to the floor. 'They've scheduled the press conference for the day of your showcase. I've tried to get them to change it but they can't. There's nothing I can do.'

I drop his hands like they're burning hot. 'What?'

'Nina, please – you know it's out of my control.'

'You promised you'd be there,' I whisper, all the good feeling I had a moment ago seeping away. 'You *promised*.'

'I know, but there's nothing I can do! I asked Mark and he said it wasn't possible. It's not that easy setting up a press conference. There are a lot of people involved –'

'Chase, for the past couple of months we've hardly had any time together and you know that my showcase is a really big deal. It's the one day you promised you would be there for me, no matter what. I need you in the audience. You have to change the press conference, please!'

'I *can't*,' he says harshly before taking a deep breath and continuing in a softer tone. 'I wish I could be there, but you're brilliant, Nina – you really are, and you're going to be absolutely amazing whether I'm in the audience or not.'

'That's not the point,' I say sharply. 'You know that's not the point. I need you there and you promised! I know you have the power to change it if you want to. You're letting Mark push you around as normal.'

'That's not fair.'

'You think you have some control, but he's the one pulling all the strings and you just let him, even if it means hurting the band. Even if it means hurting me!'

'What am I supposed to do, Nina?' he yells, his voice echoing around the courtyard. 'In case you didn't notice, this is a big step in my career and, let's be honest here, it's only a showcase!'

I feel as though he's punched me in the stomach.

'*Only a showcase?*' I whisper.

'Nina,' he croaks, his eyes suddenly scared and sad, 'I'm sorry, I didn't mean –'

'I get it. I have to go,' I say, pushing past him. I break into a run, not sure where I'm going but just as long as it's far away from him.

'Nina, wait!'

Nina

I ignore his calls and run as fast as my legs can take me until I end up in the only place I imagine will be completely empty at this moment in time and where Chase won't think of looking for me: the Milton Court concert hall.

Catching my breath, I walk into the empty, dimly lit and eerily quiet auditorium. I walk up on to the stage, right into the middle and look out at the rows and rows of empty seats. I sit down and let my legs dangle over the edge of the stage. Next weekend I'll be here with the rest of the Guildhall students, performing to a big audience.

But for now it's just me. No one will find me here. Finally, I allow myself to cry. To really, really cry.

It's the first time I've ever felt safe on a stage.

CHAPTER EIGHTEEN

NANCY

When a boy like Miles kisses you, it's very hard to concentrate on anything else.

I can't stop thinking about him and every time I think about that amazing first kiss and then all the kissing we did afterwards on the way home, I get this shiver down my spine and I can't stop grinning and I feel all giddy and dazed, and I could BURST with excitement and happiness. I've never felt this way before. Ever. I never realized that this is how it feels when you fall for someone. Like *really* fall for them. They completely take over your brain and you're constantly waiting for your phone to beep and their name to pop up on the screen. And when you see their name you feel your heart in your mouth and you want to jump up and down, even if they've only messaged to say hello.

I can't believe I ever thought I was in love with Chase Hunter. Before he started dating Nina, I was completely invested in this fantasy I had of Chase and me being perfect for one another. I didn't even know him, but was convinced that I was in love with him and as soon as he met me the feeling would be reciprocated. That's why I could write all those stories so easily. I made everything up in my head. Nothing was real.

I feel SO embarrassed about that now.

Because this spark I have with Miles, it's real. I mean, yeah, Chase is good-looking but HELLO, have you seen Miles's eyes? They are this really beautiful dark, dark brown framed by nice long eyelashes. And when he laughs his eyes get these little crinkles round them and that's when you know that you've really made him laugh – not a fake laugh but a proper laugh. I love his hair too; it's so thick. I need to ask him what products he uses. And, oh my goodness, because he's a drummer his arms are all muscly, and when he puts them round me I feel so safe and enclosed. He smells really good too. I don't know what cologne he uses, but it's the best one I've ever smelt and he doesn't use too much of it either, so it's not overpowering or anything; he uses just the perfect amount.

OK, I sound like a crazy person. I should stop talking about his smell.

YOU SEE? You see what happens when a boy like Miles kisses you? One minute you're talking about your old obsession with his bandmate and the next moment you can't stop thinking about his smell.

And now Layla is yelling at me because, instead of listening to whatever she's saying, I've been daydreaming about Miles's eye crinkles and his smell.

'Nancy!' she barks. 'Wake up!'

It's not the first time I've drifted off during this last-minute meeting that Layla called. We are very close to winning the competition and if we can make sure we have enough votes to beat Jimmy, then we will win the internship. I'd be spending my holiday working at the Disney Channel. Everyone would be so impressed that I'd actually done it. Me, Nancy.

We HAVE to win.

'Sorry, sorry. What were you saying?' I say.

'Your eyes keep glazing over. Do you need a coffee?' She raises her eyebrows. 'Something is different about you today. What's going on?'

'Yeah, you're acting strange,' agrees Sophie, sitting on the floor, painting her toenails bright blue.

'No, I'm not,' I say hurriedly. 'I'm just . . . I'm really excited about the chance of winning the competition.'

Even though I want to talk about Miles constantly, I haven't told anyone about the kiss. Not even Nina. When Miles had to go home that Saturday night, I got the bus with him to the station and while we waited for his platform to come up on the screen he pulled me close to him.

'I don't want to leave,' he'd said, as I lost myself in those dark eyes.

'I don't want you to leave,' I'd whispered back. 'Can't you stay?'

He'd shaken his head. 'I'll call you tonight when I'm home and we can sort out when I'm next seeing you. If you'd like to see me again, that is?'

'Actually, I'm very busy. I'll have to check my schedule, but I'm not sure I'll be able to fit you in,' I'd teased, making him grin.

'Any chance I can change your mind?' he'd said, before gently lifting my chin up and kissing me again.

HOW is he so good at kissing?!

Obviously, my brain went all fuzzy after that kiss and I couldn't remember what we were talking about, where we were or what was going on, so he had to repeat the question.

'Can I see you again this week, Nancy Palmer? Or next weekend if you're too busy to fit me in on a weekday evening?' he'd said, nuzzling into my neck.

Yes. That's right. Miles. The drummer from Chasing Chords. Nuzzled my neck. NUZZLED.

'Yeah, that might be nice,' I'd squeaked, wondering if I was dreaming and terrified that none of this was real.

'Great,' he'd said.

And then he'd kissed me again. When his platform number came up on the screen and he'd had to go, turning to shoot me one of those smiles of his, I'd almost melted right into the station floor. I'd stood there for ages, watching him walk away until he got on the train and I literally could not see him any more. Someone barged past me to get to the train and I guess them knocking my shoulder kind of knocked me out of my trance, because I realized I was standing there, waving sadly at him and NOT playing it cool in the slightest. I'd quickly turned on my heel and walked out of the station, with the smallest of skips because, no matter how hard I'd tried, I was too happy not to.

He'd texted me a few minutes later to say how he'd had a really good day and he couldn't wait to see me again –

'NANCY! You're doing it AGAIN!' Layla's shrill voice cuts through my thoughts. 'Your eyes are all glazed!'

'I'm sorry, I'm so sorry,' I say, sitting bolt upright on her bed.

'Snap out of it. This is serious!' She sighs, sitting down at her dressing table. 'How are we going to secure those last-minute votes?'

'We've texted everyone in our contacts asking for them to vote for us,' Sophie says. 'So that's got to help.'

Layla rolls her eyes. 'You think they'll vote just because we asked them to? That's not enough! Jimmy's website is really popular. That protest outside the town hall got a huge amount of interest – it was even in the local paper!'

'Our website was on loads of celebrity sites,' Sophie points out.

'Weeks ago! Since then, our hits have dropped to an all-time low,' Layla says, tapping her fingernails on the table. 'If we lose to Jimmy, something is seriously wrong with the world. How can we beat him? I can't bear that he might be spending a week with the stars of the Disney Channel while we're stuck at home revising like everyone else.'

'You're right,' I say, determined to get Miles out of my brain for one minute so I can focus on what's important. 'We have to think of something.'

'There is a solution and it's been there all along. Nancy, you need to ring Chase and ask him for some music news,' Layla says sternly. 'Explain what this website means to you and he'll surely be able to help you out.'

'He can tell us something about Chasing Chords!' Sophie cries.

'Yes, well done, Einstein,' Layla says, her voice monotone. 'Obviously. Or Nancy could ask Miles for some new gossip from his friend Tyler Hill.'

Just the sound of his name makes me go giddy. I pull myself together pronto.

'I've told you before, I *can't*,' I say in a strained tone, trying to get it through to them. 'He'd think I was using him. Please can you drop it?'

'But think about it, Nancy,' Layla says in a softer, more encouraging tone. 'One more exclusive like Tyler Hill's fashion line, one tiny story that makes people click on our link and Jimmy will have no hope! They'll want more! It takes two seconds to vote and it says it right at the top of our website in huge letters. Everyone would be too busy scrolling through our website to bother voting for Jimmy's.'

'I don't think we need it,' I say, attempting to be convincing. 'Your make-up and fashion posts are amazing, Layla. Everyone at school talks about them. And, Sophie, you've even had a video go properly viral!'

'Yeah,' Sophie sighs, concentrating on painting the nail of her little toe. 'I really didn't mean to walk into that glass door, but I'm glad I caught it on camera.'

'See?' I say. 'We have this in the bag already!'

'No, we don't,' Layla retorts. 'Yes, we have a loyal following and, yes, my vlogs have become an inspiration for my fellow classmates, BUT it's not their votes we need here. We need the votes of everyone else! We're talking about the weirdos and randoms who are only checking out our website today as they peruse Jimmy's too, working out which one to bother to vote for! They're the people we have to win over!'

'Layla's right,' Sophie says solemnly. 'We need you to bring us one last brilliant story that will make everyone sit up and notice. A story that will win their hearts.'

'Yes, well put, Sophie,' Layla agrees, looking mildly surprised at Sophie's unusual eloquence. 'Nancy, you could be a *legend* at school.'

'Don't be ridiculous.'

'I mean it,' Layla says, her eyes boring into mine. 'Everyone will want to be you!'

'And be friends with you,' Sophie adds. 'You're very fun to hang out with.'

'*And*, more to the point,' Layla says, back to rolling her eyes at Sophie's comments, 'you hang out with famous music stars. That makes you officially the coolest person in school.'

'Yeah,' Sophie says firmly. 'Nina *who?*'

I glance at their hopeful expressions and then bury my head in my hands. 'I wish I could simply call Miles or Chase and ask them for a story, but it's too embarrassing! I don't have the guts, I'm sorry!'

'Miles was happy to help you before,' Layla huffs, standing up and coming towards me. 'I don't understand why you're being such a coward about it. If it was me, I'd call Chase and say, *Look, please can you help me with a story for this really important project? It's a matter of LIFE and DEATH.*'

'It's a shame you're not friends with Chase Hunter, Layla.' Sophie sighs. 'Then our problem would be solved. You'd have the guts to do it.'

Layla nods thoughtfully and then gets a funny look on her face, as though she's just thought of a VERY sly plan. Suddenly she jolts forward and, before I even realize what's happening, she snatches my phone from where it's lying on the bed in front of me.

'Hey! Give that back!'

'You have Chase's number in this phone, don't you?' she says, dangling it in front of me. 'So, you won't mind if I have a scroll through your contacts and send it to myself.'

'Layla, this isn't funny,' I say, scrambling across the duvet to grab it back. She pulls it out of my reach just in time.

'It's the perfect plan!' Sophie giggles. 'Then you don't have to worry because Layla will call him for you. Sorted!'

'Don't be stupid! He'll be furious that I've given out his number,' I say, folding my arms. 'Layla, give me back my phone. You can't get into it anyway. It's got a passcode. So you might as well hand it back. I'm serious!'

Layla snorts. 'Oh, please. I've known your passcode for years, just like you've known mine. It wouldn't by any chance be the same as your school locker, would it? Let's give 9481 a try . . .'

My smugness drains away as I watch her type in the correct numbers. Nina and I have always had that same passcode – when we were little, we found this old key with '9481' engraved on it and we'd thought it was the most mysterious, magical thing ever.

I forgot that when Layla and I were friends we obviously told each other our locker codes for when we needed to get books or homework that the other one had forgotten. I can't believe she remembers it.

'And what do you know?' Her face brightens. 'I'm in!'

'Layla! Give me my phone!'

'You seem very touchy about getting this back, Nancy! What else do you have on this phone that you don't want to share?'

Panicking that she'll see the messages from Miles or make good on her threat and steal one of their numbers, I jump off the bed and rush towards her, but she dodges out of my way and runs to the other side of the room, hopping over Sophie's legs.

'Layla,' I say through gritted teeth. 'Give it back.'

'I will give it back once I've taken Chase's number and given him a call. You don't need to worry. I won't go through anything private.'

She smiles sweetly at me before she begins scrolling through the phone. 'Ah, here he is!'

'LAYLA!' I cry, leaping over Sophie's legs and basically rugby-tackling Layla to the floor.

'Hey!' she yells. 'Get off!'

I scramble to get my phone back as she holds it out of my reach, Sophie shrieking with laughter in the background. While we grapple with each other and she flails her arm around to keep the phone away from me, Layla accidentally swipes and presses the screen several times, and a video starts playing. I'm still yelling at her to give me the phone back so no one is really listening at first, but then it dawns on both Sophie and Layla whose voice it is.

'*This is a BIG exclusive, for your eyes only. Nancy Palmer, THE Nancy Palmer, has kidnapped a ridiculously good-looking drummer . . .*'

Sophie gets to her feet and rushes closer to get a better look.

'Is that Miles? Chasing Chords' Miles?' Layla says, still holding me at bay and throwing the phone towards Sophie, who snatches it up eagerly.

'. . . *and is now holding him hostage, completely LOST, in a field of suspicious cows. Nancy, what do you have to say for yourself?*'

'Sophie,' I croak, 'please give that back.'

'Oh my god! He's filming you, Nancy!' Sophie says. 'Where is this? Some kind of field?'

'*Ready for your close up? I'm zooming in on your face! Say something.*'

Layla stares at me. 'When was this?'

'*It's raining on my phone. Put it away.*'

'*She is truly mysterious. Will I ever make it out of here alive?*'

'EEEE! THERE HE IS!' Sophie squeals. 'He's in shot now! Oh my god, Nancy!'

'*The truth of this story is that MILES is the one kidnapping ME, an innocent civilian, who isn't allowed to look at her map and find us a way HOME before we both get soaked.*'

'*Will we ever really know the truth?*'

'This video is amazing!' Sophie says, showing it to Layla.

'Please,' I say, but they're so engrossed and, no matter how I try to grab the phone back, I'm no match for both of them working together to keep me away.

'*OK, stop recording now. You've made your HILARIOUS point. Now, I have this stupid video stuck on my phone, taking up valuable space. I thought you were going to give me an ACTUAL story.*'

'*Wait, I have one more thing to say! Spoilsport. I wanted what I have to say to go on the record.*'

My breath catches in my throat. Why hasn't the video stopped? It should have stopped. That's when I turned it off. I stopped recording then, didn't I?

'*Oh really? And what's that? Another exciting exclusive about mud being on your boot or something?*'

'All you can see is your jeans now, Nancy,' Sophie points out. 'Your filming technique is awful.'

'Shh!' Layla hisses.

'*No. That you're wrong about Nina being the only twin that people care about.*'

The video stops moments later. Sophie lowers the phone and both of them stare at me. I can't believe I didn't press the button to stop recording properly. I must have turned it off accidentally, holding it against his back as he kissed me.

'Nancy,' Layla begins, the colour drained from her face, 'are you dating *Miles*?'

'No,' I say. 'No, course not. We . . . he needed a break from London, that's all, and we were messing around and –'

'What happened after he said that thing about caring about you?' Sophie asks, her eyes shining with excitement and intrigue as though she's just watched an Oscar-winning performance.

'Nothing. Nothing happened. We walked out of the field and he went back to London.'

'He kissed you,' Layla says, shaking her head in disbelief. 'I can tell. He kissed you!'

She snatches my phone from Sophie's hands and clicks on something, before her eyes widen and she turns the screen round to show me one of the selfies Miles and I took together on our walk.

'There are loads of selfies of you together and your lipstick is smudged in this one!' she cries out, before examining the photo again and going through the photos with an expression of complete horror. 'I can't believe you and Miles . . . I can't believe it.'

If there wasn't anything at stake, I would have found Layla's horrified reaction really quite funny. Because the idea of me dating a famous musician would KILL her. It's bad enough that my nerdy twin sister, who she always used to take great pleasure in laughing at, is dating Chase Hunter, but if she discovered that I, her ex-best friend, was living HER dream of going out with someone famous then I seriously don't think she could handle it.

'This is AMAZING!' Sophie screams at the top of her lungs. 'That's why you don't want to ask him about any news! It's because YOU are the news!'

'No, you've got it wrong. We're not –'

'Why didn't you tell us?' Sophie claps her hands together. 'OMG maybe Layla and I could date the other two members of Chasing Chords! QUADRUPLE DATES!'

'Layla,' I say, watching her still examining my phone, 'can I have it back now?'

My phone suddenly rings. I freeze, thinking it might be Miles.

'It's Nina,' Layla tells me, holding the phone out.

I take it from her and answer under their scrutinizing gaze. At least Nina has bought me some time to work out what exactly I can tell them and how I can get out of this situation.

'Nancy? Can you talk?'

Nina's voice is raspy and wobbly, and I know immediately she's crying.

'I'll be back in a second,' I say to Layla and Sophie, before speaking into the receiver. 'Are you OK?'

I leave Layla's bedroom, closing the door behind me and walking down the hall before sitting on the top stair.

'What's wrong? What's happened?' I ask, listening to Nina's sniffles.

'It's so stupid, but I don't know what else I can do. I think I have to pull out of the showcase. Who am I kidding even trying for this summer school place?'

'Nina, calm down. Tell me what's happened to make you think like this.'

'It's Chase. He's not coming to the showcase. I can't do it without him, I just can't. And he doesn't get it. He doesn't think it's important, even though it's important to me. Things have been bad between us for a while and now this. He doesn't have time for me and I . . . I think that maybe it would be for the best if we broke up.'

She bursts into a fresh round of tears.

'Nina, it's OK. Deep breaths. Whatever happens, it will be OK,' I say in the most calming voice I can muster while feeling sick to my stomach for her. 'Why isn't Chase coming to the showcase?'

'Because he has to be at a press conference. They're announcing his solo career.'

'W-what?'

'Apparently, there's no other time they could do it. Mark is insisting that it has to be announced that day and Chase feels that there's nothing he can do –'

'Nina, are Chasing Chords . . . are they SPLITTING UP?! Chase is going SOLO?! WHAT?! I can't believe this! Oh my god, I don't know what to say!'

'I know. It's a long story,' Nina says sadly, and I suddenly feel terrible for focusing on that, which isn't even important right now.

The important thing is Nina and Chase. I don't have time to worry about the best band in the world splitting up and never hearing their music again. I'll have to worry about that colossal, horrific, life-changing news another time.

'I wish you were here. I could really do with a hug,' Nina admits. 'Nancy, I know it's a lot to ask, but could you –'

'I'm on my way,' I say, standing up and walking back towards Layla's room. 'I'll be there in a few hours. Don't worry, Nina – it will be OK.'

When I've hung up, I take a deep breath and push open Layla's door, knowing this isn't going to go down well.

'I have to go,' I say, preparing myself for Layla's wrath. 'Nina needs me. She's really upset. I'm so sorry, I promise I will work on the train. I'm sure that I can think –'

'It's no problem,' Layla says breezily. 'Nina needs you. We can handle the website.'

Sophie looks as stunned as I feel.

'You . . . you can?' I ask, gathering my stuff. 'Are you sure you don't mind?'

'Sure. If Nina's really upset, then you should go to her and help.' She raises her eyebrows at me. 'And there's no need to look so shocked.'

'No, I thought you'd be unhappy. We only have a few hours until the votes are counted and –'

'Look, Nancy,' Layla interrupts, her expression softening, 'when it comes to family, I get it. You should be there for your sister. We can handle the website.'

'Wow. Thanks,' I say, beaming at her.

'Nina may be a loser, but I hope she's OK,' Layla adds, sitting down at her desk. 'Now stop staring at me and go!'

'Thanks,' I say one last time, before racing out of the room and down the stairs.

I really didn't think there would be anything that could shock me more right now than the news that Chasing Chords is splitting up.

But Layla's just gone and done it.

Miles, I heard about the band and Chase going solo. Are you OK? I'm so sorry! No wonder you've had so much on. I just hope you're all right

I'm sorry I didn't tell you. I hope you understand why I didn't? We couldn't risk the press finding out and I'm still getting my head round such a big change. But yeah, I'm OK. Wish I could see you x

I'm on my way to London now to meet Nina. I could come find you afterwards?

I'd love that. Surely, this is going to be the perfect time

for the Sound of Music
impression? If ever I needed
to laugh . . .

Trust me, my terrible singing
would only make things worse

Can't wait to see you xxx

Same xxx

EXCLUSIVE!
CHASE HUNTER GOES SOLO!
Music Editor: Nancy Palmer

We can exclusively reveal that Chase Hunter, the lead
singer of Chasing Chords, is pursuing a SOLO career!
Although it has not yet been announced publicly, a
secret source has confirmed this HUGE NEWS that
Chase Hunter will be splitting up the famous band
known for their awesome songs, like 'Light the Way'
and 'Torn Up Inside'. Chasing Chords fans will surely be
devastated by the news but we also CAN'T WAIT for
Chase's new solo album!

YOU HEARD IT HERE FIRST!
ALL THAT GLITTERS, Number One for Hot Music Gossip!
DO YOU WANT THE LATEST MUSIC STUFF LIKE THIS
BEFORE ANYONE ELSE?
THEN DON'T FORGET TO VOTE FOR US ON THE
HOMEPAGE!

EXCLUSIVE!
CHASING CHORDS' MILES CAUGHT IN A KISS AND TELL!

All That Glitters can exclusively reveal that Miles Turner, drummer of Chasing Chords, has shared some SECRET KISSES with our very own music editor, Nancy Palmer. Click <u>HERE</u> for PROOF! Selfies together AND a video of the two on their ROMANTIC walk!

YOU HEARD IT HERE FIRST!
ALL THAT GLITTERS, Number One for Hot Music Gossip!
DO YOU WANT THE LATEST MUSIC STUFF LIKE THIS
BEFORE ANYONE ELSE?
THEN DON'T FORGET TO VOTE FOR US ON THE
HOMEPAGE!

CHAPTER NINETEEN

NINA

I pull myself together after sobbing down the phone to Nancy. Knowing that she is on her way to London makes me feel better. I don't want to handle this myself; I don't feel like I can. I decide to take Jimmy's advice and go for a wander. There is no point in trying to build up the excitement I'd had from speaking to Mr Rogers for my lesson. It had vanished as soon as Chase had told me what he was really thinking.

It's only a showcase.

All this time he has been pretending that he believed the showcase to be as important as I thought it was, but really in his head it was a silly concert compared to the real pressure and significance of his big new record deal. He's just been humouring me. With those few words, he'd made me feel so small. After I ran off, he messaged me, asking to meet him, saying he was sorry and that he didn't mean it. But I'm not sure what to believe. Maybe he did only say it in anger. Or maybe his anger revealed what he really thought.

Either way, I don't want to be around him.

After washing my face in the concert-hall bathrooms, I leave the building, walking without anywhere to go. I stop at a cafe to get a cup of hot chocolate and continue walking aimlessly until I find myself in front of St Paul's Cathedral. It's so beautiful, and I wonder why I haven't been to see it already, considering Guildhall is only a short walk away. My phone vibrates with a text from Nancy telling me that she is at Norwich station, about to get on a train. By the time she gets here, I'll have finished my lesson with Caroline and can spend some time with her before the group rehearsal this afternoon.

I get distracted from the magnificent St Paul's architecture by music and spot a busker down the way, singing and playing the guitar, drawing in a big crowd. I go over to watch her for a bit, trying to put my finger on why she is so good and then it dawns on me. The whole time I've been watching her, I haven't noticed if she's made any mistakes in the song or whether her singing is completely perfect; her love of her music is infectious and that's why all these people are stopping to listen.

My phone vibrates in my pocket and I reach for it, thinking it's Nancy. But it's Chase calling me. I ignore it. I'm not ready to talk to him. He rings again. And again. And then he sends a flurry of messages asking me where I am, saying that we need to talk. He's so determined to talk to me that I feel I need to reply otherwise he won't stop.

Nina

Maybe he is looking for me at Guildhall and is panicking about where I am.

> Chase, I'm OK. I'm at St Paul's
> Cathedral. I need some time to
> myself

I put my phone back in my pocket and continue to watch the busker dance around on the pavement to cheers and applause. My phone vibrates again.

> Don't move. I'm on my way

Part of me is annoyed that he isn't giving me the space I've requested, but part of me is desperate to see him and for him to tell me that everything is going to be OK between us; that it had just been a silly fight because we'd both felt under lots of pressure and taken it out on each other; that of course he will be there in the audience for my showcase, cheering me on and giving me the confidence to play.

But when I see him getting out of a sleek black car and walking towards me, I know that's not about to happen. His face may be partly shielded by his hoodie and sunglasses, but I can see his expression is thunderous.

'What has Nancy done?' he growls, beckoning for me to follow him, away from the crowd surrounding the busker.

'What are you talking about?'

He holds out his phone, which is open on the *All That Glitters* homepage. There are two new stories posted by Nancy. As soon as I see the headlines, my insides turn to ice. I read the posts over and over again to make sure I've understood them correctly, to make sure I'm not seeing things.

After I've read them so many times that my eyes hurt and seen the huge amount of comments building up underneath each one, there is one moment when I think: *How could Nancy do this?*

And the answer comes back straight away: *She couldn't.*

Nancy won't have published this. I don't know how the information is out there but Nancy would not have pressed upload on these posts, no matter how much she wants to win that competition.

But who could have published it but her? There are photos of her and Miles, and a video that no one else could have had. She didn't even tell ME about that date with Miles, so there's no way anyone else could have known.

I sit down on a bench outside the cathedral. My brain hurts. This day is going from bad to worse.

'Chase,' I say, looking up at him, 'you can't think Nancy would do this? There must be some mistake.'

'Who else could have done it? Who else would have that information? And the photos and the videos! Nina, the posts are under her name! Look!' He slumps down on the bench next to me. 'This is so bad. Everything's exploded. Miles stormed off; none of us know where he's gone. And the press is all over us. Trying to get here without anyone noticing was like a scene from *Mission: Impossible*. They've surrounded my home, the studios, everywhere. Mark is freaking out, trying to do some damage control. I thought Nancy was my friend.'

'She is your friend!' I protest. 'Chase, we need to speak to her. There'll be an explanation.'

'The only explanation is that she posted these stories to win that stupid competition she hasn't shut up about. All she cares about is getting attention.'

'Chase, stop. That's not true. If you'd give her the chance –'

'Come on, Nina,' he growls. 'You know as well as I do that she's hated you being in the spotlight. And this has given her the perfect chance to get ahead, so that everyone is talking about her again.'

'She wouldn't have done this,' I say desperately. 'She must have been tricked somehow!'

'How did she even know in the first place?' He takes off his sunglasses to look me in the eye, his blue eyes cold and angry. 'You told her, didn't you? Even though it was supposed to be a secret. Miles didn't tell her.'

I look down at the ground, my eyes filling with tears at his accusations. He's never spoken to me like this before.

'Yes, I told her this morning after our fight.'

'Right before the post went up,' he says, shaking his head. 'Brilliant. She didn't even hesitate to sell us out. How could you be so stupid as to tell her?'

'Because I trust her!' I yell, causing passers-by to glance curiously at us before scuttling on.

'That was your mistake, then,' he argues. 'She's not like you, Nina. Some people will do anything to get to the top. Trust me, in my industry you get that a lot.'

'She's not like that. There is an explanation for this, I know it. And I know that you know that, too! You trust her. You're just angry and upset. Please, calm down and think about it.'

'I don't have the luxury of calming down to think about it. I now have to deal with this craziness without any preparation, and so does the band.'

He shakes his head and puts his sunglasses back on.

'Tell her that she's caused a huge mess and I hope she's happy.'

He stands up, ready to leave.

'Chase, wait,' I say, grabbing his hand, but he pulls away.

'No, Nina. I have things to do.'

He walks to the car without stopping or looking back at me once. I watch the car pull away. My brain is spiralling with worry. Everything is out of my control and I'm here alone; I don't know what to do.

I start feeling dizzy and sick. It's getting harder to breathe. I suddenly feel very hot and I quickly take off my jacket, my hair sticking to the back of my neck as it grows damp with sweat. I panic as my throat begins to close up and my breath becomes short. I clutch the bench as though I might fall off it any second. I'm frightened.

I need Chase. I need him to come back.

But he's not going to come back. My phone, I need my phone. I fumble for it in my pocket and can see a long list of missed calls from Nancy and Mum. I press Nancy's name and hold the phone to my ear.

'Nina?' She answers the phone, her voice filled with panic. 'Nina, thank goodness. You have to believe me, but I didn't . . . Nina, are you OK? I can just hear you breathing. Nina, what's going on?'

'I . . . I can't . . .'

'Oh, Nina,' she says in a tearful voice. 'It's OK. You need to slow your breathing. Come on, breathe along with me. That's it. Really slow.'

'My throat . . .'

'Feels tight. I know. It's OK though. You need to slow your breathing and it'll feel better. Are you sitting down?'

'Y-yes,' I stammer.

'Good. That's good. It's OK. Keep breathing nice and slow. I'll do it with you.'

I sit on the bench, trying to inhale and exhale at the same time that I hear her doing it. Gradually, my head feels less blurry and the ringing in my ears gets quieter. Everything comes back into focus. My mouth is really dry and I realize that my cheeks are wet from tears.

'I need some water,' I whisper, my breathing back under control.

'Yes, you do. Can you get some?'

'Yes, there's a shop nearby,' I tell her.

'Give yourself a moment and when you feel up to it you can go get some. Do you feel better?'

'Yes. Thanks so much, Nancy.'

'It's all right,' she says. 'It's been a while since you've had a panic attack like that. I'm so sorry that I've caused this one. I'll be with you soon and we'll work it all out. Right?'

'Yeah,' I say, wiping the cold sweat from my forehead.

'Are you with someone?'

'No. No one's here. But I'm OK.'

'You're not OK. Is there anyone you can call to be with you until I get there?'

I think for a second. 'Yes. There is. I'll call them now.'

'I'll be with you soon, Nina.'

After she hangs up, I hesitate, wondering if I'm doing the right thing by calling Dad and asking him to come here. But there isn't anyone else I can think of right now. The first time I call, he doesn't pick up, so I try again. This time he picks up just before I'm about to hang up and tells me that he's coming out of a meeting. He has a bit of time before the next one, so he can swing by.

When a black car pulls up nearby a few minutes later, for a moment I think it might be Chase coming back to apologize and my heart skips. But Dad steps out, on his phone as usual, and I tell myself to stop being so stupid. Chase isn't coming back.

'Nina, hi,' Dad says, finishing his call and handing me a bottle of water.

'Thank you.' I smile weakly as he sits next to me. 'And thanks for coming.'

'As I said, I have a little time between meetings.' He checks his watch and then picks a bit of fluff off his pristine black city coat. 'How can I help? How's the practising going? Everything set for the showcase?'

'Oh, yeah, fine. Actually, I didn't ask you to come here because of that,' I say, a little confused that he didn't pick up on my tone over the phone. 'I just needed someone because I . . . well, I was having a panic attack.'

'About what? The showcase?' he asks, scrolling through an email. 'Nina, how many times do I need to tell you that you have it in the bag? I think the talent scouts would sign you now if they could, so the showcase is really a formality.'

'No,' I say, taken aback by his casual attitude towards me having a panic attack. 'I wasn't upset about the showcase. It's Chase.'

He looks up at that. 'What about him?'

'We had a fight. A big one. And –' my face crumples as the words come out, making it all more real – 'I'm not sure if we've broken up.'

'What? You've broken up?'

'I'm not sure, I think so. He just left and he was so cold. He wasn't himself and now I don't know what –'

'What happened?' Dad asks sharply.

My hands shaking slightly, I type Nancy's website into my phone and pass it to him so he can read the two articles. He raises his eyebrows as he scans them and then hands the phone back to me, a smile creeping across his face.

'I can't say I'm surprised! This is brilliant news, Nina. Why didn't you tell me about Chase's solo plans?'

'What? No, it's not good news. It's supposed to be a secret and they were going to do a press conference next week about it. Now, the secret is out and Chase is really angry.'

'Yes, but think what this will do for *you*,' he says, leaning back on the bench. 'Chase is doing a good PR job, I have to say. His name is once again big news. An excellent boost for your campaign.'

'My campaign?' I shake my head. 'Dad, I don't think you get it. Chase might have broken up with me over these stories. He's really angry at me and Nancy. I told him that there was no way Nancy wrote these posts and she would never do that to him, but he told me I was being stupid. He hurt me. I don't know what to do.'

Dad shrugs. 'Simple. Apologize.'

'Apologize,' I repeat slowly, staring at him.

'Apologize for defending Nancy. Whatever it takes for him to stay with you.' He swivels on the bench to face me properly. 'Look, I understand that in the heat of the moment you may have said some things, and it's understandable that your natural reaction would be to stick on Nancy's side. It's difficult to apologize after realizing you're wrong –'

'I'm not wrong,' I say sharply. 'Nancy wouldn't have done this.'

'Nina,' he says, exhaling loudly and shaking his head, 'you know as well as I do that she did.'

'No, she didn't.'

'Why wouldn't she?' He smiles, as though it's all a bit of a joke. 'This is a HUGE scoop! Handed to her on a plate. You told me that her website was doing well; think how it's doing now! It was a smart move on her part, especially if they were going to do a press conference next week. She simply let the cat out of the bag a few days earlier than planned. Hardly a problem for the band, but a big story for her. I'm impressed.'

'Dad,' I say sternly, wondering if I'm hearing him right, 'Nancy didn't do this. She would never do that to Chase. She would never do that to Miles, and she would NEVER do this to me. I don't know how this happened, but I'm not wrong about that.'

He purses his lips together.

'You don't know her,' I add quietly.

'All right, Nina, believe what you want,' he says, holding up his hands. 'I think that you'll find this is a big fuss over nothing. You'll feel better once you've made up with Chase. I can drop you at his place now, if you give me the address.'

'He doesn't want to see me.'

'Of course he does! You just need to remind him. Do whatever it takes. It's important.'

Another email pops up on his phone and he curses when he sees who it is, before grumbling about clients who won't stop pestering, typing a reply at the same time. I watch him curiously, doubts beginning to creep into my head that I can't shake.

'Dad,' I begin, without him looking up, 'why do you want me to do whatever it takes to get back with Chase? Why is it so important that we don't break up?'

He snorts, still typing on his phone. 'That's a silly question.'

'I mean it. Why do you think it's important?'

'Well, you like him,' he says, putting his phone down and looking up at me. 'And, trust me, life will be much harder if you don't have Chase by your side.'

'Why do you think that?'

'Because if you lose Chase, you're throwing everything away!' he says, exasperated at having to say it out loud. 'It's not worth losing your career over something your sister has done.'

'I'm sorry,' I say slowly, trying to work out what he's saying. 'You think by losing Chase, I'd be throwing away my career?'

'Of course. Don't be naive, Nina. It's because of Chase that you're in the limelight in the first place. Your relationship is a big pull for future agents and music labels.

You already have a platform, thanks to him, which is the hardest part. It's an excellent start, but if things go south with Chase, who knows how long that will last?' He takes a deep breath. 'The good news is that this whole publicity stunt has happened right before your showcase. I wouldn't be surprised if we have paparazzi showing up in hordes now, along with a lot of people from the industry. I might try calling a couple of contacts today, actually, while this news about Chase's solo career is breaking. Do you think he can come to your showcase? It would be good to have his weight thrown behind it.'

'So you think, even if I'm not sure how I feel, I should do everything in my power to stay with Chase because it would help my career?'

'Yes, of course,' he replies without hesitation. 'You have to stay relevant and Chase helps you to do that. Why else do you think I posted that photo of you two in the cafe online a few weeks ago?'

His words hit me so hard it feels like the breath has been knocked out of me.

'The photo of us in the cafe,' I say, feeling sick to my stomach. 'You were the one who took that photo of me and Chase through the window and then you put it up online. Right before you showed up on our doorstep in Norfolk and asked to be part of our lives again.'

He smiles, tapping the side of his nose. 'Nina, if there's one thing I've learned in my career, it's that you want people talking about you, no matter what they're saying. If they're not talking about you, you're irrelevant. It was a good photo, I thought, and got you and Chase to the top of everyone's newsfeeds.'

It's as though a veil has been lifted. Suddenly everything becomes horribly clear. I stare at him as he gets back to his phone. He was absolutely right, what he said before. I am naive. I've been terribly naive. But not about everything else. About him.

'Can I ask you a question?' I say, building up the courage to confront him. 'If you lost me right now, would you be losing a daughter or a business opportunity?'

'What?' He rolls his eyes. 'Nina, don't be so sensitive.'

'I've been so stupid. You even told us when you first came to our house. You saw the video of me and Chase on YouTube and that's what brought you back into my life. That's when you came looking for me at Guildhall.' I shake my head at him, wishing that I was wrong but knowing in my gut that I'm right. 'How could you do this to me?'

He looks at me as though I'm mad. 'I saw my daughter needed guidance and I knew that with my help you had a chance of making something of yourself! I've done everything in my power to help you get ahead. It was me who saw your potential.'

'What about Nancy?'

'What?'

'I said, what about Nancy?' I feel the anger bubbling inside me. 'Do you see her potential?'

'Well, she's certainly shown initiative today,' he says, looking confused. 'Nina, what's going on? Do you want me to help Nancy with her journalism career? Is that what this is about?'

'This is about being a dad!' I cry. 'This is about seeing me as me and not a way of making money! This is about wanting to make an effort with Nancy, no matter what her ambitions or talents are! What if I told you that I didn't want a career in music? What if I told you I don't want a career in anything?'

'I would say that you're being very dramatic,' he says wearily, glancing at his watch. 'Nina, I really don't have time for this. You need to be realistic here.'

'And what about that story you told me about growing your business. That wasn't the whole truth, was it? You didn't do so well that your ex-business partner's clients came to you. You went behind his back and took them. Then you let his company fail. He was your friend!'

He shrugs. 'That's business. That's how it works.'

'What about loyalty? You were in it together. But you were happy to tread all over him in the name of ambition.'

'That's the only way of getting to where you want to be! Nina, what's this all about? I really don't have the time to –'

'Why did you come back?' I yell, making everyone nearby stop and stare. 'Just, please, tell me why you came back into my life now?'

'Because you had a bright career ahead of you!' he cries in frustration, his cheeks growing pink at the unwanted attention from strangers around us. 'But you had to strike while the iron was hot, and I knew that I could help you do that.'

'You came back because you thought I could be famous. Another brilliant business venture for you to get your hands on.' I shake my head. 'I was going to be a big star some day, right?'

He looks at me. 'I don't know what you're expecting me to say. I think you need to drink that water. I'll drop you at Chase's and we'll get this mess sorted out.'

'Thanks, but no thanks,' I say, standing up. 'I'm going back to Guildhall. Alone. I don't need your help any more.'

'Nina,' he says, sighing. 'What is wrong with you?'

'I didn't want you to help me with my career. I just wanted you to be my dad. I thought you wanted that, too. I was wrong. This time I'm walking away from *you*. For good.'

'Don't be stupid, Nina,' he says, his expression caught between irritation and amusement. 'You need me to get you to where you want to be. How else are you going to do it?'

'You're wrong. I don't need you and I don't need Chase to get to where I want to be. I can do that myself. I'd forgotten that important fact, but you've helped to remind me. Bye, Dad.'

I turn on my heel and start walking. He doesn't call out for me to stop. He doesn't run after me telling me I'm wrong. I don't need to look back to know that he'll go to his car, make a few phone calls and drive off.

And even though the truth really hurts, even though I feel like I've lost my dad all over again, as I walk down that busy London road, I feel stronger than I've ever felt before.

At least I have him to thank for that.

CHAPTER TWENTY

NANCY

Oh my god. *Oh my god.*

Everything has gone wrong and I've never felt so powerless.

I don't know what to do. I can't go anywhere because I'm stuck on this train, which feels like it's taking forever to get to London. I know that Nina is in a state and I can't do anything about it. I can't bear that she's on her own, having a panic attack and all I can do is sit here and *wait*. Miles won't pick up his phone. I've tried a hundred times and I know there's no use in trying any more. He doesn't want to speak to me. He thinks I'm a sellout. He thinks I've used him for a story. He thinks I don't really care about him. I tried calling Chase and he won't pick up to me, either. They all hate me. They've got it all wrong and I can't do anything.

I look out of the train window, tears streaming down my cheeks. I feel so ashamed and hurt, and the worst thing is that I keep getting messages from people at school telling me how amazing I am and how brilliant the scoops are.

Nancy

Anyone would think I was having a wonderful day, judging by the comments that keep appearing under the stories:

OMG CAN'T BELIEVE THIS!! Nancy you are SO AMAZING! ILY!! XXXX

Nancy and Miles 4EVA!!! The cutest couple!!! Nancy, I go to your school and I just want to say that you are an inspiration!!! Xxx

Can't believe Chase is doing a solo album!! Nancy, do you know when he's releasing his first solo single??? Let us knoooooooow!!!!

Nancy, I am the year below you at school and your BIGGEST FAN! Can you ask Chasing Chords to do a final show in Norwich before they split up? PLEASE REPLY!! xx

My questions is, WHEN are the Palmer girls going to join together for their own YouTube channel?! Nina is with Chase and Nancy is with Miles?! THE COOLEST SISTERS EVERRRRRRRRR xoxo

Omg, that video is too adorable. Nancy and Miles are made for one another!! Someone start an Insta account of photos of them together PLEASE! XXX

OH MY GOD I GO TO SCHOOL WITH THE PALMER GIRLS!! Nancy is my biggest inspiration!!! She is so cool and pretty in real life!!! WE LOVE YOU!!

I have finally got the response I wanted, but now I don't want it at all. Not for this. I can't read any more of them.

I just want Miles to talk to me.

I called Layla as soon as my phone went mental with the stories going online, but she's not answering my calls or messages. I sent her and Sophie an essay of a message saying that they'd ruined everything and that I would never forgive them for going behind my back and doing this. They've read the message but neither of them replied.

It's so obvious from the writing that I didn't put up those posts. Who uses that many exclamation points? And capitalizes random words? No thought has been put into the writing at all. I suppose they were in such a rush to upload them that they didn't make much effort. If I wasn't so upset about the people they've hurt through the stories, I'd be furious about how badly written the stories are – all done under my name.

I begged them to take them down but it's too late. Both stories have gone stratospheric. They're everywhere. Layla and Sophie's horrible plan has worked. *All That Glitters* is the hottest music site on the internet right now. I've got DMs from every paper and magazine you can think of asking me to spill the beans on my romance with Miles, or asking for more details about Chase going solo.

I don't even want to THINK about the chaos that Miles and Chase are in, either. The press will be all over them and they're going to blame me.

Miles must think I'm the worst person on the planet. Nothing has really started between us and now it's gone forever. I use my sleeve to wipe my tears as I scroll through my sent messages and there it is, right at the top: the video and photos of Miles and me, sent to Layla's number, at the exact time that Layla was holding my phone, right before Nina called and she gave it back.

'Here you go.'

I jump out of my skin as a hand holding a tissue appears in front of my face. A man sitting on the train seat opposite has noticed I'm crying and is coming to my sleeve's rescue.

'Thanks,' I croak, taking it gratefully.

He smiles kindly at me and then takes his seat again, getting out his book. Suddenly a text from Miles comes through. My breath catches as I open it, hoping that he's realized I would never do this to him, but the blood in my veins turns to ice as I read his cold tone:

> My publicist requests you don't
> talk to any press

I quickly reply, knowing that he's at his phone and will read it. My fingers are shaking as I type.

> I didn't write those stories. You
> have to believe me. Please, Miles.
> Please speak to me

331

The longest minute in the world passes before my phone pings in reply.

> Even if you didn't, you showed
> someone those photos and that
> video. You told someone the info
> about me and about Chase.
> I'm turning off my phone.
> Don't contact me again

My face crumples and I let out a loud sob, shoving my phone in my bag and then leaning my head in my hands, wishing I could go back in time. I wish I'd never let Layla near my phone. I wish that when I'd been speaking to Nina on the phone, that I had kept my voice down. That I hadn't reacted so dramatically to what she was telling me to the point where I repeated her words out loud for anyone to overhear. I wish I hadn't been so naive when Layla said that I could go and look after Nina. By then, she and Sophie had everything they needed to cause this media storm and make our website a big hit.

As the train pulls into Liverpool Street station, I want to get on one right back to Norwich, head home and never leave my room again. But when I get off the train and go through the barriers, Nina is standing there, waiting for me.

I walk over to her and she doesn't say anything; she just pulls me into a hug. We stand like that for ages. When she pulls away, she can't help but laugh as she realizes we're both crying.

'Look at us,' she says, getting out a tissue and handing it to me. 'We're such a mess.'

'Nina, you must be so angry at me.'

'No.' She shakes her head. 'I know you didn't write those stories.'

'Layla tricked me.'

'I guessed that already,' she says. 'We have a lot to talk about. I know a great cafe nearby, if you're up for a hot chocolate?'

I nod and she links her arm through mine, leading us to the escalator. Even though everything is awful right now, I feel that little bit better seeing Nina and am so grateful for her. How could I ever have grown apart from my twin, the one person by my side no matter what?

'I've made things worse for you and Chase, haven't I?' I say as we walk down a quiet street off the busy road. 'That's why you had the panic attack. Are you OK?'

She nods, holding open the cafe door for me. 'Yes, thanks to you talking me through it.'

While I go to the bathroom to wash my face and redo my make-up, Nina orders two hot chocolates at the counter and then we find a nice, quiet table in the corner, away from the window.

'I'm so sorry, Nina,' I say, holding the warm mug in my hands. 'I've ruined everything.'

'No, you haven't.'

'Layla took my phone and she saw that video. I did try to get my phone back from her, but she and Sophie wouldn't let me. She sent it to herself without me knowing and then when we spoke on the phone she must have overheard everything. I swear, I didn't write those stories. I've asked her to take them down but she won't, and now it's too late. I'm so sorry, Nina. You had a horrible panic attack because of me.'

'No, it wasn't you. It was a buildup of everything. And, anyway, if anyone needs to apologize, it's me.' She takes a deep breath. 'I just saw Dad and it turns out that he's exactly the person you thought he was. I have been so wrong about him.'

I stare at her. 'What happened?'

'He's not interested in being our dad. Only interested in being the dad of a famous pop star.'

'Oh.' I take a sip of my hot chocolate and place the mug down on the table. 'Are you OK?'

'I think so. You?'

I take a moment to think about my answer. 'I guess I didn't have the chance to really connect with him again. I'm disappointed he has met my expectations, but I let him go a long time ago. Still hurts a bit, though. Rejection is never nice, especially not from your own dad. It made it worse that he wanted you but not me.'

'I let myself get caught up in the idea of him being around again at the cost of your feelings,' she says, shutting her eyes in anger at herself. 'I was so naive. You must think I'm such an idiot.'

'I don't think that. It makes sense that he'd be more interested in you than me. You're the interesting one with the big, bright future.'

'Nancy,' she begins, looking me straight in the eye, 'I'm really sorry that I didn't push for him to make an effort with you, too. It must have been so hurtful and he never should have made you feel like that, and neither should I. If it makes you feel any better, I'm never going to let him into our lives again. Not that I imagine he'll try that hard. I can't believe he came back just for the fame and the idea of making more money.' She shakes her head. 'I got him so wrong.'

'We don't need him,' I say quietly but firmly. 'We never did.'

'I know that now.'

'And Chase?' I say, watching her carefully. 'What's going on with him?'

Her forehead creases and I know she's trying her best not to cry.

'He's very upset about everything.'

'It's all my fault,' I say desperately. 'Don't worry, I'll tell him that you didn't do anything. I'll explain what happened and when he knows everything, he'll realize that none of this is because of you. He can be angry at me instead.'

'It's not only this, though,' she explains. 'It's everything. Tension has been building for a while and maybe this was the excuse he needed to end things.'

'I don't believe that,' I tell her. 'And I don't think you do either.'

'We'll see.'

'Nina?'

A tall woman with jet-black hair sleeked back into a ponytail and incredible bone structure comes over to our table holding a take-away coffee cup. Everything about her screams authority, even the way she holds herself. I hope I have this exact vibe some day. Nina instantly straightens up and blushes.

'Hi,' Nina squeaks. 'How are you?'

'I'm good, thank you. I've just come from a meeting.' She looks over at me. 'You must be Nina's twin sister.'

'Um, yes, sorry,' Nina says, stumbling over her words. 'This is Nancy. Nancy, this is Caroline Morreau; she's the director of music at Guildhall.'

'It's nice to meet you,' I say, shaking her hand.

'And you. I've seen your website. It's very good.'

I glance at Nina, assuming she must have told Caroline about *All That Glitters* for her to know about it, but from her expression I can see she had no idea.

'My daughter is a big fan of Tyler Hill,' Caroline explains, noting our surprise. 'She showed me the exclusive piece you wrote about her fashion line. When I realized it was written by Nina's twin sister, I was intrigued by your other music posts. It's nice to meet an aspiring music journalist.'

I drop my eyes to the floor. 'Actually, after someone posted under my name this morning, I won't be writing about music ever again. No one will take me seriously as a music journalist any more.'

'I'm sorry to hear that,' she says, watching me curiously. 'The piece under your name about how music makes you feel was very beautiful and poignant. Not easy to write either. I take it you were actually the author of that piece?'

I nod. 'Yes, that one was me. You liked it?'

'I did. You clearly have a talent for writing about music. It's a shame you're giving up. I was hoping to see more posts along those lines or perhaps invite you to write about some of the goings-on at Guildhall. It's always good to find someone who really gets it. Oh well, never mind.' She checks her watch. 'Ah, I better be getting back. I've got plenty of paperwork to do that will keep me from sitting in on your group rehearsal, Nina. Something I expect you'll be leaving for any minute, so as not to be late?'

'Yes.' Nina nods, blushing. 'Straight away.'

'I'm pleased to see your time-keeping has improved. Nice to meet you, Nancy.'

When she walks out, Nina's shoulders visibly relax.

'Caroline seems nice,' I say, watching her go.

'Yeah, if you're not one of her students,' Nina says. 'I mean, she's great, but she's ever so slightly intimidating. I'm sorry I have to leave you to get to rehearsal. I promise as soon as I get out we can talk everything through.'

'That's all right – I'll come to meet you in reception. I'll find something to do until then.'

She raises her eyebrows at me. 'Are you going to try to speak to Miles? Once you've explained, he'll understand, I know he will. He'll just need time.'

'I don't know,' I say into my mug. 'But I have to keep trying to make things right. Oh, and before you go, when I rushed home this morning to grab my bag before getting the train, Mum asked me to give this to you. Apparently Mr Rogers dropped it off at the shop this morning.'

I reach into my bag and hand her the large, thin envelope Mum had insisted I take with me. She opens it and then breaks into a smile as she pulls out what looks like a few sheets of crumpled paper with a sticky note on the front.

'What is it?' I ask.

'Some sheet music, that's all,' she explains, her eyes glistening. 'Thanks for bringing it.'

She gets up and comes over to give me another hug before telling me she'll see me in an hour or so after her practice. I wave to her as she walks out of the door, the envelope of sheet music tucked safely under her arm. I finish the last gulp of my hot chocolate, and get my phone out with a fresh wave of determination.

But I don't call Miles. I know there's no point. None of the members of Chasing Chords have any interest in speaking to me right now.

Instead I call someone who I know will always pick up his phone, no matter what, no matter how much he dislikes me. Because I know that he'll want to fix things as much as I do.

Walking into the record store, I'm hit by that same dusty smell that Nina finds so comforting. It's much bigger than the one on our village high street but I suppose that's hardly a surprise as this one is in London. I have to walk down a few aisles before I spot him right at the back, his hood up, headphones on. He doesn't hear me approach him. I tap him on the shoulder and he spins round, scowling when he sees it's me.

'What are you doing here?' Chase says, pulling his headphones down round his neck. 'How did you find me?'

'I spoke to Mark. When Nina was in that coma, you gave me his number in case I couldn't reach you.'

'Why did he tell you where I was?' he asks irritably. 'I said I wanted some time to myself.'

'He's worried about you. So, even though he hates my guts right now, he was more than happy to tell me where you'd be in the hope I might persuade you to stop brooding in an old record store and actually go and help him sort out this mess.'

Chase narrows his eyes at me. 'The mess you caused.'

'Chase, do you really think I wrote those stories?'

He pushes his hands into his pockets and lifts his eyes to the ceiling.

'Honestly,' I continue, when he doesn't say anything, 'now that you've had some time to really think about it, do you believe I wrote that story about you? And that story about Miles? Do you think I would do that to you and Nina? Do you think I'd go out of my way to destroy whatever it is I had with Miles for the chance of winning a competition?'

He lets out a long sigh and then finally lowers his eyes to meet mine.

'No,' he says, his face softening. 'No, I don't.'

'You still have the right to be angry at me, though. I was careless about something very important, and I trusted people I shouldn't have. So, though I didn't write those stories, I am really sorry for this whole mess.'

He nods slowly but doesn't say anything.

'None of this is Nina's fault. That's what I came here to say. She didn't tell me about your solo career for some gossip or anything like that. She let it slip this morning when she was upset about you arguing, and then it was me who talked about it so loudly that someone overheard who shouldn't have. You can be mad at me, but please don't be mad at her. Also, I don't really know what's going on between you and Nina right now, but can I give you my opinion on the matter?'

'Do I have a choice?'

'No, because I think you need to hear it. It's important to have an outsider's point of view every now and then. Also, I don't care what you musicians say, the answers do not always lie in dusty old record stores.' I glance around the shop and wrinkle my nose. 'Speaking of which, did you have to be so predictable and come here to do your brooding?'

He tries to suppress a smile, but he can't help it. 'Go on then, Nancy. What is this important opinion of yours?'

'Don't focus so much on the future that you mess up everything in the present. That's what I'm taking from today, and I think you should, too. It's easy to forget about what's really important, and then realize too late that you've lost it. Pop stars always sing about stuff like that. You would know.'

'Wise words. I'll think about it.'

'Promise me that, whatever else is going on with you two, you'll forgive Nina for telling me about the solo thing? It really wasn't her fault. I can't emphasize that enough. You can trust her. Chase –' I push for an answer – 'promise me.'

'All right,' he says eventually. 'I promise.'

'Thank you. I'll let you get back on with your brooding over dusty old records now.'

'Hey,' he calls after me as I'm walking away. I turn round to face him. 'What have you lost?'

'Huh?' I check I've still got my handbag round my shoulder. 'No, I've got everything.'

'You said that today has taught you that it's easy to lose something important,' he says, coming towards me, his piercing blue eyes boring into mine. 'What is it that you've lost?'

I smile sadly at him, my heart sinking as I speak.

'It's not what I've lost. It's who I've lost.'

He nods in understanding. 'You know, this is the second time you've come looking for me to fight for me and your sister. The last time I didn't even realize you existed.'

I smile, remembering when I barged into the studio to tell Chase that Nina was in a coma and he needed to come and be at her side right away.

'It's funny,' he continues, 'you were so determined then, just like you are now. Nothing was going to stop you from getting what you wanted. You weren't going to leave that studio until I came to the hospital and right now you weren't going to leave without me promising to forgive Nina for a mistake that you think is your fault.'

'Yeah, well.' I shrug. 'You know me.'

'I do,' he says, folding his arms. 'And that's why I'm so surprised you're giving up so easily on the person you think you've lost.'

'There's nothing I can do, Chase.' I sigh, wishing that we weren't talking about this because it makes everything hurt and my eyes well up all over again. 'I can't bounce back from this. That story is mortifying, and so personal with the video and everything. He doesn't want to speak to me; he doesn't want anything to do with me and with good reason. *I* wouldn't want to speak to me if I was in his shoes. He'll stay mad at me forever. There's nothing I can do.'

'Really? Nothing?' He stares at me as though I'm supposed to be getting something, but my mind is completely blank. 'Nothing you can do to stop him being mad at you?'

I'm about to tell him no, when something clicks. Suddenly, standing in the middle of that dusty old record store with Chase Hunter watching me with a knowing smile, it dawns on me what I have to do.

Well, this is going to be interesting.

School News Blog: Updated 15:00

WINNER OF THE DISNEY INTERNSHIP COMPETITION ANNOUNCED!

Votes have been counted and I am delighted to announce the winning website of our Disney internship competition: ALL THAT GLITTERS! Congratulations to Layla, Sophie and Nancy, who will all be working hard at the Disney Channel this coming Easter holiday, and congratulations to runner-up Jimmy Morton for his brilliant website, JIMMY'S JOURNAL. Thank you to all who voted and well done to all our finalists for their hard work and fantastic creativity.

Carolyn Coles, Headmistress

CHAPTER TWENTY-ONE

NINA

'I made cupcakes.'

Mum places a tray down on the sitting-room table, on which there are three mugs of steaming hot chocolate and a plate of pink-iced, sprinkled cupcakes.

'I was going to get you a congratulations cake, Nancy, like the one you got Nina,' she continues, passing us our mugs and then sitting in the armchair opposite us on the sofa, 'but I felt like baking myself. I hope that's OK! We're so proud of you for winning the competition. And I'm sorry these are a little late. I should have baked them at the weekend when you were announced as the winner, but with everything that happened, I couldn't find the time . . . Well, anyway, congratulations, darling!'

'We really are so proud of you, Nancy,' I say cheerily. 'I knew you could do it. *All That Glitters* is brilliant, and mostly because of your content.'

Nancy smiles. 'Thanks. But –'

She looks down at her hands, frowning.

'What's wrong?' Mum asks.

'I don't deserve congratulatory cupcakes.'

'What?' I laugh. 'Why not?'

'It doesn't feel right!' She sighs. 'I don't know. I didn't want to win like this. By leaking personal information about people I care about in order to get enough clicks.'

'But you didn't leak that information. We know that,' I say, as Mum nods in agreement. 'And you can't let that take away from all your hard work on the website this term. The rest of your content was really good.'

'Absolutely,' Mum says. 'I think you would have won even if those stories hadn't been posted. Everyone loved your music posts!'

Nancy attempts a weak smile. 'Thanks, Mum. And the cupcakes look great.'

As I hold up my mug of hot chocolate to cheers Nancy, Mum takes a deep breath.

'Girls, I wanted to give you some time and space after such an eventful weekend, you know, to get your heads in order, but, as it's the middle of the week and we're all home, I thought this evening would be a good time to talk about your father and everything that happened.'

She takes a moment. Her expression is full of concern and her eyes are glistening with tears that she's trying to hold back.

'I wanted to say . . . I'm so sorry, to both of you,' she says quietly, shaking her head. 'I should have protected you from him. I can't believe what happened outside St Paul's Cathedral, Nina. The way it all came out. And, Nancy, that he should have treated you so badly –' she pauses, collecting herself – 'I shouldn't have let any of this happen.'

'Mum,' I say quickly, unable to bear how upset she is, 'none of this is your fault at all.'

'Yeah,' Nancy agrees. 'You giving us the choice to have him back in our lives, even after everything he's done to you, was so brave. Seriously, you are so strong.'

'I couldn't agree more,' I say firmly. 'And you can't protect us from everything. We had to see his true colours for ourselves.'

Mum smiles weakly at us. 'I'm still sorry this happened. He really doesn't deserve you.'

'He *definitely* never deserved you,' Nancy states.

'If anyone should be apologizing, it's me,' I say, putting my mug back down. 'I'm the one who got sucked in. I'm the one who wasn't brave enough to question his motives.'

'You know what?' Nancy says, putting a hand on my shoulder. 'Let's stop blaming ourselves, shall we? This was all on him.'

'You're right, Nancy,' Mum says, getting up and coming to plonk herself down between us on the sofa. She puts her arms round our shoulders and pulls us to her. 'If anything, he's just shown that, no matter what, our family is stronger than ever.'

'Exactly.' I smile, nestling into her shoulder. 'Nothing can break us. Certainly not *him*.'

'Right, now that's out of the way,' Mum says, pulling her arms back so she can dab her eyes with a tissue from her pocket, 'who would like a cupcake?'

'I'd love one!' I say, picking one from the plate she offers.

'You're only allowed one, Nina, if you don't eat it like a squirrel,' Nancy says.

'I do NOT eat like a squirrel,' I protest, nibbling the edge.

'How is everything with Chase, Nina?' Mum asks, giving Nancy a cupcake and then taking one for herself. 'Have you sorted everything out?'

'Things are better, thanks to Nancy.' I smile, making her blush. 'I know I've already said it, but thanks for going to speak to him.'

She shrugs. 'No problem. It was my fault in the first place. Have you guys talked everything out now?'

'We've chatted on the phone a few times, but he's been really busy and I've got my performance to focus on . . .'

'Speaking of which, is he coming to the showcase this weekend?' Mum asks hopefully.

'Fingers crossed. Obviously the press conference has already been held since the news came out a little earlier than expected, so technically it solves the problem of him being free on Saturday.' I let out a sigh. 'But, because the news is so huge, there's been a hundred press requests that have come flooding in and he's swamped. The whole band has been manic all week.'

'That doesn't surprise me. They must have had even more reporters bothering them than we've had,' Mum notes, rolling her eyes. 'Thank goodness they've lost interest as the week's gone on. Some of them even pretended to be customers coming into the shop!'

'I suppose they realized that they weren't going to get any comments from us and the only pictures they'd get were of Nina and me going to and from school,' says Nancy. 'Not exactly that interesting. Although it was quite funny seeing our headmistress giving them that big telling-off on Monday when one of them dared set a foot inside the school gates.'

I giggle. 'They were terrified of her! Celebrities should hire her whenever the paparazzi are bothering them.'

'And what about Miles?' Mum says, turning to Nancy. 'Have you spoken?'

She shakes her head. 'He's still angry at me. But don't worry – I've got a plan to try to win him over.'

Mum and I share a confused look.

'You do?' I ask. 'What is it?'

'You'll see,' she says, finishing her last bite of cupcake and then snuggling into Mum. 'But trust me – if it doesn't get his attention, then nothing will.'

The sound of Caroline's heels crossing the stage echoes through the silence around the concert hall. The spotlight follows her to where she stops, centre stage.

Nina

'Good evening, I am very pleased and proud to welcome you to our showcase this evening. The students have worked very hard this term and we could not be happier with their progress. Tonight, you will be witnessing some very bright stars of the future and I'm sure that their talent will blow you away . . .'

Deciding not to listen to the rest of her welcome speech as it's making me too nervous, I duck out of the wings and down the steps into the green room where some other students, also too nervous to wait in the wings, are milling around, preparing themselves for their performance. Grace is standing in a corner doing some breathing exercises. She grins as I walk in and beckons me over to her.

'How are you feeling?' she asks, shaking out her hands.

'Like I'm about to throw up everywhere,' I say, clutching my crumpled sheet music.

'Me too,' says Grace. 'I think that's the adrenaline. Apparently, it's a good thing. Did you get a glimpse of the audience?'

'I tried but the lights are shining too brightly on to the stage. I can't see any faces. When they were all coming in it sounded like there were a lot of people.'

'Nico told me that a few journalists tried to sneak in as audience members, but the Matchmaker gave them some very stern words and sent them packing,' Grace says with a grin. 'He said one of them looked as though they might start crying. Apparently it was very entertaining. I wouldn't like to be on the Matchmaker's bad side!'

'Me neither,' I say. 'Although I think a few reporters are still lurking outside hoping for a picture.'

'Do you think Chase is in the audience?' she asks carefully.

'I don't know,' I admit. 'I hope so; he messaged this morning saying he was going to try to make it, but –' I take a deep breath and roll my shoulders back confidently – 'it doesn't matter whether he's in the audience or not. I know I can do this by myself.'

'Too right you can,' she says, before noticing someone over my shoulder. 'Oh, it looks like the Matchmaker wants a word with you before you go on.'

I turn round to see Caroline watching us by the door of the green room. She must have finished her welcome speech and the first student must be onstage. I'm up second. As she catches my eye, she gestures for me to join her.

'I better go,' I groan, dreading whatever Caroline is going to say. 'When are you onstage?'

'Right after you.' Grace smiles. 'Don't raise the bar too high, Palmer.'

I grin at her and then reluctantly leave her to her breathing exercises and walk to where Caroline is patiently waiting, her arms folded.

'Are you ready?' she asks, eyeing me up and down.

I nod. 'I think so. I don't really have the time not to be ready now. I'm onstage in a few minutes.'

'Yes,' Caroline says thoughtfully. 'I wanted to speak to you before you went on.'

'I'm not sure I'll be able to remember any last-minute corrections,' I say hurriedly, knowing that if she points a mistake out now, I might lose my focus on everything else.

'It's not a correction.' She takes a deep breath. 'Nina, did I ever tell you why I liked your audition?'

I shake my head.

'I saw something in you, Nina Palmer,' she says, prodding my arm. 'A connection to the music. And then you came here and spent your time trying to be someone that you're not. Music doesn't hide us; it opens us up. It makes us vulnerable and it also makes us powerful. That's what I've been trying to teach you, along with all the technical work. And I wanted to say that in this morning's dress run, you got it. I saw that you had finally got it.'

I smile. 'I was reminded recently why I played the piano in the first place.'

'Good. And you've been practising so much over the term that your technical ability has come on beautifully.' She leans down to look me right in the eye. 'You're a wonderful pianist, Nina, with great potential. I would like to work with you further and see what you can really do.'

'You would?' I whisper, hardly daring to believe what she's saying.

'I would,' she says without hesitation.

'Nina Palmer!' A girl with a headset on pokes her head through the door to the green room. 'Nina Palmer is on next.'

'She's coming,' Caroline tells her, before turning back to me and holding out her hands. 'Do you need your sheet music?'

'No,' I say, passing it to her. 'I don't think so.'

'I didn't think you did. Now, off you go. Good luck.'

'Thanks, Caroline,' I say, beaming up at her. 'And thank you for everything this term, for being so patient with me. I hope my lessons weren't too much hard work.'

She lets out a 'Ha!' and then shakes her head. She holds open the door for me and speaks in a low voice, so no one else can hear, 'Try teaching Jordan. Now, *that* is hard work.'

I'm still smiling to myself at her comment as I walk up the steps to the wings and it's only when I look out at the piano sitting in the middle of the stage that I realize I'm about to do this. My whole body tenses and my stomach starts churning. My hands begin to shake and I can't stop it. The loud applause – and I mean loud; there must be a LOT of people in that audience – for the first student eventually dies down and Caroline steps out to announce my name as the next performer.

Wondering whether I should run away, the concert hall erupts into applause and Caroline walks back off the stage towards me.

'You're OK,' she says. 'You're doing what you love. Yes?'

'I'm doing what I love,' I repeat hoarsely.

Nina

TJ, Nico, Florence and Grace gather around me in the wings and start clapping along with the audience encouragingly. Caroline places a hand on my back and gives me a gentle nudge forward on to the stage. I stumble into the spotlight and take my place at the piano stool. I don't look out at the audience as the room descends into silence. I don't bow or introduce myself. I close my eyes, take a deep breath and open them again, ready to focus. My neck damp with sweat and my mouth so dry that I can't swallow, I put my hands up on to the piano keys.

This is it. I've been working towards this. And here I am. On my own. At this beautiful piano. I forget about Dad and how much he's hurt me. I forget about my relationship problems with Chase. I forget about trying to get a place on the Guildhall summer school. I forget about everything except for the one thing Caroline reminded me of: I'm here, doing what I love.

I start playing my favourite Austin Golding song. The music that Mr Rogers had put into that envelope with a scribbled note that read: *I think you've been looking for this.*

I have no idea if I'm playing well. I'm so lost in the song that I don't think about whether I'm getting everything right; or whether I'm remembering all those scribbles I wrote in the margins of the music; or whether my facial expression is attractive when I play; or if everyone will think that this music is too easy and simple for a Guildhall student.

I don't care about any of that. I'm loving every moment of it. The acoustics in the hall are incredible and the music sounds so beautiful in here. A rush of warmth flows through me as I play. When I come to the end of the piece, I've forgotten there's an audience at all.

I play the last note, which echoes through the silence. I let it linger and then take my foot off the pedal. The hall suddenly erupts into cheers and applause, and I remember what's happening. Hurriedly standing up, I look out at a sea of faces and my legs instantly turn to jelly. Steadying myself by placing one hand on the piano, I do an awkward bow thing and then race off the stage as quickly as possible, straight into the arms of someone who steps out to catch me as I trip into the wings.

'Chase!' I cry, gripping on to him. 'You're here!'

'Of course, I'm here,' he says, and then, without saying anything else, he kisses me.

When he pulls away, I'm smiling so much my jaw is already aching. He brushes my hair off my cheek, tucking it behind my ear, and I'm so engrossed in his mesmerizing sea-blue eyes that I almost miss Grace passing us to take her place onstage.

'You were incredible, Nina,' she whispers. 'I'll see you on the other side!'

'Good luck!' I tell her, as she stands up straight, lifts her chin and glides on to the stage to rapturous applause as though she belongs there.

If adrenaline was pumping through my veins before the performance, afterwards it's gone into overdrive and now that Chase is here, standing right in front of me, I really feel like I might burst with happiness.

'Nina,' Chase whispers, holding me close, 'after we watch Grace's performance, can we talk somewhere?'

I nod and turn to look out at the stage, while he stands behind me, wrapping his arms round my waist and resting his chin on my shoulder. He's here. *Of course, he's here.*

Grace launches into her song, 'Listen' from *Dreamgirls*, and sings it so beautifully that my eyes fill with tears. I hear a sharp intake of breath from Chase as he witnesses her performing for the first time and remember when I first heard her sing at the start of the course. I don't know how she has got even better, but she has. When her song finishes, I whoop so enthusiastically that my throat feels hoarse. She walks offstage and nervously asks us whether she did OK.

'You have a really beautiful voice,' Chase tells her, and she covers her face with her hands in excitement.

'Chase Hunter said I have a beautiful voice,' she squeals, making me laugh out loud.

Leaving her to be congratulated by James, who approaches her with a dopey look on his face, Chase links his fingers through mine and leads me down the steps.

'There are some other rooms down the corridor from the green room,' I tell him, as he holds open the door for me. 'I'm sure one will –'

'Nina,' Jordan interrupts, coming out of the green room.

I feel Chase tense next to me, but not even Jordan can dampen my mood right now.

'Hey, Jordan, good luck for your performance. You're on in a bit, right?'

He nods. 'Thanks. And I wanted to say that I saw you play and –' he hesitates, searching for the words and then clears his throat – 'it wasn't what I expected. As in, I may have been too quick to judge you. As a pianist, I mean.'

'OK,' I say, glancing at Chase who looks as confused as I feel.

'What I'm trying to say,' Jordan continues with a sigh, 'is that you were good. Really good. Even if it was an Austin Golding piece.'

'Thanks, Jordan.' I smile at how difficult he found that to say.

He nods awkwardly and then heads through the door to wait in the wings.

'That was weird,' Chase says, as I lead him into a small practice room down the corridor. 'I think that was a compliment, but I'm not entirely sure.'

'Me neither,' I admit, taking a seat, 'but it's the nicest thing he's ever said to me, so I must have played well.'

'Are you joking? You were amazing out there,' Chase says, sitting down opposite me. 'Nina, I've never seen you play like that before. How did you do it?'

I smile, my cheeks burning. 'I'm not sure. I forgot about everything that's been happening lately and let myself love the music again.'

'Well, there's a talent scout from the Chasing Chords label here,' he says, lifting his eyebrows. 'I saw him watching you with great interest.'

'He must be here on Dad's instruction.'

Chase nods slowly. 'I'm sorry about what happened with your dad. He's an idiot.'

'Yeah, he is.'

'Are you OK about it?'

I hesitate. 'I feel sad about what could have been. I thought he really cared about me and it would have been nice to have a dad again. But I'll get over it. He doesn't deserve a family and I won't be letting him near mine ever again. Besides, I don't need him. I've got Mum, Nancy and Jimmy in the audience and I know they'll always be there –' I smile up at Chase – 'and, best of all, you're here. I can't believe you made it.'

'That's what I wanted to talk about.' He reaches forward and takes my hand in his warm grip. 'You shouldn't ever have to doubt that I will make it to be in the audience for you. I want a solo career, Nina – but, more than that, I want you. I'm so sorry that I haven't been around when you've needed me most. I've been so wrapped up in my own problems that I haven't been there for you. I really hope you can forgive me. You're the best person I know. I don't want to lose you. I was so focused on my music career that I've been missing out on what I already have, and I don't want to be living in the future. I want to be living in the now. With you. From now on, I promise to make sure that we make time for each other. No matter what is going on. You're my priority.'

He glances down at his feet nervously and continues in a quieter, less confident tone. 'Obviously, I understand if you want some time or space after everything that's happened. I said some stupid stuff and I know I haven't been a brilliant boyfriend, so if you need to think about things, then that's absolutely fine. I just wanted to let you know where I stand.'

'I don't need time or space,' I say, so happy that I'm barely able to get the words out. 'I never want to lose you. Ever. That all sounds good to me. I haven't exactly been a perfect girlfriend either, so I'm sorry, too. We'll both make this work, no matter what.'

He grins, squeezing my hands tightly, and then pulls me to my feet.

'Nina, I've been meaning to tell you for a while, but I kept getting too nervous that you maybe weren't there yet. But right now I don't care if you are or not – I'm going to say it anyway.' He takes a deep breath. 'I am head over heels, completely and utterly in love with you.'

There it is. Just like that. The L-word. And it's even more wonderful to hear than I imagined.

'Well, that's lucky.' I bring my eyes up to meet his, my heart somersaulting. 'Because I'm in love with you, too.'

He smiles, his dimples deepening in that way I adore, and then wraps his arms round me, lifting me up off my feet and spinning me round like we're in a cheesy Hollywood film, making me burst out laughing. I can't quite believe that it's really possible to be this happy.

I'm staring up at Chase's sparkling eyes, thinking about how perfect he is and how perfect this moment is, when it's interrupted by a polite knocking on the door. Grace pops her head round and smiles at us apologetically.

'They've nearly finished setting up for the group performance. Are you ready, Nina?'

'I'd almost forgotten,' I say, turning to Chase. 'I'd better go. I'll meet you afterwards.'

'I'll be here.' He grins, kissing me on the cheek. 'Oh, and in case she's wondering, tell Nancy that I did as she asked.'

I'm so dizzy with happiness that I don't really think about what he's said until he's gone back to take his seat in the audience and I'm standing in the wings with the other students, waiting to take our places on the stage. What is he talking about? What did Nancy ask him to do? And he'll see her before me when they wait for me after the show, won't he? Why can't he tell her himself?

I'm thinking about how random it was for him to say that when I spot Nancy tiptoeing up the steps to join us in the wings.

'Nancy!' I leave my place behind Jordan to stand with her at the back of the group. 'What are you doing back here? You're supposed to be in the audience.'

'I wanted to get a better view,' she explains in a whisper. 'Nina, you were absolutely brilliant. If you don't win this thing, then the teachers here are out of their minds. I'm so proud of you. So is Mum. She was crying throughout your entire performance. Like, proper weeping. Uncontrollable. I tried to get a picture of her so we could laugh at it later, but it came out all blurry because I was sitting right next to her and it was too close up.'

'Thanks, but, Nancy, you should really get back to your seat. We're about to go on,' I point out, nodding towards the conductor, who is walking out on to the stage to great applause.

'Good luck, Nina,' she says, and smiles. 'Also, after those performances, they should swap you and that Jonathan dude around for the group piece.'

'Jordan.'

'That's the one. You should be Piano One; you were a hundred times better.'

'Nancy, I'm serious, are you sure you want to stand here? The view and the sound will be better in the audience.'

'I won't get in anyone's way back here, I promise,' she says, ignoring my advice.

'OK. Oh yeah, I just saw Chase and he said to tell you that he'd done what you'd asked? What does that mean?'

A flush of pink appears on her cheeks.

'Cool, thanks, Nina,' she says, distracted.

'Nina,' Jordan hisses, gesturing for me to join him as everyone else starts filing on to the stage. 'We're about to go on!'

Nancy gives me a thumbs up and I leave her to it, rushing to join Jordan and follow him back out into the lights. Relieved that my solo piece is over and happy to be hidden right at the back of the orchestra for this performance, I'm not as terrified this time round. We wait for the instruments to check they're in tune and then the conductor raises his hands, counts us in and the music begins. I don't know if it's because of all the practice or the fact that the solo performances are over, so we're no longer in competition with each other, but we play the piece miles better than we've ever played it before.

The conductor is jumping around ecstatically through the piece and when we hit the final note, and the percussionists hit the cymbals with a loud crash, his shoulders visibly relax, and he is beaming at us as though we're his favourite people in the world.

He turns for his bow and the lights go up so that we can see the audience on their feet. He motions for us to stand and bow, too.

This is it. It's over. The course has finished. I look across the orchestra at Nico, TJ, Florence and then to Grace, whose eyes have welled up. A lump forms in my throat.

After weeks of frustration, of constant stressing and plenty of hard work, I can't bear the idea of being without Guildhall. I finally feel at home here. I was only just getting to know everyone.

Something happens that distracts me. Out of the corner of my eye, I see a movement from the wings. My jaw drops to the floor.

Nancy is walking out on to the stage. *What is she doing?*

The noise in the hall dies down as she walks right into the middle.

'Hi, I'm Nancy,' she announces to the audience, with a slight shake in her voice. 'I won't take up too much of your time. I know you're eager to hear who's won the summer school place and stuff. Thanks to Caroline Morreau for letting me do this.'

She nods to Caroline, who is sitting in the front row. Caroline smiles back.

WHAT IS GOING ON? What on EARTH is about to happen?!

'Miles,' Nancy says, stepping into the spotlight, 'this one is for you.'

CHAPTER TWENTY-TWO

NANCY

That's it. My life is over.

I have officially humiliated myself past the point of no return. I need to pack up my things and retreat from human society and become some kind of hermit. There's no going back.

As soon as I stepped out on to the stage, I regretted my decision. But it was too late. I had committed to what I was about to do and I had to go through with it.

And now here I am, singing *The Sound of Music* completely off-key and with no accompaniment, complete with actions, to a huge audience comprising professional musicians, talent scouts, aspiring music students and their family members. There's no point in doing it half-heartedly. I have to put my heart and soul into this terrible, terrible performance.

The orchestra is taking up most of the space, so I only have a small bit of downstage to work with. I fling my arms out and run to one side of the stage, belting out '*The hills are alive, with the sound of music!'* and then attempt to elegantly prance to the other side of the stage to sing the next line.

There is a sea of faces staring up at me in utter shock, glancing at each other questioningly, none of them with any clue what is going on. I should stop now. This is probably where I should stop. I've sung the first few lines. That's all I need to do. But for reasons unknown, even to myself, I carry on.

I launch into the second verse, rushing now centre stage and blinking into the spotlight. Miles had better be in the audience. That's all Chase had to do: bring Miles to Nina's concert. That's what I asked him and, according to the message Nina gave me before she went onstage, he had managed to do just that. So I hope this mortifying situation isn't a complete waste. If it turns out Chase is lying to me and Miles isn't in the audience and I am currently doing this for absolutely no reason whatsoever, well, then . . . I'll kill Chase.

This is technically all his fault in the first place. He was the one who put the idea in my head in the record store when he asked me if there was anything I could think of doing that would cheer up Miles. And that's when I remembered him saying that no one could stay mad at the combination of music and public humiliation. So that's exactly what I am doing for him.

I really hate him. Why couldn't he have said something like, no one stays mad when you text them apologizing from the bottom of your heart? No, it HAD to be bursting into song in a public place.

'*My heart wants to siiiiiing, every song it hears!*' I come to a stop as I realize that I can't remember any more of the lyrics.

You'd think I would have spent some time learning them yesterday or something, knowing that I was going to do this, but no. I didn't. I am very angry at my past self. WHY DIDN'T I LEARN THE WORDS?

The hall is in complete silence. I stand in the middle of the stage and clear my throat. I have to say something. I can't just stand here like a lemon. No one knows if that's the end or if I'm about to launch into the next line. People are shifting uncomfortably in their seats. There is nothing worse than this silence. SAY SOMETHING. ANYTHING.

'I can't remember the rest of the words,' I squeak.

OK. Maybe don't say that. The horrific silence was better than saying that. Everyone is staring at me like I'm completely MAD. Which, right now, I think I may be.

Someone laughs. One laugh. I think . . . I *think* it's Miles's laugh. But I can't be sure. I squint out at the audience trying to see where the laugh came from, but the stupid lights make it quite difficult to see individual faces. It might not have been Miles. It might be my wishful thinking. After all, even though I did just sacrifice my reputation and dignity for him, he may still hate me.

Then someone starts clapping. Everybody else slowly joins in. The applause gets louder and louder, until some start cheering and laughing. The orchestra behind me is clapping too and I glance over my shoulder to see Nina bent over double, she's laughing so hard. That other pianist, Jordan, is also crying with laughter. That's something. At least the rest of the audience found that fairly entertaining, even if Miles does still hate me.

I do an awkward bow and then salute the audience before legging it off the stage into the wings and leaning against the wall to catch my breath and let what I just did sink in. Whoa, the adrenaline when you come off stage is like coming off a roller coaster. How do people do this for a living?

Caroline Morreau comes on to the stage and cranes her neck round the curtain to wink at me.

'I've always loved a bit of spontaneous music. Thank you to Nancy for that . . . fascinating performance. And now we're going to announce the individual who has performed on a truly outstanding level tonight and therefore won a place on our acclaimed summer school programme.'

I wipe the sweat off my forehead and start fanning my face with my hand in an attempt to cool down. I feel on fire with the embarrassment still and am desperate to run away to go hide somewhere, but I need to hear these results. Nina glances at me from her piano on the stage and I hold up my crossed fingers. She smiles back at me.

'The winner is . . .'

Say Nina. Say Nina. Say Nina. Say Nina.

'GRACE BRIGHT!'

The crowd erupts and I see Nina leap to her feet, cheering for one of the singers, who is so stunned that she stands completely frozen to the spot. I can't believe Nina didn't win, but she doesn't look that upset from here. In fact, she looks really happy.

I consider hanging around backstage to comfort Nina in case she's disappointed, but then I remember that Mum and Jimmy are here in the audience, so I'll leave that to them. Mr Rogers is here, too, as he wanted to see his star pupil in her element, plus clearly Chase is somewhere if he managed to give Nina the message to pass to me. I really hope they've worked everything out.

I rush from backstage out into the reception hall, making a beeline for the toilets before the audience starts filing out. I lock myself in a cubicle and lean against the door, giving myself a little pep talk in my head.

I have to face him. I can do this.

Who cares if the *Sound of Music* thing didn't work? Who cares if he doesn't want anything to happen between us? Who cares if I messed it up for good and embarrassed myself in front of a large audience for no reason?

If Miles isn't interested, then that is fine because I have SO much going on to distract me.

For example, I have a major new website to launch. Now that I've told Layla and Sophie I'm resigning as their music editor and starting my very own site, something I am perfectly capable of and should have done right from the start. Not that Layla and Sophie seem to care all that much about my resignation. To be honest, I think they'd rather forget about *All That Glitters* altogether.

On Thursday all three of us were called to the headmistress's office. Layla and Sophie had been very excited because they thought she was going to give us all the details about the internship. Before going in, I'd told them that I wasn't going to accept it as it didn't seem right, and I was going to tell the headmistress why.

'Whatever,' Layla had said with a shrug, not looking too bothered. It was like she didn't even regret what she had done.

When we'd sat down opposite Mrs Coles, I'd launched into the little speech I'd prepared straight away.

'Mrs Coles, I appreciate it but I can't accept the Disney internship. I didn't write those stories, so I don't think that I should –'

Peering over her glasses, she'd held up her hand to stop me.

'Thank you, Nancy, but it's unnecessary for you to continue. I'm not sure any of you will be accepting the Disney internship.'

Layla's jaw had dropped to the floor. 'WHAT? But, Mrs Coles, just because Nancy doesn't want to go, doesn't mean that we should –'

'This has nothing to do with Nancy,' Mrs Coles had interrupted her calmly. 'This has to do with cheating. It has come to our attention that Jimmy's website was logged into by someone other than him and his final article was deleted on the final day of voting. You wouldn't know anything about that, would you?'

Layla sank back into her chair. Sophie kept her attention on her hands.

'No,' I'd answered, looking baffled. 'I can't believe it. Someone changed stuff around on Jimmy's website? That's awful!'

'My thoughts exactly,' Mrs Coles had said, giving Sophie a hard glare. 'Our IT expert has identified the IP address of the computer that was used to alter Jimmy's website. Would you like to say anything, Sophie? Layla?'

I had stared at them in disbelief. I couldn't believe that they'd not only posted articles under my name, they'd also gone into Jimmy's website and deleted his post!

Once they'd admitted it, Mrs Coles gave them detention for the coming term and later that day a new post appeared on the school website, announcing that due to 'unforeseen circumstances *All That Glitters* and its creators had to bow out of the competition'.

Jimmy was announced as the winner of the competition and the Disney Channel internship. I couldn't think of anyone who deserved it more. I guess everything turned out how it should.

And anyway, instead of being behind the scenes at Disney, I've got the Easter holidays to work on my own website.

Not to mention I have these tiny things called GCSEs looming. So I definitely don't need the distraction of a boyfriend. Especially one like Miles, with his strong arms and beautiful dark eyes. I wouldn't get anything done! Considering all that, it really doesn't matter what happens now when I leave this toilet cubicle. I can handle it.

I take a deep breath and open the cubicle door, heading over to the sink to wash my hands with ice-cold water in an attempt to help me cool down. The audience has left the concert hall now and the bathroom has become busy. I keep my head down, hoping no one will notice who I am. Either they don't see that it's me or everyone is too polite to say anything, because I leave the bathroom without anyone commenting on my Maria impression. When I come out, the reception hall is filled with noise and bustling with people huddled in their family groups, as they congratulate performers and discuss the show, while drinks and canapés are brought round on posh silver platters.

I spot Mum with Nina, Jimmy, Mr Rogers and Caroline Morreau. I squeeze through the crowd to where they're standing in the middle of the room. I am already embarrassed at the comments that I know are coming my way.

'Ah, there you are, Nancy!' Mum says with an amused expression. 'Ms Morreau was just filling us in on how brilliantly Nina has done this term.'

'*Mum*,' Nina whispers, looking mortified. 'That's not what she was saying.'

'Please call me Caroline and, actually, that was exactly what I was saying,' she insists. 'I have been delighted with your progress, Nina. And it's really lovely to meet the man who has nurtured her talent,' she says to Mr Rogers, who begins to blush. 'I very much hope, Nina, you will consider applying to our summer school programme.'

'I will.' Nina nods vigorously. 'Thanks, Caroline.'

'I look forward to your audition.' Caroline smiles at her. 'Now, I had better do the rounds. Enjoy the rest of the day. Nancy, I'll be seeing you soon.'

'Thank you. For everything,' I say, my cheeks burning up. She nods at me in acknowledgement and moves on to talk to Jordan's family who are lurking nearby.

'I think that's the first time she's ever smiled at me,' Nina says, looking like she's in shock.

'Well, isn't she wonderful?' Mum gushes. 'So graceful and eloquent! Nina, no wonder you learned so much from her. I already admired her from her albums you played me, but she is amazing in person, too!'

'So cool that she's encouraging you to apply to the summer school,' Jimmy says, squeezing her arm. 'Not that I'm surprised after your performance. If you don't get a record deal sometime soon, I'm going to eat my laptop.'

'Thanks, Jimmy, you're the best.' Nina laughs, before nudging Mr Rogers. 'It's all thanks to you, Mr Rogers. You didn't let me give up on myself and you reminded me of the music I really loved. Thanks so much for coming to my showcase; it was really good of you to make the effort to come all the way to London for it.'

'I wouldn't miss it. I'm very proud of you. And ... um ...' He glances at Mum and then down at his feet. 'That's not the only reason I'm here actually.'

'Yes, it's not,' Mum jumps in, placing a hand on his arm. 'Girls, I'd like you to meet the wonderful man I've been dating. Max Rogers.'

Wait. WHAT? I look at Nina whose jaw is on the floor, her eyes wide as saucers.

'You ... you two are *dating*?' Nina croaks, pointing at Mr Rogers and then at Mum.

'Yes, I really hope it's OK with you, Nina. That's why I didn't want to tell you for a bit, just until we knew things were serious. We met at the surprise party that Nancy organized for you at the start of the year and, well, we hit it off,' Mum says shyly, fluttering her eyelashes at Nina's piano teacher.

'I care about your mother very much and have never been happier, but –' he stands up straight and clears his throat – 'I completely understand if it's too weird for you, Nina, so I'd officially like your permission to date her.'

Nina hesitates and then breaks into a smile. 'I think it's brilliant! You have my permission.'

Jimmy leans in to whisper in my ear. 'I did NOT see that one coming.'

'Neither did I,' I reply.

The way Mum is beaming at Mr Rogers makes me want to cry. She really deserves to be this happy.

'So,' Jimmy says, putting his hands on my shoulders, 'are we going to talk about what Nancy did this evening? Or just pretend like it wasn't completely random and absolutely mad?'

'Yes, quite the surprise.' Mum giggles, now with Mr Rogers's arm round her.

'I would definitely like some answers,' Nina adds. 'How did you get Caroline to agree to let you storm the stage?'

'After we bumped into her at the cafe last weekend, as you know I went to see Chase and he put the idea in my head to . . . uh . . .'

'To apologize to Miles by singing the *Sound of Music* soundtrack in front of a live audience?' Nina suggests, finishing my sentence.

'Right. Yeah. Stupid.'

'Not stupid,' Mum says. 'It was wonderful. I remember you used to cheer me up by doing that and it never failed. Tonight's performance was the best you've ever done it.'

'Thanks, Mum. I will now have to leave the country because of the humiliation, but I appreciate your support.' I sigh. 'Anyway, after seeing Chase, I came back to meet you, Nina, and I was sitting in the reception bit waiting for you while you were in your group rehearsal. Caroline came in and I guess I looked a bit shell-shocked from the day we'd had as she invited me into her office for a cup of tea and I ended up telling her all about Miles and what had happened. She had been so nice about my website earlier and she was super understanding.'

'Are you serious?' Nina asks, shaking her head in disbelief. 'But she's . . . *Caroline Morreau*, director of music at Guildhall!'

'To you, maybe. But, to me, she was just a nice person giving me a cup of tea. She was so encouraging about my music writing, too. She's asked if I'd like to interview some Guildhall alumni for my website.'

'How wonderful!' Mum exclaims. 'What a brilliant starting point for your new project.'

'I know. I did question why she'd give me that opportunity over an established, experienced journalist, but she kept saying she'd like a fresh pair of eyes for a piece on the music school and how important it is to encourage new talent.'

'I guess that's why she's such a good teacher,' Mr Rogers points out.

'Anyway, it turns out she's an old romantic, too,' I say, realizing I've gone off point and continuing with my story. 'I told her about the *Sound of Music* thing and she said that I could go big with it at the showcase. Such a big gesture might change Miles's mind, she said.'

'So, you going on to the stage and singing to Miles was her idea?' Jimmy says, staring at her chatting to some parents on the other side of the room. 'She seemed so intimidating and serious onstage, but now I am seeing her in a whole new light.'

'Did Miles see it? Did it work?' Mr Rogers asks eagerly.

'I have no idea.'

'Uh . . . I think we may be about to find out,' Jimmy says, nodding over my shoulder.

I glance behind me and see Chase approaching our group with Miles beside him. As soon as I see Miles, I feel like I can't breathe. Butterflies start freaking out in my stomach, fluttering about in anticipation and making me feel sick.

'Hi,' Chase says, grinning and wrapping his arm round Nina's waist, 'found you.'

He kisses her on the cheek and Nina melts into him, gazing into his eyes. I mean, it's kind of gross to witness, but also a huge relief that they're OK. As if I ever doubted it.

I can't bring myself to look at Miles, who is now standing right there in front of me. There's an awkward silence in our group as everyone tries to think of something to say.

'Hey!' Nina says suddenly in this overly bright, enthusiastic voice. 'I want to introduce you all to my Guildhall friends. I think they're over here. Nancy, you met them earlier backstage, right?'

'No, I didn't really –'

'So you can stay here as you already met them,' Nina insists, her eyes boring into mine. 'And, Miles, you can stay here too, because . . . um . . . well, there's so many of us, let's not overwhelm them. OK, they're standing over there – let's go!'

Wow. That was the most unsubtle move in the world.

As everyone nods in agreement and shuffles away – including Mum who WINKS at me AGAIN as she goes, a repeat of the totally unacceptable, non-stealthy gesture she did that time in the shop – I'm left standing next to Miles.

'Hi, Nancy,' he says.

Blushing already, I force myself to look at him and notice that he's smiling at me. Which is surely a good thing? Oh god, why are my palms so sweaty?

'Oh, hey, Miles,' I say in as nonchalant a manner as possible. 'What's going on with you?'

WHAT'S GOING ON WITH YOU?! That's what I lead with?!

I add myself to my kill list.

'I'm not too bad,' he says, pretending like everything is normal. HOW IS HE SO CALM? 'You want to go chat outside? It's a bit crowded in here.'

'Yep. Sure.'

I follow him through the mass of people, my heart in my throat. I don't know what I'm going to do if he tells me it's all over before it even began. I can't cry. Not here at Guildhall, with all these people around. It's Nina's big night and I have to be strong for her. I can't be miserable. Luckily, the few reporters who have bothered to wait outside Guildhall for the duration of the showcase are distracted, laughing at one reporter killing time by attempting to do some opera singing, and they don't notice us sneak out and turn the corner. *Whatever you do, don't cry*, I think to myself as Miles walks a little bit away from the building down the street so we are sure of some privacy.

'I've had an interesting week,' he continues. 'I don't know whether you saw the press conference earlier in the week, but Chase has asked me to co-write his solo album with him, before we start work on the next album for Chasing Chords. I thought everything was going to be a bit rubbish, but it turns out it's the exact opposite. I have a busy, exciting year ahead.'

'Oh. That's good. Congratulations,' I say, looking down at my feet.

Unsure what to say next, I continue to stare at the ground and neither of us speaks for a moment.

'Nancy,' he says, breaking the silence and, even though I'm looking at my shoes, I can feel his eyes boring into me. 'I know you didn't write the stories. I know it wasn't your fault.'

'It was my fault,' I say, hot tears prickling behind my eyes. 'Everything was my fault.'

'Actually, it wasn't,' he insists in a gentle voice. 'I'm sorry I haven't got back to you this week. I was trying to work out what to say.'

'Stop being so nice. It makes me feel worse.' I force myself to look up into those stupid, lovely eyes of his. 'I'm really sorry, Miles. I really wish I could make things better. I mean it.'

'I know you do. I guessed that from the little show you put on this evening.'

A wide grin spreads across his face.

'You were right, Nancy. No one could stay mad after that *Sound of Music* trick. It was a truly memorable performance and I feel very honoured that it was dedicated to me. I already couldn't get you out of my head and, after that, I have no chance.'

When he says that, I feel a tiny spark of hope. What does he mean, he couldn't get me out of his head? In a good way or a bad way? Argh, WHY do boys have to be so cryptic?!

'I thought it was the least I could do,' I say quietly.

'Thank you,' he says, and I don't know whether he means to but his hand sort of moves forward and his fingers lightly brush mine.

A shiver runs all the way through me as we touch.

'So, I was thinking, I'll be needing to get out of London quite a bit with all this work I have to do on Chase's album.

378

You know, get some fresh air and inspiration for lyrics. I thought some long walks through the Norfolk countryside might be in order.'

I blink up at him. 'R-really?'

'Yeah. But only if you're there acting as tour guide. You were so good last time, what with all those circles we did without getting anywhere.'

'Hey, that was your fault,' I point out, the heavy anxious feeling I've been wrapped in all week slowly easing away with his teasing. 'You wouldn't let me use my map.'

'Maybe next time you'll remember where it is that you live and how to get back there, you know, considering you've been there for seven years.'

I roll my eyes. 'You know what? Maybe next time you should go for a walk on your own.'

'Ah, that wouldn't be any fun. If I was on my own, it wouldn't be much of a date now, would it?'

'So, it's a . . . date?' I ask hopefully, hardly daring to breathe, I'm so nervous.

'Yes, it's a date. I've liked you for a long time, Nancy Palmer.'

He takes a step forward and is now standing so close that I have to tilt my head up to look at him.

'You remember when I came to your mum's village shop to go to the record store and I asked you to come for lunch?' he asks.

I nod, aware of how close we are and finding it difficult to think of anything sensible to say. He smells so good. It's very distracting.

'The band wasn't in Norwich that weekend to meet the producer. I wasn't doing anything that day and Chase told me you were working in your mum's shop while Nina was at her course, so I thought I'd try to run into you. I pretended I was there for another reason but –' he pauses, looking embarrassed – 'I was there to hopefully see you.'

I stare at him, letting his words sink in.

'Wait . . . you came all that way . . . to take me for a lunch?'

'Yeah, I did.'

'Really,' I say, tingling with happiness. 'Kind of stalker-y.'

He laughs and then reaches up to brush along my cheekbone with his thumb.

'I really wish,' I say, losing myself in his eyes, 'that I hadn't been wearing that lobster hat.'

He puts his other hand on my waist and pulls me towards him. I can't believe this is happening to me. My heart is so full it might explode.

'I thought you looked perfect,' he says.

He leans forward as though to kiss me, but hesitates and then he does *that* smile. The smile he seems to have only for me. The smile I want to see every day from now on.

The smile I'll never risk losing again.

'Hang on a second,' he teases, his eyes twinkling mischievously. 'Is this going to end up all over the internet for everyone to see?'

'Nah,' I say, standing on my tiptoes to kiss him. 'This moment I'm keeping all to myself.'

If you want to see more of Nancy and Nina
then read on for an extract from

#Find
the
Girl

The first book from
Lucy and Lydia Connell

CHAPTER ONE

NANCY

For as long as I can remember I have been in love with Chase Hunter.

I love everything about him. The way his thick, dark-brown messy hair sticks up when he runs his fingers through it (which he does whenever he's nervous) and how he gets the cutest dimples whenever he smiles, showing off his pearly white teeth. He has the most beautifully sculpted cheekbones and chiselled jaw, but my favourite thing is his vintage indie style of dressing; he looks hot in whatever he's wearing, but I love him best in his simple, favourite combo of black skinny jeans, a white T-shirt and leather jacket, and that fedora hat he hardly ever goes without. And who could miss those piercing bright blue eyes framed by long dark eyelashes, which make your knees turn to jelly and cause your brain to go blank and forget all the words in the English language as you look into them.

Chase is also the most talented human being on the planet. He plays a whole host of instruments, but he's the best at piano. He's been playing since he was four years old, when his dad first plonked him on a piano stool. And Chase has a seriously beautiful singing voice that makes a shiver go down my spine and the breath catch in my throat.

Chase and I are made for one another. We like all the same things, including, but not limited to, the following:

1. Music (mostly pop, but we also both occasionally dip into soundtracks from the West End)
2. Fashion (we can both pull off hats, and that is something you just can't teach)
3. Dogs AND cats (but neither of us are fans of pigeons – they are pure evil)
4. Art (for me, that includes nails and make-up; for Chase, it's songwriting and, also, photography is one of his favourite hobbies)
5. Yoga (we are both totally spiritual)

Basically, we're soulmates.

'Nancy? Hello, Earth to Nancy!'

I snap my head up as my friend Layla's voice cuts through my daydreaming.

'Sorry!' I smile as she rolls her eyes, sitting down next to me and pulling her phone out of her bag. 'I was in my own world.'

I'd just been remembering Chase's birthday last year, when he went to his party wearing an open red-and-black check flannel shirt over a vest. I had inhaled so sharply when I saw him in such a great layer combination that I had accidentally swallowed my gum, making me cough and splutter all over the place.

Which is proof of how good-looking Chase Hunter really is.

He, literally, almost made me die.

'Whatever.' Layla sighs impatiently, busy texting. 'So, what's this big news you wanted to tell me?'

'You have got to see this app I downloaded.' I grin, sliding my phone across the table towards her.

Her eyes flicker towards it reluctantly.

'What is it?' she says in a bored voice. 'And who opened the window? Seriously, it's freezing in here.'

I shrug and reach up to close the classroom window, deciding not to mention that it was actually me who had opened it earlier, just before she came in. I had been spritzing my new perfume and gone a bit overboard, spraying so much that I sneezed about a hundred times and could still taste it in my mouth.

I can confirm that perfume does not taste as nice as it smells.

'Morning!' our friend Sophie says brightly, sauntering across the classroom and sitting at the table in front of us.

We don't have seats officially assigned to us in morning registration, but Layla made sure at the beginning of the year that everyone knew these three places were ours, because, being right at the back and next to the window, they are the best seats in the room.

A few weeks ago, Timothy Davies tragically forgot about this unwritten rule and we came in one morning to find him sitting at mine and Layla's desk, doodling cartoons in his notebook. Layla was furious and I had to step in quickly before she went full-on Disney villain at him. I know what she can be like. Don't even get me started on the time I took a sneaky bite out of her red velvet cupcake.

I will never commit such a crime EVER again. The punishment was so not worth the bite.

'Hey, Sophie.' I grin as she sits down, swivelling to lean on the back of her chair and face us. 'I have to tell you about this app. Basically –'

'Did you get my message?' Layla asks her, cutting across me.

'Yeah.' Sophie nods, rummaging about in her bag before passing Layla a lip gloss. 'Sorry, I completely forgot I'd borrowed it. I'm glad you reminded me. My brain has been all over the place this morning, stressing about the English test today.' She lets out a long sigh. 'Who knew Jane Austen could be so complicated!'

'*Jane Eyre*,' I correct.

'Oh.' Sophie stares at me blankly. 'Are those two different things?'

I smile. Sophie always has her head in the clouds; sometimes I think she's on a completely different planet.

She lives next door to Layla, so they've been best friends for years and I often wonder whether Sophie is ever annoyed that Layla chooses to sit next to me at school now, rather than her. However, whereas I'd be upset if my best friend since forever did that to me, I genuinely don't think it crosses Sophie's mind.

'Jane Austen was an author, and Jane Eyre is the main character of Charlotte Brontë's book. Totally unrelated except for the first name.'

'Wait, what?' Her dark eyes widen with panic.

Sophie always goes on about how lucky I am to have blue eyes and poker-straight blonde hair, but I think the exact opposite. I would do anything to have her intense dark-brown eyes and beautiful brunette curls. I get really mad at her when she straightens her hair. She has no idea how long it takes me – and how many times I burn myself with curling tongs – to achieve anything near the kind of volume her hair has. Layla has lovely natural waves too, and whenever she stays over at mine she complains about how much hair spray I use in the morning, accusing me of poisoning her lungs.

The straight-hair struggle is real.

'I was just telling my parents this morning that I've been studying Jane Austen,' Sophie continues. 'No wonder Mum looked confused at breakfast when I mentioned all the moors.'

'The moors?'

'Yeah,' she says. 'You know, all the moors in the book. I read that this morning online. It's an important theme,' she adds proudly.

'Ah,' I begin carefully, 'I think you're getting confused with *Wuthering Heights*. That's a different book, by Emily Brontë.'

Sophie stares at me blankly. 'I'm lost.'

'Charlotte Brontë is the author who wrote *Jane Eyre*, the book we're studying,' I explain slowly. 'Emily Brontë was her sister, who wrote another classic book, *Wuthering Heights*, which we're *not* studying. That book has the important moors theme in it. And neither of those books are anything to do with Jane Austen.'

Sophie slumps her shoulders forward. 'I'm never going to pass my English GCSE. I can't even get the book right!'

'Don't be silly – you'll be fine,' I say, trying to be as convincing as possible. 'It's only September, so this test doesn't mean anything. You've got the entire year to read the right book before the actual exam.'

'I suppose.' She sighs. 'What am I going to do about the *Jane Eyre* test?'

'I can give you an overview of all the important points, if you like,' I suggest.

'You seem to know a lot about *Jane Eyre* and classic literature all of a sudden,' Layla notes, watching me. 'I didn't know boring old books were your thing.'

'They're not,' I insist hurriedly. 'It's because of the

test. And I just . . . I know a lot about them because of Nina. She often talks about books at dinner.'

Layla rolls her eyes. 'That figures.'

Technically, that wasn't a lie. Nina does sometimes talk about books at dinner. But what I don't mention is that I've also read all those books myself. Twice. I just can't admit that to Layla and Sophie.

They would think I'm as big a loser as my sister.

'Did you see Chase is working in Manchester today?' I say to Sophie, keen to change the subject. 'He was meant to be taking time off this week, but he is so dedicated.'

I swirl the tip of my finger gently over my current phone background: a black-and-white picture of him laughing, with his dimples very pronounced and all these cute crinkles round his eyes.

I sigh dreamily. 'He's just perfect.'

'He really is,' Sophie says enthusiastically, as Layla nods in agreement. 'If only we knew him! Can you imagine meeting Chase? Like, face-to-face?'

She squeals loudly at the thought of it, causing Mrs Smithson, our form teacher, who has just sauntered into the room, to jump and splash her coffee all over the floor. 'I think I would pass out on the spot!'

Which brings me to the teeny, tiny snag in my otherwise perfect relationship with Chase Hunter . . .

I've never actually met him.

And the reason I've never met him is because he just so

happens to be the lead singer in the globally famous band Chasing Chords.

But that doesn't mean we're not soulmates.

I know it sounds mad but I've been loyally supporting Chase since his band first uploaded one of their songs on to YouTube, which went viral in a matter of days and landed them a big record deal. I was the first one in our entire school to stumble across the video online of the band playing a song that Chase had written, in what I now know to be his mum's dusty old garage. I lay on my bed and played it over and over on repeat, until Nina knocked on my door and went, 'Can't you put some headphones on?' in an unnecessarily narky tone.

I didn't care though because I knew then that I had stumbled upon something really special. I showed the video to everyone the next day at school, and by then the band's YouTube hits had skyrocketed. I followed them on every possible social media platform and registered for their newsletters, so that I could stay on top of all their updates, like when they signed the record deal. I couldn't stop listening to their latest song until they uploaded the next one, and then I couldn't stop listening to that one either. I have always been into music – Nina and I used to pretend we were pop stars all the time when we were little – but no songs have ever had the effect on me that Chase's songs do.

Layla and Sophie love Chasing Chords, but they don't

compete with my appreciation of Chase. They don't really get him. Which is why I write the posts for the blog we created together, the one dedicated to our amazing fan fiction about the band. When I first suggested we set it up, Layla was really keen, but she never actually contributes anything. She just lies on her bed Snapchatting, while I sit at my laptop and work hard writing the stories, with occasional helpful comments from Sophie (although I have to put my foot down when Sophie suggests stupid plotlines like Chase and Miles, the band's drummer, going on a space adventure with NASA).

It's not like I always get As on my English papers or anything, and even if I did I wouldn't tell anyone in case they thought I was a big nerd, but writing fan fiction about Chasing Chords is one of my favourite things to do. Through my stories, I get totally lost in the band's world and I feel as if I know them better than they know themselves. I get loads of comments on my stories from fellow Chasing Chords fans begging me for the next instalment and I always secretly hope that the band might actually log on every now and then and read the stories, or even comment under another name.

Once the band replied to a tweet I sent them about how much I loved their latest single:

Chasing Chords @realchasingchords
@npalmer Thnx! Without fans like you, we'd be lost xox

I took a screenshot of it, which I printed out in a blown-up size, and then I bought a really expensive frame, and set the picture up on my dressing table next to my framed picture of Chase and my mirror, so I can read it every morning while I get ready.

I just have to meet Chase, and then everything else will fall into place. And ever since this morning, when the band announced they would be playing a surprise gig in London on Saturday, with tickets going on sale this week, I'd been coming up with a brilliant plan to make that happen.

'I have to tell you both about this new app,' I say, slightly distracted by Mrs Smithson, who was attempting – and failing – to mop up the spilt coffee with a piece of paper in absence of a tissue.

'What is it?'

'It gives me priority when buying any gig tickets in London,' I explain eagerly, clicking on the app to show them. 'We'll get first dibs as soon as the tickets for the secret Chasing Chords concert go on sale!'

'Amazing!' Sophie squeals, just as Mrs Smithson raises her mug to her lips, making her jump again and spill what's left in the mug down her shirt. 'Is it expensive? Getting this priority thing?'

'Who cares?' I shrug. 'It's Chasing Chords. We HAVE to get tickets and this is our best chance.'

'Will your mum mind?'

'Sophie, you've met my mum.' I sigh, sharing a knowing

look with Layla. 'It's not like she'd understand anything about apps. She can barely work her mobile and it's ancient. It doesn't even have a camera.'

'What?' Sophie replies, stunned. 'Do phones like that actually exist?'

'Trust me, they do.'

I had tried to update my mum's phone and I'd even got so far as to take her into a mobile phone shop in town, but that ended up being a total disaster. She completely embarrassed me in front of the really cute shop assistant by asking the WORST questions, like, 'Why are young people so obsessed with your own faces? I'll never understand this selfie malarkey you go on about, Nancy. Although, I do have to say, Nancy, *you* have a very beautiful face. Like mother, like daughter, eh?'

That wasn't even her worst joke, and every time she made one she cackled really loudly afterwards when it was clear that I wasn't finding any of them very funny at all. Then she insisted on making the cute shop assistant guide her round all the phones on display so that she could 'gather all the facts', before declaring to the entire store that she couldn't POSSIBLY discard the phone that has loyally stuck with her through thick and thin for the past four years, and she wouldn't be purchasing anything today, but did the cute shop assistant want to note down his number for her beautiful daughter, standing right there next to her.

It was MORTIFYING. I literally had to crawl out of the shop and couldn't speak to her for the rest of the afternoon, making a promise to myself that I would never again attempt to lure my mum into any kind of modern technology.

Just thinking about the phone-shop incident was actually making my cheeks burn hot with embarrassment, even though it was months ago.

'What is your sister doing?' Layla suddenly says, looking towards the front of the classroom curiously.

I hadn't even noticed Nina come in the room, but she must have been in there for some time because her notepads and pencil case were open on her desk, as though she'd been working.

I watch as Nina, with her clunky purple headphones round her neck like always, gets up from her desk and holds out a pack of tissues to Mrs Smithson, who is now standing looking in despair at the coffee stain on her shirt. She takes one gratefully before Nina quickly returns to the safety of her desk. But, of course, one of Nina's shoelaces has come undone and she trips, stumbling forward and quickly steadying herself on Timothy's shoulder as she passes his desk.

'Sorry!' she mumbles, as he jolts his head up in surprise.

Layla sniggers next to me.

Oh, Nina, I think, staring at her, *you can't even walk from the front of the class to your seat without somehow messing it up. Why do you have to be so embarrassing?*

I don't think anyone noticed except me and Layla, and Nina was only at the front of the class for a matter of seconds, but still I notice the familiar crimson blush appearing on my sister's cheeks as she ducks her head down to her notebook, pulling her headphones back into place over her ears.

'What is with her?' Layla asks, shaking her head. 'She is so clumsy. I swear I saw her trip in the canteen yesterday. It's like she can't handle her own feet!'

'You two are so different, Nancy,' Sophie chimes in.

'Thank goodness,' I quip, laughing nervously.

'It's really weird. Apart from your looks –' Layla begins, leaning back in her chair, as the bell for morning registration trills loudly through the room – 'I'd never guess you were twins.'

The lovable twin duo **Lucy and Lydia** are well known for their eponymous YouTube channel and are steaming ahead in the digital world. Their uplifting platform features all things beauty, fashion and music related, and they're known for their infectious enthusiasm. They regularly upload their hugely popular 'Get the Look' videos, which cover some of their favourite music artist looks. As a result of this successful content thread, the girls filmed an exclusive series for MTV, *Lucy & Lydia: Style Sisters*, which amassed an incredible 6 million views. Following this, the girls went on to do a Snapchat takeover for growing channel PopSugar, which resulted in over 1.4 million views. With a highly engaged and fast-growing audience across all their platforms, Lucy and Lydia are certainly the ones to watch. They have excellent relationships and have worked closely with brands such as Disney, Missguided and Soap & Glory.